T0272113

Sheine Lende

Sheine Lende

A Prequel to Elatsoe

Darcie Little Badger

illustrated by Rovina Cai

THORNDIKE PRESS
A part of Gale, a Cengage Company

LIBRARY OF CONGRESS CIP DATA ON FILE.
CATALOGUING IN PUBLICATION FOR THIS BOOK
IS AVAILABLE FROM THE LIBRARY OF CONGRESS.

ISBN-13: 978-1-4205-1615-9 (hardcover alk. paper)

Published in 2024 by arrangement with Lantern Publishing, LLC.

Print Number: 1   Print Year: 2025
Printed in Mexico

This book is dedicated to the memory of Adson, a sweet, adventurous, and gentle cat with the coolest name (Adson toothed forceps)! Adson was a loving and patient little buddy to his human family (and his cat bestie DeBakey). The world is brighter because of you, Adson.

Sheiné łénde is also dedicated to Shemáá, who taught me to be brave. I love you.

~~ ONE ~~

They'd left the trail hours ago, and Shane worried that the bloodhounds were leading them astray. It seemed impossible for a six-year-old to wander this far off the beaten path without succumbing to the bull nettles and heat. There was a little shade, but the trees — squat shrub oak, juniper, and elm, mostly — didn't crowd each other. More often than not, direct sunlight baked the crown of Shane's head, burning the line of skin down her center part.

"Ma, do you have a spare bandana?" she asked. A few steps ahead, her mother — who did not look away from Nellie, the

7

leader of their three-bloodhound pack —
responded, "Did you lose yours?"

"Yes, ma'am. I'm sorry." Shane must've
forgotten it alongside the Herotonic River,
the last time she'd gone swimming with
friends. She'd have to pick up extra shifts
at Pizza Dale; Shane could spend her next
paycheck on a replacement.

Shane's mother, Lorenza, untied the
bandana around her neck. "Use mine,"
she offered. With an appreciative smile,
Shane took the patterned square of cotton,
which was damp with sweat and smelled
like aloe; she folded it in half and fash-
ioned a makeshift bonnet by tying two
corners under her chin. "Xastéyó, Ma.
Didn't expect to be outside this long."

"When you're searching for a lost child,"
Lorenza softly countered, "always plan for
the worst."

Shane had no response to that. Instead,
she checked her handheld compass, noting the direction. They'd been travelling
east the whole time, zig-zagging from tree
to tree, and she suddenly recognized that
the lost girl, Malorie, must have been hot,
too. So Malorie had turned her back to the
afternoon sun, taking relief in patches of

shade. But why had the child kept walking, on and on? Had she been trying to find a way home? What a nightmare. Malorie's desperation had only made things worse.

The girl went missing during a birthday party. At about 2 p.m., with everyone gathered around a three-layer chocolate cake, the party hosts took a head count and realized Malorie was gone. Out of the forty-eight children and ten adult chaperones present, only one person — a boy — had noticed Malorie slip under a loose board in the backyard fence and disappear into the wilds of hill country. A quick search had turned up nothing, although the adults found a couple deer trails the girl might have followed. All the parents had been called to help. One had known about Shane's mother and her tracking hounds.

It was noon the next day, and Shane and Lorenza hadn't found Malorie. Bleakly, Shane wondered how she could plan for the worst-case scenario when she could barely stand to think of it.

"Let's rest," Lorenza abruptly said, slumping heavily against an oak tree. "Heel, dogs." Dutifully, the two living bloodhounds raised their noses, tails wagging, and scampered to their human's side. However, Nellie's ghostly shimmer passed through a clump of yaupon holly and continued eastward. Some ghost dogs could become fully visible, like holograms, but poor old Nellie never learned that trick. So, he always resembled a dog-shaped heat mirage, subtly bending light as it passed through his non-body.

"He's really keyed into that scent trail," Shane commented. "Good sign, right?"

The only thing that could entice Nellie from Lorenza's side was a strong scent to follow. He'd been that way in life, too. When the family adopted Nellie from a shelter in McAllen, they'd been looking for a family dog, not a tracker. Old Nellie had been in the shelter a long time — people usually wanted puppies, not senior dogs — but when he'd gazed up at Lorenza with his deep brown eyes, she'd declared, "You're the one."

All floppy ears and jowls, Nellie also had a maze of wrinkles on his brow. If those wrinkles made him seem eternally thoughtful, his droopy eyes made him seem like a melancholy dog, but that couldn't have been farther from the truth. The moment Nellie was released from his pen, he'd shuffled up to Lorenza to request head scratches.

The day after they brought the old dog home, Lorenza went to work gathering corn, and Nellie promptly dug a hole under the backyard fence, put his nose to the ground, and followed her scent straight to the field. "I think he used to be a hunter's pet," Shane's father had suggested. "Or a sidekick to a detective like Sherlock Holmes. That's how he learned to find people."

"Why's he only following Ma, then?" Shane had asked. "You're the hunter, Pa, and I'm the detective."

"No, I'm a mechanic who goes fishing on the weekend," he'd corrected, "and when did you become a detective?"

"Today."

"Because you want Nellie as your sidekick?"

Reluctantly, Shane had nodded. She could rarely stand to lie. It made her hands clammy, her stomach sick.

"Good timing," he'd said. "My hammer's missing, and I need a detective to —"

11

"Oh, Grandpa Hugo was using it." That morning, Shane had observed him fixing the wobbly pantry shelf. "He probably left it in the house."

For a moment, her father was speechless. Then he'd picked Shane up and spun around, exclaiming, "Case closed! You don't need a Nellie sidekick, do you?"

"Not for this," she'd laughed.

"Not for anything!"

But that wasn't true, was it?

In the wilds of hill country, Shane tried to keep Nellie in sight. However, she quickly lost track of him.

"Come back!" she hollered, but Lorenza shook her head.

"Let him go. It doesn't matter if he runs ahead."

"But —"

"I can't walk farther," she explained, and when Shane looked down at Lorenza's face — which had suddenly become sallow and bright with sweat — she realized that something was very wrong. Lorenza worked in the peach orchards, picking fruit under worse conditions than hill country in the early summer; she shouldn't be so run-down and sickly after just ninety minutes of backcountry hiking.

"Drink more water," Shane suggested, quickly unclipping a mustard-colored thermos from the hook on her belt.

"Thank you." Lorenza held the thermos with two hands, took a sip, and then flinched when she swallowed, as if the cool water burned her throat. Shane realized she was breathing quickly and shallowly. Concerned, Shane knelt beside the oak trunk and fanned Lorenza's face with a folded topographic map.

"What's going on, Ma?" She pressed the back of her hand against Lorenza's forehead. "Oh, shoot, you're burning up!"

Lorenza cursed under her breath. "I caught it."

"It? Huh?"

"Mariana" — Lorenza's best friend at work, a single mother of six young children — "has been sick. Wouldn't go home to rest. Couldn't. I must have got her cold."

"Are you sure it's just a cold?" Thinking of the alternatives, Shane's anxiety spiked.

Lorenza took another drink of water, considering the question. At last, she said, "Perhaps a flu."

They couldn't get trapped in the middle of nowhere. Shane was still learning how to survive in the wilderness. "Let's get you home," she insisted. "Malorie's trail goes east. We know that now. Others can take over and find her."

"Wait." Lorenza reached out, clasping Shane's free hand and squeezing gently. "First, call the buzzards."

"You think . . . you think we really . . ." Shane lowered the map she'd been using as a fan. "Malorie's been missing less than a day."

"Just in case." Lorenza sighed in exhaustion — or maybe defeat. "It's better to know one way or the other. Wake the buzzards, Shane."

Lorenza was right. So Shane closed her eyes and reached deep, to the endless skies Below, where the dead flew together: birds and dinosaurs, bats and prehistoric dragonflies, great flocks of weightless, exuberant ghosts. She focused on one type of animal: the black turkey vulture of Texas. She thought of the vultures that roosted

14

on the windmill near her house, the community of birds perched side-by-side, their silhouettes reminiscent of tombstones. In the morning, they tucked their bald heads against the wind and took flight. Vultures were bold but quiet. Strange but dignified. She called to them with the imagined odor of rot, and, silently, they answered.

A dozen great winged ghosts, shimmering like Nellie but also carrying a faint black sheen — as if dyed by the memory of feathers — swirled up into the sky and dispersed. From experience, Shane knew that they would soar overhead for ten minutes, give or take, before returning to the land Below. Her eyes turned upward, she hoped for the best. She always tried to side with the glass half full, and let tragedy take her by surprise.

The people who asked Shane's family for help knew about their bloodhounds (the living ones, anyway). But Shane's mother never advertised turkey vultures. The implication was too terrible. In flight, the birds sniffed the air for the delectable scent of decay.

Aided by a pair of mini binoculars, Shane kept watch as Lorenza rested in the scant shade. Five minutes passed. The vulture shimmers weren't circling anything yet. Shane nibbled on her thumbnail, silently praying for five more minutes of nothing.

Then, in the distance, Nellie bayed. It was a mournful sound, but both women cried out with joy.

"He found Malorie!" Shane exclaimed. "Nellie did it! Oh, she's close! No wonder he was so determined!"

"Help me stand. Quickly!"

Shane grasped Lorenza's forearms and heaved her upright with a single firm pull. "Can I take your backpack?" she asked, but Lorenza — who was breathing more slowly and evenly now — just shook her head and forged eastward, following Nellie's baying.

Neal and Nealey, excited by their brother's call, quickly took the lead, their velvety ears flopping as they jumped over fallen trees and scampered around bushes. Shane and Lorenza followed them at a brisk walk. With luck, they wouldn't need to travel far. Nellie could run quicker and howl louder than any living dog. But, he usually restrained himself around his

16

humans, as if respectful of their physical limitations.

They'd only gone a quarter mile when they saw the edge of a pink sleeve peeking out behind a tree trunk, like Malorie was just sitting on the other side of the oak, calmly waiting to be saved. Nearby, Nellie's bay was now as loud as a tornado siren. "Quiet," Lorenza rasped. Then, when he immediately obeyed, she added, "Good boy." Nellie darted up to her and she stooped to pat the shimmery space where his head was, ruffling his nonexistent ears.

"Malorie?" Shane called, approaching the tree. "Hey, sweetie? We're here to help." There was no response; the sleeve didn't even twitch. Shane glanced up, checking that the sky was clear. No buzzards, living or dead, flew above her head. That was a good sign. Without another second's hesitation, she rounded the old oak tree.

Malorie sat against the trunk, her eyes closed, her head slumped to one side. One of her pigtails had come undone, unleashing tangled brown curls down her left shoulder. She wore the outfit she'd

17

chosen for the birthday party: new blue jeans, a pink T-shirt, and purple slippers. The skin on her face was sunburned to the point of peeling, but what concerned Shane the most was the girl's unresponsiveness. Malorie hadn't moved an inch.

"Can you hear me?" she asked, kneeling. "Malorie?" Gently, Shane pressed her fingers against the pulse point in her neck. The skin's heat shocked her; it was worse than Lorenza's feverish brow. At least she could feel a quick, fluttering pulse.

"Please," Shane begged her. "Wake up."

Suddenly, Malorie flinched away from Shane's hand with a soft, "Ow." Her eyes struggled open, their lashes tacky with the salt from evaporated tears. "I'm lost."

Shane almost laughed with relief. "Not anymore," she promised. "We're taking you home."

"Give her this," Lorenza said, joining them. She passed an extra thermos to Shane, who unscrewed the top and helped Malorie take sips of cool spring water.

"Where's my mom?" Malorie asked, once she'd finished drinking. Her voice was clearer now, slightly stronger.

"She's waiting outside the forest," promised Shane. "Can you get up?"

"No. Look." The girl pulled her right pantleg up to the knee. One side of her lower thigh was purplish and swollen, the skin taut around a pair of black puncture marks. "Hurts too much."

"What did that to you?" Lorenza asked, calmly, as if inquiring about the weather. "Was it a snake?"

"Yes." Malorie's eyes glistened; if those tears fell, she'd need to drink more water, and they didn't have an unlimited supply. "Am I dying?"

"No, dear." Lorenza's calm demeanor didn't falter. It rarely did, at least in public. Shane wondered if her mother had been born an enigma, or if she'd learned how to hide her feelings over time. "Can you remember what the snake looked like, Malorie?"

"It was brown and made a sound when I stepped on it."

Lorenza grabbed a dry mesquite pod from the ground and shook it; the beans rattled inside their long husk. "A sound like this?"

19

Malorie nodded, sniffling.

"Rattlesnake," Shane breathed, instinctively looking for movement in the brush around her feet.

"She needs a hospital," Lorenza replied. "Shane, can you carry her?"

They both knew the answer was yes. Shane hadn't been allowed to join rescue missions until she could walk five miles with a fully loaded hiking backpack. It only took her a month of training to pass that test, and the task was easier now, since her upper body strength had been enhanced by her mopping and scrubbing the floors of Pizza Dale. Malorie was smallish for six, weighing maybe forty pounds and change. But she was also dehydrated, sunburnt, and half-dead from the snakebite. Shane didn't want to jostle her, was terrified of hurting the frail child. "Let's build a stretcher, Ma. I have enough rope for a little 'un."

"Carry her." Lorenza squeezed Shane's shoulder, insistent. "Alone, you can go quickly. I'll follow with the backpacks." For a moment, Shane was perplexed. In training, she'd learned that it was good practice to split heavy burdens. Surely their escape would be quickest with a stretcher. But then, Shane felt the heat of fever through her mother's grasp, and recognized the bone-deep exhaustion in Lorenza's dark, sunken eyes. Lorenza's second wind, ignited by Nellie's baying, was rapidly fading.

"Alone?" Shane repeated. She didn't want to leave her sick mother in the wilderness, but what other options did they have? Malorie could die without quick medical intervention.

Then, she remembered the flare pistol.

"We can signal for help!" she exclaimed, dropping her backpack and unzipping its outer pouch.

"How?"

"Sorry. I was supposed to keep it secret. Grandpa Louis gave me a gun that shoots SOS flares! Bought it at a pawn shop, cheap. It's in here somewhere." Finding only bandages and a tightly folded blanket, Shane tried a side pocket. The gift was inconspicuous; it was the size of her hand and roughly shaped like a typical pistol. However, rather than firing bullets, it could shoot a flare into the sky: a bright-red flame that universally meant "We're in trouble!"

"It's a signal gun, like the kind they use at sea?" Shane's mother clarified, deadpan.

"Yes. Somebody from the other search party will see the light or hear the explosion and bring help. We won't have to move Malorie alone —"

"No." Lorenza pulled the bag away from Shane. "That's too dangerous."

"Huh? Why? I know how to aim up."

"There's been a drought. The land is dry, and signal flares burn hot."

"Grandpa says it's really uncommon for them to start fires." Why didn't Shane's mother accept that her health was worth the risk . . . and more?

Lorenza's face twitched in an expression of annoyance. "Does he?" Then, calm again, she added, "It's possible, especially during drought."

"Please let me take the chance. You're in no state to walk back alone!"

"This is greater than you or me," Lorenza countered, and then she quickly turned around to cough into her elbow. They were deep, wet coughs.

"Ma, seriously. Are you all right?" Shane leaned forward, gently touching her mother's back.

"The girl." Another cough, this one louder. "Go. I'll follow. Go!"

"I . . ." Lorenza had done a hundred rescues; this was Shane's third. She had to trust her mother's experience. "OK."

With that, Shane returned to Malorie's side. "Drink some more," she encouraged, raising the spare thermos to the girl's cracked lips. "See those dogs?"

"Uh huh," Malorie rasped between sips. Neal and Nealey sat about twenty feet away; they knew to give strangers plenty of space, unless instructed otherwise.

"They're good pups," Shane explained, still steadying the thermos as Malorie gulped down more water. "They'll guide us to safety. It's a long way, but I can give you a piggyback ride."

"What about the other one?" Malorie asked, water dripping down her pink chin. She dabbed the droplets with her sleeve, flinching at the sting of cotton against sunburnt skin.

"What other one?"

23

"The dog that found me. I heard a howl."

"Ah, yeah. Nellie." As she spoke, Shane patted her leather belt; its satchels contained a compass, a Swiss army knife, flint, a pocket-sized first aid kit, and a walkie talkie, all accounted for. Her thermos was clipped against her right hip. She sealed and secured Malorie's thermos against her left hip.

"Where did Nellie go?"

"Probably peeing on a tree somewhere." Shane lied, eying the shimmer behind Lorenza. "Don't worry. He never leaves my mother's side for long." And with that, Shane knelt with her back facing Malorie. "Wrap your arms around my neck."

Carrying a person was much trickier than carrying a weight-balanced bag with padded shoulder straps. It took Shane a couple attempts to stand with the girl on her back. She took a practice step, wobbling slightly.

"Don't fall," Malorie pleaded.

"I won't." She widened her stance and leaned forward to compensate for her new center of gravity. "There. Ready to go."

At that, Shane looked toward her mother, who was sitting cross-legged on the ground, busy combining the contents of both backpacks into one. Lorenza met her daughter's eyes. "I'll be right behind you," she promised, holding up the second walkie talkie.

"You better." Then, Shane called, "Neal! Nealey!"

The dogs jumped upright, their tails held high, their eyes glinting under droopy brows.

"Reverse course!" Neal and Nealey trotted westward, retracing their earlier footsteps. With a grunt, Shane followed. By her estimation, they were three to four miles away from the house where Malorie went missing. At her current speed, they'd reach safety in less than two hours. Maybe they'd get lucky and cross paths with a member of the neighborhood search party before then. Ten volunteers were zig-zagging through the area, looking for signs of Malorie. If Shane and Lorenza didn't have to hide Nellie, they could have brought a couple of those helpful men along. In that alternate reality, Lorenza wouldn't be alone, and Shane wouldn't have to carry a forty-pound sick kid over three miles of sunbaked hill country.

However, as far as the world knew, the skill to raise the ghosts of animals died out with Shane's great-grandmother, who was captured and imprisoned during an attack by the US. That happened in the 19th century, but Lorenza still maintained that it was safer to stay under the radar.

"Am I in trouble?" Malorie whispered, resting her chin on Shane's left shoulder.

"No way. Everyone will be happy to see you."

"It feels like I'm dying."

"You aren't. Promise."

Shane wondered if Lorenza was really right behind her, but it was difficult to check with so much weight on her back. She tried to listen for signs, but couldn't hear anything beyond her own heavy footsteps and breaths.

"What's your name?" Malorie asked.

"Everyone calls me Shane."

"Why?"

"Because they can't pronounce my real one." She sighed. "Neither can I."

"That's sad."

"Huh. Guess it is."

To conserve energy, they lapsed into silence. The dogs charged ahead, stopped, waited for Shane to catch up, and then ran again, rinse and repeat. The muscles in her legs burned like she was jogging uphill. Sweat dripped into her eyes, stinging, but she couldn't wipe her brow. Instead, Shane blinked until the pain subsided and her sight cleared; however, moments later, it happened again.

"Malorie," she said. "You see the bandana over my head?"

"Uh huh."

"Can you tie it around my forehead instead?"

It took a couple minutes for Malorie to loosen the knot under Shane's chin, but once she succeeded, she made a crooked headband that successfully kept Shane's vision clear.

"Thanks. Hey, is my ma behind us?"

"No," Malorie said. "At first, she was. Not anymore."

"OK. That's OK. She just needs lots of breaks. Nellie will keep her safe."

27

It was past noon, and the sun shone into Shane's face whenever she looked up. Her sunglasses were still in her backpack, with the flare pistol and all her maps. To take her mind off the heat, glare, and pain, she hummed a cheery made-up tune and pretended to be a turtle with a really heavy shell.

"Shane," Malorie whispered.

By now, they'd traveled two miles surely. The sun was lower, brighter.

"Shane!" Malorie urgently repeated.

"Yes?" She hoped Malorie didn't need to take a break; Shane was afraid she wouldn't be able to go any farther if they stopped and broke her momentum.

"There's someone behind us," she said. "Not your mom."

One of the search party? "What does he look like?" Shane asked, excited. "How far is he?"

"His eyes are so big and round," Malorie whispered. "They're like owl eyes. I'm scared. What is he?"

With a sharp gasp, Shane did a one-eighty turn, expecting to find a monster. But they were alone.

"I don't see anybody," she said. Was Malorie hallucinating? Dehydration and snake bites could do that to a person.

"I think he's hiding now."

Whether Malorie's condition was deteriorating — or she'd actually seen a bird-eyed man — they needed to keep moving double-time. Resolutely, Shane picked up the pace. With every step, her heart rate jumped, and she gulped deep breaths, unable to escape the edge of suffocation. Her inner ears ached, a feeling akin to an ice-cream headache, and her thigh muscles burned like she was running uphill.

"Almost . . . there!" she promised breathlessly. "Hold on." Who was she speaking to? Malorie? Her body? Her arms shivered, muscles spasming with the strain. Afraid to lose that all-important momentum, Shane sped up, charging around bushes and prickly pear cacti, through oases of shade shaped like oak leaves and branches.

Then, finally, Shane saw a flash of silver: a weather vane glinting in the distance. "The house! We're almost safe! Your parents are waiting!"

No response from Malorie.

"Hey! Hey, you there?"

Silence. Shane shifted, jostling the girl, desperate for a sign — any sign — that she'd be alright. "Malorie!"

"Whuh?"

Although meek and confused, the question was so much better than silence, and Shane exhaled with relief. "Just a couple more minutes," she promised, staggering forth, no longer reliant on the dogs' guidance. Between the trees, Shane saw the wooden fence with the loose boards, the top half of a colonial-style wood house. There were drooping helium balloons tied to the chimney, remnants from the birthday party. Suddenly, as she tried to step over a branch, her legs gave out. Shane pitched forward, landing on her knees; Malorie's arm momentarily squeezed her neck in a painful crush. Shane coughed, resisted the urge to pry the skinny arm loose, and slowly, achingly stood again.

"Help us!" she shouted, staggering toward the house, her eyes locked on the red balloons. "We need a doctor!"

A woman's voice, more welcoming than any siren's call, shouted out, "Hello?"

Shane recognized her as Malorie's aunt, part of the search efforts.

"We found her!" Shane hollered. "She was bit by a rattlesnake! Please help!"

Within a minute, other people came running through the forest; worried faces, weeping family, strong arms to carry Malorie to safety. A red-bearded man — Malorie's father! — picked up his daughter, cradling her. All at once, Shane felt so light, she was afraid she'd fly away. Instead, she leaned against an oak tree.

"What's wrong with her?" Malorie's father asked, hugging his unconscious daughter. "Mal, open your eyes. Please!"

"A rattlesnake bit her left leg," Shane answered breathlessly. "She's dehydrated and probably has heatstroke. Get her to a doctor now!"

"Oh, God!" Malorie's father sobbed. "We'll help you, Mal. It's gonna be OK." He and the other adults rushed Malorie toward the house. At the hospital, she'd receive antivenom, fluids, and bandages. *Malorie will survive*, Shane thought. She had to survive.

With an exhausted groan, Shane, now alone aside from the dogs, sat against the oak and took a deep drink of water. Neal and Nealey nuzzled her face with their wet noses. "Good girls," she softly praised.

She wondered if anyone else had noticed that her mother was missing; if anyone would return to check on her. And if the answer was "no," what should she do? Who could she call? There were no throngs of family and friends to gather round and carry them to safety, not anymore. Shane unlatched the walkie talkie, pressed the talk button, and said, "Ma, we made it. Malorie's going to the hospital. Where are you? Over."

Almost immediately, the speaker crackled, and Lorenza responded, "Good job. On the way. Over."

"Thank you, thank you, thank you," Shane murmured to nobody in particular, although the dogs tilted their heads inquisitively. Then, she held up the walkie talkie and asked Lorenza, "How d'ya feel? Over."

"Like I need a long nap. Over."

"Need help with the backpack? Over."

"No. You stay put and rest." Shane heard the beginning of a cough, then her mother's line cut off for a few seconds. Finally, Lorenza added, "Over."

Shane glanced at her wristwatch, making note of the time. She'd give her mother half an hour. If Lorenza wasn't back by one-forty p.m., Shane would go find her. Then, they could visit the house with the deflating balloons and ask whoever was still there for two glasses of sweet tea, cough syrup, aspirin. Cookies or pie would be nice, too, if they had 'em. She closed her eyes, imagining bright white refrigerators stocked with food, just like the fridges in commercials on TV. Meatloaf, fruit salad, casserole, cake, crisp vegetables, and amber soda in glass bottles. Shane's mother never charged people money for rescue jobs, but she didn't turn down gifts, either. That was a point of contention between them. Shane thought she should ask for compensation on a sliding scale: if people could afford to pay for her mother's time, resources, and work, they really oughta. However, Lorenza disagreed; Shane sensed that she was afraid — deeply, adamantly afraid — to exploit families during their most desperate moments.

There was a crunch in the forest behind her: the sound of crisp twigs snapping underfoot. "Mom?" Shane stood and looked into the trees. Nobody there. The sound could have been a squirrel jumping onto the ground. Maybe something larger, like a racoon.

She thought of Malorie's whispered warning: *His eyes are so big and round.*

A man with owl eyes.

Then, far away — too far to have made that sound — Lorenza walked into view. With a cry of relief, Shane jogged toward her mother. "I was worried! Just about to find you!"

"You did well," Lorenza answered, allowing Shane to take one of the hiking bags. "I'm proud." They linked arms, each supporting the other during the last leg of the journey. Step by slow step, the pair walked toward the house, where their truck was parked nearby.

"Thank you." She patted her mother's hand. "Ma, it pains me to say this, but you're a hypocrite."

"Quite an accusation."

"Didn't you once tell me to rest when I'm sick?"

"I might have." She side-eyed Shane. "But we saved a life today. Brought a child home."

"Just promise me you won't pick fruit till you feel better." Before Lorenza could protest that they needed the money, Shane added: "I'll take extra shifts at Pizza Dale for the week. They're always short-staffed in the summer."

A moment passed when all they heard were their own footsteps and labored breaths.

"OK," Lorenza agreed. They were nearly out of the woods. Conversationally, Shane asked, "The dogs would bark at monsters, right?"

The slightest hint of tension sharpened her mother's response. "Probably. Why do you ask?"

"Ah, it ain't nothing." Just a few more steps left. "Malorie believed we were being followed by a man with owl eyes. I think she was hallucinating."

"Oh," Lorenza whispered.

"What?"

"I think I saw him, too."

They exchanged a tense look.

"Probably your fever, Ma."

"Perhaps."

Nevertheless, exhaustion be damned, the two of them sprinted the rest of the way to safety. Most owls were simple, innocent birds. But some, the Owls of power, foretold great tragedy.

⁓ TWO ⁓

Three weeks later, Shane stepped into the employee breakroom of Pizza Dale. The boxy space was lit by a bare light-bulb, which hung over a square table surrounded by four metal chairs. To the right of the entrance was a ceiling-high wall of cube-shaped green lockers, and to the left was a porcelain sink with a bar of soap. Underfoot, the floor was pale gray concrete; above the sink, a round white clock ticked loudly, like a metronome, which was probably an intentional design choice. The senior manager of Pizza Dale, twenty-year-old Carl Bottlesmith, fre-quently and passionately explained that

37

breakrooms should be bland and uncomfortable. Otherwise, he claimed, employees unconsciously wasted too much time. Carl also made everyone call him "Sir" — even the head chef, Jose, who'd been working at Pizza Dale since the business first opened in '53.

Currently, Sir Bottlesmith was sitting in the breakroom, his hands clasped on the wooden table. "Close the door, Miss Solé," he requested, pronouncing Shane's last name as "Sohl" instead of "So-leh." She was too nervous to correct him. Anyway, it could've been worse. He pronounced the head chef's name as "Joe-say."

Carl continued, "Thanks for meeting me here. I would have preferred to speak in my office, but it's being repainted."

"That's OK," she replied. Shane stepped into the breakroom, pulled the door shut, and then sat across from Carl. "This is fine."

"What can I do for you?" he asked.

"First, I really appreciate that you gave me extra shifts last week."

"Not a problem." He smiled benevolently. "Do you need more?"

She shook her head, returning the smile. "Actually, now that my ma's recovered, I'd like to return to part-time hours."

"Oh." Carl raised his bushy red eyebrows. "We could certainly revert your schedule, but . . ." The clock ticked twice. "Frankly, I'm impressed with your work ethic, Miss Solé. Do you have any interest in joining Pizza Dale full time?"

"Me? Full time?" She'd been afraid of that offer. Lately, Carl had been dropping hints that the shop sparkled when Shane was around, and he was normally stingy with his praise. However, she couldn't possibly learn tracking, finish school, and work forty hours a week. She met Carl's unwavering stare; her boss considered eye contact to be a sign of honesty. He'd read it in a "business success" book: the source of all his managerial tricks and sketchy wisdom. "I wish I could," Shane said, "but I need time to watch my little brother when his babysitter isn't free. Like, this afternoon, Ma has to respond to a missing person situation, and Marcos's usual —"

"Stop," Carl interrupted, lifting his hands like a traffic guard. "Stop, stop, stop."

Shane snapped her mouth shut.

"I need you to understand something," he continued, and then leaned forward, resting his elbows against the slick glass tabletop.

Tick, tick, tick.

"Yes?" Shane prompted.

"You can turn down my offer." He flicked his right hand, as if shooing away a meddlesome fly. "That's fine. Just don't complicate everything with stories. Business is business, which means I only care about your life within the walls of Pizza Dale, Miss Solé. It's nothing personal. As the bossman, I need to make impartial managerial decisions. Understand?"

She nodded. "Right on, Bossman."

"But the offer remains open," Carl said. "When do you graduate?"

"Next year." Shane laughed. "Don't you remember? When you were a senior, I was a freshman. We once sat next to each other during a tornado drill." Briefly, she hunched and covered her head with both hands. "Like this." Aside from that ten-minute incident, they'd never occupied the same social bubbles at Wilson High, but

Shane could remember seeing Carl in the bandstand at a pep rally, his cheeks puffed out as he blasted the school's anthem from a tuba.

"Hey, what did I tell you about personal stories?" However, this time, his tone was vaguely amused. "In any case, if you need steady work after high school, there's always a spot for you at Pizza Dale."

Shane wasn't sure what she'd do for money as an adult, but none of her dreams included long-term employment in a restaurant with an intentionally bleak breakroom. "I'll keep that in mind," she said. "Thanks."

"We appreciate you." Standing to his full height of five foot eleven, Carl removed his glasses — which had pine-green rectangular frames — and wiped the brown-tinted lenses with his long silk tie. It was the color of an old carrot. The slender young man always dressed in oranges and greens, perhaps because they complemented his curly auburn hair and hazel eyes. In contrast, other folks at Pizza Dale wore red and black at work. There was no official uniform: the employee manual recommended purchasing color-coded outfits from the local Sears. When Shane first started the job, she'd had to borrow dress pants and a red T-shirt from her friend Amelia till her first paycheck arrived. Now, within the walls of Pizza Dale, Shane wore a black T-shirt, black pants, and a red vest; she washed them after every shift, reusing the same outfit four times a week. Shane's casual clothes were always practical, too — consisting of T-shirts, overalls, and denim pants.

Carl walked to the breakroom door, opened it partway, then paused. "Earlier, did you say missing children?"

"Yes."

He stared at her expectantly, like he was waiting for an explanation. Shane didn't provide one; she'd hate to be reprimanded for wasting Carl's time with dreaded personal stories. In the awkward silence that followed, the clock ticked adamantly, and Shane wondered if curiosity would override company policy just this once. Would he finally learn that she and her mother saved lives beyond the walls of Pizza Dale?

But in the end, Carl simply shook his head and said, "See you tomorrow."

With twenty-seven minutes to kill before her shift began, Shane drummed her hands against the tabletop. Her beat fluctuated from slow to drumroll-quick, as if mocking the clock's steady rhythm. When the drumming became boring, she stood and paced, throwing the occasional air punch, pretending to be a Hollywood boxer in a training montage. Normally, Shane occupied her free time in the outside world by doing handstands or playing with harmless little insect ghosts: monarch butterflies with stained-glass-translucent wings, ethereal lightning bugs, and swarms of bodiless gnats. They tickled her face like windblown dandelion fluffs, filling the air with colors and light. However, the restaurant had been built two blocks away from an old cemetery. When Shane was near a burial ground, especially one with tombstones and other markers of the dead, she would not call upon the world Below.

Human ghosts were terrible things, without exception. They weren't like animal ghosts, no. Sometimes, Shane wondered if they were even ghosts at all. Whatever the case, she'd hate to accidentally summon one. When she and her friends swam in

43

the sluggish river behind Pizza Dale, she'd often feel the tickle of a wing on her arm, or the brush of a fish's fin — but looking down, she'd see nothing. As if, in that place, it was easy for the ghosts of animals to visit Earth.

However, Lorenza insisted that Shane was safe at Pizza Dale, as long as she didn't visit the cemetery and look at the names on the tombstones. It was difficult to rouse human ghosts, and all but impossible to do so without disturbing their graves. That said, the cemetery still frightened Shane, especially during quiet nights, after everyone else had gone home and she was left alone to mop the checkered restaurant floor, the electrical lights humming their high-tension song of modernity. On those nights, Shane inevitably looked through the windows of Pizza Dale, fixating on the shadows in the forest beyond the parking lot. Every time they swayed, she wondered if it was just the wind blowing through juniper branches, or . . .

From the hallway, a voice as chipper as a sparrow's song called out "Morning!" Then, the door popped open, and Amelia (who was seventeen years old, just like

Shane; in fact, they were in homeroom together) swept into the breakroom, surrounded by a cloud of lavender perfume. Shane's friend's hair was long, sleek, and perpetually untangled — even at the end of grueling shifts — and her face was soft, pretty, and round. That day, Amelia wore a crisp black blouse with a red skirt; all her clothes were locally-sourced haute couture. It paid to have a seamstress for a mother. "Amelia!" Shane exclaimed. "You're early." Normally, her friend stepped into Pizza Dale at the exact start of her shift, not a minute sooner.

"Improbably, yes." She joined Shane near the lockers. "For the first time in human history, the ten-six bus was ahead of schedule. We got all the green lights, which is probabilistically equivalent to lightning striking twice, and nobody started a fight with the driver or another rider."

"That's weirder than the green light thing."

"Right? I wish I lived close enough to walk. Why can't Pizza Dale stick a fairy ring in the parking lot? I heard they're building a new one in Boerne."

"It may happen someday. On TV, they say the house of the future will be self-cleaning, with a ring in every garage. Well. Not every one . . ." Fairy rings might be a good alternative to planes, trains, and cars, since they could teleport you through ineffable fae magic, but only a fraction of the human population could use the ring transport centers. "I'm jealous you got that magical ancestor, Amelia."

As they spoke, Shane opened Locker #4, which had been hers since she started work. Within the cubby-sized space was a box of bandages, a water thermos, a brown cardigan, and a Polaroid taped to the inside of the door. Shane glanced fondly at the picture: she and two other teenagers — her friends Amelia and Gabrielle — sat on towels beside a public pool. Their long black hair fell loose, and they wore shorts and T-shirts over one-piece bathing suits. In the photo, Shane draped her arms around her beaming friends. Standing at five-foot-eight, Shane was the tallest of the group, with the correspondingly longest armspan, so she was always in the middle when they hugged. A perk of her above-average height.

"I just wish my great-great-grandmommy had lived to see the first ring." Amelia put a dramatic hand against her chest. "She got left at the altar, you know. Burned by a changeling."

"Yeah, you've mentioned that 'fore." Shane smiled sympathetically. "Pity." As the children of a fae and a human, change-lings were exceptional at shapeshifting and magic. They rarely stayed on Earth for long, though; to them, its rigid physics were like the bars on a prison cell.

"She should have known better," Ame-lia concluded. "But love isn't always convenient or logical. It's instinctual and uncontrollable." There was a sudden bit-terness to her comment, which confused Shane. The emotion seemed too extreme for a conversation about a long-ago breakup.

"Love's lots of things."

"So you're saying it's a changeling?"

Shane snorted at the metaphor. "Guess so."

"What else is love, to you?"

With her arms crossed, Shane side-leaned against the lockers. It should've been an easy question to answer; she felt love every day. Yet no sufficient description came to mind. "I'm no poet," she huffed.

"You don't need to be."

"It sure helps! What's love to you, Amelia?"

Without missing a beat, her friend replied, "The reason I can teleport through fairy rings."

"That it is. Bet you can do magic, too. Six generations isn't too far removed." It made her friend one thirty-second fae, which wasn't much, granted, but maybe enough for tiny spells.

"Probably," Amelia shrugged.

"Why don't you try and find out?"

"Because it'd be tragic kiddie-level magic, like creating balls of light. Plus, I'm afraid of . . . I don't know. Harm? That energy's pulled from another universe. We don't understand it, 'cause we have no reference. It doesn't follow the physics of our world, and I'd never forgive myself if I threw off the natural balance for a party trick." Amelia yawned wide, her eyes squeezing shut. "It's so early. I'm surprised you were here before me."

Shane sympathetically yawned, too, even though she wasn't much more tired than usual. "I had to speak with Carl," she explained. "Ma's feeling better. No need for extra shifts."

Nodding, Amelia unwrapped a stick of gum and popped it in her mouth. "How'd he take it?" she asked between chews.

"Pretty good, for Carl. Oh, and thanks for covering part of my shift today. Ma's driving to Less Crossing, and she has to leave by one."

"What's the situation?" Amelia's thick, dark eyebrows scrunched with concern. "You said something about missing siblings this time?" They'd talked on the phone last night, Shane briefly explaining the latest rescue case. Shane's friends knew about the living bloodhounds, and her mother's rescue operation, but not the ghosts, and certainly not the legacy Shane had inherited from her four-great-grandmother. A legacy less common — and more dangerous — than an affair with a changeling.

49

"Yes. A sixteen-year-old girl and a ten-year-old boy. Yesterday, they took a walk on the railroad tracks behind their house. Never came back."

Amelia's expressive eyebrows popped up in disbelief. Although Amelia rarely smiled or frowned, she could convey a suite of emotions in her dark eyes and musical voice. "How does a sixteen-year-old get lost on railroad tracks? Those go in a straight line."

"That's the weird thing," Shane admitted.

"They were attacked. Had to be. Tell your mom to be careful." Amelia tried to blow a bubble, but her cinnamon gum wasn't stretchy enough; instead, it pathetically drooped between her lips. With an annoyed huff, she spit it into the wastebasket. "What's the point of bubblegum without bubbles. I'm curious. Has your mom ever found a dead body?"

The change in subject gave Shane mental whiplash. "Has she . . ."

"During a rescue, I mean."

The solitary lightbulb flickered, six quick strobe flashes. Wide-eyed, both

50

girls looked up. Before the room went dark, Shane resolutely hustled to the center table, climbed onto a metal chair, and tightened the bulb, its glass hot against her fingertips. She was used to flipping tortillas on a flame-heated skillet, so she didn't flinch at the slight burn.

"Yes," Shane answered, turning to face Amelia. "She has."

Shane's family of three rented an old wood cabin that whistled and groaned in the wind, its walls full of boreholes and cracks. Sometimes, it felt like they lived in a musical instrument: one that badly needed tuning. Lorenza, Marcos, and Shane shared a bedroom — the only bedroom — their mattresses arranged like puzzle pieces on the creaky oakwood floor. The living room was furnished with a sofa, a coffee table, a bookshelf, and a twelve-inch television. There was a well-stocked pantry attached to the kitchen, and the bathroom had indoor plumbing, although the pipes rattled at night, and the toilet wobbled whenever Shane used it.

When the world indoors got too claustrophobic, Shane usually escaped to the backyard, where the tree line pressed against their meager vegetable plot and clothesline, which always drooped with Marcos's small pants and shirts, their mother's blouses and skirts, and Shane's overalls, work uniform, and T-shirts. They dried their socks and underpants on a line over the bathtub.

Thirty-five minutes after leaving work, Shane biked up the driveway to her house. Using the chain and padlock she always carried in her handlebar basket, she secured her bike to one of the porch's wooden posts. Then, she pushed open the front door, calling, "I'm back!"

"Shhhush," Lorenza whispered, quietly padding into the living room. Her mother wore her hiking boots, jeans, and long-sleeved cotton blouse, and Shane wondered if she expected to go far off the railroad tracks. "Marcos is taking his nap," she explained. "Just fell asleep." When Neal and Nealey scampered over and sniffed her shoes, Shane leaned over to ruffle their ears. As always, Nellie remained beside Lorenza, a shimmery extension of her shadow.

"I'll keep quiet," Shane promised. Without an hour-long midday nap, Marcos could barely function. She wondered how he'd fare in elementary school next year, when kids were expected to run around the playground after lunch. Perhaps he'd find a patch of shade near the monkey bars and sleep until the school bell rang.

"Supper's in the fridge," Lorenza said. "I'll be home by nine." She picked up her survival backpack and slung one strap over her shoulder, leaning slightly under the weight.

"Wait, Ma . . ." Shane thought of Amelia's skeptical question: *How does anyone get lost on railroad tracks?* "Is it really safe for you to go alone? You just got over a flu! What if we ask Grandpa to babysit Marcos —"

"No." Lorenza strode to the door and pulled it open. Anticipating an adventure, Neal and Nealey darted to her side.

"Wait until tomorrow, then?" Shane hurriedly suggested. "When we can go together?" She thought about their most recent rescue, recalling her mother's exhaustion and Malorie's desperate state. Even an experienced tracker could get into trouble when they worked alone. But then again: twenty-four hours often meant the difference between life and death.

As if sensing Shane's worries, Lorenza said, "Mr. Park is joining my search."

"You mean their grandpa? One guy?"

"Shane." Her voice softened. "The Parks have suffered terribly this year. If I can help, I must."

Shane understood, all too well. "Right." She rubbed her arm. "I hope you find the kids."

"Yes, hope. You're good at that." Lorenza's lips quirked in a fond expression; an almost-smile. Then, she hesitated on the doorway threshold, one foot outside. "If you need anything . . ." She jabbed a thumb at a piece of lined paper taped to the wall beside the door. The paper contained a list of phone numbers, the first four written in black ink, the fifth written in pencil, since it changed so often: HOSPITAL, FIREHOUSE, MRS. KILLEN (their nearest neighbor, a widow with two chihuahuas), DELEONS

54

(Lipan cousins, living two hours away by car), and GRANDPA (added recently).

"We'll be fine," Shane reassured her.

"Of course." Lorenza suddenly strode back into the house, took Shane by the arm, and pulled her into a tight side-hug. "See you tonight," she promised, looking her in the eye, her voice gentle.

After a final affectionate squeeze, they parted ways. Lorenza walked down the gravel driveway to her red pickup truck, trailed by Nellie, Neal, and Nealey. When she popped open the driver-side door, all three dogs hopped into the truck's cabin and climbed onto its bench. Shane watched her mother from the doorstep, only closing the door once the truck rumbled away, its tires crunching in gravel. Marcos would nap an hour longer. Once he woke, she'd need to fix him a snack, but Shane was free until then.

For a moment, she was at a loss at what to do. No homework in the summer, and Shane couldn't visit friends when Marcos needed supervision. What did other teenage girls do when they were alone and had time to spare? Well, Amelia sewed rag dolls and read thick books from the nonfiction section of the library. Gabrielle enjoyed painting and penning romances in her lockable diary, blushing as she wrote. But those hobbies didn't appeal to Shane.

To banish the silence, Shane walked around the coffee table and turned on the wood-paneled portable radio, which sat on the bookshelf. The radio was neatly flanked by stacks of old picture books and nursery rhyme collections. At first, nothing but static played, so Shane fiddled with the dial until it landed on station 98.337. A shrill shriek of electric guitar blasted from the speakers. "Aw, heck," she muttered, swiveling the volume from High to Off. "Bad idea." With bated breath, she stared at the dark hallway. When Marcos didn't scamper from his bedroom, dragging his toy bunny by its floppy arm, she exhaled with relief and moved to the kitchen.

Their boxy yellow refrigerator was a new model, purchased out of necessity when the old one spontaneously combusted. It'd happened in the middle of the night. Shane had been dreaming something half-remembered now, but vivid then — a river and a juniper tree with eyeballs where the berries should be — when all three dogs started howling from the kitchen, startling her awake. At first, she'd assumed a burglar was in the house. Maybe he'd crept through the window to steal their tin silverware? But as Shane was searching for her baseball bat — a reliable wooden slugger — she heard Lorenza exclaim, "Kó! Kó! Take Marcos outside!"

The electrical bits in the old fridge had been sizzling and spewing black smoke; thanks to the dogs, they'd caught the fire in time to extinguish it before it spread, and aside from the perishable food, the family didn't lose anything of value. However, once her next paycheck arrived, Lorenza spent all her funds to buy two things: a better fridge, and special treats for the dogs.

Shane pulled the new fridge door open; bright yellow light and winter-cool air spilled into the kitchen, and she enjoyed the chill for a moment, closing her eyes appreciatively. To cope with the summer heat of Texas, they left the windows open, and there was an electrical fan in the bedroom — but that just made the temperature bearable, not comfortable. Shane could have spent all afternoon like this, basking in the pleasant fridge light, but electricity didn't come free. She grabbed a half-eaten bowl of fruit salad — banana slices, whole green grapes, and melon cubes mixed in with little white marshmallows — scooped a portion into a clay bowl, and returned the dessert to the fridge. Then she moved to the front porch, leaving the door open so she could hear Marcos if he woke up. That was one good thing about a small house; nowhere lay beyond earshot.

After finishing her bowl of cubed fruit, Shane hummed a discordant tune, and the wild grass around her trembled as the ghosts of katydids climbed the yellow-green blades. Abruptly, she stopped calling them. Within ten seconds, half the shimmers were gone. Over the next minute, the remaining ghosts trickled back to the world Below, and then, she was alone with the living.

The previous evening, Shane had eavesdropped on the phone call between Lorenza and a friend of the Parks. Because the phone speaker was so loud, she'd overheard everything he said.

"The girl is sixteen. Name's Donnie. Strange one, that Donnie, but she's never been trouble, just troubled."

"What do you mean by that? Troubled?"

"She's into freaky things. Monsters, rock and roll, excessive hairspray —"

"Sounds like a teenager."

"S'pose so, but I don't know many girls who watch scary movies by themselves. She takes her grandma's car to the drive-in every Friday, and never brings a boy."

"What do you know about her brother?"

"His name's Bobby. Ten years old. Those poor kids. Their parents died last year — horrible accident. Maybe that's why the girl's so odd."

"I'm very sorry."

"They live with their grandparents, Mr. and Mrs. Park. I know the Parks well, from the farmer's market; they sell baked goods and vegetables, when the season's right. Mrs. Park gives free cookies to any kid who asks, and their veggies are 'pay what you can,' even if that means nothing. They won't let anyone go hungry. I need you to know that about them."

"They sound very kind."

"Absolutely are. Everyone in the neighborhood knows it. We all live in Less Crossing. It's a small town — and by small, I mean microscopic. There's a barbeque joint, a grocer, a gas station, and last-century houses with weedy lawns."

"Did anyone see anything? The day the kids went missing, I mean."

"Well, the train passes through town twice a day, and when it's safe, Donnie and Bobby walk the tracks. They follow 'em to a covered bridge over the Herotonic. There are fossils in the crumbling dirt along the bank, mostly old shells from a prehistoric ocean. Mrs. Park says that the siblings don't take any fossils home, but they enjoy looking. The world's their museum, I guess."

"The bridge is isolated?"

"Very. This morning, Donnie and Bobby went walking, and they never returned. Left at nine a.m. Their grandparents started worrying at noon. They checked the tracks and river, but couldn't find any sign of the pair. Police aren't interested. They figure that Donnie and Bobby ran off for fun and will return when the game gets old. Maybe Donnie's at a boyfriend's house, or with a *friend, and Bobby — clingy like he is — fol-lowed her. Mr. and Mrs. Park swore that the siblings wouldn't run away, as they never miss lunch without warning. But the police essentially told 'em, 'Call back on Tuesday if they're still gone.' Two days!"*

"That's unacceptable."

"You're telling me! Mid-afternoon, the neighborhood organized a community search, but it failed. No surprise there. A for-est surrounds Less Crossing. Railroad cuts through it. I personally think the siblings wan-dered off the tracks and got lost. But . . . people in Less Crossing are antsy. Locking their doors and keeping their children close. Think you can help, ma'am?"

They'd talked a bit longer, and then Lorenza agreed to look for the siblings, even though Marcos's babysitter was busy. "You'll have to watch him tomorrow after-noon," she'd told Shane. "Ask a friend to cover your shift at the pizza place."

Donnie and Bobby were lucky that Shane had Amelia.

She wondered what the bloodhounds would find. Maybe the siblings had chased down a train and jumped into an empty boxcar; Donnie and Bobby could be half-way to Chicago by now. If that was the case, their scents would vanish alongside the tracks, like they'd grown wings and flown away.

From within the house, a high-pitched voice called "Moooom?" Shane twisted to look inside. There, Marcos stood beside the sofa; barefoot, he wore his favorite black-and-yellow basketball shorts, his long hair mussed and in need of combing. He had the best hair in the family: sleek and dark, it grew past his lower back. In contrast, Shane's hair didn't get longer than her mid-back, and it was so thick and prone to tangling, the bristles on her brush sometimes snapped when she combed it after a bath. That's why she always kept it braided, especially at work.

It would be a sad day when Marcos had to cut his hair, as deep as silken obsidian. Lorenza had been searching for an elementary school that allowed boys to grow their hair below their ears, but there were none within driving distance. No matter their traditions, he'd be in violation of official policy.

"Ma's doing a rescue with the dogs," Shane answered.

"I know." Marcos walked outside and sat next to Shane, leaning against her with a put-upon sigh. "But when will she get home?"

"Late tonight." She looped an arm around her brother, squeezing him. "You're stuck with me until then. Hey, why're you awake? Shouldn't you be dreaming?"

"I don't dream," he said, which was a blatant lie, as she knew he loved recounting his dreams at dinner. Lately, Marcos did that: he'd fib about little, obvious things, with seemingly no motivation, although Shane suspected that every quirk had its underlying cause.

"Since when?" she gently confronted. "What about your dinosaur dream last week?"

He shrugged.

"You want to hear a story? I know a couple good ones. Did Ma ever tell you about the time Four-Great-Grandma outsmarted —"

"No, I want to watch TV," Marcos decided, taking Shane by the hand. With a firm pull, he led her inside. "Can we?"

Lorenza had a family rule: no television before sundown. But Marcos's usual babysitter watched daytime soaps, and, technically, Shane was his babysitter today.

"Oooookay," she said. "Find a good show. Nothing scary, though."

"Thank you!" After selecting the right channel with the VHF rotary dial, he leapt onto the brown sofa, compressing its center cushion with a *whump*. Shane sat beside him, planning to watch only a few minutes, just enough to supervise his choice of show. But when the television started blaring a comedy about a retired movie star who was trying (and failing) to run a motel, Shane got invested, and two comedies, one game show, and a medical drama later, she and Marcos were still sitting on the sofa, cocooned in hand-stitched quilts — gifts from their maternal grandmother, Bee, who'd passed when Shane was very young.

"I think it's time for popcorn," Shane decided. "You hungry?"

Marcos nodded, his eyes bright in the reflected screen-light. "Uh huh."

"OK —" Abruptly, she noticed a shimmer of light between the sofa and the coffee table. "Nellie?" Shane asked. The ghost dog wiggled, responding to his name. With a gasp, Shane stood and leaned over the coffee table to click off the television.

"Mom's home?" Marcos wondered, sitting up straight. The quilt slipped off his shoulders and pooled around his waist.

"She's early!" It wasn't yet three p.m.; Lorenza must have found the siblings quickly. But Nellie rarely strayed away from Lorenza. It seemed odd that he'd enter the house before her, or that they hadn't heard their mother's truck. Shane hustled to the front door and threw it open. The sunlit driveway was empty.

"Ma?" she called, jogging outside and down the gravel path. Nellie followed at her heels, and Marcos ran behind them.

"Mom?" he mirrored. "Mooom?"

When Shane reached the street, she glanced to the right and left. Nothing; nobody. They lived in a quiet pocket of land, their neighbors all sequestered within fences of barbed wire, chain link, and wood. Somewhere, a mockingbird ran through its greatest hits: crow, chickadee, sparrow, chicken.

"She's not here," Shane said, looking down at Nellie, as if he could offer an explanation. The dog paced around her, anxious.

"That's because it ain't nighttime yet," Marcos decided, crouching to pet Nellie, who leaned into his hand.

"Maybe . . ." She crossed her arms, thinking. "I should call the Parks, though. Just to check."

Inside, Shane pulled her mother's folder of search and rescue information off the bookshelf and flipped through its papers until she found the notes about Donnie and Bobby. Then, she moved to the wall-mounted landline in the kitchen and dialed the Parks' number.

After two rings, a woman answered. "Donnie?" she asked, her voice meek with exhaustion.

"Ah, sorry. No. My name's Shane. Is this Mrs. Park?"

The response was a soft: "Yes."

"I'm Lorenza's daughter."

"Who . . . ?"

"Lorenza. She's the tracker looking for your grandchildren."

"Oh! Of course! How can I help you?"

Mrs. Park didn't seem worried about Lorenza, which probably meant things were fine on her end. That was a relief, if not an explanation for Nellie's odd behavior. "I just wanted to check on my mom. Is everything going fine?"

"I think so. She's still in the woods with my husband, searching."

"You haven't heard from them recently?"

"No, but they'd radio if something went wrong —" There was a sound on the other end of the line: a crackling voice. Shane couldn't make out the words, although she strained to listen.

"One moment," Mrs. Park said, startled. "It's the radio."

A minute passed; Shane pressed the phone against her ear; waiting, dreading.

The answer was sudden and so loud, Shane had to lean away from the receiver to protect her eardrums.

"He can't find her!"

"What? Who?"

"They found an abandoned house in the woods, near the tracks. He went into the

67

building, while your mother checked its yard. Then, her dogs —"

"Neal and Nealey?"

"Yes! My husband went outside, and they ran up to him, alone —"

"Where's Ma?"

"We don't know. This doesn't make any sense. People can't just . . . they shouldn't just disappear!"

"I'll be right there." Shane hung up, and for a moment just stood still, her hand squeezing the receiver. Behind her, Marcos was frozen in the kitchen entrance, wide-eyed. His deer-in-the-headlights stare seemed to ask: *What now?*

"I'm calling Grandpa," Shane decided.

～ THREE ～

Shane was five years old when she first met Grandpa Louis, her maternal grandfather. At the time, Shane lived in "la rancheria de los Lipanes," with her parents and paternal grandparents, Hugo and Yolanda. The community had consisted of mostly-Lipan households in a horseshoe-shaped valley against a hill. One chilly winter evening, Grandpa arrived at their doorstep, his arms piled full of toys. There were blinking dollies, plastic horses, soft plush animals, and even an Etch A Sketch. "Out on bail," he'd cheered. At the time, Shane hadn't understood the meaning of the sentence. She'd just been thrilled to finally meet her fourth grandparent. After a two-hour conversation in the garage between the adults, where Shane couldn't eavesdrop, Grandpa Louis had promptly moved into the back room with the washing machine, which was always running. Since they were the only family to own a state-of-the-art motorized washer, the neighbors often visited with their bedsheets and clothes. He never complained about sleeping in the neighborhood's informal laundromat; if anything, he seemed to delight in the company, yakking the ear off his captive audience. For a year, he'd been a constant presence.

Then, one chilly winter morning, Grandpa Louis wasn't present anymore.

After that day, whenever Shane asked, "Where's Grandpa?" Lorenza would respond, "Wherever he wants to be, I guess." When Shane would follow up, "Is he coming back?" Lorenza always said something like: "I doubt anyone — even him — knows the answer to that question." Before long, Shane stopped asking, and her maternal grandfather became less real than an imaginary friend.

The answer to the second question, however, was yes. Eventually.

Twelve-year-old Shane had just biked home from school when a sixtyish-year-old man intercepted her on the gravel path to the front door. "Mija!" he exclaimed, raising his arms up high, as if celebrating tremendously good fortune. "You've grown!"

"Gah!" Shane almost toppled off her red bike. At the last minute, she planted one foot on the ground to steady herself.

"Who are you?" she asked, snatching a Swiss army knife from her wicker handlebar basket. With a flick of her thumb, she extended the dull two-inch blade. Shane's heart had been racing, and she'd felt light, but not in a skipping-through-the-meadow way. It had been the lightness of a body preparing for fight or flight. She'd hoped neither would be necessary. She'd never fought anyone before. Not really.

In a bind, she could always call for backup, waking the ghosts of Texas: the crickets, flies, deer, and black bears. Hares and squirrels, robins and hawks. She'd just learned how to reach deep and rouse anything below the fabric of Earth. However, that plan was a last resort, for although a menagerie of ghosts could cause a distraction, wild animals were uncontrollable — in life and especially in death. They weren't her servants. At most, they could be companions, but relationships like that took trust and years of work.

"You don't remember me?" the man's smile fell, replaced with a tenderly sad expression. "Doesn't your mother keep old photos in the house?"

"We lost our picture albums in a flood." The least of their losses that year — that cruel year.

"Oh, I gotcha." His crow's feet deepened, perhaps in sympathy. "Shane, I'm your grandpa. Do you recognize me? I haven't changed much in six years. Not like you. Wild. You're almost tall as me!" She stood at five foot six, specifically, nearly her final height. Her most recent growth spurt had launched Shane above the other kids in class.

But more than that had changed since Grandpa Louis left. Shane had mourned, celebrated, and learned addition, subtraction, multiplication, fractions, how to raise the ghosts of animals, and swimming (in that order). She'd made new friends, girls who taught her how to skip rope, dared her to climb trees, and whispered secrets in her ear. She'd even joined her mother on a rescue mission; they'd saved a hiker from his own terrible sense of direction.

And now her maternal grandfather looked smaller than the man she'd admired at age five. But his style hadn't changed. In fact, Shane wouldn't be surprised if he'd been wearing the same denim jacket, blue jeans, and black charro shirt for eight years. Beyond a doubt, his beaded bolo tie was familiar; its rosette depicted the sun in a bright blue sky.

"You . . ." Yes, she definitely saw the resemblance. "No way! Grandpa Louis! What in the world are you doing here?" Laughing in shared relief, they'd embraced; Grandpa Louis had tried to spin Shane around, just like he used to, but he could barely lift her an inch. Wincing, he stepped away and rubbed his lower back. "I'm renting a place in San Maria," he explained.

The city was a relatively short drive away. She wondered if that meant he'd be back for good this time.

"And 'fore that?" she asked. "Where'd you live?" Grandpa looked up then, deep in thought, as if solving a long division problem on the fly.

"Nevada," he'd said. "Then New Mexico. Louisiana. Florida. Iowa. California. Colorado. It's been an experience, mija. Life on the road's no picnic."

"I know what you mean."

Initially, after everything, Shane, Lorenza, and baby Marcos had drifted through Texas and southern Arkansas, renting rooms by the month. According to Lorenza, Lipan people used to live in an untethered way: following the bison, moving in great circles, and resting in family camps. But centuries ago, the land had been their home; they'd been welcome and well-fed. And respected, most of all. They'd been free to sing their stories, hold their ceremonies, and gather to heal, play, gossip, and laugh. Now, Texas officially belonged to millions of people . . . but not them. Not anymore.

It wasn't all bad. Since settling in Williamsville a few years ago, Shane had met two friends named Amelia and Gabrielle. As soon as possible, she was going to get a job, so they wouldn't have to move again.

"Will your mother get home soon?" Grandpa Louis wondered. He'd removed his straw cowboy hat to dab sweat off his brow with a bright-red handkerchief. It was late spring and already humid, with temperatures grazing the nineties. Shane had fished a key from her book bag and unlocked the door.

"Ma returns at five," she explained, rolling her bike to the side of the house. Then, she'd nudged out its kickstand and propped it against the sideboards. "Marcos is with her. He still rides on her back, but he'll be too heavy for that soon."

"Marcos . . . your brother?"

"Your grandson, yeah."

"Two hours." Behind her, Grandpa glanced at his chunky silver wristwatch, humming thoughtfully.

"She may get back earlier! You can wait in the living room. There's a sofa, and we even have a television now." Noticing her grandfather's frown, Shane hesitated, her enthusiasm sputtering like a candle's flame in a drafty room. "What's wrong?"

"Nothing," he said. "I sure wish I could stay, especially to meet the little man, but I have work. You understand."

75

She'd nodded, perplexed. What kind of job started in the evening? Perhaps her grandpa was a security guard or motel receptionist.

"Could you do me a favor?" he asked. "I know your ma's probably pissed at me . . ." He trailed off, as if searching for a denial or confirmation. Shane had shrugged. "She hasn't mentioned you in ages."

"Well," Grandpa Louis continued, frowning still, "tell her I'm in town. And give her this." He'd handed Shane a slip of yellow lined paper with a phone number on one side and a doodle of a penguin in a bow tie on the other. In a flash, Shane recalled a distant memory of shouting out animals — *Tiger! Boa constrictor! Elephant! Turtle!* — and her grandfather sitting on the floor, frantically sketching, little particles of wax flying off his crayons. At the thought, she smiled.

"Why were you gone so long?" she asked, accepting the phone number.

He pondered her question a moment. "At my age, you lose track of time. That's something you'll notice as an adult. Every year, the minutes seem faster. I didn't mean to miss so much. It just happened."

"But you're here now."

"Yes," he replied. "Frankly, your ma has every right to be angry at me. I've been a letdown. But that changes here and now. I'll make things right. Ask her to call, will you?"

"OK," Shane agreed.

"That's great, mija." Then he fished an envelope from his jean pocket and held it out. "This is for all the birthday presents I owe you."

"Aw, how sweet," she said, fully expecting a couple bucks in the card. "Thank you." However, when Shane tore the flap open, instead of a letter, she found a stack of fifties. "What the heck, Grandpa Louis! Are you sure? This must be three hundred dollars!" Enough for her to buy a whole new wardrobe, or months of groceries for the family.

"I missed a lot of presents."

"What kind of job do you have?"

"Jack of all trades." Then, as if casually noting the weather, he observed, "Almighty, this place is a dump. Your house is one gust away from collapse."

"It's a rental, and we don't plan to stay here forever. Mom's saving up to buy back our old place."

"Good," he answered. "Maybe I can help y'all with that, too."

"Seriously? Far out!"

They'd hugged; this time, Grandpa Louis didn't try to pick Shane up, but he did ruffle her hair. And with a wave good-bye, he'd retreated down the driveway. He turned the street corner, and a minute later, Shane had heard the hiccupping rumble of a motorcycle engine.

The sound stirred up another memory. In it, Shane sat on a high leather seat, her feet dangling above the footrests, her hands on bright chrome handlebars, pretending to drive, and somebody was laughing, but she couldn't remember why.

Once the rumble faded, Shane retreated inside, shut the door, and counted her money. She'd been wrong: it was three hundred and fifty dollars.

"Jack of all trades, huh?" she'd quietly wondered. "Which ones, specifically?"

Later that day, Shane — who'd been studying English grammar on the sofa — had heard the back door creak open. A moment later, she registered the clink of glass and the hiss of carbonation escaping into the air. Her mother had one luxury in life: a cold bottle of lime soda after work. With a thoughtful glance at her grandfather's phone number, Shane'd decided to keep quiet until Lorenza finished the drink. No use spoiling an enjoyable moment.

"Shane? Are you home?"

She'd snapped her English textbook shut and called, "In the living room, Ma! Doing my homework!"

"Before supper? That's very responsible." Into the room stepped Lorenza, holding the glass soda bottle in one hand and an oak walking staff in the other. Old Nellie followed her closely.

"There's a quiz . . ." Shane had trailed off, realizing that she'd left the open envelope of cash on the table. And her mother had seen it.

"Who gave you this?" Lorenza asked.

Her mother hadn't changed out of her work clothes: an old, floor-length cotton skirt, a sun bonnet, and a long-sleeved blouse, their pink fabric dusty after a long day working on the local farm, which supplied both sorghum and pitfruit to Midwest markets. On Lorenza's back, little Marcos had been wrapped within a cradleboard. He'd stared at Shane with shameless curiosity. The world of a baby was nothing but discovery, she mused. So much to learn, so much they'd never learn.

"Grandpa visited," she said. "It's for us."

At that revelation, Marcos had whined fussily, as if he could sense his mother's distress. Maybe he could; with the cradleboard pressed tight against Lorenza's back, Marcos could probably feel her heartbeat.

"And then," Shane added, "he gave me this phone number." She proffered the slip of paper. "Grandpa says you should call. He wants to make stuff right."

"What else did he want?" Lorenza asked, taking the paper and eyeing it with undisguised suspicion, first squinting at the numbers and then frowning at the penguin.

"Just that. Ma, I think he's serious. Grandpa moved nearby and everything."

"We'll see." She'd shaken her head once, slowly. "Don't get your hopes up. He only visits when he needs something."

"Grandpa Louis says it's different this time."

"We'll see," Lorenza repeated, sipping her lime soda. Then, she'd crushed the scrap of paper in her fist. However, instead of throwing it in the garbage — with the orange peels and coffee grinds — Lorenza shoved it deep within the drawer where they kept odds and ends: paperclips, pencils, and menus from local restaurants they couldn't afford to visit.

And, a few days later, she called him.

Over the next four years, Grandpa had visited the house regularly. First, he'd swung by twice a month for supper. Then, after Marcos celebrated his second birthday, Grandpa started visiting on Sunday afternoons. He'd bring hot dogs, beans, and lime-flavored jello molds full of sliced banana chunks. They'd all sit outside on a wool blanket, like families who picnicked in the park, and Grandpa would identify the birds in the trees, sometimes based on their chirps alone. "That's a yellow-rumped warbler!" he'd say. Or, "See that lovely red-throated birdie? It's called a rose-breasted grosbeak."

Little Marcos would laugh every time Grandpa imitated birdcalls.

And Shane would listen to Grandpa's adventures in Vegas, Flagstaff, and Los Angeles.

And Lorenza would wait for her father to take off his mask.

But, over those four years, he never asked for a single thing, other than their company.

～ FOUR ～

Grandpa Louis pulled up to the house in a nearly-new '73 station wagon. With an off-white base coat and brown stripes, it was no less snazzy than his typical motorcycle. He lurched to a stop and leapt outside, slamming the door shut with a hasty back-kick. "Is everyone OK? Any word about your mother?" There was an edge of urgency to his raspy voice, a quickening of his deep-south drawl.

"No good news," Shane said, toting luggage to the station wagon; in the thirty minutes it took for Grandpa Louis to arrive, she'd packed two duffel bags worth of clothes, toys, and living essentials, just in case they had to spend days away from home searching. She doubted it would come to that; with Nellie's help, they'd probably find Lorenza before nightfall. Anyhow, there was a difference between expecting trouble and preparing for it.

"Mom?" Marcos shouted, running outside, his eyes red-rimmed. "Is it Mom?" Since the dreadful phone call, Marcos had teetered between disbelief and morose weeping. Frankly, Shane was on the verge of stressed-out tears herself. At least she was certain that Lorenza was alive. Otherwise, Nellie would have howled, and considering his attachment to Lorenza, he probably would have followed her to the world Below too, instead of returning home where his second favorite humans lived.

That meant Lorenza was somewhere Nellie couldn't readily follow, which didn't leave a lot of options. Perhaps she'd fallen into a river. Dogs, even ghost bloodhounds, weren't able to track scents through running water. And yet that possibility didn't make sense. According to Mr. Park, Lorenza had been in a clearing before she vanished.

84

"Hey, now," Grandpa playfully chided, crossing the front lawn at a quick saunter. "You can survive a couple hours without Momma, right, little man?" He scooped up Marcos and swayed side to side in an exaggerated dance; usually, this made Marcos giggle, but now, he just whimpered.

"She's missing."

"It happens to the best of us," Grandpa sighed. "Don't worry, kid. We'll find her."

"Good to go!" Shane called, using both hands to shove the trunk shut.

If not water, then what?

There were monsters out there, too. Definitely. They lurked in every forest, every city, every desert and sea; on tropical islands, across the frozen north, and within dark, stalactite-toothed cave systems. Scientists even reported them in Antarctica, 1000-legged shadows writhing in the ice. Encounters might be exceedingly rare, but so were lightning strikes.

Yet Nellie would pursue anything — big or small, slithering or stampeding — if it took Lorenza.

A winged monster, then? An invasive gargoyle or endemic greatbird? Surely Mr. Park would have noticed one of those.

When everybody was secure and ready to roll — Marcos in the back, Shane sitting shotgun — Grandpa Louis tore out of the driveway, wheels kicking up gravel till they hit the concrete road. He veered whiplash-quick around curves and down dusty farm roads, sometimes driving twice the speed limit. "Grandpa, what if you get pulled over?" Shane asked after a few tense minutes.

"They'd have to catch us first," he joked, but he did chill out — and on the highway, they went just a smidge over the limit, weaving around slowpokes and tractors. The radio played country music, and as one song slipped into the next . . . into the next . . . and into the next, Shane's thoughts returned to monsters and unanswered questions.

Why would Nellie leave Lorenza's side? Why did he run home? Had Lorenza found the siblings? And if so, at what cost?

Don't expect trouble, she reminded herself. *Be calm and prepared.*

After forty minutes, they arrived at Less Crossing. "Here we are," Grandpa Louis said, parking outside a little pink house. The tin mailbox was labeled PARK, and

86

lawn flamingos lined the cobbled path to the front door, which was a fresh shade of white. The moment the station wagon's engine went silent, a white man and woman in their early sixties threw open the front door and hurried to the car. Mr. Park, wearing jeans and a wrinkled, untucked shirt, had white streaks in the hair behind each ear. In contrast, Mrs. Park had gone uniformly salt-and-pepper silver, and she wore a red sundress. Their brows were both finely furrowed with anxiety.

"Miss Shane?" Mr. Park asked, stooping to peer through the passenger-side window. He held Neal and Nealey by their leashes; they wiggled with excitement, their tails whooshing side to side.

"Yes, that's me!" Shane hurriedly stepped outside and snapped the door shut behind her. "Any sign of her?"

"Not yet. How old are you?"

"Seventeen." She took the two dogs from Mr. Park; Nellie audibly sniffed his younger siblings and then trotted around the car, as if searching for Lorenza.

"About Donnie's age." Mr. Park rubbed his face. "That's too young. I've already called the police. With another person missing, they must take us seriously. You can wait in the house, in our living room —"

"I'm well trained in tracking," Shane insisted.

"So was your mother," he pointed out. "Hon, don't go into that forest."

"Respectfully," Grandpa interrupted, rounding the car, Marcos trailing behind him. "Lorenza's family. Doesn't matter who've you called; we're going to look for her."

"I —"

"What can we do to help?" Mrs. Park interjected, resting a hand on her husband's shoulder.

Grandpa Louis gave her an approving nod. "Lead us to the railroad tracks. We'll take it from there."

"And do you have something that belonged to Donnie and Bobby?" Shane added. "Clothing, shoes . . . anything that carries their scent." She'd brought one of her mother's bandanas, but just in case, the dogs should have connections to all of the missing people.

"Baseball caps?" Mrs. Park suggested.

"Perfect. Please get them."

Mrs. Park retreated to grab the hats, her sun dress flapping with each hurried step. She returned within three minutes, breathing heavily. "Here." Slightly bent over to catch her breath, the Elder held out a pair of caps. "Red is Donnie. Blue is Bobby." Frankly, Shane could have guessed that based on their size alone. She hoped that the siblings were still together: Donnie was old enough to be a protector.

For a moment, Shane stared at the red one. It had a logo on the front, a serrated tooth in a white circle. The Houston Cryptids' minor league team. As a child, Shane had seen them play, but that wasn't the memory that enveloped her as she clutched Donnie's hat in a tightening grip.

Her father used to wear this very same Houston Cryptids baseball cap. Was this a sign? A good sign? A bad one?

"Hey!" Grandpa Louis gave her shoulder a light shake.

"What?"

"Good to go?"

"Yes," she decided, stamping down her memories. "But what about Marcos? It could be dangerous . . ."

"We can watch him," Mrs. Park offered.

"Do you want to help find your ma?" Grandpa Louis asked, and Marcos nodded adamantly. "Then that's settled. He'll stay with us." As if to emphasize the point, Grandpa Louis took Marcos by the hand. "We'll look out for each other."

"Uh huh, OK," Marcos solemnly promised.

"Welp. Right this way," Mr. Park said, and then guided them around the house. His wife remained on the porch, waiting for backup to arrive, her hands clasped worriedly. As Shane followed and approached the tree line, she looked up to note the sun's mid-sky position. During summertime, the days in Texas were long, but they still only had a couple hours to safely navigate the forest.

"The railroad tracks are very close," Mr. Park explained, setting a brisk pace. "See this path?" He pointed to the ground, where a ribbon of hard-packed dirt and trampled grass cut through the forest. "Donnie and Bobby made it with their feet. They walk here every day. Usually visit the Herotonic River to look for fossils or go fishing. Sometimes, there's bass in

90

the shade of the junipers. It's supposed to be safe."

"What happened when my ma vanished?" Shane asked. "Where were you?"

"We'd followed Donnie's scent trail into the forest. Not too far. There's an abandoned house — the man who used to live there died ages ago. It seems Donnie and Bobby had been messing around the old property. Them dogs started howling, and your mother said, 'The trail ends here.' We assumed that Donnie and Bobby were trapped in the house. I went inside, while Lorenza searched the yard for a cellar. We were only separated for five minutes. The house is small: just a bedroom, kitchen, bathroom, and living room. After finding no sign of Donnie or Bobby, I went outside. Immediately, the dogs ran to me with their leashes dangling loose. That's when I started worrying."

"You mean Lorenza was gone in a snap?" Grandpa Louis demanded. "She didn't shout? Her dogs never barked? Nothing?"

"You didn't hear a long, piercing howl?" Shane interjected. She had to be sure.

"Nothing." Mr. Park's brow furrowed, and he looked aside, as if gazing into his memories. "Wait. There was one thing. It may be my imagination."

"What?" Shane encouraged.

"The fire pit in the backyard. When your mother and I first reached the house, I noticed a circle of burnt ground. Gray, like old ashes. I . . . I think a second one appeared after she went missing. It's hard to say. Again, I might be imagining things. My attention was focused on the house."

"If you're right, though, that's very strange," Shane agreed, exchanging a concerned glance with her grandfather. "It could be something like magic." In Lorenza's search-and-rescue experience, encompassing dozens of missions, she'd only crossed paths with the supernatural twice. In the first encounter, she'd skirted a bigfoot's territory. After noticing the signs — namely, big footprints and cairns of gray pebbles — Lorenza had retraced her steps to give the creature plenty of space. She'd trusted Nellie to continue down the scent trail alone, later following his baying to the missing hiker. Apparently, after noticing a distant bigfoot, the hiker had been so frightened he'd slipped down a steep part of the mountain trail and broke his leg.

In the second encounter, Lorenza had found the remains of two hunters who'd been gored to death. The third hunter — gored but alive — had explained that they'd shot at a deer. Yet, it hadn't really been a deer. No, not really. And they'd paid a terrible price for their mistake.

"Here we are," Mr. Park said, stopping at the iron railroad tracks. "Considering the danger, I'm not taking another step, and I certainly won't blame you for turning back now." Immediately, Nellie's shimmer started pacing and snuffling, an anxious whine emanating from his chest.

"Nellie is looking for Mom!" Marcos exclaimed, pulling free from Grandpa Louis's hold and patting the shimmer. "Good boy."

"Who cursed the dog?" Mr. Park asked, his tone guarded. "Is there no cure?"

"Cursed?" Grandpa Louis asked. "Old Nellie? He's just a typical ghost."

At that, Shane flinched, and Mr. Park raised his eyebrow. If people ever noticed Nellie, Lorenza usually lied about his nature. She'd claim that he was a living bloodhound who'd been affected with a spell of invisibility.

"You didn't know?" Grandpa Louis asked. "Lorenza and Shane can summon the ghosts of animals. It's a trick my ex taught 'em. Trust me, Nellie's an asset. His nose is ten times stronger than any mortal snout."

"It's a little more than a trick . . ." Shane elaborated, chewing on her thumbnail. She thought she'd kicked that habit in sixth grade, but it'd come back with a vengeance that afternoon. Every cuticle was red, her fingertips soft. "It's sacred know-how, passed down over generations. Nellie has brought dozens of people home. That's why I'm hopeful."

"I am, too," Grandpa Louis said.

Suddenly, with a sharp bark of excitement, Nellie shot off down the tracks.

"Hey!" Shane called, startled. He normally didn't bolt after a scent. "Slow down, boy!" Still grasping Neal and Nealey's leashes, Shane sprinted after Nellie. They ran between the steel rails, stepping on the evenly spaced wooden sleepers.

"Wait a minute!" Grandpa hollered. "We're fallin' behind!"

"Don't worry!" she shouted. "I got this!"

"Shane, I told ya to wait!" His humorless tone left no room for argument. Shane stopped, turning: there was her grandfather, sprinting up the tracks in his cowboy boots, pulling Marcos by the hand. It only took a few seconds for them to catch up, but in that time, Nellie's shimmer had all but vanished in the distance. Shane itched to follow him — to reach Lorenza more quickly — but her grandfather was right: they shouldn't split up.

"Double time, let's go!" Grandpa Louis commanded, dashing past her, unfazed. "I wager the dog's on to something."

"Find Mom!" Marcos shouted, brushing a strand of hair from his face. "Go, Nellie, go!"

The faint shimmer of the bloodhound swerved off the tracks, following a narrow, barely perceptible footpath into the forest. Shane broke into a jog after them, since a full sprint would be too fast for Marcos's legs, which were already a whir of motion.

"If Donnie and Bobby made this trail, too," she commented, "they must have played at the house a lot." She transferred both dog leashes to one hand and then removed her Swiss army knife from its utility belt pocket, flicking out the dull blade with her thumb.

"You'll need something better than that," Grandpa replied, keeping pace next to her. Without skipping a step, he stooped to quickly pull a hunting knife out of his boot. Although the wooden hilt was dull with age, its blade glinted like quicksilver.

"Whoa!" Shane exclaimed. "How long has that been in your shoe?"

"Always," he said. "Take it." Without hesitation, Shane accepted the unexpected gift hilt-first. There were four slight indentations in the oak; valleys worn by her grandfather's fingers. Shane tested her grip on the knife, noting that her hand was smaller than his, but the balance felt good.

"What's this made of?" she wondered. For such a small weapon, the hunting knife was heavy.

"Steel," he answered. "You know how to use it?"

"Uh . . ." She slowed down a little and glanced away from Nellie to stare at her grandfather. "Like this?"

Shane used the hunting knife to nick a nearby conifer, scratching a centimeter-long, angled notch in the bark. It wasn't deep enough to hurt the tree; she just needed a mark to follow if they had to retrace their steps without the help of Neal or Nealey. The footpath was spotty, often vanishing in thin spots of the forest, where there were wide buffers of bare ground between the trees.

"Don't wear down its blade, Shane," he scolded. "You need a sharp edge to cut past skin."

"So it's for gutting a fish?" she asked wryly, momentarily slowing again to sheathe the weapon and secure it in her belt. Unlike her grandfather, Shane wasn't experienced in handling weapons at a run.

"Sure."

"You think we'll need to fight?" she pressed.

"Might."

At the confirmation, Shane's steps quickened back up again with her heartbeat.

What was the use of a knife — even a wickedly sharp one — against a gun or powerful magics? Some fae descendants could fight with whips of pure fire.

"I don't expect it," her grandfather said, "but you can never be too careful."

"Sounds like something Ma always says."

"Guess I taught her something," he muttered.

"Can I have one?" Marcos asked, pointing at Grandpa Louis's other boot, as if wondering how many weapons were hidden alongside his socks.

"You got shoes, kid."

"No, I want a knife!"

"Someday," he promised. "Shane, let Marcos hold one of the dogs. She'll keep him safe." Then, Grandpa Louis leaned over to whisper, in confidence, "Maybe I should have left him at the house, but . . ."

"What?" she whispered back.

"I don't know who to trust. Do you?"

While passing Neal's leash to Marcos, she considered the question. "I trust the Parks —"

"Why?" he asked. "They're strangers."

98

"If you don't trust them, why'd you tell Mr. Park about Nellie?" Although she'd meant it as an accusation, Shane's tone came out more inquisitive than anything else.

"Is that a joke?" When she continued staring at him, Grandpa urged, "What?"

"We aren't supposed to mention the ghosts."

"What do you say, then?"

"That we train living dogs. One's invisible."

"You lie to your clients?"

"Only when they notice Nellie. I'm usually bad at fibbing."

"Hey, I'm not wringing my hands, scandalized." Grandpa Louis snorted. "Anyway, that's not even lying. It's bluffing. I'm a master of the art. But why's it necessary to bluff about Nellie? If the Parks are friends, they'll be impressed that you control ghosts. If they're enemies, they'll be intimidated. Win-win."

"Ma says it's dangerous. Some people will get scared, and others . . . ." Aware that Marcos was listening now, Shane toned down her explanation. "If word spreads that our family still knows how to raise animal ghosts, we could be targeted, Grandpa. By people who'd get scared. Or who'd try to steal the knowledge."

"Oh, mija! Don't worry. This isn't the 1800s." The humor seeped from her grandfather's voice. "And if anyone tries to hurt you kids, I'll kill them."

In the years she'd known him, Shane had never seen her grandfather without a slight smirk. She'd assumed his mouth couldn't turn down, but clearly, she'd been wrong.

"Kill 'em?" Marcos exclaimed, looking up with a wide-eyed gasp. "How?"

And the switch flipped back; Grandpa chuckled, his eyes crinkling. He ruffled Marcos's hair playfully. "With my bare hands."

Shane wasn't deceived by his pal-around behavior. Her grandfather might be skilled in the art of bluffing-not-lying, but unless he was the world's greatest actor, she had no doubt that he'd gladly kill somebody to protect them. Most likely with the pistol holstered at his hip.

And why not? What would Shane do to defend her friends and family? If the search for Lorenza ended at a criminal wizard's house, and the man confronted them with an inferno shotgun, would she hesitate before summoning a writhing mass of ghost alligators? Of course not. She'd bury him in teeth.

With a thought, Shane reached out until she sensed them — the dead — their presence like an itch between her ears. Running, swimming, soaring, slithering: the ghosts of the forest waited for Shane's call. She wound through the frenzy, taking stock of her potential allies.

She didn't see, smell, or hear them. Instead, she knew them by their approach; the space they filled; the reactions of other presences; the lures that enticed them to earth. And a quality she couldn't describe with words, much like the sensation of love: to her, they were both ineffable.

Wolves, bears, mountain lions, and other large predators were too dangerous; Shane couldn't direct their aggression. A distraction would be better. She could call upon swarmers: mosquitoes, biting flies, wasps, and gnats. In fact, Shane's familiarity with insect ghosts made it easier to wake them up at a moment's notice. And there were so many . . . billions upon billions!

Suddenly, a looming presence brushed against her consciousness, as if using her as a guideline. It wasn't a bug; it was too large and unknown to her. She withdrew, yet the ghost surged forward.

What had she awoken?

Sensing danger, Nellie barked twice, sharply. And, as if burned, the unknown ghost withdrew.

"Gawd!" Shane cried, returning to her senses.

"What is it?" Grandpa Louis asked.

"Nothing. I . . ." She looked down at her shaking hands and then up again, taking in their surroundings. While her mind had been preoccupied with the dead, her body had continued walking, as if running on autopilot. "We're here?"

The wilderness tapered off into a clearing of knee-high grasses and stumps surrounding a wretched little cabin. It was in a sorry state, its foundation crooked, its walls leaning at a perilous angle, like the Tower of Pisa. The rotten door hung open, and no glass remained in the front windows. Leaves, twigs, and other windblown organic rubbish blanketed the drooping roof.

Although Nellie trotted straight for the front door, Shane hesitated, waiting for her grandfather's input.

"That shack is a hazard," he said. "Marcos, don't let go of my hand."

"I won't, Grandpa. It's OK."

"Ma?" Shane shouted, although she suspected it was useless; had Lorenza been nearby, Nellie would have noticed her. "Ma! We're here!"

Nellie walked into the cabin, unconcerned by its dilapidated state; if the house toppled, he'd simply float through the rubble, one perk of being bodiless. The living weren't so lucky. Shane, Grandpa Louis, Marcos, and the other two dogs went only as far as the stoop, which creaked under their feet.

"Anyone there?" Shane shouted, stretching out her left hand, touching the dull doorknob with her fingertips. "Ma? Bobby? Donnie? Make a sound if you hear me!"

Of course, somebody else could be lurking in the house. Cryptids, monsters, spirits. Ghosts. And for every inhuman threat, there were a hundred humans just as dangerous, if not more. Humans who'd gladly prey on children like Bobby or Marcos; on teenagers like Donnie or Shane. On women like her mother.

There was a buzz, then the hum of quick little wings; a translucent wasp flew past Shane's cheek and into the darkness beyond the cracked cabin door. She must have disturbed the ghost earlier, when she'd been distracted by the unknown presence, 'cause she hadn't intended to wake anything yet.

Cautiously, Shane opened the door all the way and peered inside. The dim living room smelled of vegetable rot and mouse droppings.

"Nasty," Grandpa said. He briskly retreated down the porch steps. "Let's find the mysterious fire pits. Just be sure to give them space."

Shane noticed that Grandpa Louis's free hand rested on his pistol now, its holster unclipped. As a group, they circled the abandoned house to check the backyard, which was partially reclaimed by the forest. To the right was a waist-high pyramid of old car tires and a stump crisscrossed with gouges from an axe head. The long-gone tenant must have used it to chop wood. To the left, a handmade swing dangled from the bough of an old elm tree. Shane paused, remembering a similar one from her childhood: a plank her father had hung behind their house. She used to love that old swing; she'd pretend to be a winged girl, kicking her legs to fly higher as her parents took turns pushing her.

Did the swing survive the flood? Yes. She remembered, now. The swing and the old oak tree. But it didn't matter.

Nellie's shimmer paced the back of the clearing, fixated on a circle of ash-gray ground. Roughly twenty feet wide, the area was bare of life, as if burned into the earth; she understood why Mr. Park had mistaken it for a fire pit. In fact, from a distance, it did resemble the base of a large bonfire. But upon closer inspection — not too close, since Grandpa Louis stopped the group about six feet away from the perimeter — Shane realized that the circle was too geometrically perfect. Plus, there were no charred pieces of wood or garbage. Just gray dirt powdered with fine, bone-white dust. There was a second, slightly smaller circle behind it. Notably, instead of ash, the area smelled faintly sweet — like vanilla.

"Kids, get back," Grandpa Louis barked. "I think I know what it is."

"Is it dangerous?" Shane asked, taking Marcos by the elbow and guiding him behind their grandfather.

"Did the circle hurt mom?" he asked, shaking off Shane's hand.

"'Course not." Grandpa Louis shuffled a few steps closer, crouched, and pushed a leaf aside, revealing a delicate, bell-shaped mushroom. Its white cap was speckled with raised red spots, like frozen drops of blood. Now that she knew what to look for, Shane started seeing the other white and red caps. In fact, a ring of mushrooms surrounded the gray circle, as if it were the oversized bullseye in a natural dart board, the swollen pupil of a trippy eye. Could it be . . . ?

"What does this look like?" Grandpa Louis asked.

"A fairy ring?" Shane shook her head. "That's not possible." Even under optimal conditions, it was tricky to cultivate fairy ring species on Earth, 'cause they came from a different realm. Plus, in the rare chance they'd stumbled upon a miraculous wild fairy ring, Shane's family had no fae descendants. That meant Lorenza couldn't use it. Fae wouldn't allow "The Unrelated" — what they called most humans — to travel by their extradimensional magic.

"The Longfire Incident," Grandpa Louis said, pacing around the anomaly, his downcast eyes sharp, his hand once again on the pistol. "Nineteen twenties. Didn't they teach you about that in school?"

"No," Shane admitted. Was that 'cause textbooks didn't consider Longfire important, or had she just missed the lesson? Their frequent moves throughout elementary and middle school had disrupted her schooling time and time again.

"Psht. Education these days." Grandpa pointed at one of the innocent-looking mushrooms. "I'd bet my hat those are mimics! They're also from the fae realm, but they don't need magic to work 'cause they take energy from the life in the ground, which means anyone can use 'em to go anywhere. I thought they dealt with mimics after the Longfire Incident, though. This ain't sensible."

"Just what happened in the nineteen twenties?"

"Complicated story. I'll tell you later." He stepped over the fairy circle's perimeter, standing in the narrow strip of green and brown earth that surrounded the dead gray circle, and looked up at her. "Right now, I'm going to find your mother. There may be enough power left for a jump. If your mom and I aren't back in ten minutes, tell the Parks about this ring, and take care of each other."

"We will," Shane said, nodding at her grandfather and holding Marcos tight. This time, he didn't push her away. What a relief: it was all an accident, just people stumbling into a transporter, and not a malicious kidnapping. "Bring her home."

With a confident smile, her grandfather commanded, "Circle, take me to Lorenza."

A squirrel skittered across the yard. And aside from that, absolutely nothing of interest happened.

"C'mon, you bastard teleporter!" Grandpa Louis stomped his foot, kicking up gray dust. "Where'd you send my daughter? Transport me there!"

"Let me try," Shane suggested.

With a muttered curse, her grandfather shook his head. "Don't bother. There's not enough power left. These rings feed off the ground inside them, and as you can see, most of it's drained. It could probably transport me thirty feet away" — he winked out of existence, only to reappear instantaneously at the swing set, still speaking — "but not . . . oh! See? It worked!"

The gray circle expanded; now, it touched the edge of the ring, whose mushrooms shriveled, their red spots darkening to black. Before Shane's eyes, the mimic — the only known link to Lorenza — was dying.

"Grandpa, you killed it!"

"Can you use that one instead?" Marcos asked, pointing to a nearby spot of land. It took Shane a couple seconds to see the other foot-wide ring of mushrooms, their thimble-sized caps of red and white obscured by weeds and dead conifer needles.

"Don't move!" Shane barked out, jumping forward and checking his feet. Thankfully, Marcos wasn't standing in a mimic circle, but there might be others; in fact, she realized the backyard could be a minefield of transporters. On the one hand, this was a good thing. They might find another ring that was big enough to send Grandpa Louis to Lorenza. On the other hand, it seemed one wrong step could also send Marcos to the moon, if the thought popped into his head. Could mimic circles do that? Could they send anyone anywhere, with enough power? Dismayed, Shane realized that the education system really had failed her. When she got back home, she'd search the library for books on paranormal, supernatural, and magical disasters, since her desired line of work was clearly rife with them.

And the question remained: *Where was her mother now?*

Not the moon or another inhospitable location, thank the creator (and Nellie), Shane told herself. Her mother was just somewhere without a phone. The same must be true for Bobby and Donnie.

Perhaps all three were together? Lorenza, intentionally or unintentionally, might've thought *I want to find the siblings* as she stepped into a ring, and had been instantaneously transported to their side.

The moment Shane had that notion, she noticed that she was standing in a well-hidden, hula-hoop-sized circle of red and white.

"Son of a —"

Then, the world seemed to flip.

At least, that's how it felt. The ground tilted forward, throwing the blue sky below Shane. For the second time that afternoon, she recalled her old swing set, vividly remembering the time she'd decided to jump at the swing's highest point, letting her momentum carry her into the air. The world had been blurry with motion, disorienting but exhilarating, and although Shane hadn't expected to actually fly, she'd hoped that the second of weightlessness before her fall would be close enough. That the landing wouldn't hurt.

But now, there was no landing. In fact, she never actually left the ground. One moment, her tennis shoes were pressed against firm dirt. The next, they compressed a crunchy bed of pine needles and loamy soil. When the sky flipped the right way and the world stopped spinning, Shane realized that she was no longer in hill country.

She'd landed in the middle of the Ozarks.

⌒ FIVE ⌒

Dizzy, as if she'd just stepped off a merry-go-round, Shane dropped to her knees and waited for her head to stop spinning. The disorientation passed quickly, letting her take stock of her surroundings.

Forests have personalities of bird-song, shade, scent, and color. Some are sharp with thorns, others soft with moss. Boulders and valleys, rivers and lakes, predators and prey; all these are as much a part of their forests as the trees. People, too, can belong — can *be* — forest. If they are home there; if they do not cause imbalance. Although Shane had been born in the plains of south Texas, she'd made friends with the Texan forests up north.

And while the Ozarks were still strangers, she recognized their face.

She'd seen a forest like this once before, during a drive to Little Rock, Arkansas. As Lorenza steered the truck down winding mountain roads, with Marcos sleeping in his baby basket, Shane had pressed her face against the passenger-side window, wide-eyed. To her, the forests of Arkansas belonged in a fairytale, like that one about Red Riding Hood. Her family's traditional lore rarely happened in deep green biomes; they'd been forged from a long history among the mountains of Big Bend, surrounded by the rattle of mesquite and the sway of vast green and yellow plains. In deserts and shrubland; on the coast of the gray Gulf; along fertile floodplains and over forested hills.

Typical fairy rings always grew in pairs, living and dying together. It was part of their alien biology: they weren't two separate rings, but one ring in two places. The fae realm, from which magic spilled onto Earth, was a place of spatial and temporal anomalies. Space and time could be stretched, refracted, and reassembled like the building blocks in a child's play pen.

Simply put, it was impossible for a typical fairy ring to exist — much less function — in just one point on the globe.

Yet mimics were clearly different. Shane crawled in ever-widening loops, sweeping pine needles, searching unsuccessfully for a doorway home. Finding nothing, she stood and planted her hands on her hips, thinking. She'd landed in the same time zone, as the sun was low in the sky, its light deepening in color from white to yellow. However, it was chilly relative to mid-Texas, and likely to become unpleasantly cold after nightfall. Shane had packed so quickly, she'd forgotten to shove a jacket into her survival backpack, which was still on her shoulders.

"Grandpa?" she shouted, hoping he'd found a ring that enabled him to follow her trip. Shane didn't know how much power a several-hundred-mile journey required. She could be stranded, like her mother.

However, unless the ring was malfunctioning, Shane couldn't be alone. She'd been thinking about the lost siblings just milliseconds before it transported her.

Shane cupped her hands around her mouth, using them to amplify her voice. "Donnie? Bobby?" When that failed to provoke a response, she grabbed a gym whistle from her bag, stuck it in her mouth, and blew a series of shrill, loud tweets.

A distant voice answered, "I hear you!"

"Donnie?" she guessed. "Donnie Park?!"

"Yeah! Keep whistling!"

Shane channeled her inner lifeguard and blew the whistle until Donnie burst into view, a lanky girl crashing through crunchy, knee-high bushes and shoving aside low branches. Although she'd only been missing a day, Donnie was bedraggled and dirty, with leaves tangled in her frizzy black hair as if she'd survived many days and nights alone in the wilderness. Her thin lips were chapped and pale, and the shadows under her downturned eyes were emphasized by old, streaked eyeliner and mascara. At Wilson High, the football jocks dabbed their upper cheeks with stripes of black grease to reduce glare. Over the course of a game, the grease would smudge, becoming diffuse and smoky, almost like a mask around their eyes. That's what Donnie resembled, only worse, since the knees of her bell-bottom jeans were grimy like she'd been crawling around the forest, and her white T-shirt was speckled with bright-red droplets. One of its sleeves was missing, revealing a sunburn-tinted shoulder. "Oh, no, you're hurt?" Shane asked, pointing at the blood spatter.

"Nah, nah, it's fine." Donnie's response came out rushed, breathless; she must have run a long way. "Cut my palm, that's all." She held up her right hand, which was wrapped in a strip of dirt-and-blood-stained cotton fabric: the missing sleeve. Its edges were frayed, as if torn by force or gnawed by blunt human teeth.

"We should bandage that properly —"

"Later." The girl looked around, skittish as a deer. "Have you seen my brother? He resembles me, but small and tan."

"Bobby? You didn't land here together?"

"No." Donnie shook her head. "Don't think so. You're the first person I've seen in the forest." At that, she openly stared at Shane, taking in her practical overalls, hiking boots, and survival gear. "Who are you?"

"Shane. My ma and I help find missing people. Your grandparents sent us. Well, they sent my ma, and then she disappeared, too, 'cause there are mimic rings — they're like fairy rings — growing at the old house near the railroad tracks. I accidentally stepped in one, thought about finding you, and sure enough . . ."

"You appeared here." Donnie ran her good hand through her mane of hair, distractedly combing the dense strands away from her face. A dry, yellow oak leaf fell out of her crooked bangs and spun to the ground. "Mimic rings, huh? OK, OK. That makes sense. At first, I thought I was losing my —" There was a soft crunch; at the sound, Donnie jolted and looked over her shoulder, gasping, "What was that?"

"It sounded like a pinecone falling off a branch."

"Right. Obviously." Her shoulders fell, their tension dispersing. "I watch too many scary movies. Keep expecting a masked killer to pop out of the shadows."

"Where is this place, Donnie? Why'd the ring send you here?"

"There's a cabin by the lake," Donnie answered. Briefly, her eyes went distant.

118

Then, with an encouraging "C'mon, I'll show you," she turned and briskly walked south. Shane followed, increasing her pace to match Donnie's short but rapid steps.

"My family used to vacation here," she explained, "before Bobby was born. The state park rents out cabins. Mom would sit on the dock, reading. Dad had his fishing rod, and I'd go swimming all day long. I wanted to live in the water. Grow gills and fins and never leave."

"Ah," Shane said. "Like that old story about a boy who became a fish."

"Seriously, he did? How?"

"Um. He . . ." She paused, concentrated, shook her head. "Actually, I can't remember anymore. It's been too long since Grandma Yolanda told me. But . . . I think the ending's bittersweet."

"Aren't they all?"

"What do you mean?" Shane asked. She could think of many stories that ended happily.

"Dunno," Donnie shrugged. "Just, I can never bring myself to finish a good book. The end hurts too much. Well, except for scary books, but those are different. They freak me out, so the end's a relief."

Personally, Shane enjoyed the satisfaction of reaching "The End" in her paperbacks, especially when the conclusion rewarded the journey. However, she understood where Donnie came from. "You want happy stories to last forever."

"Guess so," Donnie said.

They walked down a shallow incline, and Shane could see a glittering lake ahead, liquid aquamarine. A long wooden dock extended from its bank.

"Back then, I'd have grilled corn and hot dogs for lunch and dinner," Donnie continued, softly. "There's an old metal grill outside the cabin, but Dad always brought his own. It was a little grill, fire truck red. He never had time to cook at home."

They paused a moment, taking in the area. "My pa used to love grilling, too," Shane remembered. She closed her eyes, thinking of a yellow field, tall flowers bobbing in the wind. "In the early summer, we'd walk to a patch of sunflowers behind our house. They grew wild near the old oak tree. We'd look for wilting petals and soft, new seeds; those were ready to eat.

Pa called it the place where the sun always shines."

"I've had roasted sunflower seeds, but I didn't know they could be cooked like corn."

"Easily. You just have to time it right. Pa would season them with salt, pepper, and . . . a mixture of spices. I wish I knew what they were. Tasted delicious."

Donnie gently nudged Shane with her bony elbow and leaned in. "You could be scientific about it. Run taste tests until you find the right mix. Bring back the recipe."

"True."

"You know, it sounds like our dads could have been friends."

"Sure does."

The two of them smiled at the thought.

"Why did the ring bring you here?" Shane then wondered. "Were you thinking of the lake?"

"Right before I got transported," Donnie explained, "me and Bobby were gathering supplies for a treehouse. The abandoned house is too gross. Pretty sure it's rotting. We were going to make our own. I was telling him about this place — about the cabin — for inspiration."

"You were thinking about old times, longing to be here, and the mimic ring responded?"

"Yeah," she said. "Damn ring. I was thinking about the lake, how refreshing it felt to dive in the cold water. It dropped me straight into the deep part off the dock."

At the thought, Shane shuddered.

"You cold?" Donnie asked.

"No, just creeped out. I'm glad you weren't sent to the middle of the lake." On the other side of the vast, glittering waterbody, the trees resembled twigs. It would have been an exhausting, perhaps futile swim to dry ground. "I can't see any cabin," Shane realized. "Where is it?"

Donnie pointed at a patch of land near the dock, where a hand-built stone wall enclosed emptiness. "Used to be there," she replied. "They must've torn down the building."

No chance of convenient shelter or a phone, then. But there had to be other houses nearby. A road they could follow to a bigger road with cars. "Are there neighbors?" Shane asked. "Other cabins?"

"Nope, negatory . . ." Donnie made a thoughtful humming sound. "There was a town, barely. Just a few houses, a bar, and a general store. Loggers and their families lived there. It was down an access road behind the cabin. We'd visit for canned food and night crawlers."

"When you say 'there was a town,' you're speaking in past tense."

"'Cause the town's abandoned. I checked yesterday."

"You're kidding." Shane's instincts for danger began to prickle. Within the span of a few years, the cabin had been demolished, and the village had been emptied. Why? What had motivated all the people to leave?

"Nah, my sense of humor isn't that terrible. All the buildings are boarded up, like the families decided to pack 'n move. At least I didn't see any bloody handprints on the doors. Can you imagine?"

"Rather not! When was the last time you visited the lake?"

"Almost eight years ago. After Bobby was born, my family took a break from travelling. Mom and Dad were saving for a special trip to Galveston instead. You can see the ocean from Galveston."

At that, Shane smiled. "Gorgeous view of the Gulf. I've visited once."

"Yeah? What's it like?" Donnie sounded wistful.

"Galveston?"

"The ocean."

"Oh." She chewed her thumbnail, thinking. "Big."

Donnie snickered, heading toward the stone square. "No shit, Sherlock."

"Yup." While following her, Shane eyed the sky, guessing they had an hour or two before full dark. "How far's that logging town? And did you see any equipment we could use to call for help?"

"It's a mile." She abruptly stopped walking between the stone wall and the water. Shane noticed that all the amusement had drained from Donnie's voice now; her eyes no longer crinkled with sardonic amusement. "But there's something I have to tell you about the forest. You'll think I'm chicken —"

"I promise that won't happen," Shane interrupted, offering Donnie a bag of trail mix from her backpack. "Here, eat this while you explain."

"God, thank you. I haven't had a bite since breakfast. Yesterday!" Donnie shoveled a handful of granola, chocolate chips, sunflower seeds, pumpkin seeds, and raisins into her mouth and chewed.

"I brought fresh water and cheesy crackers, too," Shane said, grinning. "We can share them later. It would be great to find a phone or CB radio 'fore nightfall, though."

"Here's the thing. Forests don't scare me. I'm way more anxious in cities. You know monsters live in the tunnels under New York City? The kind from deep caverns. They're spreading."

"I might've heard something like that." Shane recalled a report on the national news with video of four men in dark cloaks. They patrolled the subway system, searching for ancient, bloodlust-driven vampires who plucked victims from isolated platforms late at night. The deep-cavern monsters were new to her, though.

"But ever since I landed here . . ." Donnie trailed off, nibbling on her lower lip.

"What's wrong? You can tell me."

"When I lose sight of the water" — she jabbed a thumb over her shoulder, pointing to the lake — "this major sense of danger builds, like I'm walking into a trap. I gave the town a quick look and called Bobby's name, but after a few minutes, everything felt too wrong. So I ran back here. And it's better here. Maybe 'cause I have nice memories of the lake."

Shane took a moment to quietly observe their surroundings, especially the tree line. "I don't notice anything dangerous," she said, and when Donnie blushed with shame, red splotches spreading down her face and neck, Shane hastily explained, "That doesn't mean you're imagining stuff! Donnie, I've never been here before. You have. You're familiar with the area, know its personality. The way it used to look, sound, and smell. Trust your instincts. That's an early lesson Ma taught me." She pointed to the bare foundation

126

where the cabin used to sit. "It's gone for a reason. So are the loggers."

"Yeah . . ." Her gaze swept from the lake to the deep forest. "I just wish I understood why my instincts are wigging out."

"Does the wrongness get worse at night?" Shane asked, eyeing the low sun, trying to make a decision: stay at the lake or search the town.

"I don't know," Donnie admitted. "I hid under a boat with my pointies when it got dark, and didn't emerge till daylight."

On the bank, there was an overturned rowboat with a hole in its hull. They walked there, and then Donnie kicked the boat over to reveal a pile of tinder, twigs, and sharpened sticks ranging in size from a couple feet to spear length.

"Ah, these must be the pointies?" Shane guessed, grabbing a small stake. "Are they weapons?"

"Not originally. Yesterday, I collected wood for a fire," Donnie picked up a mid-length oak branch and tested its balance with a couple slow swings. "When I couldn't get the flame started, I tried to go

127

spear fishing. Not my best idea." She held up her bandaged hand.

"So that's how you got hurt?" Shane eyed the blood droplets on Donnie's shirt, hoping they were from a shallow scratch, and that she hadn't accidentally speared herself through the palm.

"Yeah." With the spear, she prodded the dirt, scraping frowny faces into the ground. "I was using a sharp rock to carve the points and accidently slashed myself on the palm. But that's not all." At that, Donnie tugged one of her pantlegs up, revealing an egg-shaped bruise on her calf. "When I actually tried to catch dinner, at the first sign of movement underwater, I got too excited, tripped on algae scum, and made this happen."

After noticing a red puncture over the purple welt, Shane knelt to take a closer look. "Are you sure that's not a bite?" she asked. "Looks like a tooth mark there, see?"

"You think?" Instead of sitting to observe the injury, Donnie bent at the waist, her hair flopping down like a curtain. After a moment of stunned silence, she clicked her tongue and prodded the bruise; clear fluid and blood welled from the puncture.

"Leave it alone!" Shane warned, pushing Donnie's hand away. "Poking will only make things worse."

"What if it's from a snake?" Donnie's already high voice had now become shrill with anxiety.

"Been a day, so you probably don't have to worry about venom. Might need antibiotics from the doctor's office, though. You say there was movement?"

"Yeah, underwater. Are there piranhas in Arkansas? Maybe one escaped from the zoo."

"How would a piranha . . ." Shane shook her head at Donnie's upside-down smile. "You got me. C'mon, now."

After the pair stood straight, their attention returned to the pile of spears and stakes.

"We can use the long ones as walking sticks," Shane suggested, swapping out the stake for a waist-high oak spear. "If something large charges you, hold it pointy-side out, bracing the end against the ground, see?" She did a quick demonstration. "You want the attacker to impale itself."

"Easy. No problem." Donnie laughed, snorting. "Don't be offended if I hide behind you instead, though."

"Offended? I'd be honored."

"My heroine."

Now armed, the two turned their backs on the lake and walked briskly to the overgrown access road. It was just wide enough for one car or a pair of teenagers walking side-by-side. Under the canopy of trees, the light dimmed, and the temperature dropped, a premature dusk.

"What happened to your mother?" Donnie asked, softly, as if they were studying in a library instead of trekking through the Ozarks.

"She got transported somewhere, too. It was earlier today, so I'm not in crisis mode. There's a good chance that Ma will get home without help. Not to brag, but it's really hard for us to stay lost."

"No, brag," Donnie insisted, with an edge of desperation. "I want to hear it.

Tell me all the righteous stuff you can do to find Bobby."

"Um, well." She'd never been put on the spot like this; even among friends like Amelia, Shane only discussed rescue highlights — the moments of discovery, the exhilaration of bringing a person home. She didn't bog down stories by describing all the work required to achieve these moments. "There's this. Ma says . . . when you plunge into the unknown during rescues, there are two journeys. First, you have to find the person. Then, you have to find the way back. These journeys may seem equally important, but they're not. 'Cause if you fail to locate a missing person, you can always try again. But if you fail to return home, you're lost, too."

Donnie made a sound of agreement.

"Ma wouldn't let me do real rescues until I mastered the blindfold test."

"What's that? Sounds fun."

"Actually, yeah. It was a game. Ma would drive me to a random place. A forest, a city, a beach. Wherever. Then she'd park, get out of the truck, and give me ten minutes to observe our location." Shane tapped

131

the bandana around her forehead. "After that, I'd cover my eyes, and Ma would guide me into the unknown. After about a mile, she'd make me spin till I got dizzy. Then, she'd say, 'Blindfold off. Find the truck.' At first, I'd use maps, compasses, and everything in my survival backpack. After I got good enough, she took away half my tools. By the end of my training, I could find the truck with nothing but the clothes on my back and the shoes on my feet. Considerin' Ma taught me everything I know, she'll for sure find a way home. Shoot, I bet she's already left a message with the neighbor."

A small part of Shane worried: *But what if she hasn't?* And: *But what if she can't?* Another part of her insisted: *Then we'll find her.*

And she had to find herself, first.

They walked quietly for a moment, and Shane used the lull in their conversation to catalogue the ambient sounds. Insects and frogs were the dominant noise-makers.

"How do the mimic rings work?" The question was flavored with a hint of apprehension, but Shane couldn't tell whether

132

the forest or something else was responsible for Donnie's fear.

"I'm not totally sure," she admitted. "The large ones are more powerful than the small ones. They burn the life inside them. Bigger diameter means more fuel."

"Can they read your thoughts? Sense where you want to be?"

"Yep."

"Ah, shit," Donnie whispered, and when Shane gave her a questioning look, she elaborated: "I don't know what Bobby was thinking. I hope . . . I hope the ring transported him to a friendly little village."

"Yeah," Shane agreed. "Yeah, I hope so, too."

Again, they descended into an alert silence. The lower the sun sank, the faster they walked, till the pair were nearly jogging, Donnie carrying the water thermos and taking deep gulps. Although she was rapidly exhausting their water supply, Shane cut her lots of slack; Donnie had been dehydrated, turned off by the lake's muddy taste.

They reached the logging village within twenty minutes. A clearing the size of two football fields had been cut into the forest; log cabins were arranged around the perimeter, with two long buildings in the center of the village, where the access road ended.

As expected, there were no signs of life, the cabins well-sealed by planks, the central courtyard empty. "One of these buildings had to be a communication center," Shane said. "A place to call for help. Even if we don't find a phone, if there's a radio, we can send a distress signal." Most of the ginormous lakes in Arkansas were man-made, the result of dams. Even at a late hour, there might be people working at the reservoir. If not, somebody else might hear their call for help. Retirees in lakeside houses, visitors camping in the forest, rangers working at parks. Shane and Donnie might be the only two humans in the ghost town, but they couldn't be alone in the entire forest. People coveted lakes. Always had.

"This one used to be the general store," Donnie said, leading her to a rustic log cabin with boards nailed across its door and windows. "Great place to buy cola and worms for fishing. I learned how to bait a hook before any other kid." Shane stepped on a plank, and in the orange-tinted natural light, she observed that it was a fallen sign with the words *Food, Cigarettes, Drink* handwritten in blue paint.

"Excellent. Can you try to find a way inside? I'll refill our water supply."

"No problem." She dropped her spear and wedged her uninjured hand under one of the boards across the window. Once she had a firm grip, Donnie braced one foot against the wall and repeatedly threw her weight backward, prying the board loose with brute strength. One of the nails popped free, and the others creaked partway out of the windowsill. The gal was wiry but determined.

With a satisfied nod, Shane ran to the well and peered inside. Darkness. She patted the ground, found a pebble, and dropped it into the hole, listening. *Plink.* A soft impact, clearly muted by water. With a relieved huff of breath, Shane overturned the bucket, shook the bugs and dust out, and lowered it until she felt the rope go slack. It only took a few seconds for the vessel to fill, and the built-in pulley allowed her to retrieve half a gallon of water without much effort. As Shane tilted the metal bucket to fill her thermos, something clinked. Had she accidentally pulled up a rock, too? Reaching into the water, her hand closed around a baseball-sized object, smooth and light.

Wide-eyed, Shane held up an empty shell. It was, in the sunset, the color of a peach, the kind her mother picked in the orchards of central Texas when she wasn't picking melons. Oddly, its shape was something between a nautilus and a conch. Shane wondered: Would she hear the ocean if she held the shell against her ear?

Nearby, something heavy crunched in the brush. With the shell and half-full thermos in hand, Shane slowly backed away from the tree line. "Got that window open?" she called to Donnie.

"One more board, and we're in."

The crunches stopped abruptly. It was probably just a bold deer. Could also be a black bear, which were native to Arkansas. Although black bears were more skittish than grizzlies, and easier to scare away with an aggressive shout, Shane still didn't want to encounter one.

"Done," Donnie shouted, her voice punctuated by the sharp sound of nails popping out of the window frame. "There's no glass left."

Shane turned on her heels and sprinted to the grocery store. Donnie was already peering into the darkness, her chest pressed against the windowsill. "I think the shelves are empty," she reported. "Hard to see much, though."

"Let me take a peek," Shane suggested, extracting a flashlight from her bag. "Can you watch the forest? I heard something, probably an animal."

Donnie went wide-eyed, her head bobbing in a quick nod. She grabbed her spear and braced it against the ground, just like Shane had demonstrated earlier.

"Don't stress," Shane tried to reassure her. "If the critter didn't attack me at the well, when I was alone, I doubt it'll charge us now."

"Unless it's calling for backup," Donnie said, and although she phrased it like a joke, her lopsided smile didn't reach her eyes.

"One problem at a time." Then, she peeked into the grocery store, which smelled like cedarwood and dust. With a click of a switch, she turned on her flashlight and swept it side to side. The high-powered beam washed over empty shelves and illuminated a counter on the far side of the room; judging by its prominence in the store, it might have been the register station. The walls were bare, and although Shane didn't notice any carpets or trap doors, she did see numerous small, dark pellets on the floor.

"No luck," she sighed, quickly pulling her head outside. "Somebody totally cleared the store 'fore it was closed. Plus, it's an unsafe shelter. There're mouse droppings everywhere."

"Nasty." Donnie eyed the second long building, which faced the grocery store. "That used to be a community center. Can I borrow your light to look between the boards? The gaps might be wide enough."

"Sure."

After giving Donnie the flashlight, Shane eyed the courtyard, wondering what had driven the loggers away. The answer came a moment later, when her gaze landed on a sign beside the community center, a rectangle on a metal post.

She hadn't noticed it earlier because the building's heavy shadow obscured its mud-spattered face. But, as the light swept across the sign, momentarily illuminating a red hourglass symbol, Shane cried out, "Donnie, wait!"

"What?" Donnie immediately froze in her tracks, as if playing a game of Simon Says with life-or-death consequences.

"It's a warning! Look, to your right! What does it say beneath the hourglass?"

Donnie retrained her light on the sign and read aloud: "Dangerous xenobiology. No camping permitted."

"Monsters," Shane whispered, wishing she had Nellie to keep guard. "That's why the village is abandoned."

"Real monsters?"

Shane raised an eyebrow. Was she hearing things, or did Donnie sound a little excited now? Not "It's my birthday!" excited, with smiles and happy dancing. That would've been concerning. Rather, Donnie sounded like a gal who'd just agreed to ride the world's scariest roller coaster. Fear and macabre anticipation, combined. "Yes. That, or other supernaturals."

"They must be tough, or the special animal control would've cleared the area."

"Guess so. Especially when it comes to resource extraction, like logging. So yeah. I'd wager that the xenobiology is extremely dangerous, extremely difficult to restrain, or both."

"Well, what do we do? Turn back?"

"We'd have to move fast to beat nightfall. The critter could live in the forest." Shane eyed the village. There were no old vehicles to hide within. Perhaps they should look for a cleaner building, take shelter, and then hike to the nearest gas station at sunrise?

A gust of wind ruffled Shane's hair. Blinking, she grabbed her compass, eyed the needle, and faced due north. Then she licked her pointer finger and held it aloft. "The wind's blowing from the west!"

"So? Is that good?"

"Could be great. The lake's to the west of the dock. Ah, I hope I remembered to bring it . . ." She dropped the survival backpack, unzipped its main pouch, and rifled through her supplies. Shane had been so flustered that afternoon, she'd neglected one of Lorenza's earliest lessons: know everything you carry, and remember its place.

"Yes! Here!" She opened a lunchbox-sized metal canister. Inside, secured tightly, were the flare pistol and two cartridges.

"Whoa, you're packing heat?"

"It shoots distress signals." After hastily closing the canister, Shane jumped upright. "Can you build a campfire if I give you the necessary tools?"

"For sure! I already collected the timber, remember?"

"We could be rescued tonight!"

"Isn't the forest dangerous after dark?"

"Yes, so let's hurry!"

Donnie threw a peace sign into the air and cheered, "Run, run, run!"

Side by side, they ran down the access road; Donnie held the flashlight, and Shane explained her new plan. When they reached the lakeside, Donnie would build a roaring fire in the old stone pit. As she worked, Shane would go to the end of the dock and shoot the first signaling flare; the wind would safely push it over the water, alerting the lakeside community that somebody was in trouble. If it was overlooked, she'd fire a second time. The campfire would serve as a beacon; when the rescue boats came, they'd see its light. Once help arrived, they would call Mr. and Mrs. Park. Donnie knew their home phone number. If that failed, she'd call the neighbors. If all went smoothly, they'd be safe by midnight.

Within seven minutes — one of the fastest mile runs in Shane's life — they burst into the clearing near the lake. In the tail end of dusk, the dock resembled a long shadow. "Two days until the new moon," Shane observed. "It'll be a dark night."

"That makes it easier to notice the emergency light," Donnie said, slightly winded, and her optimism lightened Shane's heart.

"Yeah," she agreed, unclipping a small red pouch from her belt loop. Inside was a rod of flint and a steel nail file. "Here."

"What's this?" With a puzzled scowl, Donnie rattled the pouch, unzipped it, and shone the light inside. "A tiny knife and baton?"

"Flint. To start the fire."

"Uh, do you have a matchbook or a Zippo?"

Shane shook her head. Matches could get soggy, and they ran out quickly, while cigarette lighters were unnecessary. "Can't you use flint?" she asked, trying to keep her tone light and nonjudgmental.

In response, Donnie swiped the sharp end of the file against the stone, and sparks flew into the air. "Sure. It's been a few years, though, so I'm rusty."

"Hey, that's fine. Worst case scenario, I'll run back to help." Shane held up a fist, knuckles outward. "Ready?"

"Ready." Delicately, Donnie pressed her curled fingers against Shane's. It was the gentlest fist bump Shane had ever received.

"Let's go." With a smile, Shane turned and jogged toward the dock. Spurred by the threat of unknown xenobiology, she consciously remained alert, focusing on her full suite of senses and not just sight, which was unreliable in the dark. At first, all Shane heard were hopeful little frog songs, and the wind drummed a slow, encouraging beat against her back. When she stepped onto the dock, her tennis shoes clunked on the wooden planks, and the lake lapped against the wooden pilings, making a soothing, rhythmic sound that reminded her of the ocean; of waves sloshing onto sandy beaches, washing over stone jetties and seawalls.

Then, for a fleeting moment, she really smelled the ocean, too, recognizing the briny scent that used to permeate everything on the coast of Galveston.

No, Shane thought. *You're being silly.*

Sometimes, memories confused the senses. She took a deep breath, reassuring herself that the humid air smelled of pine and algae.

Splash.

Shane froze in place, staring at the dark water, wondering whether she'd just heard a fish jump. The lake must be full of bass, catfish, and other energetic species. When she didn't notice a second splash, Shane took a cautious step forward and then paused, waiting, listening. Hearing nothing but frogs and crickets, she forced herself to continue walking.

Although Donnie felt safe near the lake, the opposite was true for Shane. As she drew away from the muddy shore, her instincts warned her to turn around and sprint back to land. But she didn't know whether she could trust them.

After all, memories confused the senses. And she had so many terrible memories of water.

With gritted teeth, she bargained with her fear: she'd go only halfway up the dock. That would be far enough. After scurrying the last few feet, Shane loaded and prepped the flare pistol, just like she'd been taught. Then, she held it up, her finger on the trigger, aiming at the star-freckled sky.

"I'm in position!" Shane glanced over her shoulder, hoping to see the timid glow of a new campfire. Instead, she observed Donnie's hunched silhouette as she bent over the pile of sticks, clicking sparks into the tinder.

"Almost got it," Donnie called back. "Fire away!"

Suddenly, beneath Shane's feet, there was another loud splash. With a gasp, she pulled the pistol's trigger. *Boom!* A radiant light shot into the air, burning like a red comet. It reached its peak height and then arced downward, shining even brighter on the descent. As it approached the water, the flare cast a spotlight onto the lake. Shane squinted, convinced that she saw movement farther away — ripples, perhaps cast by the jumping bass — but before she could whip out her pocket binoculars to confirm, the flare fizzled out.

She crouched, loading the second cartridge under the faint moonlight. When Grandpa Louis first gifted Shane the pistol, he'd taught her how to load and unload it, making Shane practice until it was almost second nature to her. Thank goodness for that experience. Once Shane reunited with her mother, she'd tell her all about this ordeal on the dock. Maybe Lorenza would finally admit that Grandpa Louis had good ideas. Occasionally.

"How's that fire?" Shane shouted.

"It keeps dying! The sparks won't stick!"

"Is the tinder dry?"

"Yeah, I think." She heard several swish-clicks of iron skating down flint, and then Donnie exclaimed, "Good job, hot rock!" She watched her bend low, blowing on the spark-lit embers. Within seconds, Shane smelled smoke on the wind, the first sign of an infant campfire.

Shane aimed for the sky and shot a second flare, which arced as high as the first. For eight seconds, it burned brighter than a fairy light.

All she could do now was wait. Wait and hope that somebody — a fisherman in his canoe; a park ranger in her tower; a family camping on the other end of the lake; a retired couple on their porch — was looking up. And why wouldn't they be? On clear nights, far from the city's electrical pollution, it was possible to read the stories of constellations and see light from beyond the Milky Way.

Quickly, Shane stowed the pistol and ran back to land, her feet thudding eagerly across the wooden dock. "Where's the fire?"

"It died out!" Donnie knelt at the edge of the stone ring, her hand protectively cupped around a small tuft of smoking tinder, blowing. Fueled by the oxygen in her breath, the embers glowed bright orange, on the cusp of flame. But the moment she stopped blowing, the tinder lost its heat.

"On second thought," Donnie said, scooting aside to give Shane a better look at the failure, "maybe the sticks 'n stuff are a little damp. There was a thick fog earlier. I could almost drink the air."

"Can I give it a try?" Shane asked. With a nod, Donnie passed her the flint kit. While Shane shaved sparks into the tinder, Donnie eyed the lake.

"Wait, stop clacking," she said. "Do you hear that?"

Shane went very still. "What?" she whispered.

"Sounds like . . ." She cocked her head, squeezing her dark eyes shut. "That's a motorboat engine!"

Now that Donnie mentioned it, Shane did hear a faint mechanical rumble. "They must have seen the flare!" she exclaimed. "Quick, use the flashlight! Get their attention!"

"We're saved!" Donnie ran to the edge of the lake, jumping and waving the light back and forth. "Hey! Hey, you! Over here! Help! Help us!"

After her sparks failed to catch fire, too, Shane made a snap decision to join

Donnie instead of wasting time with soggy kindling. At the lakeside, she blew on the sports whistle until her forehead ached. They'd have to be loud to compete with the engine.

"Oh, no, no! I can't hear the boat anymore," Donnie said. "Wait . . . maybe? Maybe I can?"

For a moment, they both listened.

"The motor's getting softer," Shane realized. "They're going the wrong way."

"No, no, no! We were so close!"

The flashlight hadn't been bright enough, and the boater hadn't heard them.

But perhaps there was one last hope.

"How many lightning bugs would it take to make a beacon?" Shane wondered aloud. "Five thousand? More?"

"Well . . . I see about ten right now," Donnie replied, deadpan, "so it's a moot point."

For the moment, Shane ignored her; there'd be time to explain later. "I might not be strong enough," Shane muttered, sitting on a patch of soft grass. "Just have to try my best."

Despite all her experience waking insect ghosts, she'd never attempted to summon hundreds, much less thousands at once. But the technique should be the same; she just had to scale up. With a calm, slow breath, Shane thought about the first time she'd cupped a lightning bug in her hands. The tickle of its feet; the rhythm of its shine. Then, in her mind's eye, she transformed the lightning bug into the sun. Its glow intensified, expanding. The brighter the sun, the louder the call: Shane honed her consciousness into an all-encompassing point of light.

"Hey!" Donnie grabbed her shoulders, shook her into alertness. "Look at me! Wake up! What in the infinite realms is happening?" When Shane opened her eyes, the campsite was as bright as day. Thousands of blinking lightning bug ghosts drifted through the air; some landed on the ground. Others rested on Shane's arms and in her hair. Their invisible feet were as soft as feathers.

"It's a trick," she explained, standing. "They'll only stay here for a minute or two, though, so I hope it works." Shane gently swiped at the air, catching a handful of ghosts. One was clever enough to fly through her cupped hands, but the rest crawled on her palms, glowing in pulses. She watched them vanish, one by one, the little ghosts returning to the land Below. Incrementally, the lakeside dimmed, and within five minutes, it was dark again.

"Do you hear that?" Donnie asked, her voice soft with awe. "The rumble's getting louder again."

Together, they ran to the end of the dock and cheered as an old aluminum motorboat chugged toward them. With rescue imminent, Shane forgot to be scared of the lake, even when she heard a third and final splash.

It might be a fish. It might be something stranger. Whatever the case, it wasn't her problem anymore.

⌁ SIX ⌁

In a twenty-four-hour diner, Donnie called her grandparents while Shane described their predicament to the night-shift waitress, an Indian-American woman in a checkered dress. Although the waitress wore an ID tag pinned to her collar, it was blank, as if she'd erased her name using white paint.

"You girls were transported to the middle of nowhere?" she asked, hand on hip, her red lips quirked in a smile. "Most people wouldn't fare so well."

"Did you notice Shane's backpack?" Donnie asked, hanging up the phone and

152

joining them. "She could probably survive in the middle of the desert."

"Hey, you were doing alright without me."

"Uh, I stabbed myself with a pointy stick and then curled up under a rowboat." Donnie gestured to her grubby, blood-stained shirt. In the motorboat, working by lantern light, Shane had inspected and cleaned the injury. Fortunately, it was just a long but shallow scratch that wouldn't need stitches.

"What did your grandparents say?" Shane asked.

"They're sad that Bobby isn't here, but really glad I'm safe. Your grandpa will pick us up. He's already on the way. It's a two hundred-mile drive, apparently."

"Do you mind if we wait in the diner for a few hours?" Shane asked the waitress. "I have enough money for a pot of coffee —"

"Darling, a story like yours is worth burgers and pie. Follow me." With that, the waitress guided them to a corner booth. The bright yellow tabletop was decorated with a steel napkin dispenser, a white salt shaker, a black pepper shaker, and a fake daisy in a small ceramic vase. Aside from a coffee-drinking trucker at the counter, Shane and Donnie were the only two customers in the diner. Not a surprise, since it was an hour till midnight. They slid into opposite sides of the booth.

"Any special requests?" the waitress asked, taking out a small notepad and pencil.

"A burger and ginger ale would be great," Shane said.

"Same here." Donnie glanced at the dessert stands on the counter; three partially-eaten pies were displayed under glass domes, like museum exhibits. "Is that green one key lime?"

"Good eye. We have apple and banana cream, too."

"Key lime," Shane and Donnie said in unison; the waitress laughed, delighted.

"Great minds think alike. It's our most popular flavor." She made a couple notes. "If you need anything, shout for Maxine. It's a slow night, so I'll be prompt."

"Do late shifts ever get busy?" Shane wondered, curious.

"Sometimes." Maxine looked through the window. Beyond the mostly-empty parking lot, long-haul trucks and late-night travelers sped down Highway 902. "Not today, though. Y'all better hope it stays slow." And with that cryptic comment, Maxine winked, turned on her heels, and walked to the kitchen.

"I dig her style," Donnie commented, her voice warm with admiration. "You know, my friend Bettie says that the Weird like to visit all-night establishments. And they like to work at 'em, too."

"You think Maxine is a vampire or something?" Shane whispered, half-joking. The newly cursed were indistinguishable from non-vampiric humans, aside from a few subtle quirks — like a decreased appetite for solid food, high sensitivity to sunlight, and heightened strength and reflexes. That said, there were other, more likely reasons why somebody would take a night shift. For example, they could need the money. Which was why Shane worked late at Pizza Dale.

"She's bringing dinner, and that's all that matters," Donnie answered.

"Yeah. Agreed." Shane rested her chin on one hand. "Has my mother called home yet?"

"Nobody's heard from her."

She'd anticipated that answer. If there'd been good news about Lorenza, Donnie would have shared it already. "I have a theory," Shane said. "You and Bobby were on my mind when the ring sent me to the lake. Well . . . what if Mom was thinking the same thing, but she got transported to Bobby?"

"Hope so," Donnie muttered. "Then he wouldn't be alone."

"Did Bobby say anything 'fore you guys stepped into the ring?"

"Um . . ." She stared at the ceiling fan in the middle of the diner, lost in thought. "Not really. When it happened, he was quiet. And sad. Bobby gets sad a lot." Donnie shook her head regretfully. "I turned my back for a couple minutes, and when I looked back, he was gone, and there was a big gray circle in the yard. It hadn't been there before, so I ran to investigate. 'Round there, I felt the sun on the back of my neck, and I thought: *Wouldn't it be great to take a dip?* Then, bam: I'm in the lake."

"Your brother must have walked into the ring first; if the gray circle was big, it sent him far away." Shane rubbed her temple, wondering: What would Ma do? How would Lorenza find a sad, lost child? They didn't have a scent trail to follow. There wasn't physical evidence to track. However, Donnie's familiarity with her brother could help them make a list of all the places the kid longed to visit. "You know your family best. Did he have a favorite playground? Is Bobby always talking about living on a boat? Or an island? Does he have an imaginary friend from Sweden? Bobby's mind could have sent him to a place he likes to imagine."

"There's something . . ." Donnie squeezed her eyes shut and exhaled. "But I don't want to say it."

Shane patiently waited for Donnie to steel her nerves.

"I told Bobby about the cabin by the lake, right?" the girl continued, her words flowing in a nearly breathless rush. "Basically, everything I shared with you. The

157

fishing and swimming, the grill, the long days and dark nights. Thought it would be a sweet story."

"It is," Shane reassured her.

Donnie rubbed her eyes with the palm of her hand. "Not to Bobby."

"What d'you mean? Why?" Kids could be sensitive, take things the wrong way. Shane knew that from experience with her own little brother.

"Because Bobby never went on vacation with Mom and Dad. And he never will. I understand that sadness, now. But at the time, when Bobby started crying, all I could think was 'He's ruining my good memories.' And he wouldn't stop! So I asked him, 'What's your problem? Do you want to go home?' And he said . . ." She stopped.

"What?" Shane encouraged.

"He said, 'No. I want to be with them.'" Donnie reached across the table to clutch Shane's hands. "He said he wanted to *be* with them."

Shane inhaled sharply. "Your parents."

"Yes."

"Aren't they . . ."

"Dead." In an instant, Donnie's brown eyes shone with the beginning of tears. "What have I done?"

Before Shane could respond, Maxine walked up with a tray of ice-cold drinks. As she placed them on the table, the waitress eyed Donnie worriedly. "Darling, you OK?"

Quickly releasing Shane, Donnie nodded. "I'm fine."

"It's been a bad day," Shane said. "Thanks for asking."

"Of course, girls." And although Maxine pursed her lips, clearly still concerned, she left without another word.

"We don't know if it's possible for a fairy ring to transport somebody to the underworld," Shane whispered to Donnie.

"But if it can — and did — that means he's . . . gone?" Her voice cracked with fear. "Right?"

Something about that assumption rang false. "No. It's possible to come back." Shane rubbed her forehead, trying to massage life into long-dormant memories.

"I swear I once heard a story about a man who visited the land of the dead. He returned to Earth after two days. Maybe? It was so long ago, I can't remember how the story went."

"Where'd you hear it?"

"My grandma Yolanda. She isn't with us anymore."

"Could we ask your grandpa Louis?"

Shane had been sipping ginger ale through her red straw; at Donnie's question, she snickered mirthlessly, and an unpleasant surge of bubbles stung her nose. She scrabbled to grab a napkin, coughing into paper.

"Gah, need a pat on the back?" Donnie half-rose to help, but Shane waved her away.

"Just swallowed down the wrong pipe," she gasped, clearing her throat. "Answer's no. Grandpa Louis, um, doesn't care about that stuff."

"What stuff? The dead? Stories?"

"Apache stuff," she clarified, looking away. "It's a Lipan story."

"Whoa, you're Apache?" Donnie sounded way too fascinated.

160

"Yes?" Shane tensely waited for her verdict. It was difficult to predict how somebody who wasn't American Indian would respond.

"What's Lipan mean?"

"There's different groups of Apache people. Mescalero, Jicarilla, Lipan, so on. We have our own unique history, culture, and stuff."

"Oh . . ." Donnie opened her mouth, hesitating. Then, "Can't you ask a different Lipan about stories?"

In an instant, Shane could relax again. "I guess so. It's just . . . it'll be tricky. The other Lipan people I know? We used to live in the same neighborhood. My family and others, together. But eight years ago, we lost the land, everyone scattered, and now I don't know where anyone lives, except for a couple aunts and uncles. The Elders may not even have phones."

"It's a start, though," Donnie said.

And Shane, smiling, agreed: "It is. We should also research the mimic rings. Maybe their paths can be mapped."

Idly, she wondered about Donnie's race. Mr. and Mrs. Park were white, but Donnie had the appearance of mixed ancestry, as did many people who lived in Texas. However, Shane was reluctant to ask, *What are you?* to a virtual stranger, since she knew from experience that it was a personal and largely unnecessary question. Some people — too many people — would ask that with a sneer; to them, it was an accusation.

Perhaps, someday, Shane and Donnie would discuss their family histories in the context of friendship and trust. She warmed at the thought.

Then, the food arrived. With wide eyes, Shane and Donnie watched Maxine cover their table with plates of crispy, greasy, salty fries; burgers with fresh green lettuce and squares of cheddar cheese; and generous slices of sugar-dusted key lime pie. "Bon appétit," she said. "That's French for *enjoy the meal.*"

"Merci," Donnie thanked her.

"Muchas gracias," Shane added. Spanish was the only Romance language she understood.

"De nada." Maxine patted each girl on the head before leaving to check on the trucker at the counter. For the next half hour, Shane and Donnie ate their meals in exhausted silence. Rather than ener-gize her, the rich food made Shane groggy, so she folded her arms on the tabletop, pressed her forehead against her forearm, and closed her eyes. "Just gonna nap a minute," she said through her fingers.

"Hey, Shane?"

She responded without looking up, "Uh huh?"

"Are you ever going to explain the fireflies?"

"Hm." A moment passed. "Maybe."

"Oh." She heard Donnie shift on the padded seat as she sprawled lengthwise across the booth. In the kitchen, dishes clinked, and the overhead fan hummed. "OK. Just. Whatever it is, I won't judge."

"Good to know." Shane stared at a grain of salt on the countertop, thinking. Mr. and Mrs. Park already knew about Nellie; it was only a matter of time before Donnie learned the big secret, too.

"I'll tell you sometime," Shane prom-ised. "For now, sweet dreams."

Donnie softly replied, "You too."

The next thing Shane knew, somebody was squeezing her around the shoulders. With a cry of surprise, she jolted into a sitting position, and Marcos tightened his hug. "Shane!" he exclaimed. "We found you!" Nellie excitedly climbed onto the seat next to them; the booth's cushion depressed under his all-but-invisible body. The physics of ghosts were sometimes puzzling: Nellie had no weight, but he exerted force, resistance. He could pass through matter, but he usually didn't.

"Marcos, I'm so sorry!" Shane gave her brother a kiss on the forehead. "Were you worried?"

"Grandpa was," he said, still clinging to her shoulders. "I told him that you and Mom always get home."

"That's right," she agreed, shifting so that Marcos could sit beside her. It was still dark outside, with only one vehicle — Grandpa Louis's station wagon — now parked in the front lot. Across from Shane, Donnie was sitting up, her hair even messier and her eyes deeply shadowed. She watched Shane and Marcos with a solemn expression.

"This is my brother," Shane introduced.

164

In an instant, Donnie smiled, her posture straightening. "Hey, I'm Donnie. How's it going?"

Marcos responded, in his politest manner: "Very well, thank you. Pleased to meet you."

"Wow, you sound like a little prince!"

"Don't be tricked," interjected a familiar voice. Grandpa Louis, who hadn't changed his outfit since Shane went missing, walked up to the booth. "The kid's putting on airs. He's usually an imp, aren't ya, Marcos?"

"Grandpa, that's not true!"

"Don't get upset. I'm trying to compliment you. It's better to be an imp than a prince."

"True," Shane said, trying to keep the peace. Marcos normally had a calm temperament, but it was half past three in the morning, and he probably hadn't napped earlier.

"Mija, my brave granddaughter," Grandpa Louis said warmly, leaning over the table to kiss her cheek. "I'm so proud of you. When your mother returns, she'll be proud, too."

165

"Have you heard from her?" Shane asked.

He simply shook his head.

"We can talk rescue plans later," Grandpa Louis said. "But for now, vámanos." He turned to look directly at Donnie. "Say, is that ketchup on your shirt? Or blood?"

"It's nothing bad," she promised, standing. "Just from a scratch."

As the group made their way out of the diner, Maxine handed Shane an apple pie in a to-go box. "Good luck with everything," she said.

Nodding gratefully, Shane replied, "Thanks. You too." Although she knew zilch about Maxine's personal life, everyone needed luck with something.

A few miles away, they came upon a dreary roadside motel with VACANCIES advertised on its grimy sign. Grandpa Louis parked in the empty lot and then rented three rooms: a double for Shane and Marcos (and Nellie), a single for Donnie, and a single for him and the living bloodhounds.

After paying the bill in cash, he handed Shane and Donnie heavy skeleton keys. "You're in numbers three and four," he said. "I'm taking five. We'll leave after breakfast, so get lots of rest."

Considering the late hour, that command seemed unlikely. Then again, Shane doubted she'd be able to sleep at all with her mother still missing. She wanted to do something, not lie on a creaky old bed until sunrise. If she'd rested during Malorie's rescue, the girl might've died. How was this scenario any different?

"Bedtime, Little Prince," she said, shouldering her backpack and taking Marcos's hand. Hugging his floppy-eared rabbit plushie, he trudged with Shane to Room 3. Inside, it smelled like old cigarette smoke, and the blue carpet had a questionable dark stain, but at least the sheets were soft, the pillows decently stuffed, and the tap water clear. There were two twin-sized beds, one near the front entrance and the other tucked against the back wall, not far from the bathroom door. Shane designated that one for Marcos, in case he had to use the restroom in the middle of the night.

167

She dropped their duffel bag on a set of drawers and looked at the rose-print wallpaper. Most was a dirty yellowish shade, but there were two clean squares over the beds' headboards, as if paintings had once hung there, protecting their section of the wall from smoke stains. Perhaps they'd been stolen. The room seemed naked without art.

"Brush your teeth," Shane ordered, holding out Marcos's toothbrush and a half-full tube of minty-fresh paste. He whined wordlessly, but did as she'd asked.

"And don't forget to wash your face!" she called when she heard the bathroom sink running.

They both went to bed in their day clothes; in her hurry, Shane hadn't packed pajamas, not that it mattered. An exhausted Marcos could have slept in a bunny suit. Within minutes, he was dreaming, Nellie lying at the foot of his bed.

As she'd feared, Shane couldn't sleep at all.

She lay face-up, the covers tucked to her chin, and listened to water drip from the leaky faucet: *plip, plip, plip*. It reminded her of the ticking clock in the breakroom at work. *Damn, work!* Shane couldn't remember the Pizza Dale phone number. She'd have to call Amelia first thing in the morning and ask her to convey a message to Carl, explain why she'd missed work without any warning. Shane might also need another couple days off.

Or longer, her fears whispered. As long as it took to find her mother.

For the call, she'd have to use a quarter-guzzling payphone, since Shane doubted that a roadside motel with a leaky faucet and dubious stains on the carpet would allow her to bill anything to her room.

With no better idea, Shane counted the water drops, hoping that the process would soothe her mind, like counting sheep. But her body buzzed with an insatiable anxiety, more potent than caffeine, and as the count rose to one thousand, she gave up.

Shifting restlessly, Shane turned on her side. There was a narrow gap between the cloth curtains, through which she could view a half-inch slice of the world outside. For a long time, she stared at the black sky, countering her fears with the possibility that her mother would call in the morning.

Something clattered against the window. *Plink*. It sounded like a pebble hitting the glass. Who was messing around at such a wretchedly late hour? At first, she thought of Donnie. Maybe she was restless, too. But she couldn't help Bobby at the middle of the night in the middle of nowhere.

That didn't mean she wouldn't try, though. Shane understood the impulse.

With an exhausted groan, Shane pushed away her covers and slipped out of bed. After tiptoeing to the window, she slowly tugged the edge of one curtain aside. Outside, beyond a narrow strip of grass, the gated pool glowed soft blue, its water illuminated by porthole-shaped lights embedded in the underwater walls. And although a plastic sign warned guests POOL HOURS 6 AM – SUNDOWN, a girl was bobbing in the deep end. Shane only saw the back of her head, her silvery white hair spread across the water's surface like a golden, fan-shaped lily pad. The stranger didn't swim laps or splash around. She simply bobbed in place, facing the grassy, garbage-littered wasteland behind Ten Penny Inn. Her shoulders seemed gray, like a dolphin's belly, but perhaps that was a trick of the odd lighting. In one hand, she clutched something pink, but the water obscured the object's details.

Shane leaned closer, all but squishing her nose against the Windex-streaked glass. The swimmer turned slightly — had she sensed something? — and Shane saw the hint of a face in profile: a long nose and sharp chin. Bangs fell across her eyes, concealing them.

Strange that a girl would be swimming alone at night. But roadside inns — like forests and twenty-four-hour diners — were natural habitats for weirdness. The swimmer could be a young-looking vampire, sensitive to sunlight. An immortal siren in the desert. Or just a human teenager, like Shane, which made her wonder: *Are you lost?*

Shane glanced at the door, tempted to crack it open and shout, "Do you need help?" Then, Marcos turned in his sleep with a disquieted little sigh, snuggling deep into his pile of flat white pillows. Rabbit tumbled off the bed, plopping face-down on the threadbare carpet.

The world was full of questions, and, at the moment, Shane only had the energy for one: *Where is Lorenza?* Plus, the girl seemed fine. After a final glance outside, Shane closed the curtains. Quietly, she retrieved Rabbit, tucked him next to Marcos's head, and then returned to bed. There, she wriggled deep under the cotton sheets and intentionally turned her back to the window.

Eventually, Shane fell asleep. She dreamed of the stars blinking out one by one, and water dripping from long, silver hair.

Plip. Plip. Plip.

By sunrise, the pool was empty.

⌐ SEVEN ⌐

Grandpa Louis bought gas-station coffee for everyone, even Marcos, who made a disgusted face after the first sip and pushed his Styrofoam cup away.

"You said you wanted coffee," Grandpa Louis protested. "What's the problem?"

"It's gross."

He shook his head, as if disappointed. "Fine. I'll drink it. You can have my OJ."

The group sat around a plastic table in the motel lobby, eating a breakfast of apple pie. The filling was pleasantly tart; the chef had clearly used fresh fruit, not canned, sugar-soaked apples. At Shane's feet, Neal

173

and Nealey polished off their travel bag of dog chow and were rewarded with chewy strips of beef jerky. Nellie lingered near the treats, sniffing loudly, perhaps remembering their savory flavor.

"Any news from your grandparents?" Shane asked, dusting crumbs off her lap and then looking at Donnie.

"I talked to them when I woke up," she said. "There's still no sign of Bobby, but the feds are swarming our house now. They've even blocked the railroad tracks, rerouting trains. Grandma says they're visiting neighbors, too. It's unreal. Like something from a movie."

"Swarming?" Shane repeated, stunned. It was a major change from their initial response, when the cops had refused to investigate, insisting that Donnie and Bobby were playing runaway.

"Let's get moving, then," Grandpa Louis decided, standing. "We have to reach Less Crossing before the roads are blocked. Hell, at this rate, they may quarantine the whole town."

"Wait, really?" Donnie wondered, wide-eyed. "Because of the fairy rings?"

174

"Oh, sure. The feds love throwing around their power. In fact, I once met a badge-flashing motherf —"

"I call shotgun," Shane interrupted, loudly. Then she grabbed Marcos by the hand and guided him toward the lobby exit. To his credit, Grandpa Louis hastily corrected, "Mother friend. As in a friend of my mother. What was I saying? Forgot already. The curse of aging."

"Man, you don't look old," Donnie said. "What are you? Fifty-something?"

"He's sixty-five!" Shane called over her shoulder.

"Hey, how did you know?" Grandpa Louis asked. "Did you work at a carnival, guessing people's age and weight for money?"

"You're family, that's how. I also know that Mom's forty. Marcos is six. Pa would have been forty-one."

"And you're seventeen," he said.

"That's right."

They piled into the vehicle, Donnie and Marcos in the back, Shane in the front passenger seat, Neal and Nealey curled at Marcos's feet, and Nellie perched on Shane's lap, eager to watch the scenery through the window. Grandpa Louis turned the ignition key, shifted into drive, and pulled onto the highway. For the first hour, Donnie and Shane recounted their experience at the lake. Then, the conversation shifted to the missing.

"Maybe there are more big rings near the abandoned house," Donnie suggested. "It's risky, but we can use them."

"Not likely." Grandpa Louis accelerated to pass a truck full of hay bales. "After Shane vanished, I looked but couldn't find any. Just useless tiny ones. Not that it matters. The feds won't let us near the site. They're probably worried the mimics will spread. Last thing anyone needs is a second Longfire Incident."

"You mentioned Longfire earlier," Shane said. "What happened?"

Her grandpa scratched his whiskery beard, thinking. "I only know the official story. What they printed in the newspapers decades ago."

"Was that after you married Grandma?" Marcos asked.

He chuckled. "No. The Longfire Incident happened when we were little teenagers."

"So . . . before you left Grandma?" Shane clarified.

"Guess so." He shrugged. "When you're young, romance burns hot, which means it never lasts." At that, Shane raised a skeptical eyebrow. Her parents had been high school sweethearts, too, but their love grew stronger with time. However, she was reluctant to correct an Elder, so she held her tongue.

"As a kid," Grandpa Louis continued, "all the people you meet, the friends you make, the relationships you chase . . ." He waved a flippant hand. "They're practice for the real thing. When you're my age, you'll think back on the characters of your early years and wonder, 'What happened to those people, the friends I thought I'd die for, the gal I swore I couldn't live without?' Whatever happened to those all-important people?"

"I'm more curious about the Longfire Incident," Shane prompted; she suspected that he was stalling, but she didn't know why. Her grandpa made a sound of amusement, smirking.

"Ah, yes. Lost my train of thought. But yes. All this was a little before I met your grandmother." They passed a green field. In the distance, dairy cows grazed in clusters. They were getting close; just fifteen, maybe twenty minutes until they reached the edge of Less Crossing. "You have to remember that the first ring transport centers were built in 1923. Back then, people could only travel between LA, New York, and London. So when Longfire happened, the public was still debating whether rings were game-changing marvels or weird, dangerous, alien-realm technology. In other words, the US government didn't want to undermine trust in ring transportation. It would be a diplomatic nightmare to reject the fae's gift, especially since our royalty, diplomats, and bigwigs had been asking for ring transport since the Dark Ages."

"Times have changed," Donnie remarked. "There's a ring transport center in every state, last I checked."

"It'll be every city soon," Shane added. "Amelia — she's my friend, really smart and pretty — says they're building new centers in Dallas, Austin, and McAllen. Boerne, too." She wondered why the fae had finally changed their minds, after centuries of guarding the rings from humans, including descendants. They must have benefitted somehow. Maybe it was a source of leverage in a rapidly changing world? To Shane, recent advances in technology certainly resembled magic. For example, handheld calculators could solve complex equations in a matter of seconds, like little pocket-sized mathematicians. And there were things called computers that could decipher far more complex stuff, quicker than a human! Or so she'd heard.

"Magical transportation's big business," Grandpa Louis agreed. "The Longfire Incident could've prevented that progress. Nearly did. According to the papers, a man known as "Mr. Brooklyn" got ahold of a mimic sample; he worked at a ring transport center, and stole the mimic to grow a personal transporter in the wild. Maybe thought he could control it somehow. Damned if I know. Well, Brooklyn's experiment left a humongous gray circle of death in an old-growth

Colorado forest. Within the ring, all the trees crumbled into ash. Prime logging land, destroyed. The papers called it a failed experiment. They figured that Brooklyn had teleported to another planet. On Earth, all traces of his mimic died. In other words: 'Nothing to worry about here, law-abiding citizens. Forget about Brooklyn; everything's a-ok!' But now, I'm not so sure. Seems like a cover-up, am I right? Like the government knew more than the public."

To be fair, Grandpa Louis said the same thing about most government-adjacent situations. Shane wondered if his contemporaries shared his opinion on Longfire. "Cover-up how?" she asked.

"Well, mimics are 1) rarer than a royal flush, and 2) disguise themselves as legit ring-forming species until they start growing on Earth. There's no way to know that the supplies have been contaminated 'til then. I heard that Brooklyn was a low-level guy, with no access to the grow rooms. So how'd he know what to take? Did he steal ten thousand samples? Without getting caught? Yeah, no way. Like I said: I don't buy it."

Grandpa Louis had a point, assuming his info was accurate. Did that mean Brooklyn had gotten lucky, like a lottery winner?

Or maybe he hadn't been a low-level employee after all.

"Cover-up or not," Donnie said, "I bet the authorities have been studying mimics for decades now, in secret." As she spoke, Donnie leaned forward to rest her arm behind Shane's headrest. "They can help us. They can find Bobby."

Grandpa Louis laughed sharply.

"What's so funny, old man?" Donnie demanded, her cheeks reddening.

"Honey, do you seriously believe they'll use classified information to save a couple" — he made snippy air quotes — "ordinary people?"

"No. I think we should make every attempt to save my brother."

"And Mom," Marcos said, as if they'd forgotten. As if Shane hadn't been worrying about Lorenza all morning.

"It's worth hoping," Shane added, and although Grandpa Louis had more to say (judging by his grimace), he kept quiet, perhaps sensing that he was outnumbered.

With a bemused snort, he turned on the radio, fiddling with the dial until a saxophone blared and a woman mournfully sang, "*Who loves me like I love you?*" Shane let three other ladies sing their pieces before asking, "Grandpa, have you ever heard a story about a guy who visited the underworld and then returned to Earth?"

"Returned alive?"

"Alive and unharmed."

He clicked his tongue. "Nothing credible. My buddy Alejandro thinks he went Below and back during a bad trip in Vegas, but I don't buy it."

"That's definitely not the story I meant." Shane looked out the window. They were speeding past a field of vividly violet and yellow wildflowers now. Colors like that belonged in a Van Gogh masterpiece, she decided, and — not for the first time — wished that she could paint.

"I promise, mija," Grandpa Louis told her, squeezing her left hand, "your Momma's here, on Earth. Fairy rings can't send people to the underworld."

Normally, that was true, but mimics didn't seem to be normal.

"And if I'm wrong," he added, "we'll find her anyway. You kids don't need to worry. I have a failproof plan. Put your faith in that."

Suddenly, above the whoosh of traffic, Shane heard a roar. She pressed her face against the window and observed a group of small aircraft flying in formation. They were crop dusters, typically used to drop insecticides and other chemicals on farmland. However, looking around . . . . Shane didn't notice any farms.

"They're headed for Less Crossing," Donnie said, and a minute later, three more planes flew past.

"You're right," Shane gasped. "Hurry!"

It took fifteen minutes of white-knuckle driving to reach town. Grandpa Louis floored the accelerator, passing other cars by driving in the shoulder. The planes had triggered a race, and although Shane didn't know what they'd find at the finish line, she keenly felt the urgency. Something big was happening in Less Crossing. If they arrived too late, they might miss the chance to gather information about Lorenza's disappearance. If Grandpa Louis was correct, the feds or whoever

called the shots wouldn't be merrily sum-
marizing their activities to a bunch of
concerned family members.

At the turnoff into town, two police cars
were parked in the road, blocking traffic.
As the station wagon approached, the
red and blue lights flashed in warning. A
young officer, who'd been leaning against
the side of his vehicle, pointed at the side
of the road, directing Grandpa Louis to
park. In a field in the distance, several men
in button-up shirts watched the sky with
their hands on their hips, and two people
in white suits gesticulated adamantly, as if
directing an orchestra. More likely, they
were giving orders.

"A traffic stop?" Shane whispered.
"Grandpa, those guys up there look like
feds, don't they? Guess they're swarming
the whole town now. Not just the Parks'
place."

The blood drained from her grandfather's cheeks, leaving him unusually pale.
"Quiet, all," he whispered. "I'll handle
this." After stopping on the shoulder,
Grandpa Louis cranked the driver-side
window down and smiled at the approaching policeman.

"Howdy," he greeted, leaning into his southern accent. "What can I do for you, Officer?"

"Do you live in town?" the young man asked, leaning down to peek into the station wagon. His eyes hid behind sunglasses.

"I do," Donnie said from the back, ignoring Grandpa Louis's earlier order. "With my grandparents. Is everything OK?"

"Yes, yes. No need to worry. Simply put, the town's closed for a couple days. Everyone's been evacuated to Miller Creek."

"Evacuated?" Shane asked. "Is this related to the disappearances? Have there been more?"

"My mom's missing!" Marcos said. "Help us, please!"

"My brother's gone, too. His name's Bobby. We need to speak with somebody in charge."

"I . . . I don't . . ." The young officer glanced over his shoulder and shrugged helplessly. A moment later, he was replaced by a middle-aged policeman with a severe scowl and even larger sunglasses.

"We are not at liberty to discuss the details surrounding this evacuation,"

185

the older man said. "Residents of Less Crossing are advised to gather at the Miller Creek elementary school; there are beds and meals in the gymnasium. If you need directions, I can provide them. Understood?"

Shane could almost smell the scent of gym mats and disinfectant; hear the chatter of a hundred families, united in confusion and displacement.

"Understood," Grandpa Louis said. "We'll turn around —"

"No! Forget that! What are they doing to my home?" Donnie demanded, pointing to the sky. Through the streaky windshield, Shane observed the planes she'd noticed earlier; white chemical clouds spilled from their bellies, falling fog-like on Less Crossing. There were dozens, maybe more! As if every crop duster in North Texas had been recruited to douse the town in a mysterious chemical.

What could the chemical be? Considering the rapid response, it had to be readily available, something that farmers stockpiled. Although Shane's family had once grown corn using natural pest control methods, most big-time farmers — like

Lorenza's employers — attacked pests with chemicals. Herbicides killed weeds. Insecticides killed insects. And . . .

"Fungicides," she hissed, turning to look at Donnie. She whispered, "They're killing the mimic rings."

"What? No! If there are any rings left, we need to use them!" Donnie tried to open the side door, but the latch rattled uselessly. She plucked desperately at the lock, which refused to pop up. "Are you serious? This door's busted! Piece of junk, let me out! We have to stop the planes! They're destroying our only chance!"

"Miss," the officer warned, "please calm down."

"It's too late," Shane said, nodding her chin toward the tails of mist-fine chemicals. "The pesticides have fallen. We can't reverse that."

"Welp, that's that. Have a super day, Officer," Grandpa Louis said loudly, wrangling the gear into reverse. "We'll be on our wa —"

"Let me out first!" Donnie exclaimed. "They have to do something!" Suddenly, Shane's seat jolted as Donnie grabbed its headrest and pulled herself forward. The gangly young woman wriggled over the conjoined front seats, awkwardly twisting, her hands landing on Shane's lap. "Help me out here," she asked; she was stuck halfway between the front and back of the car. But before Shane could respond, Grandpa Louis made a tight U-turn and started driving away from town. Shane instinctively grabbed Donnie around the shoulders to stop her friend from slamming against the dash.

"Get in your seat," he barked. "A tantrum will do no good."

"Tantrum?"

"Yeah! You want to go to jail? Think that'll help anyone?"

"Calm down," Shane sighed, gently pushing Donnie back over the front bench. "Both of you."

"Hey, I'm calm, I'm calm," Grandpa Louis promised, driving them further away, his voice softening. "It's just . . . local enforcers are following orders, not making decisions. They don't know anything, kid, and they couldn't stop the planes."

In frustration, Donnie smacked her hand against the window — *thwup* — leaving a ghostly print of her palm.

"What's your plan, then, Grandpa?" Shane asked, recalling his mysterious promise that Lorenza was not beyond their reach. At her question, he smiled. Now that the police cars were blips in the rear-view mirror, his typical swagger returned full-force.

"See for yourself," he said. "Check under your foot mat."

Shane bent over to pick up the rubber mat. Beneath it was a square panel, about six inches wide. "Secret storage?" she guessed, wedging her nails in the panel's seams and popping it out, revealing a shallow compartment. It was big enough to hold a paperback book, nothing larger. At the moment, the compartment contained a dirt-filled plastic baggie.

"Is this from the forest?" she whispered, as if anyone outside the station wagon could hear them.

"There were a couple little rings around the house," Grandpa Louis said. "I snuck a sample in my handkerchief. Which

189

means we can grow our own ring. Use it to get Lorenza and the boy. You know how, right, Shane? Daughter of farmers."

At first, she thought he was joking. A tacky joke at a terrible time, which wasn't unusual for Grandpa Louis. However, even he wouldn't make light of the current emergency. Then she clicked her tongue and shook her head.

"We never grew mushrooms," Shane replied. "Especially not dangerous ones."

"So let's find somebody who has," said Donnie quickly.

"That's the spirit!" Grandpa Louis praised.

"My cousin's friend works at the ring transport center in Houston," Donnie suggested. "His name's Frankie."

"Pretty sure it's a crime to grow fairy rings on private property," Shane said, carefully closing the secret compartment. "And you can forget about mimics. That'd be like . . . like planting a garden of them carnivorous trees. The ones that can bite off a hand, if you reach into the wrong hollow. What're they called?"

"Bleeding Birches," Donnie provided, 'cause of course she knew the name of the country's most notorious monster plant. "In the old days, when people saw blood trickling down the rivulets in their bark, they thought it belonged to the trees, like sap. They learned the truth fast, I bet."

"No kidding." Shane glanced out the window at the horizon, where the planes circled like buzzards. "I think . . ."

"What?" Marcos asked. He'd been listening to the conversation solemnly, his hands clasped around Neal's neck.

"Mimics are tricky. We can't risk them spreading, but we also can't grow them in a pot. They're powered by other plants." She absentmindedly touched Nellie's head, petting the space where his brow should be. "You know, I bet Mom's already left a message with the neighbor. Right? She'll tell us she's in Paris, or something, with Bobby. Then all we'll need to worry about are plane tickets."

Lorenza could find her way out of any maze; she was a master of the blindfold test, incapable of remaining lost. In any case, it would take weeks — months, probably! — to grow a mimic ring that was large enough for rescue purposes. They couldn't afford to wait that long. Especially if Bobby was trapped Below. Shane couldn't remember the old stories, but she doubted that long-term living situations were feasible in a realm of ghosts.

"Yeah," Donnie agreed. "Yeah, you're probably right."

A message from Lorenza would fix everything. For now, what else could they do but hope?

⁓ EIGHT ⁓

As the station wagon rolled to a stop, Shane jumped outside and sprinted to the mailbox. They'd received two letters: something from the electrical company, and a yellow envelope with Malorie's address at the top, probably a thank-you card for Lorenza. Shane shoved both envelopes, unopened, into the deep pocket of her overalls. Then, she peered into the narrow tin mailbox, willing it to contain one more scrap of paper — a note from the nearest neighbor, Mrs. Killen, maybe. But there was nothing.

That didn't mean anything conclusive. Mrs. Killen lived a quarter mile away, a long walk for an Elder under the summer sun. She might be waiting until evening to deliver Lorenza's message. "Grandpa, I'm going to check on the neighbor," Shane called. Up the driveway, her grandfather and Marcos were unloading the station wagon. After reuniting Donnie with her grandparents and agreeing to touch base by phone that evening, they'd sped straight home.

"Any good news?" Grandpa Louis asked, pointing back at the mailbox.

"No. Not yet."

With long strides, Shane made it to Mrs. Killen's front door in ninety seconds flat. She knocked loudly — *thnk, thnk, thnk* — and from deep within the house, four chihuahuas yapped. Shortly after, the door cracked open, and a stooped elderly woman with lime-green reading glasses and bright-red lipstick peered up at Shane.

"Sheh-neh!" she greeted, smiling. "How are your dogs?"

"They're doing great. Actually, I wondered if my ma's called?"

"Lorenza? Not since last month, when she had to work late, and your phone was off the hook." The disappointment must have been plain in Shane's eyes, since Mrs. Killen added, "Is something wrong?"

"No. Maybe. I don't know." Shane raised her voice to be heard over the chihuahuas, which were now barking at Mrs. Killen's ankles, trying to push outside. "We haven't heard from her in a day. It's getting scary."

"That's terrible," she gasped. "What happened?"

"She was on a rescue mission. Hasn't come home yet." Shane fished Mr. and Mrs. Park's phone number out of her pocket. "If Ma calls while we're out, could you alert these folks? They know how to get in contact with the right people. I'm sorry for the trouble —"

"It's no trouble." Mrs. Killen reached forward, but instead of taking the slip of paper and withdrawing, she clasped Shane's outstretched hand and met her stare. "If the phone rings, I'll answer. Day or night."

For a moment, they stood there, hands joined. Behind her half-moon reading glasses, Mrs. Killen's cataract-yellowed eyes were wide with concern, and Shane wanted so badly to confide in her; if

Mrs. Killen could help in this small way, maybe she'd be willing to do more — to draw upon a lifetime of wisdom and connections to help bring Lorenza home.

What were the chances that the next-door neighbor, who lived in a smaller, sadder shack than Shane's little family, could snap her fingers and make it all better?

"Do you know anything about fairy rings?" Shane asked, and Mrs. Killen's sharp nose crunched with confusion.

"No. I can't use them."

"It's OK." Shane unclasped their hands and backed away, trying to smile. "It'll be OK."

One of the chihuahuas, a skinny, toothless dog who was older and spryer than Shane, pushed around Mrs. Killen. He launched onto his hind legs, his front paws scrabbling against Shane's pantleg, and begged to be pet. Defenseless against the old dog's charm, Shane scooped him into her arms and nuzzled his velvety forehead. "Good b —"

She barely had time to turn her head before she sneezed.

"Oh, dear," Mrs. Killen said, taking the chihuahua from Shane's arms. "Allergic to pets?"

"Couldn't be! I've lived around dogs mosta my life."

"Sometimes they come and go, allergies. Was a time when cedar pollen never bothered me. Now, my eyes itch every summer."

"Hope that never happens to me," Shane answered softly. At the very least, she thought, ghosts were hypoallergenic.

After thanking Mrs. Killen a final time, Shane jogged back home. Along the way, she felt the prickle of Mrs. Killen's worried stare, and the weight of unspoken concerns and questions. No doubt right now, Lorenza's absence from work was triggering gossip and speculation. As soon as possible, Shane needed to call somebody at the orchard to explain the situation, and plead for Lorenza's job; if she got fired over this, the family would have to move again.

There were other calls to make. Grandpa was handling the official stuff — Lorenza's missing person case file, and updates from the feds — but while the men in badges investigated, the rest of the world continued turning, and Shane didn't want Lorenza to return home to chaos.

When Shane stepped into the messy living room, her hair damp with sweat, she saw a pile of papers and books on the sofa, and Grandpa kneeling by the coffee table, flipping through a phone book. "Sorry for the mess," he said. "I was looking for the yellow pages."

"What for?"

"Somebody who knows how to keep mushrooms alive."

"You still think we'll need to use the mimics?" She rubbed her forehead, frustrated. "It'll take weeks to grow a ring."

"Hopefully not, but your friend Donnie had a point. We need to keep all our options open."

At that, Shane reluctantly nodded in agreement. If all else failed — if Lorenza didn't return home and Nellie couldn't find her — at least they'd have a chance. "I wonder where they came from," she mused. "Why were mimic rings growing near Less Crossing?"

Grandpa Louis grunted, a vocalized shrug, and kept paging through the book.

With a loud, shrill trill, the phone rang. In her haste to answer the call, Shane nearly tripped over the edge of a woven throw rug. She hopped twice to regain her balance, then yanked the receiver off the wall.

"Yes? Hello?"

On the other line, Amelia said, "Shane, honey. You need to speak with Carl. He's livid."

That couldn't be right. "Didn't you tell him I was handling an emergency?"

"I tried, really! He wouldn't listen. Sorry, I have to hang up, OK? Break time's almost over. How's your mom?"

"Still missing."

"I'm sorry."

"Me too. See you soon, Amelia." After hanging up, Shane turned toward her grandfather, who was holding the phone book in his lap and pointing at something in its pages of names and numbers.

"Found one," he said. "This lady's a gardener with twenty years of experience.

Can't beat that. Marcos, where are you, young man? We have an errand to run."

"On the way there," Shane asked, "could you drop me off at Pizza Dale?"

"You're going to work?" Her grandpa sounded surprised, and she didn't blame him.

"Not exactly. Just need to ask for time off."

"I thought your friend already took care of it."

A fruit fly brushed against Shane's arm, tickling. She didn't glance down to check whether it was still alive. "Unfortunately, this is something I need to handle face-to-face."

"Take a seat," Carl ordered, pointing to the breakroom table. They were alone in the room, but sounds of chatter and clinking trays filtered through the wall adjacent to the kitchen, reminding Shane that — beyond the gray box and its ticking clock — there was a bustling, vibrant restaurant.

"Yes, sir." She pulled a chair away from the table and sat with her hands politely clasped in her lap. As the bare lightbulb flickered overhead, Shane experienced an overpowering sense of déjà vu. Had it really been just a few days since her last meeting with Carl? So much could happen — could change — in just a few days.

"I can't talk long," he said. "It's a busy day, especially since you left us short-staffed."

"I'm sorry about that. Did Amelia explain what happened?"

"No," Carl said. When Shane raised her eyebrows with disbelief, he clarified, "Your friend tried to feed me an excuse, but I reminded her that I'm your manager. What does that mean?"

It took all of Shane's self-control to block her reflexive eye roll. "That I should tell you directly?"

"We went over this last week. It means I'm impartial. I can't take personal stories into consideration. Shane, unless somebody died —"

"No," she said quickly. "My mother's still alive."

He had the decency to look relieved. "Good." Then, Carl's expression went

201

stern. "Unfortunately, you skipped work without notice."

"There was no way to contact —"

"That may be so," he interrupted, "but the team needs employees who are reliable. Until now, you've impressed me, Shane. Never missed a shift. Never late."

At a loss for words, Shane just stared at the bridge of his nose, pretending to make eye contact, and waited for his verdict. Carl made a show of removing his glasses and wiping them on his tie. He seemed younger without glasses, which somehow made everything worse. She keenly remembered that pep rally in high school, when they sat on opposite ends of an auditorium instead of opposite ends of a cramped metal table.

"I'll give you a pass," he finally said. "Just this once."

She slouched with relief. "Thank you."

"It can't happen again, though."

Shane nodded quickly. "Understood." Assuming their talk was over, Carl started to stand. But hastily, she added, "I have one more thing to ask."

He slowly returned to his seat, his bushy eyebrows scrunched with displeasure.

"I really appreciate my position at Pizza Dale," Shane explained, nailing the speech she'd practiced in the station wagon, "and want to continue working here. The money helps my family a lot. However —"

"However?" he muttered. "That sounds ominous."

"Uh . . ." In her rehearsal early that morning, she hadn't prepared for an interruption, and it threw off her flow so bad, she momentarily forgot what came next. "Um, I . . . I need to request emergency time off."

"Ah. I see. How many days?"

At that, she bowed her head, staring at a chip in the table. "As long it takes to find my mother."

"She's missing? What —" Carl seemed to catch himself breaking his own rule, because he abruptly added: "Nevermind. I can approve up to one week —"

Shane started nodding; she wanted so badly to believe that, within a week's time, Lorenza would be home.

"— beginning Monday. We need you at work today and tomorrow. You know how busy weekends get."

"I . . . I'm sorry, but that's impossible."

The clock ticked adamantly.

"Shane," he warned quietly, "you're leaving us short staffed again."

Tick, tick.

"What choice do I have? There aren't better options."

Tick.

"That may be so, but if you want a job at Pizza Dale —"

"I want my mother, Carl!" Shane stood so quickly, she nearly knocked over the metal folding chair. It scraped across the concrete floor, sounding like nails on a chalkboard. As her boss stared in stunned silence, adrenaline caused Shane's hands to tremble, and her heart to quicken. She recognized the twitchiness of fight or flight, but instead of giving in to instinct — to running out the door or cursing in Carl's face — Shane took a steadying breath, looked him in the eyes, and stated, "I cannot work today. I probably cannot work tomorrow or the next day. Am I fired?"

The clock ticked five times before Carl softly answered, "Yes." Still seated, he pointed to her locker. "Please pack your belongings and leave."

For a moment, Shane felt like a criminal in an interrogation room. Guilty and wretched. Her eyes stung, tears threatening to fall.

Then, she laughed. At Carl's horrified expression, Shane snorted, "Don't worry. I just realized that there are bigger tragedies than losing a job in the local cemetery-adjacent pizza parlor."

"Very amusing." He stood and tucked his chair back in place. "I'm sure your next employer will love that positive attitude."

"My next employer will be me." Shane walked over to the wall of cubby-sized, green lockers and opened #4. "Next summer, I'll make search and rescue a proper part-time job. Me and my mom and our ghost dog."

"Ghost dog?"

"That's right, Carl. I have a ghost dog. So trust me when I say that it's been freaky working next to a burial ground. If you're curious, I can bring him to Pizza Dale when I pick up my last paycheck."

"Shane, what's going on right now?"

"Just chatting. You aren't my boss anymore; it's cool to share personal stuff, right?"

With a baffled shake of his head, Carl backed toward the door. "Well, erm . . . have a good life," he stammered.

"Will do. See ya, Carl."

At that, Shane watched her ex-manager flee. The wooden door clunked shut behind him, leaving her alone with the ticking clock, the single flickering lightbulb, and the smell of pizza. She gathered her belongings. The bandages, the cardigan, the spare thermos. Finally, Shane looked at the Polaroid photo, studying the smiles of her friends.

Gently, she unstuck it from her locker door, opened Amelia's locker — number twelve — and placed the photo on a stack of neatly folded blouses.

And with that, she left the breakroom, stepping into a narrow corridor in the back of the restaurant, behind the kitchens. The rich scent of dough and pepperoni intensified; Shane's stomach ached with hunger for a slice of cheese pizza, and she realized that she'd unintentionally skipped breakfast. Normally, her mother cooked eggs with corn, squash, tomatoes, and beans in the morning; the family ate from the pot throughout the day, pairing the scramble with corn tortillas and meat, when available. It occurred to her that she'd never thanked her mother for the food, instead treating meals like a given. In the future, Shane swore to thank Lorenza for breakfast every morning, just like she thanked the sun as it rose.

It was 10:58 a.m., two minutes before the restaurant opened for lunch. She shouldered her way out the back door, stepping into the weedy patch of land where the dumpsters were hidden. Clutching her belongings in one arm, Shane jogged around to the front parking lot, which was already half-full with customer vehicles. There, she stood outside the restaurant and stared at the bus stop down the street, considering. She had enough money for the bus fare home, and Grandpa Louis and Marcos would be running errands for a few hours, unable to swing by and pick her up.

But what could Shane do at home? Sit around waiting? That would drive her up the wall. She should be researching mimics and the Below.

207

How could she research those subjects? Where could she go, if not home? As far as she knew, the public library didn't have a secret room full of dangerous, obscure knowledge. Plus, most Lipan stories weren't in books. They were carried within people.

She thought for a moment. There was a possibility.

Shane slipped into the cardigan she was carrying, erasing her work uniform with a splash of warm brown. Although it was forty degrees too hot for long, knitted sleeves, she never wanted to wear manager-approved red and black again. Later, she'd sew brightly-colored patches onto her black pants and pair her blouses with denim overalls. Until then, the cardigan would suffice.

Now dressed like a customer, Shane pushed back through the front door of Pizza Dale and looked around the busy restaurant. Across the room, Amelia was speaking to a family of four, jotting their order into a small spiral notebook. With a pleasant little smile, she finished writing, snapped the notebook shut, and turned to walk to the kitchen.

"Hey, Amelia!" Shane called out, speed-walking between tables. "Just a second!"

"Shane?" Her friend's eyes widened and she extended her arms for a hug. "When did you get here? What's with the winter clothes?"

"I'll tell you tonight, promise." She squeezed Amelia quickly but firmly, then stepped back. "Had a quick question. Which bus line passes by the university?"

"Line zero-four. You can take the ten-six bus to the mall stop and then connect there." Her stare of disbelief locked onto the bandages and thermos in Shane's arm. "Weren't those in your locker?"

"Not anymore." As Shane headed toward the exit, the smell of lavender clung to her clothes, lingering, if only for a minute.

After she stepped into the sunlight, Shane didn't look back.

∼ NINE ∼

Shane sat beside a window in the back of the bus, where she could press her cheek against the cool glass and watch the town pass. South of Pizza Dale, Petey's Auto Repair was next to the Film and Camera Shop and Sofa Depot, all of them single-story commercial buildings with small, gray parking lots, seldom full. The bus took a right turn at a four-way stop and drove between two sprawling fields of wildflowers. The land had been "in development" since before Shane moved to town, but she hoped it would stay undeveloped forever, so she could continue to watch yellow-petaled greenthread bloom alongside violet spiderwort.

All too quickly, the colors were replaced by the gray sidewalks and buildings near the university. The businesses catered to the teen-and-twenties crowd, with a trendy roller rink and bowling alley, several bars, and a movie theater leading to the campus, which was enclosed by a wrought iron fence. The bus jerked to a stop outside the open gate, and Shane hustled down the narrow aisle into the heat, squeezing past a pair of cigarette-puffing women who were impatiently trying to board.

"Thanks, sir," Shane called to the driver, who waved.

Through the gate, Shane asked a couple of book bag-toting young men for directions. They pointed down a rosebush-lined path, where Shane found the Department of Agricultural Sciences, a boxy concrete building with large arched windows. A refreshing blast of cool air welcomed her inside the front lobby, which smelled like old books and chalk. Seeing nobody, Shane took a left down the first hallway she found, knocking on locked doors.

Finally, at an office labeled *#10: Bronson*, a man with a southern drawl called out, "Enter!"

Shane opened the door, revealing a thirty-something-year-old man in a green wool blazer. He sat behind a desk piled with folders, his face half-hidden by a stack of papers. The walls were covered with shelves full of leatherbound books. "What can I do for you, Miss?"

"Are you a professor?" she asked, standing in the doorway.

He pushed the papers aside and tapped on a copper nameplate — Dr. Oliver Bronson — on his desk. "Assistant professor. Who are you looking for?"

"Anyone who knows biology." She eyed the books, which had titles like *Principles of Cross-Pollination* and *Nitrogen Cycling*. "Like you."

"It's a vast field. I may be a biologist, but my agricultural specialty does not make me an expert in, for example, elephant behavior or human viruses."

"What do you know about mimics?" she asked next.

"As in insect mimicry?"

Shane shook her head. "No. I mean extra-dimensional mushrooms."

With a burst of laughter, he insisted, "Miss, you're pulling my leg." Dr. Bronson leaned to one side and glanced around Shane, as if expecting a group of senior pranksters to burst into his office and shout, *Gotcha!*

"I'm not!" she exclaimed. "My ma's gone missing in Less Crossing, and she's not the only one who's disappeared. All because of mimics!"

Sensing the urgency in Shane's voice, the man's smile fell. "This is a police matter, surely?"

"They were called. So far, they've doused the town in fungicides and deflected all my family's questions. They think Ma will turn up on her own, and . . . I hope so. But I'm not gonna leave everything up to hope and strangers. I gotta understand what we're facing here. How far the ring could've sent her, its sensitivity to thoughts and whims. Can you help?"

"Miss, I study corn!"

"There must be a textbook? Or another professor?" After fishing around her

213

pocket, Shane held out her remaining bus fare. "I can pay a consulting fee."

With a slow shake of his head, the professor pushed the change away. "I want to help," he insisted. "It's just a very obscure topic. Mimics are exceptionally rare, and their behavior varies between Earth and the Greatest Kingdoms." His lips quirked in amusement at the fae's most common name for their planet.

"You believe me, though?"

"Well, yes. Your story explains why the government suddenly just decided to divert half the state's fungicides to a small town. Even our department had to donate its supplies. I've been coordinating replacements all morning. Are you a student here?"

"I'm still in high school."

"Ye gads. And your momma's gone missing. What about your father?"

"Pa's dead," Shane replied, and although there was a time when Shane would cry at every mention of her father's death, she'd learned to detach emotions from those two words. "Tuberculosis."

A pained expression flitted across Dr. Bronson's face. Then, he ducked behind his desk and opened a drawer. After loudly rifling through what sounded like more loose papers, he stood again with a business card. "It's summer session, so most of the department's home, but the Ag library will stay open until five." He penned a few words on the back of the card. "Give this to the head librarian. She'll help you access the journal archives. There may be something."

"Thank you." Shane accepted the business card. In a messy scrawl, he'd written: *She's my temp research assistant. Please allow archive access. — Dr. B*

"Trouble in Less Crossing," he mused, sitting back in his creaking chair. "Uncontrolled mimics, in this day and age? What a disaster!" Then, he shoved a stack of binders to one corner of his desk, revealing a telephone that had been buried under the materials. "Excuse me, Miss. I need to make a couple calls."

"About the fairy rings?" she asked.

"Yes, but don't get too hopeful. Your best bet is still the library. It's behind the greenhouse." He jabbed a thumb over his shoulder, as if pointing to something just beyond his office wall. "Can't miss it."

"Right, gotcha."

"How can I reach you, if I do find something? Will you be on campus next week?"

"I might," she said.

But just in case, Shane left him phone numbers to reach her house and the neighbor. Then, without wasting another second, she nodded appreciatively, turned around, and jogged down the empty hallway, her footsteps echoing off the plaster walls. When she stepped outside, the dry heat felt like a magma-bellied dragon's breath; sweat beaded on her temples. She shrugged out of her cardigan and wrapped it around her bandages and thermos, using it as a bag. Nearby, the long greenhouse glinted, reflecting sunlight off its upper western panes. It was just past noon. That meant she had four hours.

As Shane ran to the library, she fretted about the task ahead. She'd always been a slow, deliberate reader. Give her six months, and she could finish and enjoy a book, no problem. But when she had to rush the process, the words disconnected from each other; she knew what each meant in isolation, but struggled to place them in the context of sentences, para-graphs, and even chapters.

Would four hours be enough time to achieve her goals?

Shane shouldn't have worried.

In the library, she'd been ushered to a small, windowless room with off-white walls and a single wooden table. After Shane explained her needs, the head librarian — a white woman who wore her graying hair in a high ponytail — left to search their archives. Thirty minutes later, she returned with one academic journal. Bound in a plain, denim-blue cover, it resembled a duller version of the maga-zines sold within every grocery store and gas station. But while those had titles like *Seventeen* and *Vogue*, this journal was called *Applications in Ecosystem Studies*.

"This is all we have," the librarian apol-ogetically said. "Our collection's limited, and I couldn't find a thing in the news-paper archive. You might check a bigger university next time. Texas A&M, for example. If I recall, they sent researchers to the site, when the incident happened. Might be primary data in their library. That'd be with the Department of Forestry, or perhaps Environmental Biology?" She placed the journal in front of Shane and flipped to page eleven, where there was the start of a scientific paper titled "Changes in the songbird community surrounding the Longfire Dead Zone."

"It's . . . much better than nothing!" Shane smiled, trying to prioritize gratitude over disappointment. A&M was in College Station, mid-Texas. It would take more than a local bus to reach the campus. "At least I won't be here till closing, poring over books."

"Well. Yes. Every cloud has a silver lining. Stop by the front desk if you need anything else."

After thanking the librarian, Shane carefully read the text. The abstract explained that there'd been subtle changes in the songbird community around the dead zone after the Incident. The researchers hypothesized that vulnerable species were moving away from the bare patch of land in order to avoid hawks and other winged predators. But, although the circle of death was referenced several times, the mimic ring itself was only mentioned once: "The novel extradimensional entity *Marasmius transpose* (colloquially known as a 'mimic') was responsible for killing approximately 17 acres of old-growth forest through a process known as biomagisynthesis, i.e., the conversion of biological matter into magical energy (Richards 1951)."

Shane flipped to the end of the article and skimmed the list of alphabetically-organized references. There, under "R," she found the following entries:

Richards, Archie. *Proposed method of biomagisynthesis in Marasmius transpose.* Western Colorado University Press. 1951.

Richards, Archie. *Simulation of fairy ring conduit activity with terrestrial species of fungus.* Western Colorado University Press. 1952.

For future research, she copied the author's name and his books' information on a square of paper from the card catalogue section. Then, Shane went to the front desk to ask the librarian one last favor: "Do you have a phone directory of other universities?"

When Shane arrived home, she fixed herself two peanut butter and jelly sandwiches, finished the fruit salad, and moved a chair next to the phone. Grandpa Louis and Marcos were still running errands, Nellie was curled up near the sofa, and Neal and Nealey were asleep in the bedroom, so the house was unusually quiet. If she hadn't had a long list of phone calls to make, Shane would have switched on the radio.

After opening Lorenza's book of important addresses and phone numbers, she sat, tucked the receiver between her shoulder and ear, and turned the rotary, bracing herself for a couple difficult conversations.

The talk with Lorenza's boss went better than expected, since he promised that Lorenza would have a job when she returned. "Your momma's a hard worker. They're always welcome here. Hope she's home soon." That settled, Shane moved on to the next phase in her rescue mission.

First, Shane called Western Colorado University Press. Various secretaries bounced her around campus until she reached the secretary at the biology department, who regretfully informed Shane that "Archie Richards is no longer a researcher here; I believe he moved to Fairleaf College."

"Is that in Colorado, too?"

"No, Miss. It's in Washington."

So Shane hung up, dialed zero, and asked the operator, "Could you please transfer me to the Fairleaf College in Washington State?" And after another series of transferred calls, she learned that, "Dr. Richards left our institution over seven years ago."

"Do you know where he currently works?" she asked. "Is he still at a university in the northwest?"

"Oh." The secretary of Fairleaf's supernatural biology department sounded embarrassed. "I'm afraid Professor Richards left higher ed."

"Huh? What does that mean? He doesn't teach anymore?"

"Well . . ."

As the woman elaborated, Shane jotted down the phone number and name of

Dr. Richards's confirmed current workplace: Skylight Comics and Collectibles, in Tanner, Colorado.

"This is it!" Shane said, after hanging up the phone. "We found him."

All it had taken was a small fortune in long-distance calls. Fortunately, Malorie's family had tucked ten dollars in their thank-you card, so when the phone bill arrived, there'd be funds for the expense.

At her side, Nellie — who'd been alternating between Shane and Marcos since Lorenza vanished, made a soft *whuff*, kindly acknowledging that Shane was talking even if he couldn't understand her words.

"One more call," Shane told him, reaching for the phone. After two rings, a soft-spoken man answered, "Skylight C and C. How may I assist you?"

"Dr. Richards?"

His response was a slow, cagey, "Who's asking?"

"I'm Shane Solé, a student from Texas."

"Well, Shane," he replied, "our hours of operation are nine a.m. to six p.m., Monday through Friday. Fair warning: we're a long drive from Texas."

"I'm not actually calling about comics and collectibles, sir."

"This should be interesting." She detected a hint of amusement now. That was better than annoyance, at least.

"Did you write *Proposed method of bio-magisynthesis in Marasmius transpose?*" she asked.

"In a former life. Yes."

"Oh, super! A wild mimic ring teleported my mother to —"

There was a click on the other line, followed by a long electronic beep. The guy had hung up on her.

"C'mon," Shane groaned. Her finger hovered over the rotary dial. But before calling back, Shane needed a plan; otherwise, he'd just hang up again. Had Dr. Richards mistaken her for a prank caller? She hoped so. Shane might be able to convince him that she was serious.

It would be harder to convince a stranger that he should care about other people.

This time, when Dr. Richards answered the phone with a hesitant, "C and C.

How can I assist you?" Shane blurted out, "Please don't hang up! My ma stepped into a ring and went missing. A kid's gone, too! I'm not joking. I can describe the mushrooms. They were white with red polka dots!"

On the other end, Dr. Richards said nothing. But he didn't hang up this time, either. This encouraged Shane to continue.

"They reminded me of spotted umbrellas."

Abruptly, Dr. Richards asked, "How many dots were on each mushroom?"

"I . . . uh . . . I didn't count."

"Could you guess?"

"More than ten?" Why hadn't she taken notes when the memory was fresh? "Oh! Here's another detail! They smelled nice. Like vanilla."

"OK," he said. "OK."

"You believe me?"

"I believe you're serious. But Miss, why did you call me?" The question sounded apologetic. "I'm not a scientist anymore."

"There's no information about *M. transpose* in the local library. A professor I met says nobody studies it anymore 'cause it's so rare. You wrote a whole paper about the species though!"

"A long time ago."

"Is it possible to estimate the distance my mother traveled based on the size of the gray circle?"

There was a sound on Dr. Richards's end: a bell ringing in the background. "Theoretically, yes," he said quickly. "I'd need pictures of the rings, or even better, measurements of their diameters, and a few topsoil cores from outside the circle."

"I can get that to you, no problem!"

"And you're sure that your mother —"

There was a muffled sound, and a voice babbling cheerily.

"Just a moment," Dr. Richards said, distant and polite, as if addressing a client. Then, to Shane, he continued, "Like I said. Monday through Friday, nine a.m. until five p.m. I'm here every day. You know what to bring?"

"Topsoil and photos of the gray circles."

"Good," he said. Then, after a moment of hesitation, he added, "And hurry. If you're right, there's no time to waste."

With that, Dr. Richards hung up the phone once more.

Shane took a long, steadying breath. All things considered, the day's investigations had gone well. There was just one problem. "How am I gonna hurry to a store in Colorado?" she asked Nellie, who wagged his tail in response.

A knock at the door signaled that Shane's alone time had ended, which was a relief. Though it was an irrational fear, she'd had a growing sense of dread that Marcos, off running important errands with Grandpa Louis, would never come home — that her life was being whittled down, person by person.

"Come in!" she called. "It's unlocked."

The front door slowly swung open. On the porch, backlit by the sun, stood Amelia.

"Hey, what are you doing here?" Shane asked, shocked. Her friend's shift didn't end for another couple hours, and there was zero chance that Carl would have let her leave early on a short-staffed day.

"I quit," Amelia said, wiping her buckled leather shoes on the woven front mat.

Perhaps noticing Shane's stunned expression, she explained, "I don't need that place. It pays no better than my mom's shop."

"But —"

"I was there because of you, Shane."

"Because of . . . me?" She thought for a second, and it occurred to her that Amelia had started work at Pizza Dale just one week after she did.

A memory blossomed in her mind's eye. Prom night, junior year. She and Amelia were working the late shift together, serving pizza to tables of high school sweethearts. Girls in long, flowy dresses and satin gloves. Guys in brightly-colored velvet suits with oversized bowties and wilting corsages. And when the ovens cooled, and the last giggling couple stepped into the night, Shane had turned to Amelia and wondered, "Do you regret it?"

"What?" she'd asked, swiping a rag across a sauce-spattered tabletop.

"Skipping the dance." Unlike Shane, Amelia didn't need every chance to make a few bucks. "Didn't Sawyer de Santos ask you out?" He was a fine young man, an ace at chess, with a mane of black, curly hair. If Sawyer had asked Shane to the prom, she would have turned him down, but with great reluctance.

"Yeah, but Sawyer has no sense of rhythm."

"What about Porter Highsmith?" Another of Amelia's suitors. "He's a drummer."

With a frown, Amelia had leaned over a plush booth seat to retrieve a discarded corsage: a yellow rose in a bed of lacy green leaves. Instead of chucking the flower into the trash, she'd stepped up to Shane.

"What about him?" Amelia asked, while deftly pinning the corsage to Shane's red blouse. There was a coolness to her voice. A hint of pain. At the time, Shane just assumed that Porter must have insulted Amelia, but perhaps the upset had had nothing to do with him or Sawyer, or any boy.

Because when Shane had responded, "Nothing. Anyhow, I'm lucky you're here," Amelia's smile had been sweeter than the rose. As if Shane had given her a gift, something Amelia appreciated more than a pretty trinket. And that'd confused Shane for a moment, 'cause she didn't know what that gift had been. But as they'd continued to work side-by-side in companionable silence, she'd come to a tentative understanding: she'd acknowledged that she cherished Amelia's company. That her life was better for it.

"Obviously, because of you," Amelia said, glancing around the room. "So there's no point in working there anymore. Plus, I want to help you find your mom."

She smiled, and walked to Shane's side and mirrored her pose, hands on hips. "What did you learn at the university?"

For a moment, Shane couldn't think of the answer, feeling overwhelmingly light. And when her awareness inevitably returned, reality felt bad, but not as bad. Amelia would help. Amelia, with her diligent plans and her big family and her unflagging sense of responsibility.

Her friend.

"A potential next step," Shane said. Then, she quickly shared that she'd found a man who understood the magic of mimic rings. "He might be able to explain their limits or estimate the distance my ma traveled. If that fails, maybe he'll show us how to grow a new ring in a safe way. We just have provide some soil samples and photos. Donnie can help with that."

"Sounds promising." Suddenly, Amelia blinked rapidly, then pointed toward the television. There, Nellie paced between the TV stand and the coffee table. "Hey, is that your ghost dog?"

"Excuse me?" Shane jolted upright, pushing away from the sofa and turning to look her friend in the eyes. "Who told you about him? Carl?" Or had the gossip web already widened beyond her former manager?

"Yes, Carl —"

"What did he say?" Shane never should have mentioned Nellie. Now, a moment of satisfaction could lead to complications, could lead to . . . forget what Grandpa Louis had said. It might not be the 1800s, but the world was a cruel place, and the forces that had terrorized her people one hundred years ago were still in play. They'd just taken different forms. Hadn't Shane learned anything from the nightmare after the flood? Why had she let her grandfather weaken her defenses? He hadn't been there. Hadn't suffered with the rest of his family. He didn't understand —

"That you lost your senses? That working near a graveyard had been too stressful? Shane, I don't believe him. About you losing it, at least. If you say that you have a ghost dog, then you have a ghost dog." She leaned in, her voice dropping to a secretive whisper. "My great-aunt's parrot died at the ripe old age of ninety, but he stuck around for another fifteen years. Only left when she did. Animal ghosts aren't actually that freaky."

In an instant, Shane's anxiety stopped spiraling. During the earlier confrontation with Carl, she hadn't actually shared the family secret. He didn't know that she could wake ghosts, and neither did Amelia. It would be easy to pretend that Nellie was a straggler, one of the rare animal ghosts that remained on earth just because they felt like it.

And the best part was, Shane didn't need to lie to her best friend. She just had to stay quiet.

"You aren't mad that I kept him secret?" she asked.

Firmly, Amelia shook her head. "We all have secrets."

They stood in silence for a moment too long. Then, Amelia clapped her hands once, decisively, and asked, "What's next? I'm here to do anything you need. Babysit Marcos? Clean? Make calls? Start a search party?"

"First, would you like to meet Nellie?"

Amelia laughed, startled. "Of course!"

"He's a good boy." Shane held out her hand and whistled. A few seconds later, Nellie pushed his head into her palm, asking for pets. She scratched the shimmer under her fingers, and vaguely felt his fur, once so soft, now only a memory carried in the odd material of ghosts. "Give him a pat."

Hesitantly, Amelia extended her pointer finger. When it made contact with Nellie's temple, right beside his floppy ear, she drew back quickly, as if zapped. "Aaaah!"

"What's wrong?"

"I just poked a ghost! My great-aunt's parrot never let anyone touch him. He was a grumpy old bird."

Nellie wagged his tail, grateful for the attention. With less caution than before, Amelia ran her hand down Nellie's back. "It's so strange!" she gasped, her mouth quirking into a slight smile. "Like the air's dense and bouncy. What was it like when he came back?"

"A relief. He almost didn't."

"What do you mean?" Amelia leaned back from the shimmer and crossed her arms. "Weren't you shocked?"

"Not at all."

Years ago, when he passed into the world Below, Shane had cried to her mother, "Use the secret power. Please, please. Bring him back!"

And Lorenza — who'd once believed that the knowledge to wake the ghosts of animals would die with her generation, since the modern world was inhospitable to most wild species, never mind wild ghosts — had nodded in agreement that day. Her time with Nellie had been too short (wasn't that always the case, with family dogs?) Then, her mother had gone to the house, where she sat in the living room and whispered Nellie's name again and again, her eyes squeezed shut, her brow creased with

233

concentration, her call slipping to the land Below, where all creatures dwell after death. The whispers had increased in volume, then transformed into calls.

But Lorenza hadn't used the ghost-waking technique in more than a decade then, and like many arts, practice was critical. As the hours passed, and her mother's voice became raspy and faded, Shane wondered whether she'd just witnessed the death of knowledge. Through disuse, had Lorenza forgotten how to wake a ghost? It was a technique Shane's heroic ancestor had developed, a power that generations of mothers had passed along to their daughters. With Grandma Bee gone, and Lorenza struggling, who would teach Shane one day?

Shortly before midnight, when Lorenza had been on the verge of collapse, a dog-shaped shimmer had appeared in the middle of their living room. No longer burdened by the aches of old age, Nellie ran in rambunctious circles, whining and barking with joy.

Most animal ghosts returned Below after a short period of time; they'd stay as long as they desired up above, and not a millisecond longer. You couldn't force an animal's ghost to manifest on Earth, either. They came and went as they pleased. However, it had been many years since, and Nellie hadn't left Earth. Not even for a second.

"The women in my family have a skill," Shane said. "We're ghostraisers, if you can believe it. Nellie isn't the only one. Bugs, rats, buzzards, elk. I can summon everything except for humans, basically." The confession made her feel a shame-laced sense of uncertainty. She should've told Amelia earlier. Would her friend forgive her? Would she be impressed or worried or . . .

"Even dinosaurs?"

Shane barked out a single, surprised chuckle. "Dinosaurs?" She'd never tried to rouse a prehistoric giant, but weren't they just really old animals? "Sure. Probably."

"Wha . . . How? How is that possible?"

"Ma taught me," Shane explained. "And 'fore that, Grandma taught Ma. Great-grandma taught grandma. All the way back to my four-great-grandmother."

"And who did she learn it from?"

Amelia crouched and pet Nellie's back as Shane spoke.

"Nobody. She's the original. Centuries ago, my heroic four-great-grandmother — Elatsoe — she figured out how to coax animal ghosts back to Earth. At first, people were scared. But after she used the skill to help others, the only ones who feared her were the horrible people and creatures she fought."

"Was she an old-time monster hunter?"

"Sort of? Hunt isn't the right word. Four-Great never attacked anyone, unless they were hurting others."

"She was a protector, then?"

"Yes. A protector; a defender. People across the desert, mountains, and plains sought her help. She had so many adventures . . ."

Shane used to know the stories: people in la rancheria de los Lipanes would share them, and many others. But it had been a long time since the last gathering. "Once, um, there was a river monster. It kept drowning folks just for fun. Same way a well-fed house cat will kill birds without eating them. That monster would lure victims into the Rio Grande."

"How?" Amelia asked, wide-eyed —
no doubt thinking of all the times she'd
gone swimming in the sluggish Herotonic River.

"I think it was imitating human voices?
I'd have to ask Ma. In any case, Four-
Great stopped the monster's reign of terror
by snaring it in a net. She was clever and
fearless. In fact, I think Four-Great would
have been a protector even without her
ghosts. But they helped a lot, especially
against stacked odds. One time, a bunch
of soldiers tried to slaughter a Lipan camp
of children and Elders. Before the invad-
ers could fire their guns, Four-Great
swept them away with a ghostly stampede
of . . ."

Of what? Had they been bison? Or deer?
Shane couldn't remember specifics anymore. Of course, she could guess; bison
seemed right, considering their size,
strength, and formerly great numbers. Yet
this was her ancestor's story, passed down
through generations, sacred history preserved in voices. Shane couldn't bear to
warp it, even accidentally. Even just once.

". . . of large animals," Shane finished,
as to be a vague storyteller seemed better

than to be an uncertain one. Still, her cheeks reddened with embarrassment, and her eyes teared up. She wished she could ask her mother this very second how the story ended.

"What's wrong?" Amelia asked, gently clasping Shane's hand in hers. "Honey, she's OK. Your mom can survive anything. Trust me. If Donna's right, and that ring sent her to the land of the dead, your mom will just grab Bobby and find the way back."

"Donnie," Shane softly corrected, looking down to stare at the carpet between their feet. "What if the ring really did send Bobby to the world Below? Is it even possible to bring him home? I'm certain that Ma would have found a way already, if they were together." Shane flexed her toes in the carpet fibers. "I already know how to bring creatures to Earth. I should be able to reverse the process, with a little instruction. If only —"

"No more *if*s or *but*s," Amelia interrupted. "They're useless, and you know it. Focus on your lead. And, tell you what. Once Donnie gets the photos and dirt, I can take them to Colorado. Maybe

Gustavo will go with me, once I explain everything. He's never traveled by ring before."

"Gustavo's still in town?" Shane asked. Out of Amelia's six brothers, Shane knew and liked Gustavo the best. Just a year older than Shane, he'd been in two of her high school classes: home economics and calculus. The other brothers all had jobs and apartments in Austin; she'd assumed that Gustavo would have moved there, too, after graduation.

"Yep." Amelia shrugged. "He's at home, considering his career goals."

"What's on the table?"

"Opening a tattoo parlor. Joining a band. Going to college. Mom says Gustavo has a year to decide. Until then, he's her button and zipper guy. If that ever gets loose" — she poked one of the round metal buttons on Shane's overalls — "give him a call and he'll sew it tight. Hey, can I use your phone? I should call Papa, since he's our family's ring transport expert."

Shane nodded, giving Amelia permission to make the call. As her friend used the rotary dialer, the front door popped open, and Grandpa Louis stepped inside, holding a large paper bag. Behind him, Marcos carried two smaller bags, one in each hand.

"You bought groceries?" Shane asked, pleasantly surprised.

"Mushroom-growing supplies." Her grandpa dropped his bag with a loud thump and then rubbed the sweat off his brow. There was a weariness in his stooped shoulders. "This will be more trouble than I'd expected. Lady at the shop says it's hard to control the size of mushroom rings. I hope that isn't true for mimics, too."

"Maybe we can ask. I found a specialist named Dr. Richards, who wrote an article about the way they change matter into magic."

"Oh?" He inclined his head at Amelia, who was speaking rapidly in Spanish, the receiver pressed against her ear. With a teasing smile, he asked, "Is that Dr. Richards?"

"No, Grandpa," Marcos corrected; he was still learning to recognize sarcasm and dry humor, which meant half of his grandfather's jokes fell flat. "She's Amelia. Shane's friend."

"Dr. Richards lives in Colorado," Shane explained. "It's a small town, so Amelia volunteered to travel there with information."

"Bad news." Amelia had hung up, and joined them now near the doorway. "Papa didn't make it to work today. Guess why."

"Oh no! Did he disappear, too?" Marcos cried, sounding on the verge of panic.

"No, sweetheart, nothing like that." Amelia leaned over to give Marcos a comforting half-hug. "The ring transport center — the one he uses to commute to Austin — was closed until further notice. All of the centers in Texas are closed. Can you believe it? That's ridiculously awful timing!"

"How long will they be out of order?" Shane asked.

"No clue. Could be a day or a month."

"We don't have a month." Pacing, she considered their options. "A train ticket isn't that expensive —"

"Trains are shut down, too."

"You can't be serious."

"I am. Papa had an important meeting, so he tried to get a last-minute ticket. The teller sent him away. It's all over the radio, but there's no explanation — not yet — and no telling when they'll run again."

"Huh. That is bad luck." In Shane's experience, however, stuff that resembled bad luck often had nothing to do with chance. It seemed too coincidental: after wild fairy rings mysteriously sprung up near the railroad tracks of Less Crossing, the authorities had closed all the ring centers and trains in Texas. There had to be a connection. But what did it all mean?

"So we drive," Grandpa Louis announced, his posture straightening.

"Today?" Shane asked.

He nodded. "Now."

≈ TEN ≈

Shane's hands tightened on the steering wheel as she guided the station wagon along the highway. Folded state maps were piled on the passenger seat, but Shane didn't need them as long as she kept Grandpa Louis in sight. On his motorcycle, with his plain leather jacket and white bowl-shaped helmet, he resembled a daredevil: one of those guys who flew up ramps to jump over cars and canyons. Shane kept the windows rolled down so she could follow the motorcycle's rumble, even when her grandfather momentarily disappeared within traffic, which mainly consisted of long-haul trucks and commuters returning home from work. Although Shane had a license, she rarely drove on highways, using Lorenza's truck mainly to run errands around town. With Marcos in the back seat, she had extra motivation to drive safely, remaining calm and observing the speed limit despite the ticking of her internal clock, which urged her to *reach Colorado now! Hurry! As quick as possible!*

In front of her, Grandpa Louis lifted his hand, his elbow crooked at a ninety degree angle, indicating a right turn. They both pulled into a wooded rest stop, just a row of five parking spots in front of a maintenance facility. A flamingo-pink convertible idled in the middle spot, its top lowered, revealing Donnie in the back seat and her grandparents in the front. They'd insisted on joining the cross-country trip, eager to help the search. The moment Grandpa Louis and Shane drove into view, Donnie leapt out by vaulting over the side of her family's car. She wore loose gray jeans that had threadbare spots over each knee — the fabric one scrape away from tearing — and a large black shirt. Her hair was twice as voluminous today, and with every step Donnie took, it bobbed around her shoulders, cloud-like.

"I got the dirt and pictures!" she shouted, holding up a manila envelope. "There was a fence around the abandoned house, so I had to take bird's-eye Polaroid snaps by climbing a pine tree."

"How'd you get past the feds?" Shane wondered.

"Went the long way, through the forest. They don't know it like I do."

"That's good," Marcos said. "Very good." Sighing, he sat back, hugging his rabbit and staring out the side window. After handing the envelope to Grandpa Louis, Donnie popped open the convertible's passenger-side door and helped Mrs. Park step outside, steadying the older woman with a hand on her elbow. A gust of wind tousled Mrs. Park's yellow sundress, but her hair was secured tightly under a pink silk scarf. The outfit's bright colors seemed mismatched alongside the woman's somber expression. After drawing herself upright, Mrs. Park pulled free of Donnie's hold and walked up to Shane's window, still lowered.

"They say you're an ace with maps, dear," she said.

"Yes, ma'am. I learned how to read maps 'fore I learned how to read English."

The Elder slipped on a pair of sunglasses and nodded approvingly. "You can navigate while I drive. Is that OK?"

"Definitely." Shane flexed her fingers, which had been gripping the steering wheel, even parked. Out of the corner of the eye, she noticed Grandpa Louis shake Mr. Park's hand. A moment later, the motorcycle revved back to life, and her grandfather tore out of the parking lot. While he'd been riding tamely earlier, he now drove like a cheetah's ghost was snapping at his back wheel, rearing for blood. He'd hightail it to Tanner and make contact with Dr. Richards while the others caught up. Unfortunately, Grandpa Louis couldn't deliver the soil samples. Near the abandoned house, Donnie and her grandpa had collected the dozen top-soil cores in sharpened PVC pipes, too unwieldy for a motorcycle's cargo. Even so, perhaps Dr. Richards could get started with just photos.

"It'll be OK. Fifteen hours is nothing. I've made longer trips before," Grandpa

Louis had reassured Shane. "Orlando to Seattle; Des Moines to Guadalajara."

"Were they for work?" she'd asked, knowing that, at one point in his forty-plus years as an adult, Grandpa Louis had been a door-to-door salesman, although he'd never gone into more detail. When she'd used to ask, "What did you sell?" he'd deflect with, "Tacky garbage, but one man's trash is another man's treasure." Over the years, he'd also apparently worked as a bouncer, a house painter, and an alligator wrestler. The last job was a point of pride, since — in his own words — "It made me a hero, like that four-great-grandmother of yours." According to Grandpa Louis, when he was in his physical prime, he got hired as the alligator man at a roadside reptile zoo. "Didn't take any past experience," he'd explained. "Just muscles and poor sense." Visitors would pay a quarter to watch him feed meat to the alligators; for a dollar, he'd climb into the pen, jump on the biggest alligator's back, and hold her long mouth closed.

"Didn't that hurt her?" young Shane had asked.

"Priorities, kid. You should be asking, 'Didn't she hurt you, Grandpa Louis?'" He'd laughed at that.

She'd shrugged. "You look fine to me."

"The alligator was A-OK, too. Wasn't real wrestling. Just held her for a few seconds."

At Shane's incredulous stare, he'd added, "Those skills came in handy later, believe you me. I saved lives!"

Her incredulity had intensified.

"Don't raise that eyebrow at me, missie." He'd spread his arms like a saint. "Decades after that, I was riding through Louisiana. Been raining hard, flooding houses. Well, a lady scampered into the road, waving her arms and screaming. There was an alligator in her backyard, scared her young son up a tree! The boy was cold and losing his grip, and she couldn't find her shotgun. Thought I might be armed, considering my Harley's reputation. Unfortunately, I'd left my pistol at home."

"Oh!" Shane had exclaimed. "So you saved her kid by wrestling?"

"Sure did. The alligator was a little fella, anyway. Half my weight. I tied its mouth shut and dragged it to the swamp, which had overflowed into the neighborhood. Spent a week in that town. They hired me to deal with all the alligators."

Suffice to say, Shane's grandfather had a strange resume.

"Ah. Were the cross-country trips for work?" he'd repeated. "Hm. Sometimes, yeah. Other times, I just wanted freedom. You get that, on the road."

Mrs. Park, who stood four feet, eleven inches tall, had to readjust their driver's seat, maneuvering it so close to the pedals, her chest almost touched the steering wheel. Then, she fiddled with the side and rearview mirrors, shifting their angles with the diligence of somebody who knew the importance of monitoring your surroundings on the road. Behind her Donnie slid into the back seat and nodded at Marcos.

"Ready to go," Shane said. She spread a map of the southern US across her lap. Rivers and roads, cities and parks, airports and ring transport centers: everything was marked in an intricate collage of symbols, lines, and color-coded regions. Mrs. Park smoothly reversed and pulled onto the highway. In the rearview mirror, Shane could see Mr. Park standing beside the pink convertible, alone. He watched them leave until there was nothing left to see.

"Where are the dogs?" Donnie asked.

"They're with friends," Marcos said. "Chihuahuas."

"Our neighbor's watching them," Shane elaborated. "Well, except for Nellie." He was curled up in the back of the station wagon, huddled over a bag of Lorenza's bandanas and blouses as if comforted by her scent. Shane had packed the clothes just in case they had to track her mother, but it was clear that Nellie would race to Lorenza's side the moment he sensed her, no encouragement needed. "Amelia volunteered to be the official dogsitter, but I couldn't risk it. Neal might chew on her mama's pincushions. He thinks they're toys. A dog only needs seconds to get into trouble, you know. Plus, Amelia can help in other ways. She's like our ground control, the person at home. She knows science better than I do . . . better than anyone in our grade."

"I gotta meet this girl," Donnie said.

As the sun set, the five of them drove through scrubland and fields of corn. In the back seat, Donnie looped a circle of yarn around her hands and made patterns with the string: the Eiffel Tower, London bridge, a spider's web. As she played cat's cradle, Marcos watched, silent in his fascination. When Donnie tired of the game, she put the loop of string on the duffel bag; a few minutes later, Shane looked into the rearview mirror and saw her brother making Eiffel Towers, too. Shane watched him for several minutes, the towers increasing in size and complexity, until they resembled nothing she'd seen before, outside of dreams.

"Does anyone want snacks?" Donnie asked, rummaging in her grandmother's purse, an oversized, daisy-printed vinyl bag. "We have Spam sandwiches, apples, and candy." Glancing up to meet Shane's stare in the mirror, she winked. "I should have made trail mix, too. Sunflower seeds and chocolate chips. They're my new favorite. You bring any?"

"Sorry, all out!" She smiled. "Somebody ate them all."

"In Somebody's defense, Somebody was starving. Maybe this will be a good replacement." Donnie leaned forward to pass Shane a plastic-wrapped cube of coconut candy. Its pink, white, and brown layers were Neapolitan-flavored. Strawberry, vanilla, chocolate. Shane remembered the taste so vividly.

"I used to eat these as a girl." She pinched the plastic between her fingers and tore the wrapper open; loose coconut and sugar crumbs dusted the open map on her lap. "My family had a house in south Texas. The rich family on the hill overlooking our neighborhood had a kid my age. A boy. Sammy Singer." Shane hadn't thought of Sammy in years, but the candy brought back memories of his large hazel eyes and hesitant smile. "He'd sneak down the hill to play on my swing or to join the soccer matches behind my cousin's house. Sammy always shared his snacks, even when there were ten kids playing with us." She snapped the coconut candy in half and handed a piece to Marcos, who had to drop his game of cat's cradle in order to eat. The deflated shape of a tower, preserved in loops of string, slumped over the duffel bag. Soon, it would untwist and become a blank circle again.

"We'd pass Sammy's coconut candy around, taking bites until it was gone. Friends don't worry about cooties. Until, one day, Sammy's mother caught us. She'd been looking for her son, wondering why he disappeared every afternoon. There was a proper playground in his yard — a little slide, swings with chain-link string and rubber seats, even monkey bars. But he'd run off anyway. I guess she spotted us from the hill. You could see all of the valley neighborhood up there, almost like living in a watchtower."

As she spoke, the car's rumble seemed to fade, her world becoming memories.

"That day, me, my cousins, and Sammy were all sitting in a circle behind my house, passing around his candy, when this tall, elegant woman in a silky white jumpsuit, pearls, and heeled leather boots stepped into the yard. I remember freezing in place. I'd only seen women like her in magazines and clothing catalogues. All her clothes new and bright, like they'd never touched the ground before. When Sammy noticed her, his cheeks went red, and he looked down, like she'd caught him with his hand in the cookie jar. That freaked me out, 'cause he was normally such a happy kid. Bashful, but happy.

"The woman looked us over, put her hands on her hips, and said, 'So this is where you've been.' Then, she smiled in this small, quiet way, like the Mona Lisa, took Sammy by the hand, and walked away.

"When Sammy returned the next day, he had a lunchbox full of coconut candy. His momma had purchased enough treats for all the kids in la rancheria de los Lipanes."

"In what?" Donnie interrupted. "Is that what they call your reservation?"

Shane shook her head. "Just the name for our neighborhood. We don't have a reservation. Never have, probably never will. Especially not here, on our homeland. Texas wanted to drive us out, destroy us."

"That can't be right," said Mrs. Park. "Your people signed them friendship treaties in the 1800s . . ."

There wasn't enough time in the road trip to delve into that complicated swath of history, so Shane just snorted and said,

"Ask Ma about it when she's back. I'm not an expert."

"You were telling us about Sammy," Donnie redirected, much to Shane's gratitude.

"Uh huh. That next afternoon, we were all so cheery and amped-up on sugar, I bet Mrs. Singer could hear us playing all the way up the hill."

"So she was cool?" Donnie asked. "You had me worried. I thought Mrs. Singer was going to scream at Sammy for giving away his snacks or something."

"Or something," Marcos muttered. He'd been nibbling on the coconut candy and listening intently, his lips bent into a scowl. He knew how the story ended; had been born and raised in its epilogue.

"For the longest time," Shane said, "my neighborhood and the family on the hill had ignored each other. The Singers owned all the farmland and ranches to the north, but we were beyond their domain. Sammy's friendship created an alliance. The Singers brought cookies and cas-serole to our community potlucks, and Sammy got invites to all our birthday par-ties. He always brought presents wrapped in colorful store-bought paper, which was almost like a second gift. I'd fold the wrapping paper into airplanes and play with them in the yard. One time, Sammy even invited me to a baseball game in the city. Our team versus the Houston Cryptids. We sat way up in the stadium with hot dogs, soda, and Cracker Jacks, and as I looked down on the green field, I thought, 'This must be what it feels like to live on a hill.' At that height, I couldn't see any details in the baseball players' faces, but I could follow the whole game as it played out below me."

"How did it all go wrong?" Donnie asked, her voice intimately close, and Shane realized that Donnie's forehead was resting against the back of her seat.

"After the flood," Shane said, "everything changed."

At the wheel, Mrs. Park hummed in agreement, as if unsurprised.

"What happened?" Donnie wondered.

And since the sun had set somewhere over Oklahoma, and there were no pretty songs on the radio, Shane told them the only story she couldn't forget.

~ ELEVEN ~

"Hurricane Alda reached us early morning, 'fore the dawn. Inside the house, 'cause all the windows got boarded, I knew her by sound. Imagine the screaming wind, the rain hitting our walls, blown sideways, and all of us huddled in the living room. Me, Grandma Yolanda, Grandpa Hugo, Ma, Pa, and Nellie. Old Nellie kept pacing around the coffee table, like he was restless. I had to concentrate to track his ghost body in the candlelight. And when everything went quiet, Grandpa Hugo ran outside to greet the sun, to pray like he prayed every morning. I tried to follow, but Ma held me back, saying, 'We're in the eye.' Which is the dead center of a hurricane, calm and bright, like an intermission. I was excited, the way kids get when there's danger, but they trust the adults to keep them safe. It's an innocence that goes away the first time life hurts you."

Both Donnie and Mrs. Park made sounds of agreement.

"It was only quiet for maybe thirty minutes, but that was all Grandpa Hugo needed. The sun doesn't want more than a quick greeting. It knows we all got work to do. So Grandpa Hugo said his prayer, checked his vegetable garden, and then ran back inside, with the shadow of a storm cloud at his heels. The wind blew the door shut behind him, smacking his rear end. 'Serves you right for playing chicken with a hurricane,' said my grandmother, but she wasn't actually mad, 'cause my grandpa was laughing, and his smiles spread like wildfire.

"When Hurricane Alda passed, we sat down for dinner. It was leftover hominy stew and tortillas made by Grandma Yolanda. She'd grind the corn into flour by hand with a mortar and pestle — is that what they're called? Think it is. Either that, or 'metate' and 'mano.' Anyway, it was made of black volcanic rock. Pretty sure the set was from generations back, 'cause the bowl was worn smooth, with corn particles embedded in its pores, turning it gray. Though it's also possible that my grandma wore the rock down herself, since she used the mortar and pestle twice a week, for long as I can remember." Suddenly, Shane mused, "How many weeks are in a person's life, assuming it's full, like hers?" It was an unimportant question in the context of her story, but she had to know the answer. Pausing, Shane tried to do the mental math. Grandma Yolanda had been sixty years old, rounding down, and there were fifty-two weeks in a year. So fifty-two times sixty was . . .

Six times two was twelve. Carry the one. Five times six was thirty. Thirty plus one was thirty-one. Stick a two at the end. Three hundred twelve. Next, add a zero.

The answer was 3,120 weeks? It seemed far too low. Was that really all the time they had? A few thousand weeks?

And how many weeks had it been since that supper? Shane, her parents, and her grandparents sitting around a table, with an electric lantern in the center since the power had gone out. When she thought about family, she remembered that table — that meal together, their faces in the light, their voices in conversation — and the moment seemed impossibly far away.

"The rain continued all night long," Shane continued, "pattering on the shingles, and when Grandpa Hugo said his prayer the next morning, the sun hid behind gray clouds. I remember Grandpa Hugo returned with mud on his shoes and water dripping off his jacket, puddling on the floor. Ma went visiting the neighbor's house; their power was running fine, and they had a television. Thirty minutes later, she was back with news. Ma said, 'Weatherman reports it'll keep raining. There's already floods. The storm surge wrecked the coast, but the rain will cause issues here.' Although Alda broke apart over North Texas, her long cape of storms would loiter 'round Northern Mexico and South Texas for a couple days; that's what the weatherman said.

"Well, at that, Pa grabbed his key ring and Cryptids cap, which hung from a pegboard in the kitchen. Didn't matter how dark it was outside, my pa never left home without a cap. Maybe he picked up the habit from Grandma Yolanda, who always — and I mean *always* — wore a wildflower behind her ear. Funny enough, Pa didn't care about sports. I mean, he'd watch games with friends, baseball and football, even basketball sometimes, but if you asked about his favorite team, he'd usually say, 'the underdogs.'

"Now, the Houston Cryptids aren't underdogs. So I once questioned him, 'Why do you wear Cryptid caps, if they win all the time?' Well, he told me, 'Red's my favorite color, Sheiné łénde.' That's all. Now and again, a genuine Cryptid fan would walk up to Pa and say, 'Did you see the game last night?' or 'What do you think about the player so-and-so?' and Pa would blush, same way he responded when a random person asked him to read. But he always thought of a good answer. 'No, I missed the game, unfortunately; had to work late.' Or, 'I'm not sure what to think; how about you?' He'd never lie, but they'd never catch on, either."

"Brilliant," Donnie chuckled.

"Sure was."

"Where was he going?"

"Ma asked the same thing. She put a hand on his shoulder and went, 'Where're you off to in this storm?' My pa said, 'If there's a flood risk, I should check on my cousins down the road.' We lived near a community of immigrants from Mexico; a couple of the men from the colonia worked with Pa and were his friends. So, not blood cousins, but still cousins."

"I don't understand, sweetheart," Mrs. Park said. "Were they cousins by marriage?"

"Grandma, I think she means cousins in a different sense," Donnie explained. "Like a friend so close, you consider him family. Am I right, Shane?"

"Yeah, spot on."

"Why was your dad so worried? Did his friends live in a floodplain?"

"We all did, basically. There were levees to stop flooding on the north side of town, but not the south. 'Fore Pa left, Ma told him, 'If you aren't back in an hour, I'll send Nellie to drag you home.' And he exclaimed, 'As if he'd leave your side!' They were joking around, but I could tell my ma was nervous, 'cause she waited near the door. Luckily, Pa came home in fifty minutes

262

flat. He hung up his cap and keys and then said, 'It's good. Everyone's A-OK.' I took that as a sign that the hurricane was old news. There'd been others, you know. Storms spinning up the gulf. They aren't uncommon. So I thought that meant the levees and whatnot were sufficient, and the weatherman was giving us the worst-case scenario just in case. My ma always said, 'Don't expect the worst, but plan for it.'

"In fact, all afternoon, I sat on my bed, played with dolls, and looked outside through a crack in the boards on my window. I was itching to go swinging again. In a couple days, the rain would stop, and the sky would clear, and we'd survived the worst part, and . . ."

In her mind, Shane could remember the sound vividly, a high-pitched: *thnk. thnk. thnk.* Knuckles slamming — not politely rapping — against wood.

"And I was wrong. There was a loud knock on the front door. From my bedroom on the other side of the house, I heard a man shout, 'The flood is coming!' Not five seconds later, Ma ran into my room, took me by the hand, and pulled me away from the window.

263

"I asked, 'Why are we running?' She said, 'To escape the water.' I got so confused; wasn't Pa just smiling because we'd be fine? So I grabbed my favorite toy, a rabbit Ma made. Nothing else. Didn't plan on being gone long. It was weird to see the frantic state of my grandparents, who were running back and forth, chucking stuff into pillow sacks. Silverware, Pa's radio, photo albums, books. Grandma swept her arm down the fridge, gathering all my terrible crayon doodles into her bag. From the driveway, Pa hollered, 'We have to go now!' and I remember Grandma's sad little cry in response. Just a wordless sound of dismay, you know? We'd run out of time. There was a large, woven basket at the door, and on the way out, she dropped her pillowcase inside, put the basket on her back, and made sure the door shut behind us."

"Are you OK, Shane?" Donnie asked, and Shane felt a prickle of frustration. Why ask that question? She wasn't sobbing, was she? Her voice hadn't cracked. And if Shane wasn't OK — if she said in reply, 'No, my heart's broken 'cause my grandmother suffered 'fore she died, and so did my grandfather, and so did my Pa; they were beautiful people with full and brilliant lives; they deserved better; they deserved so much better; there will never be justice' — what could Donnie do to help? The past was absolute. Not even the strongest fae-realm magic could alter history.

"Yes," Shane gently replied, burying her unfair resentment. Donnie was just concerned. "I'm OK."

"Who was the man knocking on your door?" Mrs. Park wondered.

"Ah, right. A stranger. Figured he was a fireman from town, 'cause he had big muscles and a booming voice. I was wrong, though. Later, after everything, we learned his story. He was a janitor from the airport, a single fella with no family in the country. He'd volunteered to spend Hurricane Alda in the airport with an old security guard, help keep an eye on things. That afternoon, their manager called with an urgent message. The Woodrow Dam was gonna overflow. Local casters had raised wards to keep the water back, but the rain wasn't letting up, and their magic couldn't resist nature forever. If somebody didn't redirect the excess water, the dam would spill into the city and wreck all its central buildings, the restaurants, banks, and department stores.

"So a team of government guys decided to divert the floodwater, send it south. Unfortunately, the airport was in the water's path. The manager told the janitor and security guard to flee north 'fore the flood blocked their escape route. But the janitor said, 'Hold on.' He knew people lived south of the airport.

"He told his friend, 'I have to warn them.'

"And what do you know? The security guard agreed. Good men, both of them. Wish I knew their names. They split up, each targeting a different neighborhood, trying to clear everyone 'fore the flood arrived. Sometimes, when you're being brave, it helps to focus on the best-case scenario, even if it's unlikely. That's what I do, and maybe they did, too.

"As my family drove away from our house, I could still hear our hero's voice on the wind. 'Hurry, hurry, there isn't much time.' In fact, there was no time. We were the last of la rancheria de los Lipanes to escape by car. Although I didn't see it, water erased the road behind us, so the janitor and the stragglers fled up the hill. Lots of the trapped people were old-timers, like our healer, who needed a cane to walk. She got carried in the arms of her grandchildren: twin boys, age sixteen. They said it was the hardest climb of their lives, 'cause the rain and wind kicked up, and they'd tied all their schoolbooks and clothes to their backs, everything wrapped in bedsheets and fastened by rope."

After carrying Malorie to safety, Shane finally understood their struggle.

"The Singers had evacuated to California, locked everything down, so somebody broke a window to get inside the house and use it as shelter. Don't know who. None of the witnesses will tell. It was a matter of survival, but the courts might not care. Anyway, everybody ran into the house. Sun above, I can't imagine the view. From the hill, they could probably see the water go over their cars and make their houses into rooftop islands.

"I thought we got lucky, by escaping. Pa in the driver's seat, Ma beside him, me between my grandparents in the back.

267

Grandma hugged the basket in her lap, while I held my rabbit. The view outside was strange, so I asked, 'Where are we going?'

"My parents swapped a look, like they weren't sure how to answer. Pa spoke first, asking Ma, 'Did you reach him?' And Ma cursed in a language I didn't understand. Well, I'm ninety percent sure it was a curse, 'cause of the bitter tone. 'No,' she said. 'None of his old numbers work. I wouldn't be surprised if he's locked up.' That clued me in; they were talking about Grandpa Louis. So I had to know, 'Why do you think he's in jail, Ma?'

"She turned in her seat, looked me square in the eyes, and said, 'Because I've had to bail him out.'

"I asked, 'When? Why'd they put him there?' I'd never heard that story 'fore.

"She just shook her head, adding, 'He's bad at walking away from a fight, especially after a drink. Then again, he's also bad at answering the phone. For all I know, my father could be on a beach in California, with the Singers, having the time of his life. Shé pa.'

"The way she spat out that last word sounded like a curse, too, but I knew it meant 'My father.' Things used to be rough between them. Still are, kinda, but they're getting better. Grandpa Louis hasn't missed a phone call in five years.

"But the past was the past, and there was nobody to house us: our other close friends and family all lived in the path of the flood. So we drove to a school-turned-shelter. Us and what seemed like a hundred other people were given cots in the gymnasium; mine was tucked against a wall. I remember that a student had carved her name into the paneling near the ground. *Lucy.* At night, I'd lie on my side, trying to sleep — it wasn't easy, with babies crying and people snoring, whispering, coughing all night long — and instead of counting sheep, I'd read Lucy's name, wondering who she'd been and where she'd gone. One night, I had a nightmare that Lucy was drowning, her hand sticking out of muddy water, and when I woke up, I was reaching for her. Sticking my hand into the air, grasping nothing. I mostly believed that dreams were make-believe, but I'd also heard about psychics who dreamed about different lives when they slept. Made me afraid that Lucy had drowned, and in her dying moment, she'd cried out for help, but I couldn't save her.

"There was one television in the gym, and it played the local news all day long, mostly showing video of the flood. Since people were still trapped in their houses, Pa and his friends took rowboats to drowned neighborhoods, while Ma spent the days in long, slow-moving lines. There were lines for donated clothing, lines for food and water, lines to use the phone, and lines for medicine; Grandma Yolanda and Grandpa Hugo had left their pills at home, so Ma had to stand in that medicine line twice a day. Mostly, Grandma didn't move from her cot, just sat next to her basket and watched kids like me play hopscotch and make-believe. Sometimes, Grandpa sat with her, and other times, he made the rounds in the gym, chatting with old friends and making new ones. He'd return with gossip for Grandma and me. A real-life soap opera, so she didn't miss her telenovelas."

Until that moment, Shane had been dry-eyed, recounting the story with a casual drawl, but as she thought about Grandpa Hugo's goofy gym gossip, it became difficult to see through the film of tears. Those weren't even the worst days; actually, they'd been pleasant, like camping indoors.

She took a slow drink of orange soda, trying to collect herself, hearing Grandpa Hugo's voice in her mind: "Do you see that fella in a red shirt, Yolanda? He's moving up in the world. Been marching around proud-chested, bragging that the men in charge are transferring his cot to a private classroom. Poor fella. If he knew why they're giving him special treatment, he might stop acting like a king."

"Do tell." Grandma Yolanda's eyes had sparkled wickedly.

"He's the one who been snoring like a buzzsaw every night."

"Him?" She'd gasped. "The man across the gym? A hundred feet away?"

"Yup. World record snoring. Maybe he *should* be proud."

Shane took another sip, and by the time the fizzle of carbonation was gone, she'd reigned in her tears.

"Six days later, Hidalgo County — that's where we lived — opened. The waters had receded.

"The drive to la rancheria de los Lipanes took longer than the drive away from home, 'cause Pa had to navigate an obstacle course of hazards. Fallen trees and standing water. The view outside seemed unreal, like something from a disaster flick, not my life. I knew how bad things were. I'd been watching the news for days, and every time Pa returned from a boat rescue, he'd tell me about the people they'd saved."

Shane remembered one such night. He'd returned to the gym late, slinking to their encampment of cots with his arms full of sopping wet clothes: his pants, socks, shirt, and jacket, dripping muddy floodwater. He was wearing a pair of shorts and a sleeveless white undershirt. They were wet, too.

"And what happened to you?" Lorenza had gasped. "Did a boat flip?"

"Do I have a story for you girls," her pa promised, and in one swoop, he'd kissed Lorenza's cheek, ruffled Shane's loose hair, and reached for his mother, who'd leaned away, exclaiming, "Oh, no! Hug me later! First, shower and change! Go, go!"

A woman nearby had hissed, "Shhush!" and Shane's father had ducked his head sheepishly, whispering, "OK, OK." A droplet of filthy floodwater plopped from the brim of his cap onto the wood floor.

When Shane's father returned, Lorenza had supper waiting; she'd set aside a plate of beans, rice, and chicken, and although they'd cooled, Shane's father scarfed down every grain of rice and pinto bean, and ate the meat to its bone. "Did you forget something?" Grandma Yolanda had asked, crossing her arms with mock indignation.

"Mama, forgive me. Your hug!" And Pa had leaned over to squeeze her tightly. Then, he passed her a slightly wilted dandelion, which she eagerly tucked behind her ear.

"What happened?" Lorenza had wondered.

"You may not believe it, my loves," he'd explained, keeping his voice soft. "Gather close." Everyone did, except for Grandpa Hugo, who'd fallen asleep earlier that evening, exhausted by a day of intense chatting.

"Me and the men went up San Jan Street, which is flooded worse than any place I've been. It was Carlos and Felix in canoes, me in the tin rowboat. There were people stuck on rooftops, 'cause they couldn't swim. Shane, my heart, when was the last time I took you swimming?"

She'd shrugged. There weren't convenient pools or lakes near home; the Gulf was too far to visit; the river too quick. She'd gone fishing with her pa, but they always stayed on shore or in his boat with life vests.

"First thing, you need to learn," he'd said. "Become an expert, like a fish. Those poor people. Hungry, thirsty, stuck in the sun. We were ferrying people all day. Down the street, where the water got deepest, I found four generations of the same family on a roof, I shit you not."

"He *kids* you not," Lorenza had softly corrected, smiling.

"That too."

"A set of great grandparents, their daughter, her daughter and son-in-law, and a baby. They'd built a shelter — a lean-to made of a tin sheet and somebody else's laundry. The son-in-law had fished a clothesline from the water, and there were a couple of bedsheets and dresses still attached. Must've been industrial-strength clothesline clips. We need that brand for windy days."

"For sure," Lorenza had agreed.

"None of the family could swim, except for the great-grandparents, who were too weak, anyhow. Carlos climbed up there with a rope, and all the boats gathered 'round, our little fleet."

"What's a fleet?" Shane had asked.

"A group of boats," he'd said.

"So like a flock of boats?"

"More a pod."

"Beans in a pod?"

"No, pod of whales."

"Huh?"

"That's how you say it. Flock of birds. Pod of whales. Fleet of canoes and tin boats."

"Makes sense."

With that resolved, he'd continued the story. "There was a six-foot drop between the edge of the roof and the water, so we had to get everyone in life vests and lower them with harnesses of rope. Oldest generation went first; they sat in my boat, since it was the steadiest and biggest. Then the second-oldest generation. She was lowered straight onto Carlos's canoe. Next came the momma and baby. She carried the little guy in her arms, since we didn't bring doll-sized life vests for a newborn. Well. All was going fine, until she got her feet into Felix's boat. Must've landed funny, 'cause the canoe started rocking, and that made her panic and scream; the babe sensed his mother's fear, I guess, and started wailing. Felix tried to put his weight against the tilt —" Shane's father swayed to the right, and everyone leaned forward expectantly. Shane, Lorenza, Grandma Yolanda, and even Grandpa Hugo, who'd awoken during the story and listened with his head propped on one hand.

"I shouted, 'Pull her up,' and thank goodness she was still connected to the harness. In the nick of time, her husband

heaved on the rope and held her sus-
pended 'fore the canoe capsized. I paddled close, took the baby, passed him to
his great-grandmother, who just had to
coo a few times to stop his crying. The
baby's parents asked me to row to safety,
quickly. 'Don't wait,' they said. So that's
what I did. Took about thirty minutes
to reach land. I made sure everybody
was safe 'fore turning around. As I
approached the deepest stretch, I saw
Carlos and Felix in their canoes with the
rest of the stranded family, and they were
frantic, paddling like they'd entered an
Olympic race. As they zipped past me,
they all shouted, 'Turn around, and go,
go, go!'

"I wanted to know, 'What's the rush?'
and Carlos hollered over his shoulder,
'There's something in the water!'" Shane's
father spread his hands as wide as they'd
go. "'Something big, with teeth.'"

"An alligator?" Shane had gasped.

"Could have been. Could have been
a monster, too. Like the river monster
handled by your great-great-great-great-
grandmother . . ." He'd paused. "That's
a mouthful, isn't it? What if I start calling

her Four-Great? What do you think, Lorenza? Is it respectful to abbreviate?"

"I'm sure she'd appreciate the efficiency."

"I guess I could call her 'heroic ancestor,' but your family line's got so many of them. Like your mother."

At the reminder, there'd been sadness in Lorenza's eyes, but there'd been pride and warmth, too. Grandma Bee had lived a full life, and her passing had been gentle. That's why they spoke her name.

"So does yours," she'd countered.

"Oh yeah?"

"Such as the man who rescued four generations from their rooftop."

"That guy? He's no hero, be serious." But her pa had grinned, and Lorenza had smiled back, and when they continued smiling fondly, Shane couldn't stand the wait. She'd asked, "Papa, what was it?"

"Ah, the creature in the water. We had no clue, which might've been the scariest part. The canoes shot past me, and I struggled to turn. That's the trouble with my tin boat. It's stable but slow."

"They left you?" Shane gasped, horrified. They were his friends!

278

"Honestly, I don't blame them. They had other people to protect! Plus, I'm powerful. Imagine me paddling like this." He swung his hands back and forth in fast, frantic arcs. "I kept glancing over my shoulder, looking for movement, but the water was dark, and it was getting late, the sun sinking. Couldn't see a thing. But then . . . well, my boat scraped something. Or more appropriately, something scraped my boat. It started taking on water. Fast. There was a slash down its belly. The thing tore it open like a knife through tin foil. What could do that to solid, thick metal? I didn't care to find out. Instead of going down with the ship, I dove as far and fast as possible. Then, I swam toward Carlos, who'd returned for me, brave man. He grabbed me by the arms, chucked me on board, and we rowed double-time. On the way, I made the mistake of looking back — never do that, when you're racing to survive. You know what I saw?"

"What?" an unfamiliar voice had asked. It was the woman who'd shushed him earlier.

"Miss," Shane's father replied, "my boat was flipped over, like a turtle shell half-poking from the water, and was following us. Something must've been under it, swimming closer. Me and Carlos screamed, I'm not afraid to admit. Never in my life have I rowed so fast. Luckily, when we got near land, my boat stopped. Then, inch by inch, it sank into the murk."

He'd concluded: "All kind of trouble washed up in the flood. Shane, you promise me something."

"Uh huh. What?"

"First? Learn how to swim, and learn well. Doggy paddling doesn't cut it. You got to get powerful and fast. I'll drive you to the lake in Mercy."

"OK, Pa. I promise."

"And when you're strong enough, we'll visit Galveston again and swim against the waves, OK? There might be dolphins."

"Really?"

"That's my promise." He'd gathered her into a tight hug. "You'll never sink, my love."

And she hadn't. Not yet, anyway.

"He saved many people," Shane told Donnie, Mrs. Park, and Marcos. "More than I knew. More than he knew, probably."

Spontaneously, the radio crackled and then bubbled out a jumble of music and static. Mrs. Park slapped her hand against the dash, trying to find the dial without peeling her eyes away from the road.

"I got it," Shane said, clicking the sound off.

"How in the world did that happen?" Mrs. Park muttered. "Did the ghost dog fiddle with my dial?"

Before Shane could respond, "I doubt it," the radio switched on again. As Shane watched in disbelief, the red station indicator moved from the left to right until it abruptly stopped on 97.3 FM. A male announcer with a southern drawl reported, "— seven instances of unsanctioned ring travel. Authorities advise people in Texas and the southwestern United States to exercise caution outdoors."

"Unsanctioned ring travel," Shane repeated. "Wait! Is this about us? I think so!" The word "unsanctioned" was an odd choice, making it seem as if Lorenza, Bobby, and the other five "instances" had used an underground, off-the-books ring transport center instead of accidentally stepping into wild-growing mimic rings. But at least the story was getting news coverage. Public attention could be game-changing in the search for missing people.

A second host with a high, sweet voice commented, "As a mother, I'm very concerned, Boris. How serious is the risk?"

"Fortunately, because of the rapid emergency response, all known hotspots of mimic growth have been neutralized. Before your boys play outside, teach them to recognize the warning signs. Don't play inside mushroom rings."

"Hey," Donnie shouted at Boris from the radio, "Easier said than done, smart guy! I didn't even see the rings!"

"And what is the news on little Bobby Park?" the female host asked.

"Shh, shh!" Mrs. Park shushed. "Listen, everyone."

"He is still missing," Boris informed the public, his voice deepening with concern. "According to his grandfather, ten-year-old Bobby Park was last seen in Less Crossing, Texas, wearing red shorts and a white T-shirt. Bobby is four feet and five inches tall. He has short black hair and brown eyes. In addition, a forty-year-old woman, Lorenza Solé, is also missing. If you have information about either person, call —"

As he rattled off the tip line phone number, Shane wondered if Boris knew that Lorenza had vanished in blue jeans and a cotton blouse, and that her hair was so long, it touched her mid-back, and that it was so dark, it resembled the space between stars . . .

"— and for information on the ongoing investigation and up-to-date safety recommendations, continue listening to KDLB Austin 97.3, your source for extraordinary news and music."

Suddenly, the volume dial spun to the maximum volume. Boris the radio host boomed: "Representatives from the fae realm are cooperating with ongoing search and rescue efforts —"

Click.

The radio fell silent.

"They're looking for Mom, too!" Marcos exclaimed.

"Did they say faerie realm?" Donnie asked. "Those guys have big magic!"

"Oh, that's wonderful," sighed Mrs. Park. "Thank goodness."

"Big magic," Shane muttered. "Does anyone else think it's strange that the car just played a news report about our family? A news report from Austin?"

At that moment, Shane noticed a flash of color out the window: two people in slick yellow suits stood along the road, their thumbs out; they each carried a briefcase and wore tiny round sunglasses with vivid green glass.

"Hitchhikers," she said, because Mrs. Park didn't seem to notice, her eyes locked too tightly on the gray road.

"Somebody else can help them. We have quite enough trouble already," she replied.

"I, um, OK . . ." As they zoomed past the people in yellow suits, Shane twisted to see their faces. One was a tall woman, taller than Shane; she had a small, sharp nose, downturned lips, and white hair in a French braid. The other was a short man, five feet and change in height, with slicked-back black hair. When he smiled at the passing car, his teeth were vividly white, and he raised his hand in greeting. The woman simply stared.

"Mrs. Park," said Shane, "I don't think they're your standard hitchhikers."

As if confirming Shane's suspicions, the radio crackled alive again and boomed, "Representatives from the faerie realm —"

Click.

Silence.

In front of them, on the distant horizon, two points of bright yellow appeared between the highway and a cornfield.

"Yeah . . . they're most definitely some representatives from the faerie realm," Donnie said. "Grandma, pull over."

"You really think so? Oh! OK, dear. OK." The older woman's voice was taut with anxiety. Her eyes flickered to the rearview mirror before she slapped a hand against the turn signal.

Nellie whuffed softly, a whisper-like bark, as they slowed and pulled onto the shoulder. Mrs. Park stopped about ten feet away from the hitchhikers; with a grin, the man from before waved and jogged close, while the woman strode after him, her arms swinging languidly. Shane cranked her window down all the way.

"Good evening, hello," said the man in a yellow suit, no tie. He folded his arms on the windowsill and bent to peer inside the car. Up close, he looked no different from a human; at least, Shane couldn't pinpoint any otherworldly features. She'd heard that people from the fae realm were unusually symmetrical, the right side of their face an exact mirror image of the left side. However, she didn't get that sense from the man. Up close, she could faintly see his eyes through the circles of clear green glass. They were crinkled at each end, mirthful and friendly. "As you've surmised, we're the representatives in question."

"Whoa, no way," Donnie said.

"Yes way, Miss."

"I'm Lorenza's daughter," Shane introduced herself. Did the representatives have information for them? Perhaps good news? "Do you know where our family's gone? Bobby and my mom?"

"Not yet," said the woman, who elbowed her partner aside to steal his place in the window. "But we need information from you." She pointed down the highway. "Take the next turnoff. Six miles down

286

the road. It leads to a rest area. We can speak more there."

"OK," agreed Mrs. Park.

"Now, hold on!" The man nudged his partner, and she begrudgingly gave him space at the window. "Is that a dog? What's the matter with him?"

"You can see him?" asked Shane, turning to look at the back seat, where Nellie shimmered next to Marcos. "He's a ghost."

"A ghost!" The man tugged on his partner's tailored sleeve. "Look, Orlanda. Have you ever seen a ghost before?"

"Of course I have, Reggie," she replied. "However, this one is brighter than the others."

"He's bright to you?" Shane wondered.

"Like sunlight on a beetle's wing," Orlanda clarified.

"Earth and its ghosts," laughed Reggie. "What a marvel."

In unison, the representatives both stepped back.

"We'll speak again in seventeen minutes," Reggie promised, waving as the car rumbled back onto the highway. Shane blinked, and they were gone.

Exactly seventeen minutes later, Mrs. Park pulled in front of two log cabins surrounded by picnic tables and metal grills. A rustic wooden sign read: *Safety Rest Area–Modern Amenities.* Two tall metal lamps flanked either end of the building and cast flickering semicircles of light over the edge of the parking lot. The facilities were empty, with one exception: Reggie and Orlanda sat across from each other at a six-person table; between them, in the exact center of the leaf-dusted table, was a root beer float with two red straws.

"Oh, I'm so nervous," Mrs. Park said while turning off the ignition. "They're real fair folk. How good of them to help us. I hope I don't commit a faux pas."

"They're just people like us," Shane reassured her, while looking at the pair through the front window. Together, the representatives leaned forward, took a long sip from their drink, leaned back, and then turned their heads to return Shane's stare. Reggie waved with an encouraging grin.

"Let's do this," Donnie said. She was the first out of the car, followed by Marcos and Nellie. Shane was fourth; she circled to the driver-side door and helped Mrs. Park step outside, placing a steadying arm under the older woman's elbow.

"I'm glad you found this place," said Reggie, as everybody took their seats. Mrs. Park and Donnie sandwiched in on the middle of the bench; Shane was between Marcos and Orlanda, who smelled of roses. Was it perfume? Or did the fae naturally smell of flowers, like the poets claimed?

"Oh, Orlanda, look at the ghost dog now," Reggie said. Nellie was standing near an oak tree, probably smelling the other dogs who'd marked it earlier that day.

"Nellie, c'mere, boy!" Shane called. Immediately, the bloodhound scurried back and flopped underneath the table, against her feet.

"On the radio," Shane said, "in the report you sent to us . . ." She paused, waiting for confirmation that they'd been the ones to control the radio. When Reggie nodded, she continued: "The host said there were five other people who got transported by a mimic. I had no idea. Who else? Were they all near Less Crossing?"

"Ah, yes and no. There were others, yes. But they were not in Less Crossing, no. Luckily, we've located all five of the others."

"Not lucky for them, Reggie," Orlanda reminded him. "Their loved ones are still missing."

"How true, Orlanda. I misspoke."

"Who were they?" Donnie asked. "The other victims, I mean."

"Various people," Reggie said, almost dismissively. "Ah! You may be amused by this story. One man was walking to work. He stepped in a ring and appeared outside his job site. Twenty minutes early!"

"Reggie, please concentrate," Orlanda scolded.

"Yes, of course." He clasped his hands contritely. "It's not my intention to be flippant."

"Rather," said Orlanda, "it is his nature."

"Can you help us?" asked Mrs. Park, her voice taut with anxiety.

"With magic!" Marcos added, and Donnie nodded adamantly in agreement.

"Well, that's the thing," Reggie said, his smile drooping.

"The vexing thing," scowled Orlanda.

"When our organization learned about the incident —"

"Mismanagement of ring material through negligence."

"The Queen Herself took interest. She sent Merlin the Third to Earth —"

"Oh, she *did*?" gasped Mrs. Park.

"Which queen?" asked Shane. According to her grade school knowledge on fae politics, they occupied four continents on an inverted globe, and each land was governed by monarchies — not unlike the systems of Earth.

"Our Fierce Queen Titania," Reggie answered. "And of course she recruited her finest magician to help. By that time, there were only three people still missing: a woman, your brother, and your mother. Merlin's visit was not publicized, as he despises paparazzi. However, through his scrying, he located the first woman. She'd been transported from Austin to her childhood home of Mumbai, and was confused but unharmed."

Somewhere, an owl cooed, and Shane shivered in the chilling air.

"Unfortunately, your family remain undetectable," Orlanda said.

As a murmur of dismay passed among the humans, the representatives took another synchronized drink of their root beer float.

"What does that mean?" whimpered Mrs. Park.

The representatives exchanged a serious glance. Then, Reggie spoke: "There are a number of explanations. They could be concealed by extremely powerful magic. In another dimension. On a different planet." He counted the options on his long, thin fingers; his white nails were filed into points. "Deceased."

"No!" cried Mrs. Park.

Half standing, Donnie cried, "My brother isn't dead!"

"I know for a fact that Ma is alive," Shane added, calmly but firmly, for Marcos's sake. "So what's your next step? Our next step?"

"We've considered growing a mimic ring ourselves," Reggie said, "but that option is currently too dangerous. Firstly, the mimic's behavior on Earth is completely novel; our scientists have very little insight. And logic suggests that your family members are both in the same place. Neither has returned. Neither can be located. Until we know where they are, we cannot endanger our agents by sending them through a ring. Understand?"

"What can you do?" asked Shane, her patience straining. Had the representatives flagged them down just to shrug in bafflement and admit defeat?

"Our organization is investigating other avenues," said Orlanda, secretively. "However, your husband" — she looked at Mrs. Park — "informed us that you are conducting an independent search?"

"Y . . . yes?" Mrs. Park hunched her shoulders, shrinking under Orlanda's scrutiny. "Is that OK?"

"Of course, Madam!" Reggie reassured her. "In fact, it's perfect."

"You know your family best," Orlanda agreed, and two bright white business cards appeared in her fingers. Shane couldn't determine whether she'd pulled them from her sleeve or from the air itself. "Given the enigmatic nature of mimic rings, and their connection to the psyche, your personal relationships with Lorenza and Bobby are invaluable. If you find a lead, or have any concerns, please call us." She passed one card to Mrs. Park, the other to Shane. In bright green ink was a thirty-digit number.

"This will work on Earth phones?" Shane asked, baffled.

"It will." Orlanda and Reggie both swooped down to take one final, long sip from their drink; after a couple seconds, their straws gurgled as they drained all the root beer and melting vanilla ice cream. Then, they stood and brushed off their yellow suits.

"Wait," Donnie said.

The representatives stopped, turned toward her, and waited: Reggie with an affable smile, Orlanda with an eyebrow raised.

"What if Bobby is in the afterlife?" Hastily, the girl added: "Not dead. I mean. Still alive, but trapped in the land of the dead, with Lorenza. Because of the ring."

Mrs. Park shook her head slowly, as if she couldn't accept that possibility.

"Ah," Orlanda replied. "That would be unfortunate."

"Indeed," agreed Reggie. He reached over to grab the empty cup. "You'd be on your own."

"We have no business there," Orlanda explained. "Among the gleaming ghosts."

"And now," said Reggie, glancing at his golden wristwatch, "our business here is done. Good luck, my new friends." The representatives started walking toward the rest stop facilities.

"You really will help us, right?" Mrs. Park reiterated, her hands clasped worriedly. "Really?"

"To the best of our abilities!" Reggie called over his shoulder, waving; this time, the gesture was quick and dismissive. In front of him, Orlanda held open the swinging door of the modern rest stop facilities. As she waited for her partner to walk inside, she glanced back at the confused-looking group of humans and nodded once, quickly, before following Reggie.

"Hey, wait!" Shane said, rising. "How much would a phone call to y'all cost?" She was running dangerously low on change; if the special thirty-digit number was classified as "long-distance," Shane might not have enough funds to contact the representatives. Hoping to get an answer from Orlanda and Reggie before they dissipated into the ether, she ran after the pair, Nellie trotting at her heels.

Inside the building, Shane found a small lobby with colorful roadmaps on the walls.

The representatives were gone.

❦ TWELVE ❦

"Those guys were strange, right?" Donnie asked. "Or is it just me?" They'd all piled into the car again to resume the drive; this time, Shane sat in the back with Marcos, who rested his head on her lap, his eyes drifting closed as the car's hypnotic motion soothed him to sleep.

"I don't know," Shane admitted. "I've never met fae representatives before. They might be acting according to protocol."

"Merlin the Third looked for Bobby," Mrs. Park exclaimed. "How could he fail?"

"They're magical, not all-powerful," Donnie figured. "Maybe the second attempt will save us, though. Merlin the Third is probably inventing a spell right now. Like a magical fishing pole." She flicked her hand, as if casting a line. "Angling through spacetime. Hook Bobby by the collar and reel him home. Wait, was that genius? Could it actually work?"

"Call them tonight!" Mrs. Park urged. "Tell the fair folk about your idea."

As Mrs. Park and Donnie brainstormed more potential spells, Shane tried to share their optimism. It was a relief that other people — magical people, no less — were looking for Lorenza and Bobby. However, she couldn't help but worry. Orlanda and Reggie must have hit a wall in their investigation; why else would they ask for clues from a bunch of civilian humans?

"Everything will be alright," Mrs. Park sighed; was she reassuring them or herself? "At this point, I'm half-tempted to drive home. We can tell the fae about Dr. Richards, and let them ask the questions."

"We forgot to mention him," Donnie muttered. "Probably should've."

Shane sat up straight, jostling Marcos awake; he squinted at her accusatorily, and then squeezed his eyes shut. After giving her brother a pat on the head, Shane said, "Mrs. Park, I'm not giving up the search. Us and the reps can work in harmony, but I wouldn't put all our eggs in their basket."

From the driver's seat, Mrs. Park softly wondered, "They'll help us, though. Right?"

Each time she posed that question, it sounded less confident. Shane wished that she could reassure her. Wished she could believe, like a child, that somebody else — the big, strong others — would make everything OK. Instead, Shane observed, "I never finished my story, did I? About the Singers."

"No," Donnie said, with a furrowed brow. "How does it end?"

"We returned home. In the house, I saw" — Shane raised her hand until it brushed the car roof — "a waterline nearly up to the ceiling. The place reeked like mildew and rot. An inch of filthy water covered the floor, so Pa carried me to my room, wouldn't let me get my feet wet. 'That's what fathers are for,' he said. I hadn't been carried since I was small, and thought it was great fun. Well. Until I saw my room. All my clothes and toys were soggy, and there was mold growing on my curtains. Killed the vibe. Pa ran back outside, me crying in his arms, and told Ma: 'We can't sleep here.'

"Like I said, Pa hadn't carried me like that since I was really little. I wish I'd . . ."

Shane should have cherished that moment, appreciated it, instead of weeping over her toys: things she didn't miss anymore, could barely even remember. When Pa put her down, she should have held his hand and never let go, but instead, she'd scurried around the house to check on her swing and the old oak tree.

"What?" asked a soft voice.

Marcos, listening; just pretending to sleep.

"Wish I hadn't wasted my tears," she said. "The houses could be fixed, and that's what everyone did, over the next few days. Kids like me weren't allowed to be indoors, so we stayed with the old folks in the shade; I'd fan Grandma Yolanda with a palm leaf and get her cups of cota and green tea while she relaxed under the oak tree. Grandma Yolanda had a bright-red beach chair, while I sat on a store-bought polyester sheet, which was thin and ugly compared to the wool blankets we'd lost in the flood, but it did the trick, kept me safe. 'Cause the ground was still prickly with debris, these sand-small pieces of metal and glass that were sharp as thorns on a prickly pear. My cousin cut his foot on a splinter of metal, just a little slash, but a couple days later his leg swelled and turned purple, smelling rotten. They had to remove it from the knee down. Said he was lucky to survive with just one amputation, can you believe that?"

"Is he OK now?" Donnie asked, and it occurred to Shane that she hadn't heard news about Cousin Joe in years. Last time he'd called, to wish her a happy fifteenth birthday, he'd been living in Los Angeles, working at a department store and dating a waitress.

"He's doing great," she said, making a mental note to confirm that answer.

"So you were able to repair everything?" Mrs. Park said.

"We did our best, but the house wasn't safe for a while. When the mosquitoes and biting flies moved in, I turned the palm leaf into a weapon, swatting the air around Grandma's head, but the swarm only parted 'round it like a second flood.

"Well, my grandma eventually said, 'Sheiné łénde, you aren't a cow's tail. Find a mosquito coil and burn it between us.' So I—"

"Wait, what did she call you?" Donnie interrupted. "You said it earlier, too. Is that your real name?"

"I . . . yes. Uh. Shane is an abbreviation of Sheh-ee-neh lehneh." The name had come so naturally during the story, but now, when Shane tried to repeat her own name, it felt awkward, especially the "L," which was supposed to roll off the tongue like the "L" in "well," not the "L" in "long." And she was overthinking things, blushing at her ignorance. How could she fail at saying her own —

"It's beautiful," Donnie replied, her voice fierce with earnestness.

Since she couldn't see Donnie's face, Shane smiled at the darkness beyond her window. "Thank you."

"Did the coils work?"

"Sure did," she nodded. "And the next day, we hung insect nets off the oak tree's branches. It was like camping in a clear tent. Way better than camping in a gymnasium.

"At night, my family slept in the truck, with all the windows open to keep cool; we taped nets over them, too. I still got a few bites, but that's the nature of tiny critters. They find ways to slip through your defenses."

Shane looked away from the dark outside her window and stared at nothing in particular for a moment, remembering.

"But this story isn't about insects. I meant to explain about the Singers."

"Oh, yeah," Donnie said. "Those guys."

"A couple days after we got home, I noticed police cars around the Singer house. It was the first sign of life up there since before the flood. 'Is Sammy OK?' I asked Ma. 'He hasn't been down to play.'

"She explained that he was still in California with his mother, and that the police were checking the broken windows. My ma said, 'If anyone asks — even Sammy — explain that we were evacuated during the flood, so we didn't see anything.'

"I agreed. It was the truth, after all. But fortunately, the police didn't ask, and the glass got repaired fast. And everything was alright. For a while."

The eye of the storm.

"Then people started coughing blood," Shane continued. "First the family across the street. Then a couple of my friends. Cousin Joe. Aunty Alicia and her daughter, Candela. My Great-Uncle. My Great-Aunt. So on. People who'd stayed in the gym got sick first, but it quickly spread through the rancheria. One of our neighbors, a midwife, knew how to recognize the signs of rough breathing and fever. That made us feel better. It wasn't the olden days, when people always died from consumption. With antibiotics from the hospital, we'd all survive.

"Except . . ."

Except they hadn't.

She'd only shared this part of the story once, while sitting with Amelia along the river, under a juniper tree. The memories already shaped Shane's nightmares; she hated voicing them, releasing her darkest days into the world.

"A second sickness," Shane continued. "Something in the water. Happened all at once. We couldn't stop vomiting, and worse. With a stomach bug like that, you can drink water all day and still die of thirst.

"Only people who boiled all their water, like Grandma Yolanda — her cota and her green tea — escaped. It was everywhere. All of us drinking the same bad water, hacking up our lungs, and not enough resources to go around."

In one of her sharpest memories of those days, Shane looked across the living room and saw her grandmother feeding soup to her grandfather, both sitting on a blanket alongside the coffee table. His head was cradled in her lap, and her arthritic hands were shaking, but she still managed to get the spoon to his mouth. He pushed it away, saying, "Not now." But she insisted. "Please try." For her, he took the soup.

And Shane whispered to her father, "Why is this happening to us? What did we do to deserve this?" He looked her in the eyes — his face was gaunt now, his cheekbones were too sharp, and his chin was rough with patchy stubble, but his expression was so tender — and he said, "Nothing. Tragedies aren't punishments."

And then, he coughed into his elbow.

"After a few days, my father and grandfather were sent to a quarantine clinic. They got it worse than the rest of us. They weren't allowed to leave the clinic, and we weren't allowed to live with them."

Shane keenly remembered the first time she heard Nellie's mourning howl, a sound so piercing, she'd felt it in her bones. He'd howled once for her grandfather. Then again for her father.

She thought of those moments often. They didn't make her sad like other memories — the pleasant memories, the memories that reminded her of all the beauty she'd lost.

Rather, her family's suffering made Shane angry.

"My father and grandfather never came home."

"God, I'm so sorry," Donnie said.

Coolly, Shane continued, "When he learned about our losses, Mr. Singer descended from the hill to visit to our home with a basket of food. Canned soup, rice, flour, and a chocolate Bundt cake." She grinned mirthlessly. "And on our doorstep, that man hugged my mother as she wept about the horrors we'd experienced. And how we couldn't pay our medical bills. And how the mold had come back. And how Grandma Yolanda needed better care. And how Ma was going to have a baby without any help. I hid in the hallway, eavesdropping. Ma never cried around me, so it felt good to know that I wasn't alone. But terrible, too, 'cause Ma was in pain, and I couldn't make things better. That's why I thanked the sun when Mr. Singer said, 'I want to help you.'

"It turned out he'd already made deals with other families in the valley. 'By the grace of God,' he explained, 'the flood did not touch my house, but I cannot ignore the suffering outside my window. I have a plan, Lorenza. It's not charity — I would never offend your pride.'

"My mother asked, tearfully, 'What is your plan, then?'

"Mr. Singer offered to buy our house. But he promised, 'Not forever.' In his words, he was giving us a loan without interest. He said, 'You can use the money to prepare for the baby. You'll need a crib, won't you? And new toys? There will be enough to pay off debts, too, and get medicine for Shane's grammy. In the meantime, I'll fix the mold problem, and when your house is ready, you can move back and pay rent until we're even. Won't take long. A month, maybe. Your place is in better shape than others.'

"I don't know whether Ma fully trusted Mr. Singer, especially since what he offered was a small fraction of the land's value. Claimed it'd be easier for her to repay that way. When she asked for more anyway, he said, 'This is the best I can do; the storm hit my bottom line, too.' Thinking back, there were no good choices. We were desperate, and he was a friend. Not a close one, but he'd never done us wrong, and he'd eaten our barbeque, taken me to a ball game, let Sammy play on my swing, and sent cards during big holidays. With the money, Ma got us a room in a motel — all our remaining belongings fit in the truck. Mr. Singer said it would only take a month to make the necessary fixes, and then he'd draw up a rental contract."

Shane paused for a moment. Then, "That never happened. Instead, he tore down the neighborhood. When Ma drove up the hill to confront Mr. Singer, he claimed that it was more efficient to start from scratch — that there was affordable housing elsewhere, that he planned to build new houses, and that she shouldn't shout in her delicate condition. He placed a bag of canned soup into her arms and shut the door.

"The soup fed us for a week."

Shane grabbed her half-empty bottle of orange soda and drank deeply. It had gone flat.

After Mr. Singer's betrayal, they'd relocated from the motel to a campground near Big Bend. Life in a tent had confused her grandmother. She'd ask, "Where am I? Hugo? Where's Hugo?" No matter how many times Lorenza explained that they'd moved, Grandma Yolanda would forget. Her mind had been scattered for a while, but after the flood, everything got so much worse. They'd let her think that Pa and Grandpa Hugo were still alive; no point in breaking her heart every day in a monstrous cycle. No. Sometimes, they'd pretend that the men were buying food in town. Other times, they were repairing our house in a rancheria de los Lipanes.

As a child, Shane often wished she could believe the lies, too, just to make the pain go away.

"We moved to a campground surrounded by a massive forest. Every morning, after breakfast, I put Grandma's chair in the shade of an old oak and sat beside her with two glasses of tea. Usually, I'd read nursery rhymes from the only book we had, an old Mother Goose collection I'd rescued from a rest stop. I'd read it out loud from cover to cover; Grandma didn't say much, never told stories anymore, but she'd listen and sometimes tap her foot to the rhythm of my voice.

"One day, I had a desperate need for the outhouse. It was just a couple minutes away, would take no time at all. So I kissed Grandma on her forehead and promised, 'Be right back.'

"Ma says it wasn't my fault, what happened next. I was just a child, and Grandma rarely left her chair, so how could I anticipate that she'd be gone when I returned? Instead, Ma blames herself, said she never should've left us to refill our water jugs at the well. Blame doesn't change what happened.

"I called Grandma's name and checked inside the truck. Nobody there. To the north, the forest was dense and dark, miles of unbroken wilderness between our tent and the sacred mountains. It was a weekday, with no other campers in sight. I shouted so loud, Ma heard me and came running.

"'Grandma's gone,' I told her.

"Ma said she must've got confused and tried to walk home, which no longer existed, least not in the way she remembered. So Grandma would keep walking, looking, lost. We went into the forest, hand in hand, and called her name. We called her name till our voices went scratchy.

"Desperate, Ma told me to get help from the ranger's station down the road. 'Sprint fast,' she said. But at that moment, Nellie took off, moving quickly. At the time, he wasn't trained for searching, but I remembered how Nellie used to find Ma in the cornfields by using his nose, so I said, 'Follow him!'

"Nellie lead us to a shallow gully, not far away but well-hidden, where Grandma was sitting. Oh, I laughed with relief and wrapped her in a hug. 'Mia?' she asked.

'Why are you crying?' Mia. It was her sister's name.

"We couldn't tell whether Grandma had a head injury or was confused for the usual reasons. To be safe, Ma and I helped her to the truck and booked it to the nearest hospital, a one-hour drive. Along the way, Ma began to cry. Grandma asked, 'What's wrong? She zhá tse'a. ¿Estas enferma?' Ma explained, 'I was just worried.' Then, my mother screamed with pain and added, 'And the baby's coming.' Maybe it was the stress, or maybe just a coincidence. Either way, Marcos, that's how you became the first person in our family to get born in a hospital.

"You probably can't remember, but Grandma met you. Held you. She rocked you gently and smiled."

This was how Shane wanted to end the story. It was a sweet memory: everyone together in a sunlit room, Marcos swaddled in a blue baby blanket.

However, Donnie asked, "Did Mr. Singer build new houses?"

"Nope. Turned la rancheria de los Lipanes into farmland."

Shane took a bite of the coconut candy. It was as sweet as she remembered.

"Just like a treaty," she bitterly mused. "A promise made to be broken."

⫷ THIRTEEN ⫸

"What are you doing?" Marcos exclaimed. "It's late!" He pointed at the clock hanging over a rustic set of drawers, the only furniture in their motel room, aside from two twin beds. Shane sat on the floor with a map of Texas spread across the brown carpet in front of her. They'd reached Kansas before Mrs. Park tiredly announced, "That's all for tonight, sweeties."

But before she could rest, Shane had to check something. "I'm curious," she explained. "Mom, Bobby, and Donnie all disappeared in Less Crossing. What about the others?"

Marcos, who was already dressed in pajamas, his teeth brushed and his face washed, crawled to the edge of his bed and gazed down at Shane's work. Using information she'd learned from reports on the radio, she'd marked the locations of the other ring incidents with Xs of blue dental floss. Three of them were in towns, and two were in the suburbs of Austin.

"Why do you care so much about the other people?" Marcos asked. "They're already found." As he spoke, he scratched Nellie's shimmery head. The old hound had plopped down at the foot of the bed, too, as if wanting to join the conversation.

"I'm looking for a pattern. And I think I've found one. All the points are near a thin gray line with dots, see?" She double-checked the legend. "That's a railroad track. They shut down the railroads after everything happened, so . . ."

"What?"

"Guess the authorities noticed this, too." She waved at the Xs. "You think somebody was riding 'cross Texas, spreading rings like a Johnny Apples?"

At that, Marcos cocked one eyebrow incredulously. He had thick, dark eyebrows, which heightened every expression on his serious little face.

"What?" Shane asked.

He shrugged. "How does this help us find Ma?"

"I don't know." It probably didn't, if she was honest. However, trains might explain why Lorenza went missing in the first place — how the rings were distributed.

Marcos nodded in acceptance, his somber eyes skimming the map, as if he'd find Lorenza's location marked somewhere among the multicolored lines and symbols. "Shane," he went on meekly, "what if . . . Mom's . . ." After a moment of hesitation, he mouthed the word: *dead.*

"No." Quickly, Shane stood. "She's alive." She walked across the room and gently nudged Nellie aside, making room to sit next to Marcos. "I know that for a fact."

"You do?" For the first time since Lorenza went missing, Marcos's eyes seemed hopeful, and he even smiled faintly, as if Shane had offered him a gift. "How?"

"When somebody in the family dies, somebody Nellie knows and loves, he howls. Doesn't matter where they are. It ain't a normal howl, neither."

"You've heard it before?"

"Three times," Shane said, and her clever brother must have understood the implication, since he didn't ask *When?*

"Ma is out there," she promised him again.

Shane usually had trouble sleeping in motel rooms, even when the beds were soft and the pillows were fluffy and cool. It was psychological: in unfamiliar environments, her mind became wary. A motel room might seem safe — with no logical reason to believe otherwise — but her subconscious remained distrustful and resisted the vulnerability of sleep. At least, that's what Lorenza believed.

Later, it would bother Shane that she fell asleep within minutes of folding up the map and crawling under her bedsheets. Either she was so exhausted, her brain couldn't remain vigilant any longer, or she'd become overly familiar with rooms away from home. Neither possibility was comforting.

She'd been dreaming of a city; it was the type of city she visited often, but only in dreams, with empty streets and endlessly tall skyscrapers. Aimlessly, she wandered, until a hesitant, frightened voice asked, "Shane?"

In an instant, the dreary city was replaced with the near-total darkness of the motel room. Vaguely, Shane saw her brother's silhouette standing at her bedside. He'd been poking her sheet-covered shoulder.

"What is it, Marcos?" she whispered.

"I hear a sound," he said. "It's coming from the closet."

"What? Are you sure?"

"Uh huh. It's quiet . . ."

Beside the front door, there was a narrow closet containing an ironing board, three clothes hangers, and their luggage. At first, Shane assumed that Marcos had only heard rats skittering in the walls, or people talking outside. But then, she heard it too: a high-pitched babble, like children giggling under a quilt. Wide awake with shock, she patted the bedside table until her fingers brushed the lamp cord. Quickly, Shane turned on the light and stared at the closed closet door. Nellie stood at the foot of her bed, and although she couldn't see him clearly, his shimmer seemed watchful.

"The walkie talkie," Shane said, rising. "Maybe it turned on." Barefoot, she padded to the closet door, closely followed by Nellie.

"Then who's talking?" Marcos asked. He exchanged his rabbit plushie for his left tennis shoe and held it up, as if brandishing a weapon, prepared to attack anything that popped out of the closet. Shane thought about her hunting knife, which was tucked within her belt in the closet along with the sound. She should have kept the weapon at hand. But she'd had no logical reason to expect danger in a motel room.

"Let's find out." With a fierce burst of speed, Shane whipped the closet door open. It smacked against the wall — *thud*! All at once, the babbling went silent. Aside from the expected hangers, ironing board, backpack, and duffel bag, the closet was empty. Still, she swept her hand through the air, checking for invisible threats. Feeling nothing, Shane pulled her backpack into the open and checked the walkie talkie.

"It's off," she reported, baffled.

Then, from the depths of her bag, came a burst of whispers. With a cry of dismay, Shane kicked the heavy backpack and sent it thudding into the wooden hotel door. A second later, Marcos's shoe flew through the air, narrowly missing its target. "Is there a gremlin in the bag?" he gasped, running to grab his second shoe.

"Better not be!" It did seem like she'd picked up a magical or supernatural critter; what else could make such distinctive, speech-like sounds? Well, aside from ghost parrots. "Hey, listen," Shane said, speaking in a calm, firm tone. "We don't want trouble. I'm going to open my backpack now. Sorry about the kick. It was instinct."

Slowly, she unzipped the hiking backpack. The sound stopped for a moment. Then, from the depths of her gear, something murmured, "Ten thousand and and twenty." Afraid to stick her hand into the unknown, Shane overturned the bag and shook its objects onto the carpet.

"Ten thousand and and twenty-one." The counting was definitely louder now, exposed. Shane rifled through her survival gear, stopping when her hand landed on the pink seashell from the abandoned well; under her fingertips, it vibrated. "Ten thousand and and twenty-two."

"Is the shell talking?" Marcos asked, crouching next to Shane.

"You found me," the shell whispered, and then, it giggled: a bell-like, bubbly sound. "Ready or not, here I come."

"What the . . ." Shane raised the shell to her ear, treating it like a walkie talkie since the voice came from its hollow, hidden center. "Who are you?" she asked.

"I am a girl who lives in water," the shell voice said.

"What water?"

"Water everywhere."

"Like lake water?"

"Yes."

"Ocean water?"

"Yes."

"A cup of water?"

There was a pause. Then, "If the cup is big enough."

Still holding the speaking shell, Shane walked to the motel window and peered through the curtains, searching for a pool. However, it wasn't visible. "Were you in the drinking well?" she asked. "Three nights ago, did you put your shell in the water bucket?"

Another pause. Then, "Yes?"

"Why?" Shane asked.

"To listen," the voice explained. "Are you the one called Shane?"

Thinking of all the hours she'd spoken within earshot of the backpack, unwittingly overheard by this creature, Shane couldn't help but shiver. "That's me."

"I don't hear Donnie anymore."

"Yeah. That's because she's not here. Can you use all shells as spy devices? Or is this pink one special? Just curious." Unlike delicate, fan-shaped seashells, the speaking shell was heavy and solid; to break it, Shane might need a hammer. In a pinch, she could use a heavy rock.

322

"Oh, it's very special. This is what my mother told me . . ."

In any case, the shell would have to go. With Lorenza and Billy missing, Shane had vitally important mysteries to solve; she couldn't waste time stressing over the motivations of a disembodied voice that probably belonged to a monster.

"At the bottom of the ocean, in trenches deep and cold —"

There were a pair of cinderblocks in the parking lot. She could run outside, prop the shell against the curb, and shatter it in a couple solid hits. "Stay here, Marcos," Shane whispered into her brother's ear. "I'll be right back." The unknown entity didn't seem to hear her, since it continued chattering about the depths.

"— beyond the domain of sunlight, where the world is so heavy, it'll crush a turtle's shell —"

Quietly, Shane slipped into her tennis shoes and opened the front door. In one hand, she held the speaking shell, and in the other, she clutched her flashlight.

"— live an ancient species of animal —"

Leaving the motel door open so that she could see her brother, Shane jogged across the strip of parking lot asphalt. As expected, the cinderblocks were near Mrs. Park's convertible.

"— a cross between a nautilus and an octopus, older than the dinosaurs, older than the first breath —"

Shane paused, listening. Octopus nautilus? She'd never learned about that animal before; was it even known to humankind?

"— they're always born in pairs. And you want to know the most interesting thing?"

"Yes," she said. "What?"

"Twins share the same egg, and inside the egg, they each grow shells. They're special pink shells, like the one I gave you. Through their shells, they are connected, always, even after hatching. No matter the distance between them. No matter where the currents flow. They sing to each other, and the shells transmit songs across space, like radios. The animals are not telepathic. Their armor is."

"The shells receive and transmit sound?" They really were like walkie talkies.

"In the way of deep-sea things, twins live hundreds of years, but when one sibling dies, the other will, too. We go into the trenches to find their empty old shells, which are always lying side by side. Sometimes, when I put the shell against my ear, I hear the echo of a song. It's probably my imagination, though. What do you think? Can songs make ghosts? Can ghosts sing songs?"

"I suppose they can," Shane said, gazing down at the shell in her hand, amazed. "But why would you give me such a valuable item? What if I'd thrown it away?"

"Shells are discarded, and shells are found. Along the way, I listen."

"What are you, really?" Shane asked, slowly turning around. Marcos was a watchful silhouette in the open doorway. "Why were you counting earlier?"

"I tried calling to you, Shane, but you didn't answer. It's OK. Humans have bad ears. So I counted until you noticed. I can count to a trillion, probably. It's a good thing you heard me earlier than that. What number did I reach? Ten thousand and twenty-two?" Although she'd always had keen hearing for a human, unless

Shane put the shell against her ear, the voice was soft: easily lost in the rumble of a car engine or the whistling wind.

"Yes. I hear you now."

"You do."

"But it's late, Shell Girl, and I'm exhausted. Please, no more games. What do you want?"

"To help."

"Help find our mother?" She held the shell close, pressing her ear against the smooth curl of its lip. "Why?"

"Because."

"Because?"

"Yes."

Assuming Shell Girl was telling the truth, there were worse answers. "How would you help us?" Shane asked.

"Uuuuummm. If you give me a taste of her blood, I can sense her. All living things are connected through water."

Shell Girl had asked where Donnie was — but had said nothing of Mrs. Park. "That's how you followed us here? Donnie's blood?"

"Yes. I'm a better tracker than your dog. Maybe fate brought us together."

Shane's grip tightened on the shell; a more fragile shell would have crumpled in her fingers. "I want to trust you . . ." Hadn't something hurt Donnie in the lake? Tangled around her leg, nearly pulling her under the surface? At the time, Donnie had assumed that the fall was an accident, the result of clumsiness, but it could have been an attack. Or was that just how Shell Girl collected blood for tracking purposes? Still creepy, but less worrisome than a murder attempt.

"Why did you give us the shell in the first place?" she asked.

"Bored."

"That's all?"

"People used to swim in the lake. I'd watch them gliding over me. Then, when I tried to make friends, everybody went away."

Shane thought back to her day in the Ozarks. What had Donnie sensed as they moved deeper into the forest, away from the water? Danger, wrongness. A second dangerous entity near the logging camp?

Or had there only been Shell Girl, all along?

"What are you, really?" Shane asked, slowly walking toward the open door. "A . . . a siren?" No, that was ridiculous. Everyone knew that sirens were gone, slaughtered in the 1800s by whalers, merchant sailors, and pirates. There were rumors that a population of survivors still lived in the Pacific, sheltering on isolated islands. Yet even if that was true, why would a siren live in the Ozarks? And why would she need a shell to communicate, when a siren's voice — according to legend — could pierce through a storm? Shell Girl was no siren. She was something else; perhaps something stranger, more dangerous.

"You can see me, if you want," the unknown entity promised. "I'm right here, beside you."

Shane whirled around, looking side-to-side. The parking lot was empty; the long building's windows dark, except for hers. Then, she remembered the pool on the other side of the motel.

"I think I've already seen you," she whispered into the shell. "The night you gave me the shell. You have bangs, right?"

"Yes. Do you like them?"

"They're —"

"Shane?" Marcos called, leaning outside. A disheveled strand of hair dropped between his wide eyes. "What's wrong?"

"Nothing!" she called, jogging back to the light. Quickly, Shane ushered Marcos inside, closed the door behind them, and shoved the deadbolt into a locked position. Then, to the shell, she said, "Unfortunately, I don't carry a vial of my mother's blood, which means there's nothing for you to track, unless I find an old bandage, and that's unlikely." Lorenza didn't leave medical waste sitting around the house, and they took out the trash once a week.

"Ummm," the unknown entity hummed, "maybe your blood is close enough? We can always experiment."

"What's your name?" Shane asked, stalling. The tactic might yield useful information, too, since names were powerful. They could reveal secrets about their person, like any trait. "My brother and I are curious."

"Along the lake where I hatched," the shell reminisced dreamily, "is a little patch of flowers. They're bright yellow, with round, flat faces and long, green stalks. Their sunbeam petals grow around a black disk, like a solar eclipse. And although my mother never named me, I've always wondered, what do they call those flowers, which look at the sun and look like the sun and turn sunlight into life? They must call them sunflowers. Can I be called Sunflower, too?"

How did she . . . ? Maybe it was a coincidence.

"I'm exhausted," Shane said, grabbing an old sock from her duffel bag. "We can talk more tomorrow."

"W —"

Quickly, Shane muffled the creature's response with the sock and buried the shell at the bottom of her backpack, then shoved the backpack into the closet.

"Why did you —" Marcos started to ask, but Shane hushed him with a finger against her lips. Then, she grabbed Lorenza's address book, turned to a blank page, and wrote in pencil:

She may hear us.

Quietly, Marcos mouthed each word, sounding them out in his head. Once he'd finished with "us," he looked at Shane with a questioning tilt of the head, as if asking, *So?*

I do not trust her yet.

After Marcos finished reading that sentence, Shane erased the page and wrote:

She might be playing games.

Not all games are kind.

Cats play games with mice.

We need to talk to Donnie.

Tomorrow.

"Now go to bed," Shane said, kissing her brother on the crown of his head. "There isn't much night left."

Nodding, Marcos wriggled back under his bedsheets and squeezed his rabbit. With a calm sigh, Nellie snuggled at the foot of his bed. Not for the first time, Shane wondered if ghosts could dream. As a living bloodhound, Nellie would nap for hours, kicking his legs and snuffling as he chased imaginary animals. He didn't do that anymore. Instead, when the family slept, Nellie curled up beside Lorenza,

Shane, or Marcos and stayed very still until his human family was ready to move again.

Perhaps he daydreamed; perhaps he thought about the world Below, where he'd dwelt for mere days before Lorenza called him back to Earth. Had he been puzzled by the afterlife? Had he searched for his humans, his little pack, confused by their absence? He must have been anxious. Why else would he refuse to return Below?

"Is it loyalty?" Shane whispered. "Are you here because we need you?"

"Whaaaat?" Marcos mumbled, his voice heavy with exhaustion.

"Nothing, sorry." She pulled the bedsheet to her chin, trying to enjoy the air conditioner and abundance of pillows, two luxuries she didn't have at home.

In the backpack in the closet, the seashell remained quiet.

~ FOURTEEN ~

For the first five hours of the trip today, Marcos slept with his cheek against the car door, Mrs. Park listened to the news on the radio, and Shane and Donnie exchanged notes to converse quietly. And even after Marcos woke up, energized by a late lunch at Millie's Famous Hot Dogs, the girls discussed some topics in writing, afraid to scare him with their thoughts. So naturally, when the subject turned to Shell Girl, Donnie grabbed her writing supplies. Although Shane couldn't see Donnie's face, she imagined an expression of feverish interest whenever she heard Donnie's pen rapidly scratching across the notepad.

333

She can teleport between pools of water, Donnie wrote. **That's not a mermaid or a siren. They swim.**

What is she, then? Any ideas?

Have you seen the movie *Blood Bath*?

No.

It's about a monster that can appear in jacuzzis & bathtubs to eat people. But I don't think it's based on reality. The director makes stuff up.

To be safe, don't take any baths until we figure this out.

I'm going to smell really gross after two or three days.

Shane twisted in her seat to pass Donnie the final note.

Dude, showers are an option.

Donnie nodded sagely and flashed Shane a thumbs up.

"We've arrived," Mrs. Park announced. And there, along the forested road, half-concealed by a long Ponderosa Pine branch, was a green sign announcing: *Welcome To Tanner, Colorado.*

Skylight Comics and Collectibles was sandwiched between a laundromat and a travel agency, and none of the shops were bustling. Behind the strip mall, the Colorado forest stretched beyond the horizon; the edge of the parking lot, where trees leaned over the commercial clearing, was carpeted with pinecones and dry brown pine needles. To Shane, it seemed like an odd location for a comic book store, with infinitely more trees than customers. Here, at the outskirts of town, there wasn't even through-traffic from one part of Tanner to the other.

Mrs. Park parked directly outside of Skylight C & C, and she turned off the engine with a sharp twist of the key. Although the comic shop had large windows, every inch of glass was papered with brightly-colored movie posters and sun-faded signs advertising stuff like "Comics – New and Old" and "Baseball Cards" and "Kung-Fu Movie Sunday – 1$ Entry, FREE POPCORN." As she exited the car, Shane swept her gaze up and down the long parking lot. There were a couple convertibles in front of the laundromat and a cluster of kickstand-balanced bicycles on

335

the sidewalk, but she didn't see Grandpa Louis's motorcycle. As Donnie grabbed the soil samples from the back of the station wagon, Shane stretched her arms over her head, wincing at the pain that twinged in her lower back. She could hike with a heavy backpack for miles, but two days in a car made her muscles stiff. If Shane wasn't careful, the tension would creep up her neck and transform into a headache. If Lorenza had been there, she would've given Shane a pair of aspirin and orders to "take them with lots of water."

Pushing back a surge of loneliness, Shane led the way to Skylight C & C and pulled open the poster-papered swinging door. A bell jingled overhead, announcing her presence. Air smelling of old paper and chalk, much like the perfume of libraries and classrooms, engulfed Shane as she entered the brightly lit store. There were memorabilia-filled cabinets against the walls, and the interior was crowded with revolving comic racks and waist-high shelves containing alphabetically-sorted comics. Behind the front counter stood a thin, middle-aged Black man with an afro and round-framed prescription glasses.

He wore a lime-green turtleneck and white bell-bottoms. As the group entered his store, he looked up from the book he'd been reading, glancing over the top of his glasses.

"Are you Dr. Richards?" Shane asked.

"The one and only," he replied, snapping his book shut. "And based on that accent, you must be the caller from Texas." Dr. Richards enunciated each word with crisp, exacting clarity, like a lecturer at a podium.

"Yes, sir."

"Who are the others?"

"Mrs. Park and Donnie," Shane introduced, nodding at each member in her group, "are family of the missing boy, Bobby. And that's my brother, Marcos." Unnoticed by Dr. Richards, Nellie slipped through the door and sat beside a rack of horror comics. On the covers, red-splattered skeletons, ghouls, human prey, and monsters — both imaginary and real — were drawn in gritty detail.

"After you rang, I read the despicable news in the paper. It's happened again, like I knew it would. I warned them."

"Warned who?"

"Everyone!" Dr. Richards pinched the bridge of his nose, under his glasses' nose pads. "Maybe now, somebody will listen. Correction: they've always listened. The risk's just never been a priority." He rapidly strode around the counter to shake hands with Mrs. Park, who'd removed her sunglasses, revealing piteously dark crescents under her eyes. "We cannot talk in front of an audience, though," Dr. Richards continued, glancing at the far end of the shop, where a group of teenage boys were thumbing through the comic archives.

It was 3 p.m., two hours before the official closing time at Skylight C & C, but Dr. Richards flipped a sign on the doorknob from "OPEN" to "CLOSED". Then he called out, "Lucas! Charlie! Damian!"

In unison, the teenagers looked up from their stories, blinking, as if waking from a collective dream. To Shane they resembled alert prairie dogs. "Yes, sir?" one asked.

"Are you going to buy that issue?"

The three customers exchanged awkward glances. "No, sir," their spokesman reported.

338

"In that case, clear out. I have to lock up early today."

Lucas, Charlie, and Damian returned the comic and then walked single file to the exit, eyeing Shane's group with unreserved curiosity. Before the last boy stepped through the door, he stopped, reached into his pocket, and held out a wriggling, black-brown insect with tiny rear pinchers. "Mr. Richards, I found a bookworm on your shelf," he said. "You better do something. Last year, they got into my dictionary and ruined sections *A* through *F*."

Shane took one look at the insect and shook her head. "That's an earwig nymph," she corrected him. "They're harmless. Throw him outside."

Dr. Richards nodded with approval as the boy walked out. "You know your insects."

"She's basically a bug goddess," Donnie commented, her smile knowing and lopsided. Under each arm, she carried the PVC pipes filled with topsoil cores.

"Are you a future entomologist?" wondered Dr. Richards, leading them to a door labeled *Staff Only Beyond This Point.*

339

He unlatched a jingling key ring from his beltloop and rifled through the keys, searching for the one that'd unlock his office.

"Ah, no," Shane laughed, looking at her feet with mild embarrassment. "I just like 'em."

"Why's that?" he asked, finally finding the right key.

"Why do I like bugs?"

"Yup." He slid the key in the lock and turned. There was an audible click of a heavy-duty bolt sliding free.

"I guess . . . I just started noticing them." She shrugged. "And then I started watching them. Which made me appreciate them."

She hesitated.

"When I was a girl," Shane went on, "I'd always play beneath an old oak tree. Red ants made a hill between two of the oak's surface roots. It was near my swing, so I had to be careful not to jump on 'em. That meant I was always alert. At first, they were bitey little menaces, nothing more. But over time, I came to like how

340

well they worked together, never fighting, least not that I saw."

With a smile, she shrugged again. "After a picnic, I was sitting on the grass when a red ant walked past my foot, and she carried a potato chip that resembled a butterfly's wing. It was fifty times bigger than her and wobbling back and forth like a flag in the wind.

"In my sandals and summer dress, I crouched there, watching. Every pebble blocked the ant's journey to her hill. It would have been easy to scoop her in my hand and carry her home, but I wanted to know if it was possible for something so tiny and awkward to succeed on her own. She wouldn't drop the chip to find a lighter piece of food. Ants are driven. They struggle until the end, whatever that may be.

"At sunset, she reached her colony, the hill between two roots. The other ants swarmed and helped drag the chip up the slope. In the chaos, I lost sight of her, but I'm glad I didn't overlook her."

"The natural world can teach us many lessons," Dr. Richards concluded.

"Guess so. She definitely taught me something."

"Perseverance." He shouldered open the door and flipped a wall switch, illuminating his small office. "Welcome, everybody."

Like the main store, there were memorabilia-lined shelves along the side walls, but the items showed signs of wear, none of them in mint condition. The collection seemed curated for somebody who dug model robots, kung fu movies, and sci-fi comics. There was a hand-painted revolving globe on a tidy white desk, and an orange shag rug in the middle of the floor.

It occurred to Shane that the office was no larger than Pizza Dale's breakroom, but unlike the miserable gray tomb at her old workplace, this space felt welcoming, and best of all, the wall-mounted ceramic clock ticked so quietly, she couldn't hear it.

"Is that real?" Marcos asked, pointing at a silver robot on the lowest shelf. It had a boxy body, zipper-shaped teeth, and wrench-shaped arms.

"Hal?" Dr. Richards picked up the model. "Sadly, he's just a figurine, not

342

an android. Those don't exist yet, far as I know. Maybe someday. Here. He needs a friend." With that, he passed the toy to Marcos, who cradled the robot, awe-struck. The sight made Shane smile.

"I brought soil from the site," Donnie said, carefully arranging pipe-enclosed samples across the carpet, where they couldn't roll around.

"One moment!" Dr. Richards bolted out of the office, calling over his shoulder, "I have to lock up, secure the area!"

"Uh . . ." Donnie turned toward the others, shrugging. "So, about the elephant in the room. Your grandpa has all the pic-tures, Shane."

"It's weird that he isn't here," she replied slowly. "He should've reached town this morning."

"Why did we split up again?"

Shane flinched at the hint of accusa-tion in that question. It had been her idea to send Grandpa Louis ahead with the photos. "Because every hour matters," she explained, willing her response to be gentle, calm. "Dr. Richards might've had answers for us by now, if he'd gotten the photos early."

"What happened to Grandpa?" Marcos solemnly asked; he was sitting cross-legged beside the desk, with Hal in his lap. Mrs. Park had taken the office chair. Quiet as always, she stared listlessly at the office door, her eyes red-rimmed with exhaustion.

"Probably took a long break," Donnie muttered. "It's hard to ride from Texas to Colorado without sleep, and your grandpa's no spring chicken."

"Yeah, maybe." Still, Shane was concerned. If Grandpa Louis had spent the night at a motel, he could've left a message. And he should be here by now anyways. What if he'd gotten in an accident? Or lost? Or was sitting in jail for breaking the speed limit? Could you be arrested for that?

Shane thought about the last time he vanished without warning. There'd been no word for years. If Grandpa Louis died on the road, would Nellie howl? Did Nellie consider him family, even with all his absences?

With a shake of her head, Shane pushed the worst-case thoughts aside. Donnie was probably right. And if not, there were a hundred mundane reasons why Grandpa Louis would run a few hours late. Still, her heart rate sped up with anxiety. Each time something frightening or tragic happened, it became more difficult for Shane to reassure herself that worst-case scenarios were unlikely.

Suddenly, Dr. Richards returned with several bottles of root beer, a tub of popcorn, and a little green chalkboard.

"Let's begin," he said, passing out sodas. "Tell me everything."

After Shane, Donnie, and Mrs. Park shared their stories, Dr. Richards grabbed a piece of chalk from the desk drawer and drew several labeled circles and an equation on the chalkboard.

"Since we know that circles *A* and *B* sent you to a lake in the Ozarks, which is about 230 miles away from the rings," Dr. Richards said, jabbing his chalk toward Shane and Donnie, "it's possible to estimate how far circles *C* and *D* sent your mother and your brother, respectively. There's just one problem."

"Missing information," Shane guessed, crestfallen.

"Yes. Until I know how big A and B are, in comparison to C and D, there's no way to make the necessary calculations."

"What about the dirt?" Donnie asked, crossing her arms and glaring at the chalkboard as if trying to make sense of a vexing mystery. "Isn't it good for something?"

"Of course. Tonight, I'll analyze the topsoil's organic content. If it's significantly variable across space, we'll know we can't compare A, B, C, and D at all. However, the topsoil will not give us anything else. We need photos or direct measurements of the circles."

"Where is Grandpa?" Shane worried, glancing at the clock.

"Lost, is my guess," Dr. Richards reassured her. He stooped to gather the soil samples. "Tanner's out of the way, hard to find. Just bring me the photos tomorrow."

"There's one more thing," Shane said. "We have a living mimic sample."

Dr. Richards nearly dropped the tubes in shock. Then, "Incinerate it! Destroy every trace! God, did you bring it here?!"

"No! Don't worry. My grandpa stored it in a freezer —"

"So the mimic is isolated?"

She nodded. Specifically, he'd transferred the specimen to a lockbox within a plastic box within the freezer.

"Good." With two long strides, Dr. Richards crossed the room and clasped his hands in front of Shane, as if begging for her cooperation. "The mimic cannot spread. Understand?"

"I . . . yes, I do." She didn't want other families to suffer like hers. But . . .

"Burn every trace, and then disinfect anything that touched the sample. Clothes. Shoes. Canisters. Heat or bleach." He stepped back, turned, started pacing. "On second thought, maybe I should supervise the disposal. I'd have to take a flight. Next week? Too late? No, that's fine. It's fine."

"Isn't there a way to grow it safely?" Shane asked. "A controlled, isolated greenhouse, maybe? We can destroy it after —"

"You have no idea how dangerous it is on Earth!" Dr. Richards whirled around; he sounded panicked now. "Nobody does. Not even the fae!"

"Yes, we do!" Marcos shouted, and all eyes turned to him; Shane's mouth dropped open in surprise. "It took my Mom! I hate it! I hate it so much!" Her brother dropped Hal and squeezed his hands into fists; they trembled with his rage. "I want to kill all of the mimics, and I want to kill the person who put fairy rings behind Miss Donnie's house, and if you don't help us . . ."

A tear slipped down his cheek.

". . . then what are we going to do?" he sobbed.

Shane scooped up her brother and lifted him off the floor. With a miserable sniffle, he threw his arms around her neck and cried against her shoulder. Warm tears seeped into her T-shirt. "We keep trying," she whispered. "We fight for her."

"I am monumentally sorry. I never intended to suggest . . ." Dr. Richards trailed off, while awkwardly rubbing the back of his head.

"It's been a very long day," Mrs. Park chimed in, softly.

"I want to show you something," Dr. Richards said, thrusting his hands into his pockets. "Need to show you, actually. It's a quick walk."

"What?" Shane asked, patting Marcos's back, relieved that he'd stopped crying.

"The Longfire site." He raised an eyebrow at their expressions of surprise. "You didn't think I opened a shop in Tanner because of its inaccessibility and miniscule population, did you? Here, I can keep an eye on things."

"I'm just surprised you live near a disaster site," Shane explained.

"And why not? It's inactive, not radioactive."

"The government doesn't care?"

He laughed sharply. "If they do? I don't know about it. To them, now, it's just another blighted piece of land. Nothing but gray dirt."

Behind Skylight Comics and Collectibles, a footpath cut through the dense forest. To Shane, it resembled a narrow capillary winding through a vast green body. Because of her sore hip, Mrs. Park could not join them on the one-mile hike, so she'd volunteered to remain at the store with Marcos where they'd keep watch for Grandpa Louis. Before leaving, Dr. Richards had heaped Marcos with action figures, airplane models, Hot Wheels, and comic books. Perhaps out of guilt, perhaps out of pity, he'd even offered Marcos the gift of a toy; it could be anything in the shop, including the high-shelf, pricey memorabilia, like a glass-encased baseball signed by Jackie Robinson. And when Marcos had shyly asked, "What about Hal?" Dr. Richards exclaimed, "Excellent choice! He likes you better than me, anyway."

As she followed Dr. Richards down the footpath, Shane glanced over her shoulder. The store was already obscured by trees. Hopefully, Grandpa Louis would arrive during their visit to the Longfire site. Then they could make the calculations immediately, instead of waiting for the morning.

Although Shane's wristwatch was hidden beneath her sleeve, the drooping sun reminded her of time's relentless passage. The gulf separating Shane from her last farewell to Lorenza was ever-widening.

How many days had it been since she'd last hugged her mother? And how far would the gulf spread before they hugged again?

"What do you know about the Longfire Incident?" Dr. Richards asked. "Or . . . I guess a more appropriate question is: what do you think you know?"

The girls exchanged a puzzled glance. Then, Shane answered, "It happened in the twenties. A guy named Mr. Brooklyn, who worked at the ring center in Denver, took a mimic sample and grew it. He probably wanted to travel somewhere far away —"

"Like Mars," Donnie helpfully supplied. "Or an alien planet that wouldn't kill him outright, hopefully."

Could the mimic find another planet with a breathable atmosphere, drinkable water, nourishing food, suitable shelter, and company, whatever that entailed? If so, it was leagues more advanced than current human astronomers. There were psychics and mediums who claimed to sense the echoes of aliens whose thoughts were so strange, they caused migraines and psychological breakdowns. However, beyond those stories, extraplanetary lifeforms were still in the realm of science fiction.

"In the end," Shane summarized, "Mr. Brooklyn's mimic ring vaporized a bunch of trees, and he disappeared."

Because Shane hadn't yet found old newspaper clippings with reports about the incident, she had to rely exclusively on her grandfather's memory. He'd lived through the twenties, was present when the country apparently buzzed with sensational news about the criminal scientist who'd perished because of his own careless hubris. It was astonishing how quickly people became indifferent to disasters. Breaking news had an expiration date, after all.

"Part of that is undoubtedly true," Dr. Richards said, and there was a bitter quality to his voice. "The Longfire Incident did happen in '23, and a man named Xander Brooklyn was involved." The trail took a sharp right. Single file, with Shane in the middle, they proceeded up a slight slope. "However, Xander didn't steal anything. I doubt he knew what a mimic was."

"Wasn't he a self-taught scientist?" Donnie asked. "My grandpa said that the police found a bunch of science papers in his house, and he got a job at the ring center to do evil genius research."

"The boxes of *suspicious* literature they recovered from his apartment" — when he said the word 'suspicious,' Dr. Richards made air quotes, as if reciting a line from a newspaper — "were science fiction novels. Mary Shelley, H. G. Wells, and pulp *Weirdest Tales*. Half the men in Tanner got jobs at the ring center when it opened. A long commute, but there were not many options for employment."

"It sounds like you knew him personally," Shane observed.

"Hey, now. I'm not that old." Dr. Richards snorted, amused. "However, you're almost right. My father did."

The terrain was getting rougher, rocks and roots sprawled across their path. When they reached a steep, slippery part of the trail, Shane wordlessly reached toward Donnie. Hand in hand, they steadied each other during the climb. In contrast, Dr. Richards bounded from rock to rock — as if he'd made the journey so often, he'd mastered its obstacles.

"Huh! Were *they* friends?" Donnie asked, once they'd reached flat ground again. Shane loosened her grip, and after a couple seconds, Donnie let go. However, they still walked close together, as if mentally holding hands now.

"Barely acquaintances." Dr. Richards stopped suddenly, tensing, like a deer before it bolts. Shane got the sense that he had been startled; perhaps he'd heard a strange noise. After a moment, he resumed walking. "Tanner's a small town. Everyone knew Xander. Unfortunately, I doubt anyone knew him well. If they had, if he'd had just one good friend, the official story may be different."

"How d'you mean?" Donnie encouraged.

"Instead of a villain, he'd be known as a victim," Dr. Richards explained. "Like your brother. Or Shane's mother."

"You mean he accidentally stumbled into a ring?" Shane wondered. "If that's true, then who planted the mimic?" Throughout the walk, she'd spoken at a soft volume, as if afraid to disturb the forest, which was unlike any place she'd visited before. Shane felt like a guest in

354

a stranger's home, afraid to cause offense and unsure of the house rules.

"Nobody," he answered. "Not directly, anyway."

They passed through a natural corridor of towering ponderosa pines, with trunks the width of wine barrels.

"Whuh?" Donnie spread her arms as they walked, as if gesturing to the entire forest. "How'd that strain appear in the middle of nowhere? Does it, like, spread magically? Or on the wind?"

"Thankfully, no. That would be cataclysmic." Dr. Richards pointed north. "Walk this way, and you will come upon a meadow. Xander Brooklyn had a telescope, advanced by the standards of his time. The lens was treated with an alchemical film of clarity. Every Saturday, he would carry it to the meadow. Before the Longfire Incident, my father and his friends walked with Xander to the meadow one night, and he showed them Saturn and the moon. The whole time, Xander pontificated about science fiction. As a youth, my father didn't read much. You can thank boarding school trauma for that aversion. Yet. Yet the way Xander described far-out stories of time machines and spaceships persuaded my old man to purchase a paperback about aliens on Venus, and he never stopped reading after that."

"Is that why you care about Xander's disappearance?" Donnie asked. "Because he taught your dad that reading's fun?"

"Not really."

"Wha?"

"Do I need a personal connection to care about a man?"

"S'pose not," Donnie conceded. "But most people do."

"These days," Dr. Richards continued, "employees of ring transport centers have to disinfect their shoes and clothes if they handle the mushrooms."

"Oh," Shane breathed. "You mean . . ."

"Yes. The protocol — not near stringent enough, in my professional opinion, but better than nothing — was created to prevent another Longfire Incident. Because at some level, they acknowledge the possibility that it was an accident. There were zero such safeguards in the twenties.

I think Xander unwittingly tracked a mimic to the forest; it might have become lodged in his boots. After over a week of rain, the ring flourished. Consequently, the next hike Xander took was also his last. They never found him or his telescope; he must have been holding it when he vanished."

"Where do you think he went? Do you really think it was another planet?" According to Grandpa Louis, there'd been speculations that Xander had gone to a different galaxy based on the immense size of the dead zone. Considering his fascination with the stars, that now seemed like a tragic possibility.

"Perhaps." Dr. Richards didn't sound convinced, however.

"The more important question," Donnie interjected, "is how in the infinite worlds did mimics appear behind my house? It's in Texas, and we aren't near a ring transport center. Nobody works with extra-dimensional mushrooms. We don't even grow button mushrooms!"

A possibility was forming in Shane's mind. "The train . . ." she said. "It passes through your neighborhood twice a day, but where does it come from? Where does it go? Who or what does it carry?"

"I . . . I seriously don't know."

"What about materials for the new ring center in Boerne?"

"Oooooh! You might be on to something!"

"All the other disappearances were near the same railroad track." Shane put a hand on Donnie's arm. "You know, my pa made a living by fixing cars, but he was a fisherman at heart. That side of my family, they're southeast Lipan, used to live near the Gulf Coast. 'Fore visiting a new lake, he'd wash the underside of his tin boat. By that, I mean he'd scrub it with a sponge in our garage, and then rinse everything down with a hose. First time I saw Pa do that, I laughed, 'cause it seemed a waste to rinse a boat 'fore it went into the water . . ."

At the thought, Shane smiled.

"He told me, 'Sheiné łénde, this isn't for the boat. It's for the lake.' And I asked, 'What for?' So my father explained, 'Every lake is a bowl full of lifeforms, and the communities aren't always the same.' Then, he told me, 'Sometimes, a mollusk, piece of

358

algae, or baby crab will get attached to a boat's belly. They can be hard to see, very small. It's easy to accidentally carry stowaways from one body of water to another, you understand? We don't want that. It might cause an imbalance."

"He's right," Dr. Richards said.

"That's what happened with the mushrooms, isn't it? An accident. First, a mimic slipped into the normal fairy ring samples, undetected. Then the train was moving materials for the new ring center, and somehow, it wasn't cleaned right."

"That's what I suspect," Dr. Richards mumbled grimly, "but whatever the case, there never should've been a second incident. History does not have to repeat itself. Not when we know better, and can do better."

"How?" Donnie asked. "Should we just abandon the whole ring transport thing?"

"Potentially, but not necessarily." Dr. Richards tapped his temple. "Due diligence. Study the mimics and other rings, understand how they'll interact with Earth's systems, determine whether mimics can be neutralized or identified before they spread. What else? We can develop much more effective safeguards; the potential for human error during decontamination is too great. And ideally? Find a significantly less risky alternative to extradimensional ring species — something sourced from Earth. I believe it's possible."

"You've thought a lot about this," Shane said, impressed.

"I'm not the only one, Bug Girl. There's a few other scientists and layfolk on my side. Unfortunately, our concerns are always weighed against shiny, immediate boons. What's one man, one plot of forest? How can they compare to the incredible convenience and economic power of ring transport? Longfire was a warning. The wise pay heed."

"He's never been found, has he?" Donnie asked.

"Xander?"

"Yeah."

Dr. Richards's shoulders fell slightly. "No." He shook his head. "But he may be, someday."

"You think so?"

"I do." He looked up as they walked, like he was trying to peer through the gaps in the leaves, where the sky was a rich shade of blue.

"Even if he was transported to another planet, like they say?"

The biologist hummed in consideration. Then, he explained. "My father didn't buy the planet theory."

"You said he barely knew Mr. Brooklyn!"

"One meeting was all it took. Want to hear why?" After they both nodded, he continued, "The night Father viewed Saturn and the moon, he commented, 'I wish I could visit all those planets. There has to be something more than this.' But Xander disagreed: 'You won't find a prettier place than home.' At the time, his answer was surprising. My father had assumed that a fan of science fiction would be into space travel, you know? And this country can be pretty, I'll grant you that, but it's got ugliness, too. Its ugliness runs deep. My father said as much. And then Xander told him, 'Science fiction is about the future, and our future is Earth.' You want to know my suspicion?"

"Go ahead," Shane encouraged, already guessing what he'd say. With the context of one simple conversation, Xander's destination seemed obvious.

"We know that the mimic is from a dimension of malleable space and time."

"It's like a time machine?" Donnie interjected.

"A one-way time machine, yes," said Dr. Richards. "The ring probably did not launch Xander into the past, as that breaks the tenuously known laws of magical physics. Furthermore, its radius is so large, and the forest's biodiversity is so rich, it couldn't have sent him anywhere on Earth. That leaves two possibilities: another planet, which Xander had no interest in visiting, or . . . the mysterious future, which was his dream."

Shane had learned about magical time travel in a freshman course on weird phenomena. According to the textbook, even the fae could not go back in time, but the strongest were able to jump forward ten minutes.

"How far did it send him?" she wondered. "And . . . and how much energy did that take?"

"See for yourself." He swept his hand in a flourish. To Shane, he resembled an unenthusiastic ringleader announcing the world's emptiest circus.

And abruptly, they stepped into a circular clearing. Larger than a soccer field, the space was as flat and dull as a parking lot. Nothing grew within its boundaries; Shane had seen more plant life in Death Valley.

"The dead zone," she gasped. Crouching at the edge of the circle, she grabbed a handful of the powdery gray ground and let it slip between her fingers; it coated her hand with a dry, chalky substance. Shuddering, she dug deeper, scooping up fistfuls of fine gray material. She continued digging, desperate to find a layer of undrained soil beneath the dead earth.

"Shane, stop," Donnie warned, placing a concerned hand on her back. "Your clothes are getting filthy." But Shane couldn't stop. She hadn't found the end of it yet; she was elbow deep and still pulling up chunks of gray. "How far does it go?" Donnie asked.

"At least four meters. I've never successfully reached the lower boundary."

In terms of surface area, the dead zone was giant, especially compared to the circles behind the abandoned house. But clearly, its true size was hidden; it was three-dimensional, extending into the earth.

Shane was the child of farmers, and knew the value of soil. Without soil, no crops could spread their roots and flourish. And soil — the soil of prairies and forests, on mountains and in valleys — accumulated slowly . . . achingly slowly. Soil formed through the gradual breakdown of rocks, and the life and death of lifeforms as small as microbes, and as large as redwoods.

The mimic ring had drained eons of history from the ground. And for what? Where had it sent Xander? The dead circle was so large, Shane understood why most people believed he'd zipped to a different planet. Damn. If mimics spread out of control, consuming the Earth circle by circle, they would all need to find a different planet. Not even worms lived in the gray remnants.

"Fifty years," she whispered, "it's been like this? Nothing's grown?"

Dr. Richards nodded solemnly.

"You're right," she said, shaking the powder off her hands. "We have to destroy the sample."

"What about —" Donnie started to protest.

"We can find our family another way," Shane said firmly, her voice thick with emotion. "If this . . . this extradimensional blight gets out of hand . . ."

"What will happen?"

Shane stood. "It's the death of us all."

∽ FIFTEEN ∽

During the return to C & C, Dr. Richards raced down the trail, his thin arms swinging hurriedly. "I want to show you a video now," he called back to Shane and Donnie. "In just a few minutes, it elucidates the vexing nature of mimics."

"We have time," Shame said. She suspected that they'd find Grandpa Louis waiting in the parking lot or store, but if he hadn't arrived, she was eager to hang around C & C a little longer. The pictures were necessary for their calculations, and Shane wanted to know that her grandfather was safe

Anything could happen on the road. There were stories of highways that appeared and vanished like mirages; they took you nowhere, forever. And what about the convoys of vampire truckers who drove big rigs through the night? Sometimes, they rode too long, worked too hard, and succumbed to bloodlust at sixty miles per hour. Then there were the monsters without names, 'cause nobody had survived to name 'em.

"Is the video about another ring accident?" Donnie wondered. She took Shane by the elbow, and, together, they jogged to catch up with Dr. Richards.

"Ring?" Ahead, he chuckle-snorted. "Yes, actually. But not the kind you're thinking of."

The girls exchanged a puzzled glance, and Shane replied, "Well, OK then. What kind?"

"The ring of a bell?" Donnie guessed. "Ring around the rosie?"

Dr. Richards held up his right hand and pointed to a bulky silver ring on his pointer finger; it had a vivid purple stone clasped within a dragon's talon. In unison, both girls said, "Oooooh."

"Jewelry," he confirmed.

When they reached the end of the trail, Dr. Richards pointed to a metal door at the back end of the strip mall. It didn't lead into C & C, as far as Shane could tell. "This is where I host movie nights," he explained, while fishing his jingling key ring from his pocket. "It's the best theater in Tanner." He made a beeline for the door and turned a heavy key in the lock, which clicked as the deadbolt slid to one side.

"The town must be grateful," Donnie earnestly said.

"It's how I make a living. Movie nights are the money-makers, while comics are just for fun." He pushed the door open with his shoulder, and sunlight spilled into the "theater," a single, cluttered room. Within, three rows of assorted metal, wooden, and plastic chairs faced a blank white wall, and beside the door was an eight millimeter projector on a metal stand. With a flip of a switch, Dr. Richards turned on the white fluorescent ceiling lights, two rows of long, bright tubes. The side walls were papered with framed, hand-painted movie posters, some with signatures. Cowboys sat upon horses; scaley monsters roared at screaming crowds; kung fu masters battled on cobblestone streets; green women posed alongside silver robots with red lightbulb eyes and pinchers for arms. There was even a poster of a glamorous man and woman kissing in front of the Eiffel Tower. To the right, a line of waist-high, pea-green metal cabinets were marked with handwritten labels, marker on yellow electrical tape. *Action, Science Fiction, Comedy, Thriller, Drama, Mystery/Noir, Unclassified.*

"Take a seat," Dr. Richards suggested. "The blue chairs are the comfiest. Best view, too. I reserve them for VIPs." He kneeled in front of the ACTION section, grabbed the cabinet by its frame, and pulled it away from the wall. The metal legs compressed lines into the thick red carpet.

"Need help with that?" Shane volunteered.

"No, thank you. It's not heavy. Just unwieldy." Once he'd moved the cabinet a few inches, Dr. Richards folded himself over the top and fished around the gap between the wall and the metal backing.

Momentarily, he said, "Aha!" then held up a key.

"I trust you," he explained, "as well as I trust any friendly acquaintance. That is to say: not fully. When I hide this key again, it will be in another location."

"Professor, we aren't thieves," Donnie replied, sounding more peeved than offended. "But for your added peace of mind, if I was a thief, I wouldn't steal from a man who helped my family."

"Me, either," Shane agreed.

"Consider my mind at peace. Sit tight." Clutching the secret key, the man headed out the door.

"Wait!" Shane called, twisting in her seat.

"Yes?" Dr. Richards paused in the doorway, dramatically backlit by the sun.

"Look for a Harley motorcycle, will you? My grandpa rides one. By now, he's gotta be in Tanner."

"Certainly." Dr. Richards tapped his forehead twice, then left with an energetic whirl.

"The forest's thick in these parts," Donnie observed. As she spoke, she scooted her chair close, closing the two-inch distance between them; she smelled like hairspray, apples, and sweat, and there was a smudge of gray powder on her cheek. Instinctually, Shane pulled a folded handkerchief from her pocket and asked, "Mind if I wipe your face? There's dead zone powder onnit."

"Gross. Yeah, please get it off. What if this shit's toxic?"

"Don't stress. The people in this town live next to it. They aren't sick."

"Yet," Donnie stressed, and Shane had to admit that she had a point. Still, there'd been decades to analyze the gray dust, and Dr. Richards was a local expert. Surely, he'd know whether the chemical components were dangerous.

As she dabbed Donnie's cheek, transferring the gray stain from her freckled skin to the cotton square, Shane made a mental note to ask the man, anyway.

A few minutes later, the door clicked open, and Mrs. Park led Marcos into the movie room. "Grandpa?" Shane wondered, trailing off when she didn't see him.

"Not here yet," confirmed Dr. Richards, who carried a disk-shaped, gray film reel case behind them. Behind him, Nellie's shimmer walked through the closing door and then flopped on the floor against Shane's feet; she heard a whoosh of ghost breath, a gentle sigh of contentment. Fortunately, Dr. Richards was busy feeding eight millimeter film into the projector; Shane wasn't sure how he'd react to Nellie. With suspicion? Fascination? The delight of a comic book fan?

"We left a note on the door," Mrs. Park said, "in case your grandfather rolls into town." Judging by her pinched expression, she doubted that he would.

"Uh huh," Marcos agreed. He sat on the wooden chair in front of Shane, with Hal on his lap.

"In any case," said Dr. Richards, "this won't take long." With that, he turned off the overhead fluorescents and flipped a switch on the projector. A large square of light flashed onto the blank wall. Another switch sent the machine's wheels turning, and, frame by frame, the celluloid film unspooled and ran in front of the intense beam of light, projecting a moving picture in front of them.

A middle-aged man in slacks and a polo shirt crouched beside a granite rock, which was approximately one foot wide and six inches tall, lumpy and completely unremarkable. The setting was a yard of thick, well-trimmed grass. Boxy hedge-rows grew in the background, and wispy clouds drifted through the blue sky. The man poked the rock with a sharp pencil. Nothing happened. Then, he held up a black velvet ring box, flipped it open, and showed the contents to the camera.

"Looks familiar," Donnie muttered to herself and possibly Shane. "Where've I seen that before?"

Inside the box was a gold band with three teardrop-cut stones. While the first two were glistening, pine-green emeralds, the third stone was a cloudy white, the color of quartz or frosted glass. Carefully, the man removed the ring and placed it on the gray rock. Then, he walked out of shot, and a moment later, the camera moved closer to the rock and ring, until they encompassed the entire shot. At first, nothing much happened. A red ant crawled up a blade of grass.

After a couple minutes of riveting ant business, Shane noticed a subtle change in the third stone. Its color was darkening from white to gray, the same hue as the granite rock.

"See?" asked Dr. Richards.

"Like a chameleon," Shane observed.

"Close. A chameleon merely changes color." He paused for a second. "It does not also change substance."

Suddenly, the gray rock crumbled into fine powder, which billowed out and momentarily clouded the view. When the haze cleared, the ring was cushioned in a pile of dust. Its first two stones were still emeralds, but its third stone was granite.

At that, the clip ended.

"Boise, Idaho, nine years ago," Dr. Richards explained, as he expertly rewound the tape. "You just witnessed rare home video of the Alchemy Ring, or so it's called."

"Did the rock disintegrate into this?" Shane asked, holding up the gray-streaked handkerchief. "Dead zone material?"

"Right on, Bug Girl. You got it."

"So?" exclaimed Mrs. Park, and she helplessly threw up her hands. "Sir, how is this relevant?"

"You just witnessed a mimic, Madam." Dr. Richards paced in front of the blank wall, a performer in the projector's spotlight. "No different than the mushrooms that stole away your grandson."

"The Alchemy Ring is a mimic?" Donnie clarified.

"Specifically the third gemstone, the one that changed from white to gray."

"OK, I got ya," Shane said. "The stone's got a magic power. It can transform into different rocks, but destroys them in the process."

"Correct!" He tapped his temple. "If you're interested, the man in the home video is Christopher Wiley, and he inherited the Alchemy Ring from his great-grandmother, once a vaudeville dancer in France. The ring was originally a gift from the Faery King's third jester, who enjoyed watching performances on Earth. Great-grandma Wiley wore the ring for seventy-five years, and when she died, Christopher had it appraised for auction by an expert jeweler at Southernbee's."

Although Shane didn't know much about fancy jewelry, Southernbee's had a reputation as a big-time dealer of antique magical and otherworldly artifacts. Every few years, the papers reported on an attempted theft or record-breaking sale in their London offices.

"The jeweler suggested that a ring with three emeralds mined from the fae realm would receive a sum of ten grand, but on the day of the sale, before any bid could be placed, the auctioneer observed that the third stone had turned to red instead of green, and the Heart Ruby, a 200-year-old brooch that had been stored alongside the ring, was missing. In its place: a pile of gray dust. The Alchemy Ring was returned, an investigation was launched, and just two days after Christopher filmed his little backyard experiment, the US Bureau of the Unknown confiscated the heirloom for additional study, after which the fae demanded its return, claiming that they hadn't known about its special properties before it was given away as a gift. All this is public knowledge. What we do not know — what inspired my interest — is the nature of the gemstone."

"Dude!" Donnie interrupted. "I do recognize that ring! There's a movie about it, right?"

"Are you referring to Stephen Loch's *The Vampire Stone*?"

"Yeah, that one. Only, instead of turning rocks into dust, it drained the blood from everyone who wore it. The stones kept getting redder. So . . . it's really based on a true story?"

"Loosely," Dr. Richards said. "As far as I know, the Alchemy Ring never hurt any living person, and is inert when it's worn on a finger. That's why its special properties on Earth were inactive for decades."

"Is the mimic stone the same species as the mimic mushroom?" Donnie asked.

"It's widely believed that all mimics are indeed the same entity, yes. One that permanently transforms into the first object it encounters. So what can the Alchemy Ring teach us about the mimic mushrooms?"

For a moment, everyone lapsed into a thoughtful silence. Then, Shane suggested, "They're hard to identify until they start turning stuff to ash?"

"Yes! And . . . their magic that turns objects to ash is unique to our dimension. It does not demonstrate itself in the Greatest Kingdoms, so the fae cannot even study it on their home turf! That lack of knowledge is dangerous." He spread his arms for emphasis. "There will always be more to learn. *Always.* Existence is an endless puzzle."

Suddenly, from outside, an engine rumbled. *Vrm, vrm.* Although the walls muffled its sound, Shane had been alert. With a shout of "Grandpa!" she pushed back her chair and charged toward the door. In fifteen seconds flat, she had sprinted around the long building and stopped outside of the C & C storefront, which overlooked the almost-empty parking lot.

"Is it him?" called Donnie excitedly, who'd followed with the others.

Shane's shoulders fell. The only vehicle in sight was a golden Monte Carlo with a thunderous muffler. "No."

He'd make it before morning. Shane refused to expect the worst.

However, as always, she'd prepare for it.

And yet, without pictures, what could they do?

Slowly, Shane pulled a sheet of paper out of her pocket. "Dr. Richards," she asked, glancing at the former professor who was carrying the eight millimeter tin under his arm, "could you double-check these notes? Make sure I copied your equations correctly?"

"Will do," he agreed.

Worst-case scenario, they'd do the math themselves when they got home. And as worst cases went, that wasn't so bad.

⚍ SIXTEEN ⚎

There was just one inn in Tanner, a half-ring of log cabins surrounding a butterfly garden. Each single-room cabin was equipped with a crusty outdoor grill and a magnificent view through the back window of the forested mountains. According to the chatterbox attendant who took their names and gave them their keys, most people who rented the cabins were tourists, families from Denver and beyond who wanted a camping-lite experience. They'd get the fresh air and birdsong of nature, without the vulnerability of a night outside. In tents, there'd be nothing but flimsy canvas between them and the dark.

Shane mainly liked the cabins because they were tucked alongside the main road in and out of Tanner. If her grandfather drove past, she'd hear him; that motorcycle's constant *vrm*ing and chugging would cut through the sounds of crickets and frogs like cymbals at choir practice. After finishing their business at Skylight C & C, Shane, Donnie, Marcos, Nellie, and Mrs. Park had raced to the cabins. They'd parked, checked in, unloaded essential luggage, and then Shane had lugged a picnic blanket and three PB&J sandwiches to the grass alongside the butterfly garden, sitting where she could watch the road. A few minutes later, Donnie shuffled to the garden, carrying a heavy cardboard box full of comic books and magazines, "research material" she'd collected from Dr. Richards's shop. She'd borrowed every issue of *Twilight Realm Digest, Weirdest Tales, Chillers: Real Stories,* and *Body Horror, Beasts, and Nightmares* that featured creatures of the water. Dr. Richards had also loaned her a vintage copy of *Monsters of America*, first printed in 1843, subsequently reprinted in 1914. It contained over five hundred illustrated descriptions by a man named

James Keeley, a gold prospector and wildlife artist who'd documented all the monsters he'd encountered during multiple trips between the east and west coasts.

"This is more nonfiction than the comics," Dr. Richards had explained. "Just take it with a grain of salt. The man probably saw a couple monsters on the Oregon Trail, but most of the illustrations are based on secondhand information. He spoke with a lot of Indians and French trappers. Collected their stories, passed 'em off as his own. Plus, by now, half the monsters are likely extinct or nearly gone."

Currently, the encyclopedia was balanced on top of the stack; Donnie rested her chin on its thick, leather cover as she wobbled next to Shane.

"Time to solve a mystery," she declared. "What is Shell Girl? She must be rare. I've never seen anything like her before, and I watch a lot of movies." With a grunt, Donnie lowered the box between them. "Your brother's inside the cabin, playing robots with my grandma. Ghost dog's with 'em, too."

"Keeping watch," Shane supposed. She drummed her fingers against her knee and side-eyed the empty road. Where *was* he?

"So . . ." Donnie drawled.

"Uh huh?" Shane prompted when Donnie didn't finish her thought, no doubt distracted by the cell-shaded art.

"What do you think it's like in the future?"

"Good question." Shane searched the garden for signs of movement, but the daytime pollinators were already resting. With a vivid thought, she woke the ghost of a monarch butterfly; it fluttered around a head of violet aster, before returning to the world Below. "I don't know. Guess that's the allure of science fiction."

With a pang of heartache, Shane imagined her ideal future: she was in la rancheria de los Lipanes again, pushing Marcos on the swing behind their house. Lorenza watched on, smiling, surrounded by dogs. Her father was there, too. And her grandparents.

It was a future that could have been, but would never be.

"Maybe Xander clears his name," Donnie speculated. "In the future."

"Hope so." Shane called another butterfly, but it only lingered a second. Perhaps they didn't like the deepening twilight. Did that mean their home Below was bright? Was it always? She hoped so. Butterflies deserved sunlight.

Lorenza had once shared, "The first time I went on a date, I summoned ghosts. Now, they were the prettiest ghosts I knew: butterflies. But still ghosts. It's a miracle that your pa asked me on a second date."

"I'd loved you before," he chimed in, "and that only made me love you more."

Such a distant memory.

"Sometimes," Shane whispered, because she could barely stand to speak the thought aloud, "I'm afraid we won't be there."

"Huh?"

"In the future," she clarified. "The twenty-first century."

"Stop that." Donnie dropped the comic and clasped Shane's face between her rough hands. She leaned adamantly close. "In the year 2030, we'll be side-by-side in a pair of rocket-powered rocking chairs,

384

watching the cars fly by. Our brothers will have wrinkles. Can you imagine?"

With a laugh, Shane brushed Donnie's hands aside. "Unfortunately, yeah," she snorted. "Thanks for that image, but . . ." A mosquito bobbed around them, swooping near and far, its distance decreasing as its confidence increased. Shane tucked her overalls into her boots, giving the bloodsucker less access to her skin. "That's not what I meant."

"What, then?"

With a shrug, she tried to explain, "By 'we,' I was referring to . . . my family. My people."

"Apaches?"

"The light gray people," she softly clarified. "Lipan."

"That's grim."

"Sometimes," Shane continued, "it feels like there's an emptiness inside my heart that keeps getting bigger. Every loss chips away at its walls. And I'm scared, Donnie. Will the world hollow me out? Will I be myself in fifty years, or just a shell? Will I be alone?" The mosquito landed on her wrist, and Shane felt a surge of fury, shocking in its suddenness and intensity. She'd never hated a bug before. They were innocent and blameless . . . so why did it feel like the mosquito was part of a cosmic insult, yet another force of a world that wanted to bleed her dry?

"Hey, buzz off," Donnie muttered, swatting the mosquito away. Then, she sighed deep. "I have a secret. Wasn't going to say anything, 'cause it's embarrassing, and maybe a little sad, but you ought to know."

"Yeah?"

"Did Grandma Park ever show you a picture of my parents?"

Shane shook her head: *No.*

"Here, take a look." Donnie pulled a silver, heart-shaped locket from under her yellow T-shirt. Barely one inch wide, it dangled around her neck on a fine linked chain. She opened the locket, which unfolded like a clamshell, revealing two portraits, each the size of a driver's license photograph. The picture on the left depicted a young white man with curly brown hair and a calm, reserved smile. Based on his resemblance to Mr. and Mrs. Park, Shane easily ID'd him as their son: Donnie's father.

So the brown woman on the right, whose skin was the same shade as Lorenza's skin, must be Donnie's mother. Indeed, the woman and Donnie had similar round noses and large brown eyes. However, something else caught Shane's attention.

"Is that a T-necklace?" she gasped, leaning closer to better observe the photo's details. Donnie's mother wore a distinctive piece of jewelry: a loom-beaded strap around her neck, with a second, wider beaded strap hanging down over her chest. Unfolded, the necklace would resemble the letter *T*.

"I have one like that!" Shane exclaimed. "Wait, is your mom . . . are you . . . ?"

Donnie shrugged. "Growing up, Mom was different from the other parents in our neighborhood. She told me different stories and cooked us different types of supper. Don't think she wanted to be different, though. When I was a girl, maybe six or seven, the kid next door called her a savage witch. I punched him in the chin, so he threw me down and knocked out two of my teeth. Luckily, they were baby teeth, so I had spares." She touched her cheek. "Later, I asked Mom, 'What are you?'"

"How'd she answer?"

"'Nothing, anymore.' That's what she said. So I kept asking. 'What *were* you?' I was such a brat. The questions hurt her, but I just couldn't stop. I could never let stuff go. How'd she put up with me?"

"That's a mother's love," Shane said, smiling gently.

"Guess so. I'll never have the patience for mothering." Donnie returned the smile, but it was a bitter expression, like a chuckle before the gallows. "After a couple days, Mom finally cracked. 'We're descended from naked Apaches,' she said."

"Naked? Why'd she use that word?"

"No clue. It was a random Spanish term that means 'no clothes,' or something. I had to look it up in a dictionary."

"Poca ropa?" Shane guessed. A second mosquito landed on her ear, but she was too excited now to care.

"Yeah, sounds right. Apaches de poca ropa."

"No freaking way!" Shane covered her mouth in shock. "Poca Ropa! The Little Breechclout band. They're Lipan!"

"Wait. Aren't you Lipan?"

"We both are! I can't believe it!" What were the chances? Even though Donnie and Shane both lived in Texas, their traditional homeland, the state's Lipan population was miniscule compared to the whole. "Wait, how did your grandparents learn about our rescue operation?" she asked joyfully.

"A friend of my grandma — not the one you met, the other one — knew her number."

"So the connection is through your maternal side," Shane said. "Yes! That checks out. Ma's well-respected among the Apaches in Texas."

Slowly, Donnie looked down at her locket, her eyes settling on the precious little faces. "She was buried in that necklace. It was her favorite."

"I can teach you how to make your own," Shane offered. "All you need's seed beads, wax, a long needle and thread, and a beading loom, which is easy to make with three pieces of wood and a couple of combs." Lorenza had taught her how to bead, while Shane's father taught her how to craft the loom.

"Really? That'd be excellent," Donnie thanked her, while carefully snapping the locket shut and tucking it back under her T-shirt. "You're something special, you —"

Her compliment was interrupted by distant, sputtering thunder.

"Is that your Grandpa?" Donnie asked, straightening alertly.

"Sounds like his Harley." Shane hopped upright. "Wait here, OK?" She sprinted toward the road. The motorcycle was travelling quickly — at least sixty miles per hour by her guess, based on the sound of its engine, which was so loud, a flock of grackles that'd been roosting on an elm tree scattered into the sky. As Shane ran up the dirt road connecting the ring of cabins to the throughway, she waved her hands and shouted, "Hey, hey!" There was a chance that the motorcycle belonged to a random traveler, and Shane was about to flag down a complete stranger, but she'd rather embarrass herself a thousand times than waste a single minute. And, in any case, she'd heard her grandfather's motorcycle often enough to recognize its sonic fingerprint, and would be surprised if the person zooming closer, seconds away from reaching the turn-in to Tanner Cabins: Bed and Breakfast, was anyone but —

"Grandpa Louis!" Shane shouted, just a few steps away from the street. "Grandpa, stop!" It *was* him! He wore his trusty helmet, with a bandana around his neck and his worn leather jacket, dulled by dust from the road. Behind him, in the motorcycle's passenger seat, was an orange bag Shane had never seen before; it was secured with a bungy cord.

For a few milliseconds, Shane's synapses fired with anxiety, convinced that he'd speed past without noticing her. But then, Grandpa Louis turned his head and they made eye contact; he excitedly mouthed her name — *Shane!* — or maybe spoke it aloud, his voice smothered by the roaring engine.

Up the road, Grandpa Louis did a sharp U-turn. So sharp, in fact, that the motorcycle's spinning back wheel painted a curved black streak across the asphalt. Instead of taking the turn-off to Tanner Cabins, he parked along the main road and deployed the kickstand. Did he have somewhere else to be?

"You beat me here!" Grandpa Louis called, while removing his helmet. His gray-black hair was slick and pressed flat. "Did Missus Park burn rubber or what?"

"No, she drove the speed limit." Shane rushed forward and threw her arms around her grandfather, who smelled like motor oil. He hugged her tightly in return. "We were worried," she explained, her voice muffled against his shoulder. "What happened? Is everything OK? It didn't seem possible for a station wagon to beat your Harley, unless there was an accident or . . ." She stepped back to look at him, his easy grin and cowboy boots, to remind herself that he'd made it to Tanner, photos in hand. There'd been no crash along the road. ". . . Or you got pulled over, and sent to prison again."

"Again?" He chuckled mirthlessly. "Kid, they haven't trapped me there yet. Come on. Let's find the comic book store. You can carry this in your lap." He started unfastening the neon-orange bag from the back seat.

"No, wait. We already visited C and C. It's been closed for hours. Dr. Richards went home to study Donnie's soil samples." She crossed her arms, frowning now. It was sometimes hard to tell when Grandpa Louis was joking. "You have been to prison, though, right?"

He stopped messing with the bag and propped the motorcycle on its kickstand. "You get put in the drunk tank once . . . no. No, mija, I've been to jail, not prison. One time. OK, three times."

"Wait, seriously?" People didn't stay locked up in the "drunk tank" for years. Her shock must have been visible, because Grandpa Louis stopped smiling.

"What?"

"But Mom always said you were in prison during the flood. That's why you didn't . . ."

And then she remembered his story about the alligators. How he'd helped people deal with the animals, after they'd washed into a residential neighborhood. Why had emergency services been over-whelmed? Why had there been flooding?

"Where were you after Hurricane Alda?" she asked.

"What's with the third degree, Shane? That happened years ago. I can barely remember last week."

"Maybe removing alligators from southern towns?"

"Yeah. Maybe." He looked up. "You kids eaten yet? I saw a burger place —"

In another circumstance, she might have let him change the subject. But not today. "If you never went to prison, Grandpa, then why'd you disappear?"

He gritted his teeth. "When?"

"When I was a child."

"Shane. Your parents housed me when I needed help, but it was never supposed to be a permanent living-dealie. I was sleeping in the laundry room."

"But you never visited after. Not even —"

"I don't get your disappointment here." His eyes hardened. "Do you wish I'd been locked up?"

"No!" She stepped back, stumbling over a root but catching her balance in the nick of time. "Just —"

"Did your momma tell Marcos that I've done time? Who else believes that fantasy?"

"Are you . . ." She put a hand against her forehead. "Are you acting like a victim right now?"

"My reputation's affected here, Shane. Years in prison? That's a major assumption."

"Why would she question it? Why would any of us?"

"Whuh —"

"It made sense when we thought people were keeping you from us. Forcibly! But no. You were *free*, which means you chose to disappear, Grandpa. We needed you. When the flood happened —"

He raised his voice a tick, matching Shane's volume. "By the time I learned about Hurricane Alda, it was too late, Shane. I was in Florida when it struck."

"Too late? The flood was only the beginning!" She swiped a hand across her cheek, swiftly brushing away a tear. "Grandpa, it's everything that came after. You didn't miss your only chance to help us. There were months of chances. We might still have a home . . . Pa might still be alive . . ."

"Hey! Don't put that badness on me! What am I, a miracle worker?"

"You could've been there to fight with us! For us!"

"That's what I'm doing now!" He spread his arms, exasperated. "You think I want to play babysitter? I've put my life on hold! I'm trying my best!"

Was he? Was that why he'd arrived hours late, with no good explanation?

"Great! Thanks for that! Xastéyó! But your betrayal's not a debt that can be paid off with good deeds." Shane's heart was beating so quickly now, she felt like she'd sprinted a mile.

"Betrayal?"

"Yes!" She was unable to meet his eyes, afraid of what they'd reveal. "All this time . . . we thought . . ."

"Well, you thought wrong. I was a self-centered piece of shit. I caused the whole state to flood. I sent the plagues. I scammed your mother, stole her land. I'm a killer. Is that what you need to hear?"

"I needed to hear the truth, years ago!"

"You could've asked! You know how to talk."

"So do you!" Her eyes whipped up, fiercely. "So why haven't you apologized? Why haven't you explained yourself? Is it because every time you abandon us, you know our assumptions will be kinder than the truth?"

"Unbelievable." He shook his head firmly. "Unbelievable." Then, Grandpa Louis swung a leg over the motorcycle, kicking up the kickstand, revving the engine awake. "I don't have anything to feel guilty about, Shane."

"You're leaving us again?"

"I'm buying a damn burger. Is that allowed?"

"Just give me the pictures!" she shouted.

"You'll get them when I return from supper."

"No!" Did he appreciate the importance of haste during rescues? Obviously not; he'd arrived at Tanner over thirteen hours behind schedule. "We must —"

Her protests were smothered under the whip-crack rumble of the Harley. The commotion seemed intentional, as if Grandpa Louis was sticking his fingers in his ears and shouting "La, la, la! I can't hear you!" His immaturity might have been amusing in less urgent circumstances, but Shane's mother — his daughter — was missing, and now he wanted to delay their search for a petty tantrum. Perhaps he mistakenly believed that they couldn't analyze the photos without Dr. Richards.

"We have an equation!" Shane tried to explain, breathless from shouting. "If you give us the photos . . . Grandpa, wait!"

He was turning on to the road, the bike's rear wheels kicking dirt into the air. A spray of grit flew against Shane's face, landing in her open mouth and stinging her eyes. Gagging, Shane spat onto the ground and then, through wet, irritated eyes, watched Grandpa Louis attempt to leave. Her pulse drummed in her ears.

Tick, tick, tick.

"Don't you dare!" With her arm outstretched, her hand grasping, Shane sprinted after Grandpa Louis. Before he could accelerate beyond reach, she lunged and grabbed the back of his motorcycle. Shane hunched over the back seat, clinging to the vehicle's frame, her shoes dragging across the rough concrete road. Flecks of white rubber scraped off the treads.

"Are you out of your senses?" Grandpa Louis shouted, coming to an abrupt stop, then switching off the engine. "You could have been hurt! Mangled!"

"We need those photos, Grandpa!"

"Take them!" He reached inside his jacket and shoved the Polaroid-filled envelope into her grasp. "Happy now?"

"Yes." She snatched the envelope away and strode across the street. "Enjoy your dinner," she called back. But when Grandpa Louis didn't immediately drive away, Shane paused, turning.

"Why did it take so long for you to reach Tanner?"

He said nothing; just stared at her like she'd grown a pair of antlers; like he didn't recognize her anymore.

"Did you stop for that orange bag?" Despite everything she'd learned about her grandfather that evening, everything that was surging inside of her, Shane couldn't help the prickle of hope. "What's in it?" Perhaps he'd found something useful — like an enchanted divining rod that could lead them to Lorenza or a compass pointing to your greatest wish. Although most known supernatural artifacts were in the care of governmental organizations, or shady private collections, there were stories about people who found rare treasures in thrift stores and pawn shops.

If Grandpa Louis had been a travelling salesman, maybe he'd have connections in the weird underground market.

Say I'm right, she willed him. If he'd found a shortcut to Lorenza, Shane would forgive everything. She'd even apologize!

"My clothes," he grumbled. "I replaced my old bag at a gas station in Laredo."

"So why are you a day late?"

He couldn't pretend not to hear her this time. "Overslept. The motel forgot my wake-up call." Shane didn't say anything in reply; she just stared. "What? I'm old and tired. Tell me how great you feel in forty years." Old and tired? Seriously? The man who could run through the forest with knives in his boots? Only time Grandpa Louis seemed tired before was after he drank too much at the family barbeques. Was that it?

"The motel made a mistake? Not you?"

"Yes." The response was terse, his eyes sharp with indignation. It didn't sound like a fib, but with Grandpa Louis, that didn't mean anything. The two of them were very different. Shane understood that now.

Nodding, numbly, Shane turned around and headed for the cabins. When she was halfway to the butterfly gardens, she heard the motorcycle rumble back to life. The engine's roar softened with distance, then everything went silent.

"Sweet, you got the photos!" Donnie exclaimed as Shane returned to sit beside her. "Where's your grandpa?"

"Wherever he wants to be, I guess."

"Huh? Is . . . he returning tonight?"

Shane doubted that anyone knew the answer to that question. "Return or not, it doesn't matter. We don't need him."

To her credit, though Donnie raised a puzzled eyebrow, she didn't press the issue.

"C'mon," Shane encouraged. "Let's go inside and run the numbers."

"Go through the values again," Amelia patiently instructed. It was half past nine, and Shane and Donnie sat cross-legged on the floor of Cabin #2, overlooking an organized chaos of photos, strings, and number-packed sheets of paper. They'd done the calculations several times themselves already, but the results were so unusual, Shane had ended up calling Amelia. Her friend always aced math tests; in fact, Amelia earned extra cash during finals by tutoring underclassmen in algebra, calculus, and trigonometry.

"The farthest distance between two points on Earth is less than 13,000 miles, if you have to travel over the planet's surface. Ring magic — according to Dr. Richards — isn't dependent on surface travel."

"You mean it takes the shortest path between two points, even if that path goes through the Earth?" Amelia clarified, using her "tutor giving a lecture" voice, which was crisp and decisive.

"Yes, that's right."

"So by that logic, and assuming the Earth is perfectly spherical with a radius of 3,959 miles — which is a simplification, since it's an ellipsoid, and —"

"But for our purposes," Shane gently interrupted, "the simplification is fine."

"Uh huh. Anyway, the farthest distance between two points on earth is about 8,000 miles. However, according to the equation, Bobby and Lorenza both traveled much farther than that. Much, much farther, even going by the lowest estimate." Because the Polaroids had been shot at slight angles, they'd included standard deviations to account for the imprecise measurements. "I suppose the topsoil values could negate our results." If the big circles were in a less fertile area than the little circles, the comparisons were useless.

"Doesn't seem likely," Shane said, acknowledging something they'd suspected — and dreaded — for days.

"Then something else might be wrong. A variable we haven't accounted for."

"Or, we could be right . . ." Shane allowed herself to acknowledge. She willed her voice to remain steady, channeling a doctor at a patient's bedside, packaging frightening news in her calm, compassionate bedside manner. "They both traveled beyond Earth." Looking down at the scattered Polaroids, Shane realized that those circles of ash might have contained Lorenza and Bobby's last footprints on their planet, and her voice cracked. "To another time. Or the world Below."

"Where the dead belong," Donnie clarified, and although she also spoke quietly, her voice was taut with hatred. "Essentially, I killed Bobby." Her eyes glinted wetly. "My brother. I . . ." Abruptly, Donnie jumped to her feet and stalked to the back window. Flipping aside its blue cotton curtain, she pressed her forehead against the glass to stare at the darkness outside.

"That's not true! It was a freak accident, and" — Shane tried to approach Donnie, to comfort her friend, but the phone line only stretched halfway up the room — "I think they can survive Below."

"For how long?" Donnie softly wondered. It was the question that had been haunting them since Bobby and Lorenza disappeared.

From the phone receiver, Amelia's voice shouted, "Forever! Assume forever!"

"We don't give up," Shane agreed. "This is a good step, Donnie. We know where he is now. I'm confident." She closed her eyes, willing herself to recall the old stories of humans who'd crossed the boundary between Earth and Below. If the stories existed, others had to know them too. That was the purpose of stories: to be shared and remembered. To draw wisdom from them. Maybe, if Shane cold-called every number in Lorenza's ancient contact book, she'd find the answer. It would be time-consuming and frustrating; by now, most of the numbers would be useless, her people continuously scattered by the flood's ripples, washing into any hospitable town or city they could afford.

"Wait." Shane lowered the heavy brown phone receiver. "Donnie, are both your maternal grandparents still around?"

"Grandpa passed, heart attack before I was born." Still gazing into the shadowy woods, she added, "Grandma's in a care home. She doesn't know about Bobby yet. I told her we're looking for your mom and a little kid now."

"What's her phone number?"

"I can get it." A pause, then: "We aren't close, though. After Mom and Dad died, she tried to be more, uh, present, but . . . whatever. That stuff doesn't matter. It's complicated family shit."

"Trust me, I get it. Does she ever tell you stories?"

"Not really, but I never asked for them."
Donnie's tone lightened. "You think
Grandma knows how to get Below?"

"It's possible. We should call her first
thing in the morning and check. Might
save a lot of time. We —"

"Hey!" Donnie interrupted, squishing
her nose against the windowpane. "Hey,
why is Marcos outside? Dude, he has a
knife!"

"He what?"

Dropping the phone, Shane bolted to
the window. Sure enough, Marcos stood
in the grassy yard between the cabins and
the forest. Lit by the silvery moon, he
carried the pink shell in one hand, and a
hunting knife — where the heck had that
come from? — in the other hand. Lumi-
nescent Nellie shimmered at his feet.

"Marcos!" Shane hollered, and he
jumped, looking over his pajama-clad
shoulder.

That's when Shane noticed the stone
well: positioned beside a rusty water pump,
it was tucked alongside the forest's edge.
Marcos had been staring at it.

"Stay where you are!" she commanded
through the glass. Then, instead of

wasting time by running to the front door and around the cabin, Shane slid open the window, kicked out its bug screen, and vaulted through the compact square opening, somersaulting into a run.

Behind her, Donnie awkwardly followed, cursing when she landed shoulder-first on the ground. By that time, Shane had reached Marcos. "What are you doing?" she asked, reaching for the knife.

"The Shell Girl says she can find Mom!"

"I told you not to trust Shell Girl!"

"I don't!" He let Shane disarm him, but pulled away when she tried to hold his hand. "I was going to find you before doing anything."

"Marcos, it looks like you were about to jump in a well."

"Just staring at it! That's where she is."

"What if she'd grabbed you?" Shane knelt in front of her brother. "What if she'd climbed outside to hurt you? She almost drowned Donnie." Although the Shell Girl seemed confined to water, some creatures were amphibious, and others — rare, sacred dragons, for one — could live in water, on land, and in the sky. "If something bad happened to you, I'd never stop crying!"

With a soft "I'm sorry," Marcos threw his arms around Shane's shoulders and squeezed. "I'm sorry, I'm sorry."

"I'm sorry, too," Shane whispered. "I love you, she ké'se."

For a moment, she yearned for time to stop, freezing her arms around her family, protecting him forever.

"Shane," the shell gurgled from Marcos's other hand, interrupting the moment, "I'm just trying to help. It only takes a drop of blood."

"Is that so?" She took the shell from him and held it against her mouth. "Prove it. Where's Bobby?"

The Shell Girl didn't respond.

"You have Donnie's blood. If that's enough to track her family, too, where is her brother?"

"I . . ." The Shell Girl made a thoughtful clicking sound. "I don't actually know."

"So you can't tell."

"Maybe Bobby is dead?"

"Liar!" Donnie proclaimed, next to them now, wresting the shell away from Shane.

"I don't know what your goal is, creature, or even what you are," she yelled. "But you tried to involve Marcos in a blood ritual, so" — she spiked the shell against the ground; it rolled a couple feet, unbroken — "I'm revoking your shell privileges!"

"Don't do that!" Shell Girl cried; splashes now echoed off the well's narrow stone walls. "I'll stop bothering you! Just return my shell! It's rare!"

"So you can manipulate somebody else?" Donnie picked up the shell and punched it, wincing as her knuckles grazed off the smooth surface.

"Calm down," Shane cut in, adamantly taking Donnie by the arm. With a jerk of her head, Shane indicated the cabins. It was unsafe to provoke an unknown entity so close to its territory, and they stood less than a stone's throw from the well. "Marcos, Donnie, let's go inside."

As if picking up on Shane's fears, Donnie nodded quietly and started backing toward the cabin. Shane and Marcos held hands, with Nellie pacing between them and the well; the dog was agitated, alert.

"You won't actually destroy it, will you?" cried Shell Girl.

"No," Donnie hesitantly answered, almost questioned, and Shane nodded in encouragement. "I just lost my temper. Sorry."

"Promise?"

They were halfway to safety.

"Yeah."

Marcos stumbled over an uneven patch of ground, but Shane pulled him upright. It was difficult walking backward in the dark; could they turn around and run? Would that be risky, given all the unknowns about the creature in the well? Or was it riskier to move slowly?

"Then give it back," Shell Girl said, her tone low and gurgling. "Give it back."

"We will," Shane reassured her. "After I put Marcos to bed."

"Liar."

"I'm not —"

"You're lying," Shell Girl insisted. "You can't hide anything from me. I've been listening for days."

Nellie barked once: a warning. In her bones, Shane knew that the monster was coming. Forty feet away, the well was difficult to see, smudged into the shadows.

But she could hear the splashes and the scrape of hard scales against rock, getting closer by the second.

"Run!" she shouted. "Go through the window!"

With a startled shout, Donnie lifted Marcos over the windowsill and into the bright cabin. A pale face — pretty nose, glinting eyes behind a curtain of wet bangs — popped out of the well, followed by a long, twisting torso. From the shoulders up, the monster resembled a young woman, but the rest of her was shaped like a gigantic, scaled eel, wriggling and well-muscled, the color of iron. Shell Girl flopped onto the ground and then shot forward with snakelike speed, her mouth clicking open and shut, as if trying to eat the distance between her and Shane. Her flashing glassy teeth were long and thin, like icicles. Within a second, she passed through the barking Nellie, who darted side-to-side in confusion. Had he forgotten that he wasn't solid? Shane almost felt sorry for the little ghost.

"Hurry!" Donnie shouted, trying to pull her toward the window, but there wasn't enough time.

Yet as Shell Girl lunged forward, and she steeled herself for impact, Shane realized that the creature wasn't futilely biting the air; she was desperately gasping for breath.

That changed everything.

In a single, fluid movement, Shane pocketed the hunting knife and removed her denim jacket. Then, she sidestepped; Shell Girl collided with the building, her hands skittering against the wood. With a twist, Shane straddled the monster's back and pinned her, same way Grandpa Louis wrestled alligators, according to his tips.

"Calm down!" Shane shouted. Then, more softly, "Calm down."

"Give it back!" Shell Girl rasped. With a muffled curse in an inhuman language, she thrashed, and Shane struggled to keep her pinned; the monster's strength didn't seem to flag. If anything, it increased with her growing desperation. Nellie scampered in circles, barking, frantic. An attack dog might have bit the creature by her tail, but Nellie had always been too gentle for physical confrontations.

"Let me go," Shell Girl gasped. "I'll leave!"

Was that the truth, or a ruse? If Shane let go now, would the monster return another day? Would she hurt Marcos? Had that always been the plan?

"You nearly convinced my brother to cut himself with a dirty hunting knife!" she shouted, while keeping hold. "He's a child!"

"I'm sorry," Shell Girl wheezed. "So am I."

A child?

In shock, Shane leaned back. "You're . . . oh." With her bangs swept aside, Shell Girl obviously had a teenager's face. By human standards, she was fourteen, max.

"I'm . . . dying . . ."

"Hang on!" Quickly, Shane grabbed the gasping girl under the arms and pulled her toward the well, straining to move her considerable weight. "I'll get you to the water."

"Shell," she breathlessly insisted. "My shell."

"We can talk when you're safe." They were nearly there. "What were you thinking? Don't beach yourself for no reason!"

"Shell."

"Objects aren't worth your life! Even rare ones!"

Shane lowered her against the side of the well and then scrambled back, just in case the eel tail lashed out. It did not. Instead, with a final, powerful thrash, the monster flopped upward and over the stone lip. She dropped fully into the darkness, landing with a tremendous splash.

"I'll return it," Shane shouted, "but you seriously have to leave us alone. Deal?"

The cicadas sang, and the toads croaked. Then, a gurgling response echoed up the stone chamber. "Deal."

"Are you OK?" Donnie asked, jogging up to Shane and passing her the shell. "Righteous, dude. That was incredible! You wrangled a monster!"

"A juvenile monster," Shane corrected, while rubbing her eyes. "Who didn't want to hurt me, otherwise I'd probably be in rough shape."

"So what did she want?"

"Who knows?" With a shrug, Shane chucked the shell into the well. "Whatever the case, she won't be back."

~~ SEVENTEEN ~~

When Donnie called the nursing home long-distance that morning, she spoke to her maternal grandmother for much longer than planned. Fortunately, Mrs. Park had paid a hefty phone deposit. Although Shane was keenly aware of every passing minute, she didn't feel impatience. It was as if, at an instinctual level, she understood that every moment of the call — even the quiet lie, "Everything is fine. Just fine," and the promise, "I want to visit. Someday. Soon," — was an important step in Lorenza's rescue.

Idly, Shane wondered why Donnie hadn't spoken to her maternal grand-mother in years. Had there been a falling out? A horrible schism? Or was it by design? Donnie had been raised without knowledge of her mother's people. What deep pain would lead a parent to deprive their children of their history?

During the call, Shane sat beside the window, where she could feel the warmth of sunrise as she waited. It was difficult to follow the conversation. There were long stretches of silence, as if the Elder had a lot to say, or spoke very slowly. Considering that she was in poor health, Shane suspected the latter. Helpless to do anything but wait, Shane bounced her foot against the floor; she drummed her fingers on the windowsill; a parade of ghost ladybugs entered and exited the cabin.

She'd felt like this before. Anticipatory. Powerless. Dread and hope fused together, two sides of the same coin. And as an invisible ladybug tickled her cheek with its wax paper wings, Shane remembered the place without sunlight: the second-floor waiting room of St. Mary Hospital.

There had been another group in the waiting room, two middle-aged women — aunties, she thought — and a girl Shane's age. The strangers sat in a row across from

Shane and her mother, everyone avoiding eye contact. A white, round clock hung on the wall, and the magazines in the wire magazine rack had been defaced, somebody inking out all the eyes of the glossy cover models. The air smelled like disinfectant and cigarette smoke, and when one of the aunties lit a Marlboro and inhaled deep, the cherry burning red, Shane had thought of dragonfire.

It was midnight, and Shane decided that the girl's name could be Lucy — the same Lucy who'd carved her name into the gymnasium wall in the hurricane evacuation center. The white door in the corner of the room remained closed, although the occasional burst of nurse chatter seeped through, and every time it did, everybody in the waiting room sat a little straighter.

It was 1:00 a.m., and Lucy probably understood Shane better than any other girl. They hadn't spoken a word to each other, but the ordeal of The Wait defied description. The auntie with the cigarette began to drift off, her eyes slipping shut, another lit Marlboro drooping between her lips and dripping ash onto her blue floral dress.

It was 2:00 a.m., and Lucy dozed against her second auntie, a stout woman in a red blouse and denim pants. Across the room, Shane couldn't sleep, couldn't remember the last time she'd slept through the night. She glanced at Lorenza, who wasn't sleeping, either. Her mother's eyes were dark with exhaustion, like somebody had tried to scratch them out, too.

"Are you thirsty?" Lorenza asked.

"No."

Still, Lorenza had rummaged through her woven bag to fetch a jar of peanuts and a canteen of cota tea.

At 3:00 a.m., a doctor in a lab coat stepped into the waiting room. Everybody looked his way, searching his face for clues — was the news good or bad, and who was he there to see? — but he was unreadably stoic, like many a battle-worn medical professional. When he approached Lucy's group, Shane wasn't sure whether she felt relieved or envious. Did Shane want her wait to end? It really depended on what lay beyond the white door.

In retrospect, the answer was no. No, she didn't want to leave that sunless, stinking room, because at least, within its walls, she still had hope for a good outcome. She'd felt the same way four days ago, before her grandfather died.

This time was going be different. Her father was younger, his body stronger; he could survive. She had to believe that.

At 3:10 a.m., Lucy and her aunties stood, smiling wearily, and followed the doctor past the swinging door. Shane felt a pulse of happiness for her friend, whose loved one — a parent, grandparent, sibling, somebody — must be doing well. Why else would they smile in the waiting room of an ICU?

Shane took it as a sign: it would be OK.

At 3:15 a.m., she leaned against her mother's soft shoulder, waiting. And waiting. And . . .

Standing abruptly, Shane walked to the cabin door, planning to excuse herself from the stifling bedroom, but as she passed Donnie, her friend held out the phone receiver and said, "Hey, wait! Grandma wants to talk to you."

"Oh!"

"Hey . . ." Pressing the phone against her chest to smother her next few words,

419

Donnie whispered, ". . . don't forget, she doesn't know about Bobby."

With a thumbs-up to show her understanding, Shane gathered herself, took the phone, and said one of the few Lipan greetings she knew: "Hooyii."

Static crackled. Then a reed-thin voice stated, "Your women live with ghost dogs." Shane could sense the question in her tone, the implicit: *Why would your family do this?*

"For six generations, yes. And other animal ghosts."

"Never humans?"

"Never." That was a boundary even Four-Great Elatsoe, Shane's heroic ancestor, wouldn't cross.

"Even so. It's dangerous, what you do. Bringing ghosts to Earth."

"It can be." That's why Shane was always practicing her skill by waking insects, whose fleeting, miniscule ghosts were incapable of doing more damage than a living insect. In fact, after death, mosquitoes were unlikely to transmit bloodborne diseases, which reduced their potential for serious harm.

Was it possible for viruses to become ghosts? The sudden thought made Shane goosebump with dread. No, no. That breed of horror didn't exist outside of nightmares and fiction, thank creation. Living plagues were already bad enough.

"I heard of your family," said the Elder, and did Shane detect a hint of amusement in her fragile voice? "My friend talks about you. And your mother. And all the women before her. But I did not think you were real people. I thought you were like Paul Bunyan. Tall tales." Her sentences were clipped by raspy breaths, as if she couldn't speak too long without getting winded.

"I guess my ancestors are pretty unbelievable," Shane admitted, smiling. "They were heroic."

"You are, too," the Elder corrected. "Donnie told me. You and your mother save lives." The pauses for breath were growing in frequency and length, and the woman's volume was flagging. Shane winced, sad that the phone call was taking such a clear toll on her strength.

"We rescue people when they're lost," she replied. "Our bloodhounds help. Nellie, Neal, and Nealey."

"Né łe," the Elder said, laughing. "Not very creative." She was the first person since pre-flood days to appreciate Lorenza's little joke; her mother named all their dogs "dog."

"My mother has a strange sense of humor," Shane explained. "Did Donnie also tell you that she disappeared while she was searching for a child? We think the kid got sent to the world Below. Through magic. My mother might've gone there, too."

In the background of the Elder's call, somebody coughed, and a television babbled incoherently. Donnie's grandmother must be in a common area, where the residents gathered to watch *Rockford Files*, take family calls, and otherwise pass the hours together or alone. There'd be nurses in the room, too, carrying trays of water and candy-bright pills in paper cups. Would there be racks of magazines against the wall? Would the air smell like disinfectant and cigarette smoke? Shane's hand tightened on the receiver as she pressed it snug against her ear, and hoped that the Elder would speak again before her thoughts dragged her back into the waiting room. To 3:34 a.m., the moment . . .

"And now you want to know how to follow them. How to go Below." No mirth remained in her voice. "It's an unnatural thing. The living are not meant to be with the dead."

"But —"

"Think what you're asking."

"Shemáá was sent Below against her will. Am I supposed to accept that? Do I give up on family?" Shane shook her head, even though the Elder couldn't see her. "An unnatural thing already happened. Please, help me make it right!"

"You are certain." A long breath and a rattling cough. "You're certain they're Below?"

"Absolutely. We have very convincing evidence." Dr. Richards's calculations, coupled with Bobby's last words to Donnie, made as strong a case as they were gonna get.

"Lucky you. For a girl who lives with ghosts, it will be easy. Easy to go Below. Only, I'm afraid that you'll find it . . . difficult to return."

Shane's grip tightened once more on the phone. "How so?"

"For us, it's easy to mistake the Below for home."

"Us?" She shook her head, uncomprehending. "No, no. Please don't worry about that. I'm not dead. Neither is Shemáá or the missing child. We don't belong Below, Grandmother. We belong to the Earth, and I'll remember that. Always."

If there was one thing Shane's ma had taught her, it was the importance of returning home.

"OK." The Elder exhaled loudly. "OK."

"You'll help me?"

"I will tell you. People have visited the land of the dead." She took a long break to breathe, and in that time, Shane motioned for Donnie to lean close and listen. The girls stood side by side, nearly ear-to-ear, with the phone receiver between them. "However, their stories have no directions. They aren't shared."

"Just like dangerous backroads aren't printed on maps," Shane supposed.

"But backroads exist, and can be found. If you know the signs." A cough. "I am

424

not an expert. All I can tell you are my hunches. I think the boundary between our worlds is like a sponge. In some places, it is easier to cross. Also. Juniper trees are in many of these old stories."

"Juniper? They're really common."

"Yes. They grow well in Texas. Even when other plants die. I will never forget. In my youth, a drought. It killed our crops, made the world yellow and brown, except for the juniper. Their leaves remained the richest shade of green. Is this why they are in our stories of death? Or are they . . . sometimes . . . a sign . . ."

A high-pitched voice on the other line chirped the question, "Isn't it time to rest, ma'am?"

"No, no. My grandbaby called, and —"

"You've been talking a very long time," interrupted the unknown woman, probably a chipper young nurse. "Tell her just a couple more minutes. She can ring tomorrow. OK?"

Donnie and Shane exchanged a horrified glance. "Grandma —" Donnie began to say.

"I'll hang up when we're done." The Elder's voice still trembled, but her tone was resolute. Then, speaking to Shane, she continued, "In certain places, is it easy to wake ghosts?"

"No. The difficulty level is about the same everywhere . . ." And she trailed off as she realized that her assumption wasn't completely true. There were occasional, very rare, "hotspots" of activity. Places where Shane found herself surrounded by ghost bugs, even though she hadn't consciously called them. Like near the railroad track, before she first encountered the dead zones. "Wait! Yes!"

"Go to one. It may help."

"What should I do once I'm there?"

"You know how to bring the dead to Earth. Learn how to follow them back. In the stories, people don't fall Below accidentally. It takes concentration. Desire." Donnie's grandmother wheezed, her voice rattling. "Your family's skill will be useful. But promise me . . ." Another cough. Somewhere nearby, the nurse exclaimed, "Really, that's quite enough!"

"Grandma, are you OK?" Donnie urgently asked. "Do you need water?"

Loudly, as if she'd taken the receiver from the Elder, the nurse replied, "Sweeties, your grammy needs to rest now. Say good-bye, OK?"

"Shane," cried the Elder, far away, nearly shouting to be heard. "Shane, promise me! Stay away from the humans Below. Don't speak to them. Don't look at them! Avoid their cities and dwellings, or —"

The phone call disconnected.

"Call back!" Donnie shouted, frantically spinning the number into the rotary dial. "I didn't say goodbye!"

However, the nurse who answered this time simply said, "You can reach your grandmother tomorrow, between the hours of eight a.m. and three p.m. There will be no more excitement for Missus Larena today."

"Is she OK?!" Donnie asked.

"Absolutely. She's tired, that's all. As I said, call another day."

After Donnie hung up, Shane sat on the edge of her bed; she smoothed the quilted comforter beneath her fingertips and considered the Elder's hurried words of advice.

"That place," Donnie muttered, pacing and glaring at the phone. "They dragged her away from the phone like she was a prisoner . . ."

"I'm sorry."

"Please tell me Grandma's advice was useful."

"It was." Before the call, Shane had felt lost. Now, she knew where they needed to go. "Your grandmother made a good point. In some places, it's common for ghost bugs to visit Earth. Not sure why. Maybe the barrier's extra porous. Maybe the path between Below and Earth is shorter, simpler to navigate. Guess we'll find out."

"Where are these spots?"

"I've noticed . . . four, maybe five of them in Texas. All been near running water and juniper trees." Shane started packing; there'd be time to plan once they got everyone in the car, heading home. "You like pizza, right?"

"Uh, yeah?"

"Fantastic. Because the ghostliest place I've ever been" — with her duffel bags hanging from each shoulder, Shane opened the cabin door and stepped into the sunlight — "was a hangout spot behind a pizza restaurant."

～ EIGHTEEN ～

The drive back to Texas passed in a flurry of planning. During stops to refuel the gas tank, Shane had called Dr. Richards to bid him farewell, then Amelia (collect; Amelia's parents had insisted), relaying instructions to prepare for the journey Below. For most of the trip, Mrs. Park drove without rest, and when her head began to droop and her steady eyes drifted away from the road, she pulled over to let Donnie hop behind the wheel. "I do have a license!" Donnie exclaimed. "Just don't use it for much, aside from watching movies."

"But you've been on a highway before, right?" Shane confirmed, before she pulled back out.

"Of course. Couple times. And, unlike, Grandma, I'm wiiiide awake." Donnie had vaguely gestured at the empty soda bottles and coffee cups littering the floor in the back seat. "Going to need another cola, by the way."

Two and a half bottles of cola, and a few hours later, Donnie jolted to a stop outside Shane's house. Aside from Mrs. Park's flamingo-colored car, the driveway was empty. No motorcycle, no station wagon, no sign of Grandpa Louis. Not that she'd expected any.

"Time for rest," Shane said. With that, she popped open her door, stepped outside, and stretched her arms, her hands reaching for the silvery moon. Although she'd dozed fitfully in the car, Shane wanted a solid night of sleep. Groggily, Marcos shuffled outside with his rabbit and held her hand. She gave him a gentle, reassuring squeeze.

The rescue started at dawn.

Behind Pizza Dale, the Herotonic River flowed shallow and sluggish, its gray water crosshatched by shadows from the trees along the bank. In the early morning, before the restaurant opened to customers, Shane, Donnie, the Parks, and Marcos snuck around the building. They wore dull clothes and gave the storefront windows a wide berth, to avoid detection. Technically, the river was public property, where people often fished for dinner, but Shane wouldn't put it past Carl to call the police if he noticed an ex-employee near his business.

Amelia was waiting for them in front of the tree line; she wore a black skirt and a rose-embroidered blouse.

"No way," Donnie said, her expression brightening. "Are you the math girl from the phone? That's not fair . . ."

"What do you mean by unfair?" asked Amelia.

"A brainiac with perfect hair. Some people get all the luck."

Amelia shook her head, nearly smiling. "Good to meet you, too, Donnie." Then, she softly added, "And I like your hair."

"Aw, thanks. I grew it myself."

"This way," Shane announced, leading the group to the water's edge. "We can set up at the pebble beach. Me and Amelia, it's one of our favorite swimming spots. Whenever we go there, I feel lots of ghost bugs, without intentionally calling them."

"I can't believe we used to have picnics in a ghostly zone," Amelia muttered. "Honestly, I think I sensed them, too. There'd be a tickle on my arm, and I'd look down, seeing nothing. Or I'd feel a fish brush against my ankle, but the water would seem clear and empty. I always assumed that I was too slow to notice 'em. You knew the truth, though. That must have been freaky. Why didn't you mention it earlier, Shane? We could've gone to the pool instead."

"Honestly, I didn't understand the significance of them ghosts, why they were so common here."

In the past, when Shane had inevitably felt the prickle of invisible mosquitoes on her shoulder here, or heard the cries of long-dead frogs, she'd thought it was her fault that ghosts were rising. Not the nearby cemetery. No. But because the water reminded her of dark things: floods and flooding lungs, drowning, grieving, gone. So she'd forced herself to ignore the dead, and thoughts of death. She'd focused on her friends' laughter instead as they waded in the cold, calm water. It was important to become comfortable in the river. She'd promised her father.

And yet, all this time, Shane and her friends had been gathering near a bridge to the world Below.

And every time she'd mentally scolded herself for dwelling on death, convinced that her own weakness was calling ghosts to Earth, she'd been blameless.

Within minutes, the group reached the picnic spot, which was a short walk down-stream of Pizza Dale. The 100-square-foot pebble beach was tucked between a calf-high swath of water and a line of juniper trees. Nobody could spy on them through the screen of dense, deep green leaves.

"Shane and Amelia?" Donnie asked, pointing to a little symbol on a juniper trunk: the letters "S + A + G" were etched into the bark. To Shane, they resembled the arrows she carved into trees when she needed to mark her path during a rescue mission. Only these letters were deeper, more lasting. Dark sap beaded on the S, which had been created with five slashes; it was a fresh marking.

"Must be someone else," Shane said, glancing over her shoulder and looking, suddenly worried that another group of highschoolers or fishermen used the beach as a hangout too.

"No, it was Gabrielle," explained Amelia, casually, unrolling a woven blanket over the pebbled ground. "Last week, after Shane quit. She used a pizza knife. I told her that you wouldn't approve, since it hurts the tree . . ."

"It was a sweet thought," Shane said, and Amelia smiled.

"That's true."

As the others prepared the rope and the walkie talkies, Shane put her hand against the sap-filled letters and imagined their initials enclosed in amber. Even if her grandfather was right, and early friendships were destined to fade over time, the tree would carry the memory of them, encapsulated and protected in its hardening wood.

The thought dispersed like a startled flock of grackles when Donnie gently poked Shane's shoulder and asked, "Hey, are you OK?"

"Uh huh. We ready?"

"Everything's set up." Donnie stepped back, her arms spread dramatically. "It's your show now."

With a nod in agreement, Shane circled the supplies on the picnic blanket. There were three fully-stocked hiking backpacks; a pair of walkie talkies with long silver antennae; rope; and food for Amelia, Mrs. Park, and Marcos, who'd remain on the beach during the rescue.

"I doubt that we can trust the walkie talkies," she reiterated for the third time. In the past twenty-four hours of planning, they'd discussed the problem of Earth-to-Below communication extensively. The devices were worth a shot, if nothing else. There were well-known urban legends about radio transmissions from beyond the grave. But nonetheless, their walkie talkies had a range of just half a mile.

Suddenly, there was a splash, and something hit Shane's hiking boot. When she looked down, she found the pink speaking shell on the mud.

"You again? Kiddo, we don't have time for games." She grabbed the shell, held it up, and opened her mouth to say something stern.

But Shell Girl spoke first.

"Borrow them," she said. "For your journey."

"Wait, really?"

In response, a second shell launched out of the water and plopped on the muddy bank. Shell Girl's slender blue-gray hand waved once before vanishing under the river's surface.

"What just happened?" Donnie asked. "Are those . . . ?"

"I guess she really did want to help," Shane murmured, smiling. "Thank you, Sunflower."

After a moment's hesitation, Shane stepped to the edge of the Herotonic. With no instructions to follow, she glanced over her shoulder, seeking guidance in her friends and family, but they were watching her with wide eyes and bated breath. In this situation, with her experience raising ghosts, Shane was the expert, and that threw her off. It was difficult to think, as if her synapses were frozen, her skull a time capsule.

However, through all tragedies and fears, all accomplishments and first steps, the world kept spinning; Shane knew that well. There was no way to suspend a moment. Time went forward, and so must she.

"This may not work," Shane told herself. And in the back of her mind, Lorenza's voice chided in reply, "Don't admit defeat already."

"This *can* work," she rephrased a little louder. Then, Shane met her brother's gaze. "Back before you know it," she promised. "See you soon. I love you, little brother."

"Uh huh," Marcos agreed, smiling hesitantly. Then, although she'd asked him to stay away from the water, he darted forward and squeezed her in a crushing hug. "I love you, too."

She kissed his forehead and stroked his hair. Reluctantly, Marcos released her.

With thoughts of roses, Shane called to the butterflies; flashes of semi-transparent color, like misty wisps of stained glass, rose from the water and fluttered around her.

No, not just the water: the ghosts emerged from the darkness too, that clumped mass of shadows cast by the juniper trees. The insects' bright wings shimmered over the rippling river. If there was a doorway, it resided in the shadows, but was shut to the living.

In an attempt to push the door open through brute strength, Shane shut her eyes and concentrated on colors. Her mind popped and fizzled in explosions shaped like the flowers outside the Tanner cabins. A single butterfly could be crushed by a pillow, but thousands of them, all flying in a single direction, might be strong enough for her purposes. If they weren't, she'd call to the turkey vultures. If they were too small, she'd go even bigger. Although she'd never raised a stag or whale before, it was a day for new experiences.

Luckily, Shane didn't need to awake giants. As the air filled with an impressionist frenzy of yellows, oranges, and blues, each butterfly ghost appearing and vanishing as quickly as a firework's spark, the color of the junipers' shadow deepened into absolute blackness. It was as if a hole had opened in the world. Or perhaps it had always been there, but she'd just never seen it before. If so, did the doorway have to be noticed to exist? Was it some type of . . . of . . .

"Amelia," she called out, "what do you call the paradox cat?"

"Paradox? Um, you mean Schrödinger's cat, which is simultaneously alive or dead, according to quantum superposition?"

"Yes!" Shane pointed at the water. "Exactly. That guy. Do y'all see it?"

The others gathered close around her. "There were a load of glassy butterflies," Mr. Park commented, and his wife agreed with a hum. "But they're mostly gone now."

"No, I mean the shadow. Under the trees. Do you see how it's changed?"

"Yeah. It got darker," Marcos muttered, hugging his bunny plushie and new robot, who were now best friends. "But just by a little bit."

"Really?" Donnie asked. "Looks the same to me."

"You don't notice anything strange?"

Everyone else voiced their variations of "Huh?" or "No."

"Strange how?" Amelia wondered.

A mist of ghost gnats rose from the passageway and spilled over the bank. Small wings tickled the exposed skin of Shane's forearms and face.

"Like there's a chasm in front of us," Shane explained, keeping her eyes on the shadow. "It goes through the river, and the riverbed, and the stone under the mud, and maybe even farther. Give me Ma's handkerchief."

Quickly, Marcos passed the red bandana to Shane, who held it toward Nellie. "Scent!" she commanded. He shoved his nose against the fabric and made snuffling sounds; Shane wondered if ghosts could breathe, drawing air in and out of their chests. How would that even work, with insubstantial ghosts like Nellie?

In any case, she knew his scent receptors were still reliable. In fact, Shane hoped that his senses would be enhanced near the Below, where ghosts flourished. "Track!" she commanded, and Nellie started around the pebble beach. His movements were quicker than usual, as if he couldn't wait to find Lorenza on the

440

other side of the trail. Everyone waited in expectant silence.

However, as the minutes passed, it became clear that Nellie wouldn't be successful that moment.

"He's got nothing," she sighed, and seeing Marcos's gutted expression, she hastily added, "but that doesn't mean we should give up. Their scents could be too distant for Nellie to notice."

"Even with his enhanced senses?" Donnie asked, scowling at the juniper shadows. "Is it worth trying Bobby's hat?"

"Couldn't hurt." Her fingers gentle against the worn red cotton, Shane folded her mother's handkerchief and tucked it in her chest pocket. Then, she pulled Bobby's baseball cap from her bag and called to Nellie, who whined and yapped in frustration. "I'm sorry, boy," Shane apologized. "Let's try one more." She held out the cap. "Track."

Nellie sniffed the hat . . . then barked once, sharply, and went very still. He lifted his right paw.

"Unreal," Shane gasped. "He did it! He found Bobby's trail! All this time, Donnie, you knew! The ring sent him to be with your mom and dad!"

"No. Way." As if wounded, her friend bent over and squeezed her eyes shut. Then, with a groan, she stood again. "He's been there a week! Tell me that we aren't too late. Bobby can come back, right?"

"I don't know."

"What are the odds?"

"It's . . . greater than zero percent?"

"That's good enough for me." Donnie looked from Shane to the shadow. "How does this work? Can Nellie lead the way? Can we still follow you, even if we don't see the passage? We have to rescue my brother fast, right?"

Shane didn't respond. They still hadn't found Lorenza.

But, Bobby was Below.

What did it mean? How was that scenario even possible? Lorenza and Bobby had both been transported beyond Earth. If Lorenza wasn't Below, where else could she possibly be? The moon? No, that would kill her, and she wasn't dead! Shane had been over this a million times. She wasn't dead, and she wasn't among the dead.

"I don't know," Shane repeated, feeling like a broken record, a clueless chanter.

"Where's Mommy?" Marcos asked timidly.

"I don't know."

"What are you going to do?" Amelia wondered.

"I . . ."

Shane stared into the shadow.

Hadn't the Elder warned Shane to be careful? It was easy to get lost in an alien world, and easier to become trapped in the inevitable home of all people. If Shane didn't return, who would take care of Marcos? Grandpa Louis? The man who routinely abandoned his own daughter?

Plus, Shane couldn't ignore the possibility that it was too late: that Bobby no longer belonged to Earth. One week was a long time to resist the dangers Below. Shane hoped that his parents had protected him somehow, but even that could be dangerous. If he had become too comfortable in the land of the dead, it would prematurely claim him.

So, yes: they'd finally found Bobby's trail. She wanted to save him, believed it was possible. However, part of Shane also worried about abandoning Marcos. Was she leading Donnie and Mr. Park into unsurmountable danger? Was her hope naïve and misplaced?

Wasn't it often misplaced?

"Shane?" Donnie repeated, interrupting her thoughts meekly. "Me and Grandpa can go alone. Just tell us how to see the path? And how to command the dog."

"I . . . no. That's impossible. You'd need months of training to work with Nellie, and he probably won't leave my side. Anyway, I —"

"Please help!" Donnie exclaimed suddenly, tightly clasping Shane's hands in her own. "We're so close. I can't lose him, Shane. My heart's already broken, but if I abandon Bobby, it'll destroy me. Please, please, please. I just want my brother back, and you're strong. So strong. Descended from heroes! You can save him. Everyone here knows it!"

After days of searching, researching, and driving across the country, they'd found a trail, which was something the feds and fae representatives, despite all their big resources, had failed to accomplish.

If Shane could do that, then she could bring Bobby home.

"I'll try my best," she promised. "Is that OK, Marcos?"

Somberly, firmly, her brother nodded.

"OK. No time to waste. The shadow will get smaller as time passes, and I think I need it to go Below. In this place, it's like the doorway." She knelt next to a duffel bag full of supplies. "Even if you can't follow me, we should prepare for a three-person descent. We need to stick together."

Donnie and the others nodded quickly.

"And we have to be cautious."

More nods.

"And we can't stay longer than forty-eight hours."

The third round of nods were slower, more hesitant.

"In the old story," Shane explained, "the man who went Below returned after two days. Possibly. That gives us a safety buffer. If he did it, we can, too. Anything longer is a risk."

"I understand," Donnie said. "You can count on us." And Shane felt like she really could trust her — as if the two of them known each other for years. Was that because the desperate, hopeful look on Donnie's face was the same one Shane often saw in the mirror?

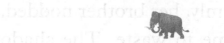

Not much time later, Mr. Park, Donnie, and Shane stood back alongside the Herotonic River, ready to go Below.

"What time is it, Marcos?" Shane asked. Her little brother scrutinized the oversized watch around his wrist. The band was an inch too loose, and the face was nearly larger than his palm, but he'd grow into it someday; that's what Lorenza always said.

It had been their father's watch, and when Shane asked Marcos to help "make sure we return within forty-eight hours," he'd insisted on wearing it.

"Ten fifteen," he reported, "and thirty-one . . . thirty-two seconds."

"Now speak into the communicator," Shane gently corrected, holding one of the pink speaking shells against her ear. As if using a walkie-talkie, Marcos lifted his matching shell to his mouth and repeated, "Ten fifteen and fifty-one seconds." A moment later, his voice, with the resonance of a distant echo, flowed from the hollow belly of the shell: *Ten fifteen . . . and . . . fifty-one seconds.* There was a slight delay, a detail Shane had to remember during the rescue mission, assuming the shells even worked across the two worlds.

"Ready?" Shane asked, looking at the Parks. Donnie and Mr. Park would follow her into the Below, while Amelia and Marcos remained on Earth to monitor their progress. And if Grandpa Louis returned to the rickety old house within forty-eight hours — something Shane wasn't counting on — he'd find a note on the door, courtesy of the neighbor:

Nellie found Bobby's trail.
I'm finishing Mom's mission.
Marcos is safe with friends.
— Shane

"We're ready," Mr. Park said, shifting under the weight of his hiking backpack. Earlier, Shane and Donnie had offered to carry his supplies, but Mr. Park wouldn't permit it; said he was used to lugging around 100-pound baskets of vegetables.

"One moment." Donnie jogged over to the juniper tree; they'd tied one end of a 100-foot coil of manila hemp rope to the trunk. The other end was fastened around Shane's waist, a lifeline. It probably wasn't long enough to reach Bobby, unless he was miraculously standing near the passageway, but if Shane got into immediate trouble, the group on Earth could pull her to safety.

"OK," Donnie, said, experimentally tugging on the tree-end of the rope. "It's secure."

"What's the time now?" Amelia asked, putting a gentle hand on Marcos's shoulder. He was staring at the wristwatch, muttering each second that passed.

"Ten seventeen," he reported.

"It's one hour and forty-three minutes until noon," Amelia added. "That means you have less than thirty minutes to go Below." After roughly estimating the height of the tree and the distance between its trunk and the water, she'd determined that the passageway would close at approximately 10:45 a.m. Anyone who claimed that trigonometry classes were useless

448

clearly hadn't needed to calculate the movement of a juniper tree's shadow.

In any case, it was obvious the rescue party had to hurry: the passageway was now just a couple feet long, its area collapsing into the tree trunk as the sun moved from the east to the west.

"Will you tell me about the rescue?" Marcos asked. "When you get back?"

"The moment we get back," Shane promised. "You got it." Looking at her ghost pup, she said, "Nellie?" The shimmer wiggled slightly in response. Smiling, Shane held out Bobby's baseball cap to remind him of the goal. "Scent," she commanded. Then, once he'd snuffled the brim, she finished, "Track!"

With an excited yap, Nellie dove headlong into the passageway. A moment later, there came a couple eager barks, not far away . . . as if Nellie was standing just out of sight. Emboldened by his closeness, Shane crouched, lowered her hand Below, and felt cool, dry air against her fingers. When nothing burned, bit, or stung her, she checked the rope around her waist, ensuring that it was fastened well.

"Hold it steady," she asked the others. "You may need to stop a fall."

The four adults took the rope, like one half of a tug-of-war team. They wore gardening gloves to prevent injuries.

"Ready?" Donnie called.

"Ready!"

After a final, lingering glace at her friends and family, Shane followed Nellie into the darkness.

∽ NINETEEN ∽

Marcos, they say it's risky to dwell upon death, that morbid thoughts are a poison to the spirit and a beacon to hurtful forces. For better or worse, our maternal line, by raising the ghosts of animals, have long skirted the edge of taboo. Still, Ma is very clear that there are boundaries we shouldn't cross. That's why we never disrespect human burial grounds. Oh, and remember when she told you to look away from that car accident? The one with an ambulance and two fire trucks around a crumpled old truck? The other drivers kept slowing down to gape at the scene, treating it like a spectacle. Gawking at a human body, somebody whose life and dreams got ended by a slippery patch of asphalt. We averted our gaze. Always do. It's our way of showing respect.

Thing is, these matters aren't black and white. You're going to struggle with your choices, growing up. You probably already have. For example, does the macabre include scary movies? Myself, I intentionally avoid them 'cause they give me nightmares. Donnie's different. She loves creature features full of Hollywood blood and guts, and she decorates her bedroom with posters of gasping women surrounded by shadowy figures. In many ways, me and Donnie are similar. By that, I mean our traumas. So I know how difficult it must be for her to thrive, despite it all. If horror movies bring Donnie some kind of catharsis — or maybe just a brief escape — who am I to judge? How is her happiness a bad thing? It can't be. Right?

And what does it mean to dwell upon death? People are allowed to grieve. To be angry and heartbroken and hurt. We aren't expected to forget the people we love, just 'cause they've walked on. I remember Pa every day. And . . . and it bothers me. The way he died is wrong, unjust, unnecessary. That's why we don't say his name. It was a bad death. He should still be here. You should know him, Marcos.

There's a point to this ramble. You'll see. When I went Below, the land of the dead, I was scared, but not because the place creeped me out. Quite the opposite. Sun above, Marcos . . . it reminded me of home. Well. After the first bit.

After stepping through the passage, I felt like I'd dropped into a hole; for a terrible second, I dangled feet-first, lowered slowly as the rope ran through gloved hands. Then, gravity gradually flipped — it was as if "east" became "down" and "west" became "up". Do you remember when Ma took us to that big playground in Houston? It had a wooden tower, with a decently high tube slide at the top. Bright yellow plastic. Three corkscrew twists. You were really little, so I climbed the tower with you, even though I felt too mature for it. When you looked into the slide, you whimpered with fear because it was impossible to see the end. "I'll go first," I said, like it was nothing, because I was thirteen years old, a teenager on a jungle gym for kids.

And when I tumbled out of the slide and onto the woodchip ground, I laughed and shouted, "It's so fun, Marcos, c'mon!"

Thing is, I'd been scared, too. Because the bigger you get, the smaller those tubes seem. I remember thinking, "What if I get stuck in here?" The smell of plastic, the heat of the sun, the claustrophobic yellow walls, the sensation of dropping, no end in sight.

That's what it felt like to go Below. Like being on a claustrophobic slide, except I had no reasonable expectation that there was an end to the drop. With the grace of a turtle on its back — or backpack, in my case — I slid across an unseen floor in a void. By the time I stopped, the tree-shaped passageway, my only source of light, was smaller with distance.

After rolling to my feet, I clicked on my flashlight and tried to get oriented. The ground must have been the darkest shade of black, because it absorbed every particle of light, reflecting nothing. Around me, the stagnant air was cool and dry, like early spring in Death Valley.

I shouted, "Bobby!" on the off chance that he'd respond, making it the shortest rescue mission in the history of Texas. Instead, there was an inquisitive bark.

A few paces ahead, Nellie waited for me. And I could see him, Marcos! In my flashlight beam, he was a visible, colorful dog, no different than Neal or Nealey. Nellie stared at me with his bright eyes; his fur was graying along the muzzle, but he stood straight, showing none of the hip pain that'd bothered him late in life. It was as if Nellie carried all the beauty of aging, with none of the physical aches. If we hadn't been on an important mission, I would've gathered him in my arms and kissed his soft forehead a hundred times.

Instead, I praised him for waiting, saying, "Good boy." It was a treat to see his tail wagging at the sound of my voice.

The rope hadn't gone taut, meaning I was within 100 feet of the passageway. I shouted, "Be careful! It's like a slide!" And then stood there, waiting, hoping that Donnie and Mr. Park would tumble next to me. But they never did.

That's when I heard you. Well. Nellie did first. In fact, I think he could hear you speaking across worlds; Below, his senses were indeed amplified, which is probably how he smelled Bobby's scent from so far away. Our doggie tilted his head to one side, and, fifteen seconds later, your voice came from the speaking shell. Just like this: "— hear me? Over."

I responded, "Yes, I hear you." And then, "What's going on? Where're the others? Over." Deep down, I knew the answer. They weren't gonna make it. I'd been the only person to see the passageway clearly, although you'd sensed a change in the shadow. Stands to reason I'd be the only one to cross over, too. Still, part of me hoped that I was wrong. What is it about me? A lab rat gets shocked a couple times, and the poor creature will stop reaching for an unobtainable piece of cheese. Yet, I can't silence my heart, which yearns for good things, even after a million shocks.

The next person to speak was Donnie. She explained, "Is everything OK? You disappeared! Just blinked outta existence. It looked like you'd fallen into another dimension." In a way, she wasn't wrong. "When I tried to follow," Donnie told me, "my foot went straight into the water. Same thing happened to Grandpa. It's

456

like the river and the doorway exist in the same place. Any ideas? Over."

It wasn't like I'd had much experience with realm-hopping. However, if I was able to bring my clothes and backpack along, maybe I could pull Donnie into the Below. After briefly describing the void, I instructed, "Hold your hand over the juniper's shadow. I'll try to guide you. Over. Heel, Nellie."

Ever hopeful, I grabbed the line and jogged to the bright passageway, which resembled a window in an infinite, unlit cavern, through which I could see the brilliant blue sky. Right away, Donnie's face appeared. She was kneeling on the bank, looking down. When I stuck my hand and arm through, she gasped, and said, "You're like Thing from the Addams Family!" Clearly, she could only see me from fingertip to elbow. I heard other sounds of surprise in the background, although the words were unclear. It was like trying to eavesdrop on a poolside conversation from underwater.

I beckoned to her, like Thing would do, and she bravely clasped my hand. I slowly stepped back, pulling Donnie toward the void.

But the moment we crossed that threshold between worlds — between light and dark, life and death, there and here — my hand was empty. Her human warmth lingered on my palm for a second. Then, even that became a memory.

I was on my own.

Well. Not quite.

At my side stood Nellie. He looked up at me, as if waiting for my next move. That's a sign of trust in a dog, y'know. I wanted to deserve it. The window shrank as the sun kept rising, and I turned my back on it.

Do you remember what I said then?

"Watch the clock, Marcos. I'll be back 'fore you know it."

～ TWENTY ～

At the end of the line, 100 feet from Earth, Shane untied herself and placed all her trust in Nellie. There'd been a subtle lightening of the world around her, as if her eyes were slowly adjusting to the Below. Emerging from the gloom, towering shapes now clarified into cacti. The passage home hovered beside a massive saguaro with a dozen upraised, prickly arms and a base large as an oak's trunk.

Although Shane was grateful for the distinctive landmark, which would mark her escape route even after the shadow door closed, it was frightening to think that she'd almost just collided with earth's biggest species of cactus. Her paternal grandfather used to warn her that they were deadly; a friend of his friend's friend once got drunk and tried to chop down a saguaro with a hatchet. Unfortunately, it fell the wrong way, and crushed him. Whether that story was true or not, Shane, who used to play outside barefoot, had had her own bad experiences with prickly plants. In fact, she'd once stepped on a little pincushion cactus, and its spines went through her heel, piercing her callused pad and becoming lodged in the soft underlying flesh. For an hour, her parents took turns plucking spines out of Shane's foot with a pair of eyebrow tweezers, but they couldn't reach them all. Shane walked with a limp for days.

If she'd slammed into the twelve-armed saguaro, it would have taken more than an hour of tweezing to fix the damage.

It took about ten minutes for the world Below to fully reveal itself, bright as day. There was a sky overhead, now vividly blue and cloudless, but no sign of the sun, and therefore very few shadows, since the light did not radiate from a single direction. It was certainly hot, though, and she realized her surroundings roughly resembled a fusion of the Sonoran and Chihuahuan Deserts, with sandy yellow soil, emaciated creosote, and a haphazard sprinkling of scrub, cacti, and drought-tolerant grasses. Shane also noticed a species of flowering shrub she'd never seen before. Maybe it'd gone extinct on Earth. There were plants in the time of dinosaurs, and not all of them still grew.

In front of Shane, the distant horizon was blue and jagged, split by a mountain range. Behind her, the desert stretched endlessly.

"OK," she said. "Track, Nellie."

With an excited tail wag, he took off toward the mountains. Out of curiosity, Shane checked her compass. Unfortunately, the needle stayed pointing north, no matter how she turned it. Accepting that her standard navigational tools — the sun's position and the Earth's magnetic field — were useless here, Shane kept her head down and focused on Nellie, who was moving at a steady trot. As they traveled, she collected pebbles from the ground and regularly marked her path with arrows. Hopefully, they wouldn't be disturbed or followed. There were no obvious signs of monsters or other humans, but that didn't mean Shane was alone.

Using the mountains as reference, Shane determined that Nellie was going in a straight line, only diverging from the path when he had to walk around a big shrub or cactus. Unless Bobby had done the same — which Shane seriously doubted, since he was a child, not a train on an invisible track — that meant Nellie wasn't following in Bobby's footsteps. Instead, he could actually sense the lost boy from across the empty desert and possibly farther. Nellie had never been so powerful. Was he extra strong in the land of the dead? Or was it just easier for him to access his true strength?

For a while, Shane distracted herself by imagining a future where Nellie could find anyone, anywhere, on Earth. And why limit it to people? Dog noses could detect tons of stuff. Like land mines, truffles, other animals, smoke, food! When Nellie was alive, Shane's family had to store all the candy in the top kitchen cabinet, 'cause he could detect the faintest trace of sugar, even if it was sealed. She'd never forget the day her father brought home a bag of fruit candies from the local dulcería. They hadn't been for a special event; it wasn't a birthday or holiday. Shane's father just liked surprising the family with treats after a long day. Their happiness reminded him why he worked part-time at the city garage, repairing engines and changing tires until his callused hands became dark with motor oil. Their little farm didn't usually generate enough money for luxuries like store-bought desserts.

Well, that evening, the family was eating supper around the television when they heard an apocalyptic crash. Somehow, Nellie had sniffed out the full bag of candies, climbed onto the kitchen counter, and knocked over two frying pans and the fifteen pound metate, which cracked a floor tile in half when it landed. The sound must've scared Nellie more than it scared the humans, since Lorenza found him hiding under a coat in Shane's closet, the now-empty bag of candies stuck to his muzzle.

Maybe, with more training, Nellie could expand his senses on Earth. Then, when Lorenza came back, she could open a real rescue business — no need to worry about secrecy anymore, since people now knew the truth. It'd be full-time work, ghost dog investigations. The days of back-breaking, sun-scorched, inconsistent labor would be over. If Lorenza didn't want to charge people for search and rescue, fine! They could teach Nellie to smell gold and take him to the beach, where vacationers lost their jewelry in the surf. Shane might join her long term. Or maybe pick a different career when she got older. The future wasn't set, but now that she was free from Pizza Dale, and nearly done with school, she could focus on building a happier life. For herself, and for her mother and brother. True, Marcos would never hear her father laugh at Nellie's guilty, crumb-speckled face. But Shane could be the one who brought home boxes of candy instead. She knew there was a patisserie near the library . . .

"One hour," Marcos said, wrenching Shane from her daydreams. "You OK? Over." The speaking shell hung from a mesh of yarn around Shane's neck.

"Nellie is still on the trail. All good. Over."

"What does it look like down there?" asked Donnie. After a moment, she added, "Over."

"Still resembles a desert. It's really quiet. There's no wind, just rocks and dry-weather plants." Even the flies from earlier were gone. "It's a little freaky."

It seemed like time had passed quickly since Shane had become wrapped up in her thoughts. Normally, that level of obliviousness was in direct contradiction with Lorenza's survival lessons. In the wilderness, an alert person was a prepared person. However, Below, whenever Shane looked too hard at the horizon, sky, or surrounding desert, a faint pressure throbbed in her head behind her eyes, and her stomach soured. Once, Shane had tried her grandfather's prescription reading glasses, and the warped view had been nauseating. Focusing on the Below caused a similar, albeit less intense sensation, she realized.

"I don't think I'm supposed to be comfortable, though. Over."

"Zero signs of Bobby?" Donnie asked. "Over."

"Nothing yet." Shane took a drink from her thermos. She'd packed enough water

465

for three days just in case, and although the extra supplies weighed a ton, it seemed wise to be prepared, especially here. She couldn't rely on natural sources of water. On Earth, Shane knew how to collect moisture from prickly pears and other desert resources. But could she eat the cacti here? Should she? Judging by their abundance and diversity, this was their kingdom beyond death. It was a land of spikes and burrows.

"We're heading toward mountains," she continued. "Bobby may be there, where the land's kinder to humans."

If he was over the mountains, Shane didn't know what she'd do. Push the forty-eight-hour limit? How long could she keep pushing? An hour . . . two? She'd need to find water and shelter, eventually. She'd need to sleep. And as the days passed, the Below would replace her bedroom on Earth. It would feel more reliable than the half-dozen apartments and shacks Shane's family had rented after the flood. And when that happened, the passage between worlds would not reveal itself to her anymore.

That's what Shane feared, most of all. That she wouldn't recognize Earth as home . . . 'cause it hadn't been home in years.

Looking up, Shane realized that the mountains seemed no closer. An image flashed into her head: a row of beaming, lipsticked women, jogging on Staub treadmills. She'd seen them on television, the pretty young ladies demonstrating aerobics on personal conveyor belts that could probably be used as instruments of torture. You could take a million steps, walk till you collapsed, and not progress an inch.

Was it just an optical illusion, or did the mountains seem even dimmer, smaller with swelling distance?

"One hour and thirty minutes," Marcos said. "Over."

"Thank you. Over." Resolutely, she looked at the ground again and focused on taking the journey step by step. Although Shane's watch ticked in-sync with earth, she didn't tell her brother to stop sending updates.

Because her eyes were downcast, she noticed the glittering black beetle. With an impressive one-inch length, it had sharp mandibles, ridged wing cases, and bulbous compound eyes.

"Nellie, pause!"

Crouching, Shane put her hand in front of the beetle's path; its antennae wiggled over her fingers, lightly brushing her skin. Then, the disgruntled beetle spread its wings and took to the sky with an aggressively loud hum.

"What is it?" Marcos asked, overhearing her order to Nellie. "Over."

"I . . . don't know. A bug. A mystery."

Although Shane recognized the beetle (or its close relatives) from illustrated encyclopedias, she'd never seen one in person. That's 'cause these ones were cold-weather insects, native to northern North America. So where did the little guy come from?

Shane grabbed her binoculars scanned the horizon, searching for any signs that the desert ended before the mountain range. Normally, she wouldn't expect to find a wintry tundra within a hot southwestern desert, since stuff like climate and geology affected ecosystems on Earth. But the Below must run by its own inconceivable rules.

Sure enough, there was an indistinct line of thin, dark trees growing in the distance, separating her from the mountains. She adjusted the focus of the binoculars, trying to make out more details, but the trees were too far away . . .

Nausea clenched Shane's stomach, and wooziness spun through her head; dry-heaving, she dropped the binoculars, which clattered on the hard ground. She squeezed her eyes shut.

"Are you OK?" came Amelia's voice.

"Yeah, yeah." The desire to vomit slowly passed. "It's just this place."

"What do you mean? Maybe you should come back now. We don't know anything about the afterlife. It could be radioactive!" Amelia's anxiety started to rub off on Shane, who couldn't afford to panic.

"Feels more like mild seasickness," she explained. "Nothing serious. Go, Nellie. And y'all on Earth: keep talking, please."

As she resumed walking, Shane kept her eyes downcast and focused on her friends' voices, which kept the nausea at bay.

"You don't have to be on a boat to get seasick," Donnie interjected. "A kid in school, Pete, went snorkeling 'round California for summer vacation. The ocean was so choppy, Pete got sick, and he couldn't spit out his snorkel fast enough —"

"Do not finish that story," Amelia groaned.

"Sorry. No more ocean talk. What do I know, anyway?" Donnie joked. "I've never even visited Galveston."

When she mentioned Galveston, Shane thought about its gray waters and towel-patched beaches, the boardwalk, and a vanilla ice cream split she'd once shared with her father, since it had been too big for one girl to finish alone. Back then, she didn't swim so well, so her mother had rented an inflatable duck from a wooden shack on the beach and told Shane to stay around the other kids, where the Gulf was shallow and murky with sand, rolling like glitter in a snow globe. In that moment of memory, Shane's pace quickened.

"Donnie, you once asked me what the ocean is like," she replied. "To me, it's a friend you can't trust. One day, he'll show you incredible sights, entertain you, and feed you — but the next day, he'll slap you in the face with all the fury of a hurricane."

"Doesn't sound much like a friend," Amelia commented. They weren't bothering with "over" anymore.

"It's an imperfect metaphor." Perhaps Shane should have used the word "family" instead.

"I'd still like to visit someday," Donnie decided.

"We can go together," Shane promised. "All three of us."

And when Shane looked up, the forest now loomed impossibly closer, as if she'd walked a mile in three minutes. In fact, Shane could see, with her naked eye, that the towering plants weren't even trees at all.

The enormous cacti were ten times bigger than any she'd encountered before. Some had a thousand arms, raised skyward. Others were larger than old-growth redwoods, with spikes the size of daggers. Clusters of the giants had grown into each other, fusing into walls of spiky stalks. It was as if Shane and Nellie were approaching the heart of the desert, where its oldest residents grew.

"I wish you could see this," she whispered into the shell. Lowering her eyes, Shane's gaze bounced between Nellie and the ground, which was becoming treacherous with burrows. The rodents, reptiles, and insects who called the southwestern deserts home were greatly accomplished burrowers, having spent millennia needing to find shade underground during brutal summer days. To the right, a hole the size of a tube slide was angled into the ground. Seeing it, Shane instinctively darted to the left; she didn't know what animal made something that big, but one thing was clear: she didn't want to be in the desert when it woke up.

~ TWENTY-ONE ~

This is what I will tell you, Marcos, when I get home. I'll describe sights and sensations with no references on Earth, and when I find myself at a loss for words, I'll use imperfect comparisons, referencing experiences you can understand. It's a story. It happened. It just didn't happen exactly like this. But I promise that every word I say is truth. Every word will help you understand all that I felt and all that I endured and all that I overcame.

So the story goes

~ TWENTY-TWO ~

Over the next two hours, the amount of cacti around Shane increased. The towering, fused saguaro, the fields of paddled prickly pear, and the spiny yucca were troublesome enough. But countless pincushion-shaped balls of spines jutted from the sandy dirt. Between them and the burrows, the desert had transformed into an obstacle course. In certain areas, Shane had to jump hopscotch-style to patches of empty ground, grateful for the skills she'd learned in the playground.

"I wish I'd known you as a child, Amelia," she commented. The base team on land had decided to monitor the speaking shell in shifts; that way, there'd always be somebody with Shane, even at night, while the others tried to sleep in tents along the river.

"I was much the same, only smaller." There was a smile in her voice. Gosh, Shane loved that about her friend. You might not see joy play across her serious lips, but Amelia's every word sang with emotion. "Believe it or not."

"Honey, I believe it."

In front of Shane, Nellie stopped walking and looked side to side; he couldn't find a path through the spines anymore. Pincushions blocked the way forward, as dense as the fibers in a carpet. Since he'd bounded through the juniper shadow, Nellie hadn't walked through any object, as if the world Below was more solid to him than Earth. They'd have to retrace their steps and find another route. With a frustrated sigh, Shane turned around.

Was that movement in her peripheral vision? Something darting behind a fused pair of saguaro and hiding from Shane's view? With great restraint, Shane stopped herself from shouting out, "Who is that?" It couldn't answer. Couldn't! Please, don't let it be something that can answer. The shy creature had been an animal, that's all. A coyote, maybe.

Even so, she was reluctant to go back now. If Nellie noticed a threat, he'd bark. Right? Or was he fixated on tracking, to the detriment of his other senses? If so, she couldn't trust him to sound the alarm.

After a quick period of indecision, Shane stooped over to wrap her arms around the dog. As she lifted him into the air, she felt his heartbeat beneath her hand; he rested his soft muzzle on her shoulder, trusting. With careful steps, Shane tiptoed between the pincushion cacti. Twice, she carefully pushed aside a spiny plant with her rubber-soled boot.

"What were you like?" Amelia asked. "As a kid, I mean."

Idly, Shane wondered how far back she should go. Before the flood, or after? "I could've been two different people," she explained, lowering Nellie onto a clear patch of ground that had resurfaced. Without the need for prompting, he continued following Bobby's scent, his steps slow and deliberate.

"At first," Shane said, "I was this loud, fast, noisy child, always in everyone's business. I could convince all the kids in the neighborhood to play my games. I even charmed a rich boy, lured him away from his fancy monkey bars to play on my old tire swing instead. That Shane was . . . light."

"Light as in bright?" Amelia clarified. "Because you're still radiant."

"Oh, stop." Snickering, Shane leapt over a knee-high prickly pear and landed on a flat-topped gray rock.

"That's what your name means, isn't it?" Amelia asked softly. "Sheiné łénde? Sunflower?"

Balanced on the rock, her eyes on the treacherous ground, Shane gasped, "Yes, but how did you know?" She hadn't ever shared the translation with anybody.

"Donnie told me."

"Uh. OK. But how did *she* know?"

"Her grandmother, on the phone."

"I'm glad my pronunciation was close enough for a fluent speaker to understand. Not many of those left." Almost none, to her knowledge. Would any remain in ten, twenty years? Or would her language become a tongue of the dead? A language of the world Below, and the wretched ghosts on Earth.

"By the way," Amelia said, "Donnie isn't really short for Donna!"

"Huh! What is it short for?"

"You'll have to ask her later. I can't pronounce the words."

"Ah, sure." Looking up, Shane cried out in surprise.

"Wha? What's wrong?"

Shane felt a gust of cold air blowing around her, chilling the sweat on her brow. It was a baffling sensation; heat radiated against her back, while nearly freezing temperatures pressed against her face. Somehow, she'd reached the abrupt end of the southern desert, and now beheld a sprawling steppe-tundra. Tufts of yellow grasses and leafless woody bushes sprouted between bright white snow, and hills rolled across the land like gentle waves in a frozen sea. Beyond the tundra, the mountains were close, as if she'd leapt miles in a single bound. Here, Shane no longer thought of treadmills; instead, she pictured a conveyor belt, speeding her toward her destination. But how?

And more importantly, if space could shift like this in the Below, could Shane rely on Nellie to lead them home? So far, he hadn't been thrown off by the changes in the environment, which sometimes seemed to stretch like taffy, and other times — now, for example — jumped to a completely different biome. However, Shane ought to keep track of direction too anyway, just in case she had to find her way home. She'd trusted the pebble arrows to help, but what if the distance between two arrows stretched while her back was turned? Would there be stars in this place? Constellations? Surely not. After all, the sun was a star, too.

"Shane?" Amelia repeated, with terror in her voice. "Answer me!"

"Sorry! It's OK! I just, uhm . . . I'm closer to Bobby than I realized."

"Can you see him?"

"No." She looked toward Nellie, who'd paused in front of the tundra, his stance rigid, waiting. "But I'm more optimistic about the search. With the desert dragging on and on, I was worried that we wouldn't reach him within twenty-four hours."

From her bag, Shane removed gardening gloves and a pair of wool socks. They'd be useful to protect her delicate fingers and toes from frostbite. After quickly slipping into the second socks and retying her hiking boots, Shane unfolded a high-collared imitation racing jacket and a loose denim jacket, which she layered over her T-shirt. Lastly, she folded her bandana into a headband to protect her ears from the wind. The temperature of the tundra hovered around freezing; in the night, if it dropped much lower, Shane would need to build a fire or find insulated shelter to survive. Was there enough fuel? Thoughtfully, she surveyed the rolling landscape. The most common plants were grasses, which weren't ideal kindling. They'd smoke a lot and fizzle out before a proper fire could light. However, the woody bushes could be useful if she collected enough dry, dead sticks to get the flame going.

Shane looked toward the mountains, which were clearer now, their slopes green with the tint of trees. The highest peaks were capped with snow. If Shane could reach the range before nightfall, she'd find more options for shelter, such as caves. However, they were still many miles away, and the hills and valleys would add steps to her journey.

Nausea twinged through Shane. It must be the mountains, she realized, that had been repelling her gaze; when she looked down, the sickness vanished. She'd been fine during the hike, chatting with Amelia and focusing on the hazardous desert terrain.

What was it about them? On Earth, the mountains were sacred places, but she knew very little of the Below. Perhaps she'd get lucky and find Bobby in the tundra.

That possibility seemed unlikely. He would have landed near his parents.

He'd be around humans.

Based on her understanding of the old stories, Shane believed that humans Below weren't terrible things; they weren't like human ghosts on Earth. Still, as the Elder warned, they could make her return difficult, especially if she interacted with them.

It occurred to Shane that half the people she'd ever loved were here, somewhere.

481

"Track, Nellie," she urged her dog, who trotted forward without hesitation, his paws crunching over powdery snow and crispy grass. His movement frightened a beetle, which took flight with a noisy hum.

"What about the second you?" Amelia asked.

"The wha . . . Oh, right. As a child."

"Yes. You said you changed. Was that after the flood?"

"After," she softly replied. "During. Because."

"I don't think she's completely gone."

"Who?"

"The Shane who could convince all the kids in her neighborhood to play her games."

"I haven't played games in a long time." Shane stooped to grab a couple dry sticks, and then continued walking.

"Well, you persuaded me to get a job at Pizza Dale."

"Hey!" she protested, laughing, her breath visible as puffs of smoke-gray condensation. "I never asked you to work with me."

"Didn't have to. I wanted to. It's nice, in your orbit."

Vividly Shane thought of yellow roses in beds of green. With gloved fingers, she touched her chest, where a corsage might be pinned. Around her, the yellow and green landscape seemed to merge with her memory of flowers. "Amelia," she whispered, too softly for the shell to catch.

Ahead, Nellie reached the top of a low hill, but instead of continuing down its slope, he halted and looked back at Shane. It was a gesture of uncertainty, the dog seeking guidance from his human friend, which worried her. What did Nellie see from his perch? Another barrier? Shane hurried to catch up.

"Whoa," she gasped.

Shane and Nellie now stood at the edge of a vast, deep valley. Far away, a silvery river cut the land, the water running parallel to the mountain range. But that wasn't Shane's greatest concern.

A herd of animals filled the valley; from high, they resembled toys in a diorama. They were elephant-shaped, but larger, and furred, and lumbering. The oldest, biggest ones had heavy white tusks, which curled upward and ended in points. Within the center of the herd, babies clumsily trotted after their mothers and other relatives. They moved at a leisurely pace; none grazed, but the valley was rich with grasses. The water must have attracted life, because birds, indistinct with distance, settled in flocks along its bank, and antelope-shaped mammals with long faces trotted near the edge of the herd.

Although the animals were similar to elephants and antelopes, Shane had only seen them in a museum. With a growing sense of foreboding, she thought back to a display on "giants of the Ice Age," which featured a woolly mammoth standing over a pair of snarling saber tooth tigers and a short-faced bear that made grizzlies seem compact in comparison.

"I'm in a prehistoric sanctuary, Amelia," she said.

~ TWENTY-THREE ~

Do you remember that exhibit, Marcos? It was rare for Ma to get a day off; even when she wasn't working for money, she was working for us, keeping house and preparing enough food to last the week. But it was her birthday, so we took a bus into town and walked to a grand stone building with a sprawling green lawn. A broad staircase led to a row of marble pillars outside the entrance. And through the heavy doors, past a gray-haired man at the front desk, we stepped into the hall of dinosaurs. Skeletal giants — T. rex and triceratops and other iconic species — were posed like they were fighting or grazing.

They didn't bother you. Maybe that's 'cause they looked so dead.

However, deeper in the museum, we saw the giants of the Ice Age, an exhibit with life-size wax replicas of prehistoric mammals. They had wiry fake fur, white teeth, and glinting glass eyes. And you stood in front of the woolly mammoth, which was bigger than an elephant, with tusks the length of cars, and broke out crying. I'd heard you cry a hundred times 'fore, but this was different, 'cause you were bawling at a goofy-looking wax statue, not anything serious. So maybe I sounded amused when I asked, "What's wrong?"

And you hid behind Ma, clinging to her skirt and pointing up. They'd given the mammoth a bland expression. To me, it seemed more dead than the dinosaurs, but you disagreed, whimpering with fear, like the figure would lift her tree trunk leg and smoosh us.

Well, Ma picked you up, made you feel taller, and said, "They're related to elephants."

"But bigger."

"Big animals can be gentle, and they usually are, if you give them space."

I wasn't smiling anymore, since the inverse is also true: little things can be dangerous. The most dangerous. I thought then about viruses and bacteria, the diseases that spread like wildfire through a human body, hidden in the blood, the lungs, the heart, embedded within the person we love. I thought about that a lot when I was young, and guess I still do. I bet you do, too.

"The mammoths are all gone now," Ma said. "They went extinct."

And you asked, "Like us?"

I've never seen Ma look so . . . so . . . you may not understand this word, but it's the best I got: *aghast*. "No!" she said. "Extinct means dead."

And you very stoically replied, "I know."

So she carried you away from the hall of dead things, and out of the natural history museum, which displays wax Lipan Apaches in the hall next to the dinosaurs. Instead, we found a minigolf course. Since you were small, Ma let you roll your ball with your hand, and I got a hole-in-one, and later, after we'd eaten ice cream and gone home, I lay in bed thinking of woolly mammoths, wondering why you'd cried so hard, and I felt a bit like crying, too.

≈ TWENTY-FOUR ≈

After deploying her binoculars to scan the valley, Shane estimated that there were one hundred adult woolly mammoths near the river, with a handful of other grazers in their periphery. Although she didn't notice any carnivores, the uneven patches of ground — including boulders and grassy mounds — could hide a dire wolf or large cat from view.

"What do you see?" Amelia gasped, astounded. "Dinosaurs?"

"Extinct mammals. Woolly mammoths, and the like. Do you suppose they behave like elephants?"

"Possibly?"

"I wish I knew more about elephants." Lorenza had prepared her to encounter twentieth century North American animal species. Wild elephants lived on different continents. "They cluster in matriarchal groups, right? Families led by the oldest females?"

"No idea, Shane. Sorry."

"There's a really big herd standing between me and Bobby. It looks like many generations of woolly mammoths are coexisting together."

"Do they notice you?"

"Not yet," Shane said, "but it'll be difficult to sneak past, unless I take a major detour."

In a less time-sensitive situation, she would have walked around the valley. However, it was already early afternoon, Bobby was nowhere in sight, and Shane wouldn't make her deadline if she wasted half a day circumnavigating all the big animals. There was no guarantee that she'd find a clear crossing, anyway. Shane might encounter other herds — or worse, because woolly mammoths were formidable. A predator would struggle in a skirmish with one full-grown adult, much less a hundred of them. Yep, Shane wagered that the Ice Age bears and big cats would avoid the valley, instead clustering in quiet spaces where they could pick off isolated prey, if the mood struck.

She'd cross here, then.

All of Shane's instincts urged her to give the mammoths plenty of space. They were wild animals, after all. Even Below. Plus, some of the big ones could've died at the hands of ancient humans.

How did the saying go? An elephant never forgets?

If Shane kept small and nonthreatening, perhaps she could slip past without upsetting the mammoths. They seemed fine around the antelope things. Plus, the herd was moving to the left, and might be gone by the time she reached the low part of the valley. She'd get a little closer and reevaluate from flat ground. From elevation, everything looked small and compact, making it difficult to judge distance. According to Lorenza, it was good practice to stay 150 feet away from bison, unless protected by a reliable barrier.

Although bison were not exactly woolly mammoths, they were heavy, herbivorous beasts that could break bones, if provoked, so she assumed the same logic applied.

"I might need to be sneaky for a bit," she told the speaking shell. "Let's go radio silence."

"OK," Amelia whispered. "Over."

For a minute, Shane watched the mammoths as they ambled along, unhurried. They certainly resembled living animals, although none grazed; perhaps the dead did not need food. In contrast, Shane's stomach prickled with hunger. After forging the river, she'd break to eat late lunch. To tide herself over, she scarfed down a handful of trial mix, chased it with water, and then repacked everything tight.

"Heel, Nellie." The bloodhound quickly moved to Shane's side and looked up at her with eager trust. He could continue tracking once they'd passed the mammoths. Until then, she needed him close, to avoid startling the herd, which might recognize the bloodhound as a descendant of wolves.

Shane had been stationary for too long: the cold had infiltrated her layered clothes.

Fortunately, while she'd been eating, the 100-mammoth herd had split into two segments; one cluster lingered, while the other marched on. Between them, a gap opened, a corridor to the water's edge. If Shane hesitated, it might close. To avoid detection, she'd stay low to the ground, and move with caution, with Nellie by her side.

But was that really the correct call?

According to Lorenza, it was also dangerous to surprise large animals. That's why you made noise during deep-wood hikes. For the most part, bears and bigfoots wanted to avoid people, mainly attacking because of fear. Mammoths should operate by similar rules, right?

Shane wished that she could ask her mother for advice. Should she be sneaky or not? Should she turn back or forge onward? She'd never been around a woolly mammoth before. Never been Below before. Never tracked alone before.

At Shane's side, Nellie cocked his head, as if wondering, "What now, human?"

The unknowns overwhelmed her.

Then, as clear as a bell, she remembered her mother's voice: *Observe*.

Within the valley, there was very little cover. It was unlikely that Shane could get near dozens of tall, watchful animals without detection.

What else do you see?

The antelope-things and birds were largely ignored by the woolly mammoths, who must not consider them threats.

And?

It was doubtful that Shane could outrun a mammoth, even without a heavy bag strapped to her back. If one started charging, she'd need a large head start to get away.

So what now? What does your experience tell you?

The mammoths would either consider her threatening or harmless. Whatever the case, it was unwise to sneak into the valley. The sooner they noticed her, the more time she had to assess next moves. They might react with immediate aggression. If so, with enough distance, Shane could safely retreat. They might be wary. In that case, Shane would slow down, act innocent, and give them extra space. Or they might barely glance her way. Gosh, she hoped that'd be the case.

Out of an abundance of caution, Shane took out the flare pistol, which had one charge in its cartridge. Although she couldn't hurt the dead, the red flame might frighten them.

"Amelia?" she softly asked.

"I'm still here."

"Can we keep talking, actually? In calm tones."

"Yes, of course."

Slowly, crouched low for balance, Shane started the hike into the valley. Underfoot, the frozen ground crunched, and a couple pebbles clattered downhill, stopping after a few feet when they collided with a tuft of yellow-green grass.

"What's everyone doing on Earth?"

"Busy setting up camp," Amelia explained. "Well. Almost everyone. Marcos fell asleep on the picnic blanket. He tried to stay awake for you, but his head kept drooping, and then he slumped over like a rag doll —"

"It's his nap time," Shane explained, smiling at the mental image of her brother. "When Marcos wakes up, tell him that sleep is important to stay clever and alert."

"I will," she promised. "And it is. Donnie and her grandparents are putting up a couple new tents too. The riverside is home till you're safe again."

"Why do you need more tents, though?"

"For my family. Mama and Gustavo are bringing extra food."

"They know about all this?"

"Most of it."

"And are they cool? With the ghosts, and everything?" She hadn't asked Amelia to keep Nellie secret. The days of hiding her past — her power — were over. Sure, Shane did incredible things. So what? She wasn't the only one. In fact, there was a kid in school who could summon flames above his fingertips. After the class voted him prom king, he'd set a bonfire alight, to the sound of exuberant cheers.

If the prom king was allowed to be extraordinary, why not Shane? Hadn't the world changed since the persecution of her ancestors? There weren't armies pursuing the Lipan anymore.

Maybe it hadn't changed enough, sure. There were still people like the Singers who'd try to crush her underfoot, treat her like a bug they despised. Well, let them try. Shane was sick of living in fear. From now on, she wanted to live in power.

Gravity urged Shane to move more quickly; it would be easy to give in to inertia and hasten her steps into a chaotic sprint downhill. She resisted the pull, leaning back to put weight in her heels. Step by step, the low part of the valley drew closer, but the mammoths hadn't noticed her yet.

"They're worried," Amelia said. "We all are. I wish . . ."

There was hurt in the silence.

"What?" Shane asked.

"That you weren't alone."

"I'm not."

"Have I ever told you . . ."

"What?"

"I love you."

Shane felt summer's warmth against her face; smelled the sweetness of lavender. In the space of three words, she existed in two worlds.

"No, you haven't. Not directly."

She'd nearly reached the fertile valley. Around her, jewel-dark beetles clamored

496

over pebbles, fleeing her steps. Although Shane was technically closer to the mammoths now, without the advantage of height, she couldn't see the full herds; just the edges of their clusters, to the right and left.

"Friends don't say that enough," Amelia said, wistfully. "There are so many rules about the way love should feel, and who deserves it more than others. But who agreed on those rules, anyway? The same people who decided that forks should go on the left side of a plate, and spoons should go on the right?"

"They should?" Frankly, when Shane set the table, she just made sure that everyone got silverware. She'd never been to an event with actual place-setting rules.

"Do I make sense? Or is this me overthinking?"

"No, I mean yeah. I get it. You're right. And . . ." Toward Amelia, Shane knew she felt a deep sense of affection. Once, the feeling had puzzled her, as its intensity was unexpected and strange, until she realized that she hadn't trusted a person outside her family since the pre-flood days. It had been difficult to forge new connections with people when she was bouncing from community to community like a pinball in a Texas-sized game. ". . . I love you too."

"You don't need to say it back, honestly."

"I want to." Shane hesitated. Over the years, many boys had told Amelia "I adore you," and other declarations of proto-love, but she'd never returned their affections. Instead, she'd always turned them down gently. In private, as she and Shane cleaned the closed restaurant or sat along the river, their bare feet in the cool water, she'd hinted at a secret. Amelia, who was so bold and open about everything else. Could it be . . .

"Do you mean it in a friend way?" Shane asked. "Completely?"

"What other way is there?" Amelia sounded guarded, but not upset. Not yet.

"I don't know." She did, though. "Love can be romantic, too."

"Are you serious?" An astonished question.

"Yes. It happens. It's always happened. I don't feel that way about girls, but when others do, it's OK. Really."

For a long beat, Amelia didn't speak. Then, gentle laughter.

"Well, lucky for us both, I do mean friend-friend," Amelia said. Hesitantly, in a softer tone, she added, "And in any case, you aren't my type."

"Yeah?" Shane smiled. "Who is?"

"I'll tell you later."

"Sure thing. I —"

One of the woolly mammoths, a large female in the stationary cluster, abruptly turned toward Shane. The animal's cumbersome tusks curled upward like ski ramps. Immediately, Shane froze, held out her arms, lowered her gaze, and waited for the mammoth to pass judgment.

When nothing startling happened — the mammoth did not charge, bellow, or stomp her heavy feet — Shane took a slow step, heading toward the widening gap between the two segments of the herd. The matriarch's small ears flared, and her trunk curled restlessly.

"About to pass a bunch of woolly mammoths," Shane said in her gentlest tone of voice. "Unfortunately, gotta get closer than comfort."

The matriarch made a low sound, and the other adults tightened their formation around the babies and lanky adolescents.

"Whoa, whoa, it's OK," Shane cooed, and she sidestepped to the left to demonstrate that she and Nellie had no intention of approaching the herd. "Just want to cross the river."

"How close is that, exactly?" Amelia whispered, her voice as tense as a bowstring.

"Less than a football field." Considerably less, at the tightest point. "Don't worry. Right now, they're cautious but not aggressive."

"And did you say river?"

"Yep. Let's take it one obstacle at a time, though."

"I don't like this, Shane."

"Not a big fan, either." Shane was now between the two halves of the herd. About seventy feet to the right, the matriarch raised her trunk high. "Easy, easy." Her heart hammering, Shane took a couple steps to the left; she wished she could go farther, but that might aggravate the other cluster of mammoths. In a moment of anxiety, she touched the pistol on her hip and considered firing it into the sky — as a warning, like a rattlesnake shaking its tail.

But would that push the mammoths away? Or would it cause a different reaction?

She imagined the two halves panicking, stampeding. They'd crush her underfoot, spear her on their tusks.

The matriarch's raised trunk curled into an elegant *C* shape. Her nostrils flared as she smelled the air, which blew from the left to the right, and Shane had a sudden idea. Very slowly, she lowered her backpack, unlatched its back pocket, and pulled out a red apple. After taking a big, crunchy bite to release the fruit's scent, she placed it on the ground. An offering, of sorts. One treat for safe passage. Even if they didn't need to graze, they might still delight in the taste and smell of fruit. Same way Nellie enjoyed snuffling Neal and Nealey's dog food. Maybe the mammoths' senses were enhanced, too. They'd smell the apple, and know that Shane was a safe human, one who gave treats, not one who spilt blood.

When Shane continued walking toward the river, the matriarch did not challenge her. Instead, after Shane and Nellie had passed through the gap in the herd, several curious mammoths encircled the apple. They prodded the fruit with their prehensile trunks, rolling it between them.

"Made it," Shane told Amelia. "What's the time?"

"Fifty past three."

On earth, there were hours left until sunset. No telling when darkness fell Below. However, after crossing the river, Shane would collect timber in earnest. Just in case she had to spend the night in the open.

In front of her, the shrubs and grasses grew up to the river, which was as gray as the sky. Shane threw a twig into the water to judge its speed and was relieved when the scrap of wood floated sluggishly to the left. The current wasn't powerful. However, she didn't notice any natural bridges, and with temperatures in the thirties, she definitely shouldn't try to swim across.

There might be a better spot downstream, Shane decided, and then she started hiking along the bank. Inland, a few mammoths calmly glanced her way, but the majority ignored her. To them, Shane was now just another harmless species in the valley, like the beetles or the antelope-things. At that thought, she felt a surge of wonder. Had she successfully communicated with an extinct species of giants? Won their trust with gentle movements and an apple?

"Can you build a bridge?" Amelia asked.

"No chance. There isn't enough material. I'm surrounded by grassland. The river's shallow, though, and I see a few rocks under the surface."

"You plan to walk across?"

"If I can." Ahead, she observed the white glint of foam on the water, a sign that something broke the river's surface? Her steps quickened into a jog. Soon, she saw a gray boulder submerged about five feet away from the bank. A rounded dome of granite jutting into dry air, creating a small platform.

Sadly, though, the potential crossing point was not suitable. With a running leap and extraordinary balance, Shane could reach the boulder from her side of the river, but it was twenty feet away from the other bank, an impossible jump for her. If she landed in the water, she'd risk hypothermia, especially if the current, slow as it was, knocked her over. Shane had to continue looking.

"Wish I'd brought galoshes," she mumbled. "They'd make this so much eas —"

There came a rumble, and with a soft gasp, Shane whirled around. The once-serene mammoth clusters ran together, fusing into a single powerful herd, their footfalls heavy enough to shake the land. Babies scurried after their aunts and mothers, and were efficiently guided deep within the crowd of bodies, until only the tallest, heaviest adults stood along the herd's perimeter. Shane's first thought — that she'd upset the mammoths somehow — was replaced with a more chilling fear, when she realized that they were all turned toward one specific point in the valley.

They were facing an unseen threat.

Once again, Shane thought about the Ice Age exhibit at the natural history museum. The great, grinning skulls of prehistoric lions, sabertooth tigers, and short-faced bears. Dead predators might not hunger, but would they kill? Like a well-fed house cat killed mice and insects just for the thrill of the hunt? She'd been confident in the mammoths' ability to scare off all the carnivores, but . . .

There were large, claw-tipped prints near the water.

A lumbering matriarch broke away from the group and charged at the thing in the valley . . . animal, monster, another human? Shane couldn't see. The unknown was hidden behind the herd.

Suddenly, the charging matriarch took a sharp turn and stopped, stomping in place. At Shane's side, Nellie tensed and growled low.

A muscular prehistoric lioness, with fur the color of golden grass, swiftly outmaneuvered the matriarch and raced directly toward Shane.

"Nellie!" she screamed. "Come!" At most, Shane had ten seconds to escape, but how? She couldn't outrun or fight the beast. From the speaking shell, Amelia cried, "What's happening?" No time to answer. No time to think. Spurred by instinct, Shane leapt for the boulder in the river. Her feet skittered on its wet surface; she teetered, and then her right foot slipped back and plunged into the water, which was as cold as an ice bath. With a gasp, Shane fell and landed belly-first on the small platform, her fingers digging into the boulder's natural grooves to stop her body from sliding fully into the river. With a grunt of exertion, she pulled herself up and tucked her soggy feet under her, kneeling.

"Nellie, come!" she shouted, opening her arms. "Jump!"

On the bank, the bloodhound darted back and forth, whining and yapping anxiously. Behind him, the mammoth herd was in motion; a tall, scraggly mammoth with a bristly tuft on her head charged at the lioness, who veered off-course to dodge the defensive attack, which bought Shane a little more time, but not enough. As she urged Nellie to spring into her arms, Shane wondered whether the dead could also hurt each other. Were the mammoths just acting out of vestigial instincts from their former lives? Or did the lioness actually pose a threat to their families? It occurred to Shane that, even if she didn't answer those questions now, there'd be time, someday, to learn all the secrets Below. More time than she could comprehend. For everyone, eventually.

"Nellie!" Shane commanded once more, infusing her tone with every scrap of authority she possessed. "Nellie, heel! Come!" With a final bark, Nellie took a flying leap toward his human, who leaned forward, reaching for his forelimbs.

With a splash, he landed in the river just a foot away from Shane's grasp. He started doggy-paddling, trying to resist the current, struggling to reach her. But even though the river was relatively slow, its power swept him away from the boulder. If the river carried Nellie out of sight, who knew how far he'd go. Desperately, Shane removed her backpack, coats, and gloves, and flung the bundle to the other side of the river, where her supplies landed on the edge of the bank. Then, she jumped toward Nellie.

Simultaneously, the six-foot long lioness, who'd outmaneuvered the mammoth guards, pounced.

One second, the dog was in the water, the human on the boulder, and the lioness in the air.

The next second, they were all in the water.

∽ TWENTY-FIVE ∽

The shock of plunging into the cold river made it difficult to breathe, so Shane couldn't turn around to confront the horror on her trail, even when she heard a heavy splash behind her. As her clothes became saturated and heavy with near-freezing water, she gasped for air, her chest spasming. Shane had to stay afloat, to breathe, to reach Nellie before the dark river stole him away. With a sharp bark, Nellie twisted and doggy-paddled against the current, while Shane kicked her legs and front-crawled toward him. Her fingertips brushed his sleek forehead, but they were too numb to feel his silky fur.

With a quick lunge, she grasped Nellie's scruff and pulled him toward the bank. Her knees brushed gravel; they'd reached a shallow section of the river. Shivering, Shane stood and heaved Nellie up and into her arms. The water crashed against her knees, but she resisted its attempts to knock her over. Just a few steps, and they'd be on dry land again.

Then, Shane saw the cave lioness. Saw her clearly, for the first time. Broad muzzle, bright brown eyes, long canines — features very similar to those of twentieth-century lions. The animal's head was tilted above the water, and she swam by kicking her legs, like a dog. The current had swept the lioness downstream, but she moved toward Shane with extraordinary persistence, drawing closer inch by inch, resisting the river through sheer physical strength. Although house cats were known to panic in bathtubs, the lioness was the image of deadly, collected grace.

What did she want? Surely, the dead couldn't starve. There didn't seem to be other lions around, no family to guard, and the mammoths would pose a greater threat to cubs, anyway. The lioness must be attracted to Shane for reasons other than desperate hunger or protectiveness. If this was a frivolous game of cat and mouse, then Shane had to ruin the beast's fun.

Still carrying Nellie, who'd begun to wiggle, Shane ran up the bank. Then, she lowered Nellie to the ground, let him free, and picked up a baseball-sized rock.

"Go! Get!" She threw the rock, which landed with a "plop" near the lioness's head. At Shane's side, Nellie barked at the approaching threat with uncharacteristic viciousness. In numb hands, Shane scooped pebbles from the ground and flung them over the water, causing the lioness to flinch and blink but not stop. No, no, the beast had nearly reached the shallow shelf in the river. If Shane thought about home — concentrated really hard — could she leave this cold and dangerous nightmare? Fall from one world to another? Return to Earth, where steppe lions had been extinct for over ten thousand years?

There wasn't enough time to try. Instead of tapping her shoes together and hoping that the universe would kindly return her home — it wouldn't; it never had — Shane unfastened the flare pistol from her belt and took aim. The rocks hadn't frightened the lioness, but a loud crack of sound and a bright flash of light might do the trick.

With luck, the pistol wasn't fouled by river water.

As the lioness cat-paddled close, Shane pulled the trigger.

Crack!

Red flame zipped over the lioness's head and landed in the river. The effect was immediate; the lioness yowled, reared back, and was pulled away by the current. However, after losing ten feet of distance, she spun around and started paddling in place, as if she couldn't decide where to swim. And maybe, had that flare been Shane's only line of defense, she would have found the courage to resume her playful hunt. But the gunfire had awoken a strange strength in Nellie, who bounded down the bank to get close to the predator. From the water, the lioness regarded him with bright jasper eyes.

Shane felt a vibration in the air, a low hum that caused her teeth to ache. A growl, building into a rumble, exploding into a flurry of barks, which were sharper, louder than the explosion of Shane's pistol. Wincing, she covered her ears to protect them from the sound. Ripples creased the river's surface, as the water tension bent against Nellie's power. On the other side of the river, the mammoths trumpeted in agitation and stomped the grass flat.

The lioness surged a foot closer to the bank, testing Nellie. He didn't back down. On the contrary, as Shane watched with horror, the bloodhound lunged forward. His front paws splashed into the shallow water.

"Go away!" Shane shouted, trying to throw another rock at the lioness, but her numb fingers wouldn't grip the heavy, frisbee-shaped piece of granite she found on the bank. Could she grab Nellie and run? No. Cats loved a chase.

Shane had to trust that Nellie would defend her, and hope that she wouldn't lose him in the process.

Nellie lunged a second time, going chest-deep in the running water, froth and debris swirling around his body. As his barks reached an apex, blood trickled out of Shane's nose and cooled on her upper lip.

The clock was ticking; she urgently had to change into dry clothes before hypothermia set in. However, Shane stood rooted in place, unwilling to turn her back on Nellie. "Good boy," she whispered.

The lioness lifted her paw and brought it splashing down, petulantly swiping at nothing.

Then, she simply turned and swam away.

Nellie stayed half-submerged in the river until the lioness reached the other bank. Panting and tail-tucked, he backed into Shane's waiting arms. She squeezed him in a fierce hug.

"You did it. You did it . . ." Shane lifted one arm to wipe the tacky blood off her face, and Nellie twisted to lick her cheek. From the speaking shell, a chorus of voices — everybody at camp, it seemed — spoke at once: "Shane!" and "What's happening?" and "Are you OK?"

"Have to get warm," she told them, shivering. Afraid to turn her back on the lioness, even now, Shane backed toward her pile of jackets and hiking backpack. Fortunately, she'd packed long johns for the night and a change of clothes for day two. Quickly, Shane removed her damp socks, overalls, shirt, and underwear and stepped into the two layers of dry clothing, pulling a pair of jeans and a flannel shirt over the full-body sleepwear. Then, she shoved her numb hands into the gloves, slipped on the double jackets, and fastened a dry bandana around her head. Not much Shane could do about her soggy shoes; they'd make the hike painfully uncomfortable, but as long as the temperatures didn't fall too low, her toes would survive alright.

Shane didn't see the lioness anymore. Had she fled? Was she hiding? Were there others in the nearby tundra; didn't lions live in groups, too? The rescue had become a desperate scramble for survival, and that frightened her. With a bored predator on the other side of the river, Shane couldn't attempt a retreat. Couldn't flee to the warmth and familiarity of the desert. It wouldn't be safe there, anyway. The sky was dimming, imitating late afternoon; whatever lived in those massive burrows between the saguaros would emerge at twilight. She was sure of it.

There was only path: forward.

"What's the time?" she asked, hoping that her brother would answer.

"Four ten," Marcos said.

Despite the dry clothes, a chill clung to Shane, who hoped that movement would warm her up. "We're going to keep tracking," she told Marcos, and then Shane surveyed the unbroken tundra with her binoculars. There was another mammoth herd in the distance; she'd monitor them for defensive behavior. They and Nellie could be trusted to provide fair warning if another predator got boldly curious. Hopefully, that wouldn't be an issue.

"I don't know if me and Nellie will reach the mountains 'fore it's night. This tundra seems to go forever."

And who said it didn't? The mountains could be a thousand miles away; rules were different Below, clearly. Maybe they rose from the edge of eternity. If so, Shane hoped that the tundra shifted into a more habitable zone soon.

To remind Nellie of their goal, Shane held Bobby's cap under the bloodhound's nose. "Scent," she asked, willing her teeth to stop chattering. "Track!" At least her hair was dry, except for the tip of her braid.

Dutifully, Nellie resumed his quick trot toward the mountains.

"Why were you screaming?" Marcos asked.

"I was screaming? When?"

"You said, 'Go, get,'" he imitated. "Before all the barking. Are there monsters?"

"It was . . . a big lion," she hesitantly explained.

"Wha?!"

"But Nellie protected me! He's strong in the Below."

There was a pause. Then, "Can Nellie smell everything, no matter how far?"

"Good question."

"Maybe Ma's there, too, but he just doesn't know it."

"It's possible." Shane stooped to pick up a couple small twigs; they'd fallen off a calf-high, leafless bush. "But if Ma isn't Below, that means she's definitely alive. So don't get discouraged if I return without her."

"Dis-what?"

"Dis-couraged. It's a feeling. Like you want to give up because something bad happened." Shane was an expert at defining words for Marcos, who would borrow "big kid" books from the library and bring them home for Shane to help read. The day he learned how to use a dictionary would be bittersweet.

"Oh." Marcos paused. "I feel that a lot."

She resisted the urge to reply, "Ditto." Instead, Shane sympathized, "Things have been rough." As she walked, something brushed her cheek; she looked up, surprised to see wispy snowflakes dropping languidly from the cloudless gray sky. Snow dusted Nellie's back like dander.

"It's five o'clock," Marcos said.

❧ TWENTY-SIX ❧

At your age, I never visited the public library — didn't have a lending card with my name and clunky signature. The nearest library was beyond the airport and over the railroad tracks, in the county half that didn't flood during hurricanes. But us kids in the valley found other ways to read. Every family had a few good books, and they'd go back and forth between houses. Pages got worn with creased corners, dirty fingerprints, and doodles scrawled in crayon and marker over the pictures. Secret messages appeared between the printed text. Handwritten codes of English, Spanish, and even attempted Lipan, which had never been constrained by an alphabet, not fully, and maybe never will.

With no big sibling to teach me words, I'd bring books to our mother and grandparents instead. Even Grandpa Louis read to me, during the year he stayed in our laundry room. He'd use goofy voices for different characters and change the ending when the whim struck. The only person who never read to me was Pa. I'd ask, and he'd say, "Grandma does better." Or, "Your mother hasn't read that one yet. Give her a chance!" His reluctance confused me since Pa normally loved telling stories. It wasn't until later, when I was older and more observant, that I noticed he always gave mail to Ma, and she'd read the letters aloud; that Pa had to stare at an instruction manual for ten minutes, his brow creased in frustration, 'fore he was able to set up the television; that I didn't know his handwriting, 'cause Ma did all the writing in the house, jars labeled with her bold penmanship.

Pa went to school, up to grade four. But I guess the lessons weren't enough, or maybe he'd never been taught the right way.

In grade one, I borrowed a book about trucks and handed it to Pa, but 'fore he could tell me to ask somebody else for help, I asked whether I could read to him; explained I knew most of the words, but wanted a grown-up to listen. We sat under the oak tree, alongside the swing, and when I struggled over new phrases like "tractor trailer," he encouraged me to sound them out and could identify everything by image. It became our new tradition. Sometimes, he'd interrupt a book with stories of his own, which I enjoyed more than anything in a book.

I can't remember them all, his stories. They're down here somewhere. In the land of the dead.

～ TWENTY-SEVEN ～

The snow continued falling, but it remained light, like dust motes, not clumps of white ash. Shane passed more herds of woolly mammoths, and saw, through her binoculars, a gigantic furred rhinoceros. Wary of his four-foot-long horn, she diverted Nellie from their trail to give the rhino extra space. All the while, Shane chatted with the camp on Earth and collected timber, carrying the sticks in a sling made from her discarded overalls. Her old clothes weren't technically wet anymore, since they'd frozen stiff.

It was difficult to judge the temperature. Shane felt overwhelmingly cold, her toes, fingers, and nose aching. Could've been anywhere from thirty to twenty degrees Fahrenheit, decreasing gradually but noticeably, as the light overhead dimmed. By six, the mountains were indistinct silhouettes against the deep gray sky. They seemed no closer. Just more mysterious.

With every aching step, Shane felt a growing sense that something, somewhere, was watching her. At first, she had chalked it up to paranoia, her survival instincts overloading to compensate for the loss of light. Nellie would bark if he felt threatened. Just like he'd barked at the lioness. So she turned on her flashlight and doggedly kept walking, planning to follow the trail until full dark. Eventually she'd set up camp, eat, light a fire, and rest. Not sleep; how could she sleep, when there were lions in the grass? What nightmares would she have in the world Below?

Then, Nellie abruptly stopped walking. He swiveled around, looking back, his tail tucked.

"What is it?" Shane asked. She couldn't see anything behind them. Just bare tundra, lightened with a dusting of snow. Perhaps he'd heard a hare or mouse. It was odd, though. Nellie rarely became distracted during a search. To be safe, Shane took out her binoculars and surveyed the distant land. Nothing jumped out, but . . .

What was that against the horizon behind her? She fixed the lenses on a vague irregularity in the landscape. By adjusting the focus, Shane tried to coax out details, but the shape was too far away. It could be a narrow boulder or a tree without branches. Maybe even a tall animal, standing still. When she lowered the binoculars, Nellie wagged his tail once and then continued tracking.

Whatever the shape was, it didn't get closer. Which was great, except it didn't seem to get farther, either. Every few minutes, Shane checked.

Was she being followed?

Over the next ten minutes, the sky, which had been dimming slowly, remained a tenuous, barely-bright shade of gray.

Then, abruptly, it went dark. With a cry of surprise, Shane grabbed Nellie around the neck and crouched beside him. They were still in the tundra, but without the moon, it resembled a void. "Is it night in

Texas?" Shane asked the speaking shell. This time, Donnie responded.

"Not yet."

"Our days aren't synced." That made sense, considering the extremely different landscape and weather. Yet Shane hadn't expected to rest so early; with a forty-eight-hour window, every hour of active tracking was critical. She couldn't continue hiking in the dark; Nellie might lead them near a herd of resting mammoths, or worse. It was time to find a clearing and set up camp. She'd packed a sleeping bag and rudimentary one-person tent, and had collected enough twigs for a small fire. Hastily, she found her flashlight by touch and clicked it awake, illuminating the circle of gravel around Nellie.

"Can't see a thing," Shane whispered into the speaking shell. "Nightfall is like the total darkness of a cave. There's nothing in the sky."

"Pretend you're in a movie theater," Donnie suggested. "That's nicer."

"Considering the freaky stuff you watch?" she joked. "Nah, I don't think so."

However, Shane had been wrong; as her eyes adjusted to the dark, her expanding pupils registered pinpoints of light overhead. One by one, a universe of stars revealed itself. "Wha . . ." she gasped. Whose sky was this? Her head tilted back, Shane viewed constellations without names. "I'm in another galaxy," she gasped.

"Huh?"

"There's no Big Dipper, Venus, or anything I know. Just strange lights scattered across the sky."

"Holy cosmic horror." A thoughtful, almost awe-stricken pause later, Donnie whispered, "What if they're the ghosts of dead stars?"

"Stars die?"

"All the time!"

"Even ours?" Shane couldn't fathom the death of the sun. She'd always taken solace in his eternal presence; as long as he held the Earth in his steady orbit, life could persist. He'd remember Grandpa Hugo's prayers. He'd rise and set over generations beyond hers.

"Eventually. In the massively distant future, but still. Did you know that black holes are real too? They eat stars."

"Yeah?" Shane squeezed her eyes shut. "Don't like that." With renewed determination, she looked downward and swept her flashlight beam across the ground, searching for a cozy spot to camp.

"There isn't one near us, don't worry. I mean. Astronomers just measured a supermassive anomaly at the center of our galaxy, so that's probably a black hole, but we're safe."

"Can we talk about something less existentially terrifying?" Shane requested, with a nervous laugh.

"Oh! Totally! Guh. Sorry. I was trying to distract you. Did I make things worse?"

"It's fine," Shane reassured her. "I just . . ."

Behind her, in the distance, a bright orange light was bobbing near the horizon, too low to be a star.

"Donnie," Shane hissed quickly. "I see something weird."

"What?"

"Fire? A torch? It could be another human."

"Bobby?"

"No. Nellie gets excited when targets are nearby." If anything, he currently looked timid, uncertain. The orange light was drawing closer, a quick approach. Should Shane run away? Hide? Stand her ground and wait? She drew her grandfather's hunting knife, her fingers large enough, while gloved, to fill the grooves on the wooden hilt.

Nellie barked twice.

Then, his tail began to wag, and he dropped his head low in a playful stance.

"They're dogs!" Shane exclaimed, laughing with relief. "Just dogs!"

The light emanated from a glass lantern dangling from a metal hook on a curious wooden sled pulled by three dogs, one in front of the other. Unlike the huskies of the north, the pups were a medium-large breed with triangular ears, short brown fur, and pale faces. The leader had a large dark spot on her side. As the group darted closer, Shane searched for signs of a rider, but the sled's lumpy contents were hidden under a dark blanket.

"Who's there?" she called. There came no answer. Instead, the new dogs drew to a stop alongside Nellie, who sniffed their muzzles and tried to entice them into a game of chase by hopping side to side. In response, they looked toward Shane, as if they expected her to explain Nellie's unprofessional behavior. The shorthair dogs were fastened by rope and leather harnesses to the wooden cargo sled, which was the length of a small kayak.

"What did you bring me, guys?" Shane asked, re-sheathing her knife. Their body language set her at ease. The dogs were calm, well-trained, and healthy. Slowly, she circled the sled, which resembled a long cart on skis, and checked its cargo for movement. Seeing none, Shane pinched one corner of the brown wool blanket and drew it aside, revealing a folded stack of clothes: a white poncho woven from a fine, soft wool; high boots; a brown pelt; fur-lined mittens; and a checkered hat with flaps to protect her ears. The outfit was sourced from such a wide variety of materials and styles, Shane imagined that its pieces came from a bazaar of many times and cultures, all humans mingling Below. Idly, she wondered how leather and pelts were acquired in the underworld. Did they come from dead animals? Were they renewable, like sheepswool? Or did people trade their burial clothes, a finite resource? If so, the pelt was a precious gift.

Near the front of the sled were several large, dry branches and a bulbous, cork-sealed clay jar, which sloshed when Shane picked it up. The bottom of the sled was padded by a fibrous, tightly woven mat.

"What's happening?" Donnie asked. "I don't hear shouting. That's good, right?"

"Somebody used a dogsled to deliver warm clothes, firewood, and a drink," Shane explained, puzzled. "They're concerned about me, but know enough to stay hidden."

"Mr. Somebody wants you to get back to Earth."

"Yeah." After glancing, questioning, toward the dark, Shane removed her wet socks and hiking boots, flinching at the sight of ten pale, pruny toes, her nails purplish in the cold. She stepped into the boots, which were a couple sizes too large, and then layered the poncho over her jackets. Gardening gloves were efficiently replaced with the well-insulated, fur-lined mittens. They would better protect her hands from frostbite, which cleaved unprotected fingers. Lastly, she slipped the hat over her head and ears.

"Much better," Shane sighed, and all four dogs tilted their heads as they attempted to understand the human babble. It was astounding how a few extra layers could warm a body.

Nellie, finally accepting that the new-comers were not eager to play, trotted to a nearby bush and bent to sniff its lower branches. Curiously, the sled dogs walked after him. They'd initially stopped next to Nellie, too, as if instructed to deliver their cargo to him, the floppy-eared dog without a harness. Was Nellie their temporary leader? Would they follow him anywhere?

Shane eyeballed the sled, confirming that it was large enough for a single human rider.

"I'm going to try something," she told Donnie. "It might get me to Bobby faster." And out of the prehistoric tundra.

"Ride the sled?" her friend guessed.

"Exactly, yes." She put out a hand. "Nellie, stay." Then, Shane slowly climbed into the long cargo area, which was boxy, as if a wheeled cart had been converted into a vehicle that could slide over snow. Sitting with her legs out, she put the pelt and backpack on her lap and wrapped the wool blanket around her shoulders like a shawl. Then, Shane rocked side to side, testing the stability of her seat. The ski-like runners remained steady despite her shifting weight; the lantern, which dangled from the hook behind her head, barely swayed.

"Track, Nellie!" Shane commanded. Her bloodhound tilted his head back to sniff the air, his breath expelled in quick white puffs. As Nellie honed in on Bobby's scent, Shane clasped each side of the sled with her gloved hands, tightly, as if clutching the bar of a roller coaster cart before the first big drop.

Nellie's head whipped toward the mountains, which resembled irregular voids in the sky. Then, he yapped once and started tracking at a steady pace. Unquestioningly, the train of dogs followed. To help Nellie navigate, Shane turned her flashlight forward, using it like the headlights on a vehicle; she imagined an unseen sea of mammoths and lions parting around them. It was a comfort to think that her faceless protector was also somewhere in the dark.

"Idea successful?" Donnie asked. It was her turn on shell duty.

"So far so good. We're moving slow, which makes it easier to stay balanced, I guess."

"Channel your Grandpa Louis and pretend you're on a Harley. Riding's in your blood."

"Forget him," she bitterly replied. "This is an adventure for my four-great-grandma. She got ghost dogs to carry stuff. Not people, though. Pretty sure Four-Great trained horses for that."

Wondering, Shane closed her eyes and listened for the distant thump of hooves, but heard only the scrape of treads sliding over the snow-slick ground. After a moment, she tabled that train of thought and fished a sandwich from the hiking backpack.

"Supper time."

"We're eating pepperoni pizza and cheesy bread."

"From Pizza Dale?" she chuckled. "Guess it's convenient."

"And free."

"What? Free food? From the Dale?" Had policy changed in the week she'd been gone?

"One of the dish guys noticed our camp. He does smoke breaks along the river, says it's meditative. Well, he returned with your friend Jose and two large pies."

"Carl didn't cause a scene?"

"Carl doesn't know!" shouted Amelia distantly.

In the background, a young woman chirped too, "Is that her talking through a shell?"

"Gabrielle?" Shane asked, recognizing her former coworker's soft voice. But what was she doing at camp? They were friends, sure, but Shane never asked Gabrielle for favors.

"Yes, it's me! I'm here!"

"I'm here, too," said a young man's voice, who she identified as belonging to one of Pizza Dale's part-time delivery boys; prior to that moment, they'd only exchanged pleasantries such as "Afternoon," and "How ya doing?" and "Fine, thanks. You?"

Well. She should have expected news to spread; Jose was notoriously chatty. She wouldn't be surprised if every staff member and longtime customer of Pizza Dale would now catch wind of "the girl in the underworld."

Well. Except for Carl; he had a rule about personal stories, after all.

The cart jolted over an extra lumpy tuft of grass, and Shane was grateful for the mat, which cushioned her tailbone during the bumpy ride. There was little shock absorption built into the elevated structure, which wasn't as low and stable as a traditional dogsled. At least Nellie set a calm pace; if he started running, Shane gave herself a fifty-fifty chance of overturning within the first minute, even on the flat tundra. After a while, she hunkered down, using the backpack as a pillow and tucking her knees to fit in the four-foot-long cart. The layered bison pelt and wool blanket were thick enough to protect her from the cold, which froze moisture on her eyelashes.

"Eight o'clock," Marcos reported.

"Thanks, buddy."

"Shane?"

"Yeah?"

"What do the dead stars look like?" He must have been listening to her earlier conversation with Donnie.

"Same as living stars. They're just in different places."

"Look up," Donnie said, and Shane almost protested that she already was, until she realized that Donnie was speaking to Marcos, all the way on Earth. "Some of the stars you see are already gone. We just don't know it yet."

"Why?"

"Because they're very far away. It takes time for a ray of starlight to go from one solar system to another. And the farther a star is from Earth, the longer the journey will be."

Donnie's voice went soft when she spoke to Marcos; was she thinking of her own little brother?

"I still don't get it," Marcos said.

"Do you remember when Grandma passed away?" Shane asked. Then, she realized: of course not. He'd only been a baby. Yet Marcos still answered, "Uh huh." And perhaps he thought that he did. How often did family stories of trauma make such a poignant impact that through empathy, and repetition, and their ripples through time, they transformed into hand-me-down memories?

"Mom sent a letter to our friends in Canada," Shane continued, "to let them know the sad news. The letter went to the post office on a Thursday, and it arrived in their mailbox on a Tuesday. It took days for sad news to travel two thousand miles. Well, when a star goes dark, it can take a very long time for that darkness to reach earth. We see their old light, and think everything's alright, because we don't know better."

"Oooooh!"

The lantern rattled and went dim; the dogs marched tirelessly, shouldering more weight than living dogs should ever pull, especially without food, water, and rest. Shane hoped that they were happy and comfortable; Nellie showed no signs of tiring himself, and hadn't seemed overly cold or achy. Unfortunately, that wasn't the case for Shane. At least she could rest. As the time passed, and the sled crept toward the mountains, she catalogued all her sore spots, signs that she still belonged to a world of sensations, of pain.

Shortly after Marcos drowsily reported, "Ten o'clock," Shane fell asleep under the primordial constellations.

≈ TWENTY-EIGHT ≈

There was no tickle of dawn against my eyelids; daylight flooded my dreams, as fast and bright as a camera's flashbulb. I jolted awake and sat up; the world was passing in a disorienting blur of movement, dogs running. We hit a bump, and the cart teetered to the left. Rather than overturning, it balanced on the edge of one long runner. To compensate, I threw my weight to the right — but too quickly! The wobbling cart flipped over and threw me onto soft, warm grass. It skittered a few feet 'fore the dogs realized that their cargo had spilled. They stopped and looked at me with their tails tucked anxiously.

First word out of my mouth was, "Nellie!" I couldn't see him; couldn't see much of anything. Well. Until my pupils adjusted to the intense light.

Like I said, this is a story. It's truth and symbolism. You'll study the words "symbolism," "metaphor," "simile," and "allegory" in English class someday. Learn how we use one thing to represent another, for various reasons, and through various methods.

I'd awoken in a place like home. Is that a simile? Honestly, I'm not sure. Is it the truth? Haven't decided. I'm rehearsing the story I'll tell you when I return. It might evolve between now and then.

Sorry. Going off the rails. Let me start over.

I awoke in a familiar place, Marcos. In many ways, it resembled our community in la rancheria de los Lipanes, as if all the people we'd lost after the flood had washed up and built anew. Now, you were born on the road, long after our neighborhood was taken. But you've seen old photos: faded snapshots of family and friends, our houses, our crops, even my swing on the old oak tree behind our house. Thank goodness for Grandma's incredible foresight. If she hadn't grabbed a photo album during the hurricane evacuation, there'd be no pictures left.

Use the pictures to visualize my surroundings in the world Below. I won't go into more specific detail. It doesn't feel right; like maybe you aren't meant to know what I saw. I probably shouldn't know what I saw, either, but it ain't like I can banish memories on a whim. Trust me. I've tried. Sometimes I wish I could take a piece of steel wool and scrub my brain — wash away all the moments that still hurt me and make it hard to sleep. What would remain, once they were gone? An abbreviated life, I guess, though I wish that wasn't so.

The new place was empty. Quiet, too. I was afraid to speak with you on the shell, unsure whether my voice would call others. Terrified that Nellie had become distracted by the scents of his former life and hadn't taken us to Bobby at all.

Who'd he led us to?

Nellie was being antsy; although he obeyed my command to heel, he leaned forward, as if my authority was a taut, invisible leash. After unhooking the sled dogs, who also stayed close, I quickly changed into warm-weather clothes and then held out the baseball cap. "Scent," I told Nellie. Then, "Track."

Nellie took off like a racing grayhound. The sled dogs dutifully pursued their leader, and I tried to keep up, but got left in the dust. Soon, I was alone.

I stopped in my tracks. That's what Ma taught me; Nellie only runs fast when his target is close. I was supposed to let him go and wait until he howled. But what if that tactic didn't work Below, where deserts expand and contract around you, or because of you? How would I find my way back without Nellie? No compass, so I'd have to use the stars, navigate in the night. Would the unseen watcher help? Maybe. But how could I leave Nellie behind? He was family, and Ma was still lost; without Nellie, who would find her? Could I do it alone?

To calm my thoughts, I closed my eyes and focused on the sound of my breathing, which was slightly labored because of the sprint. I promised myself that Nellie would howl 'fore my heart rate returned to a relaxed pace.

In the darkness, the world was inhales, exhales, and the sudden, soft crunching of footsteps, coming closer; behind me, closer; beside me, stopping. I didn't open my eyes.

Then, somebody gently touched my shoulder.

When I looked — I couldn't help it — I saw a man and a woman who resembled Donnie so closely, they had to be her parents. They were the couple in her picture, the one she showed me in Tanner. The woman opened her mouth to say —

To the right, Nellie howled, and a dense flock of passenger pigeons exploded into the sky, their wings the color of rainclouds, their bellies the blush of sunrise. The woman's lips said, *Bobby.* Although I couldn't hear her voice over the chaos of birds and Nellie, I imagined that she sounded like Donnie.

It struck me, suddenly, that she'd returned to her people, with the man she loved. Maybe that's why the community reminded me of home.

"I'll help your son," I promised.

Not long ago, there were billions of passenger pigeons. They're extinct now, just like the woolly mammoth. As I followed the voice of my hound, the flock zipped overhead. At first, it was odd to see them around people, but then I remembered that our grandparents had lived in the time of passenger pigeons. The birds' slaughter had been quick, since settlers had been insatiable.

By the time I reached Nellie, still howling, the sky was empty and giving me a well-lit view of a boy in blue jeans and a red baseball jersey. He was tall, taller than you, and thin as a rail, with doe-big eyes and frazzled black hair. His skin was a shade darker than Donnie's, and he had a slight overbite that'll probably get adjusted with braces when he's older. The dogs surrounded him, their tails wagging, and he didn't notice me 'cause he was busy covering his ears and fussing at Nellie, saying, "What's wrong? Stop crying! I won't hurt you!"

Nellie went quiet when I appeared, so I heard the tail end of Bobby's pleas. He smiled at him, probably assuming that he'd successfully persuaded the dog to behave.

"Bobby?" I called. "Bobby!"

Poor kid went still and then swiveled, searching. "Mom?" he shouted, not yet seeing me. Doubt I sound like his mother, but he was young when his parents died, and you can forget the way a person sounds with enough absence. I try to think back, recall our father's voice, and it's like my head is full of echoes. Soft and sketchy, nothing like the original sound. Sometimes, I wish Pa had been a big-time performer, so I could listen to him singing on the record player.

When Bobby finally saw me, he made a shrill sound of joy, and then he ran to me, hugged me tight. I thought about you, Marcos, and how you embraced me in the diner after I was lost. "It's OK now," I said, putting the baseball cap on his head and giving him a reassuring squeeze.

He asked, "Why is everyone hiding? Who are you? Where are we?" One question ran into the next, a week of confusion unleashed in a babbling avalanche. I clasped his warm hand firmly, afraid that he'd slip away like sand through my fingers.

"It's OK, it's OK!" I told him. "If anyone is hiding, it's because they don't want to accidentally hurt you. Do you want anything to eat or drink?"

When he shook his head no, I internally freaked, worried that he no longer needed sustenance or anything else from Earth. That I was too late. But then he explained: "I already ate breakfast."

Somehow, I doubted that he'd prepped all his meals for a week; somebody, unseen, must have helped.

"Good, great! I'm Shane, Donnie's friend! Let's go home, OK? She's waiting! Your grandparents are, too." I hadn't heard a peep from the shell, and figured that it was dawn on Earth and my communications were muffled. I'd have to speak directly in the shell to get Earth's attention. They'd be ecstatic that Bobby was safe. He should've been ecstatic, too. His fairy ring ordeal was nearly over.

However, Bobby wasn't glad. Instead, he pulled on my arm and insisted, "We can't leave without Mom and Dad. They're here! I know they're here! They left me banana pancakes today! Why are they hiding? Why won't they talk to me? I'm not lying! They didn't die! They've been here all this time! Where is this place? It has no sun!"

He called for his mom and dad with the anguish of a child who thought he'd been abandoned. How could I explain that wasn't the case?

"Bobby," I said, kneeling in front of him and clasping both his hands in mine. "I'm sorry. I'm so sorry. If your parents could be here, they would. They can't, Bobby. They did pass away."

Tears welled in his eyes, and I braced myself for more sorrowful denials.

Then, from the speaking shell, Donnie asked, "Bobby, is that you?"

"Donnie?" he gasped. "Yes! Where are you?"

"Bobby!" His sister screamed with joy. "I missed you so much! You have no idea! Are you OK?"

Quickly, I passed Bobby the shell. He answered, "Donnie, I can't go home yet. Mom and Dad are still alive, and —"

She interrupted, "No! You need to trust me, OK? Do you trust me?"

Kid went, "Uh huh."

She asked, "Remember the woods? The last time we were together? You stepped in a magic trap. It sent you out of this world, to a place you do not belong. So I asked

546

the best adventurer in Texas to rescue you. Her name's Shane."

Bobby looked at me. "An adventurer?" he asked.

"Yes," Donnie insisted. "Best in the universe."

"That's a stretch," I interjected. "Texas is big enough for me."

Donnie ignored my modest interruption. "Go with Shane. Do what she says. When you're home, we'll watch all the movies you want."

"Even my baby movies?" he asked, beaming.

"I never should have called them that." I think I heard Donnie's breath catch, like she was holding back tears. "But yeah. Even them."

"I missed you, too," Bobby told her, hugging the shell tight. "OK. Me and Shane will be back soon."

With all my heart, I hoped that what he said was true. But as Ma always says: the return is half the journey.

⁓ TWENTY-NINE ⁓

They'd left the community hours ago, and Shane was beginning to worry that they'd never reach the portal home. They weren't even in the tundra yet! To be fair, the return trip was slowed by the extra person. Bobby rode in the sled — which functioned passably well over the dry land, although Shane wasn't sure how long the runners would hold out — with the bags and the speaking shell. He'd been chatting with his family up above all morning, his cheer relentless, even as Shane's optimism began to deflate. Walking alongside Bobby, she tried to eavesdrop on his conversation with the people of Earth, but the wind

548

stole fragments of his voice. Sometimes, Shane smelled blossoming sunflowers, which made her wonder how far the wind had traveled, and where it came from. There were no sunflowers in sight. The intermittent breezes pressed against her back, gentle touches urging her forward.

Further, there were no old sled tracks to reassure Shane that they were taking the correct route, but Nellie seemed confident.

"I'm thirsty," Bobby announced. "Is this water?" He held up the cork-sealed jar and gave it a shake.

"I don't know. That came with the sled. Here, take this." Shane passed him her thermos. "Only drink what you need, OK? We have to be very careful." With two people sharing the remaining water, their supply would probably run out within twenty-four hours. At the river, she'd have to refill the bottles. Although Shane was reluctant to eat or drink anything from Below, she'd swallowed a mouthful of frigid water during her escape from the prehistoric lion, and it hadn't made her sick, or drained her life.

She just hoped that they reached the river in time.

"Can you hand me that jar?" she asked Bobby. After he gave it to her, Shane inspected its construction. The vessel was made from a pale tan clay, with a bulbous belly and a tapered top. She wiggled the cork seal loose and sniffed its contents. The drink had a unique, earthy aroma.

Cota. Greenthread.

Slowly, Shane lowered the jar. It had been a long time since she'd had cota tea. Grandma Yolanda used to make a chilled version of the amber-colored drink to share with the family, especially when they were feeling under the weather. In the spring and summer, whenever their leaf stocks ran low, she'd grab a woven basket and then drive north, where bunches of cota sprouted along the road. She'd return with bundles of bright green plants with fine, thin leaves. Once dried, the leaves could be stored in the pantry. To serve many people, she'd boil water in a large pan, steep a little bundle of cota, add a handful of sugar (Grandma Yolanda's hands scooped about half a cup each) and a blob of honey, and then pour everything into a big glass pitcher. Grandma Yolanda would prepare the drink in the evening and let it chill in the refrigerator overnight. The next day, there'd be no ice in their cups, just cool tea. Ice cubes melted too fast in South Texas, and they made drinks taste watery. That's what Grandma Yolanda said, anyway.

How many years had it been since Shane last drank cota tea with sugar and honey? Without Grandma Yolanda to gather the plants, there weren't any in the pantry. It wasn't like Shane could swing by the grocery store and buy cota in easy-to-dunk Lipton baggies either. Driven by longing, she held the jar against her lips and took a small sip. It was exactly like she remembered: earthy and subtly sweet.

For the hundredth time, Shane wondered: Who'd filled the sled with supplies? Who'd sent the dogs? Who'd brewed the tea? Was Grandma Yolanda helping her, or was the drink from a stranger? Cota wasn't a family secret; far from it. In the valley, most adults had brewed it, although other households drank it hot, not cold. In fact, people across the continent's southwest and south had consumed different species of cota since practically forever. And although Shane was Below, the surroundings reminded her of South Texas, complete with all the resources they'd had in the valley.

The dogs led her past yaupon holly, juniper, mesquite, solé with crisp stalks and mild purple flowers, fruiting prickly pears, and wildflowers with buds and blooms. All of them were raw ingredients of a feast.

"Are you OK?" Bobby asked, perhaps noticing the distant expression in her eyes. Or maybe he just worried that the jar was full of poison.

Shane stooped to pick up a dry old mesquite pod. It was curved like the sliver of a waning crescent moon. "Did you know that these can be eaten?" she asked, jogging to catch up with the sled. "When they're fresh." She inclined her head to indicate a mesquite tree adorned with yellow-green pods.

"No," he said. "I play with the dead ones like they're instruments, though."

Smiling, she gave hers a shake, the dry beans rattling.

"Yea, like that!"

"They're great, aren't they?"

"Uh huh. But me and Donnie 'ave never eat them."

"Neither has my brother, Marcos."

"Are they sweet?"

"Depends on how you prepare them. There's lots of ways. Where I come from, everyone in the neighborhood got together. We'd pick pods from the trees, dry them, and grind them into flour using a metate and mano." When Bobby wrinkled his nose with confusion, she explained, "Crush them between a little rock and a bigger, bowl-shaped rock."

"Huh. I thought flour came from wheat."

"You're right. It does. There's different kinds though."

"Do all the mes-keet trees around us make you hungry?"

"A little." Shane resealed the jar and returned it to the sled. "Mostly, they make me think about the past."

Bobby looked down at the speaking shell in his lap. "I'm going to tell Donnie that flour comes from trees sometimes."

"That's a good idea," she said. "Tell Marcos, too. Make sure they're both listening carefully."

After Shane got home, she'd teach her brother how to gather food from their backyard and incorporate the edible plants into a delicious meal, something even Grandpa Louis, who called most vegetables "weeds," would enjoy. But first, she'd make cota tea. Why hadn't she done so already? He was old enough to learn, and she could make the time.

There was one small problem, though, a detail she'd forgotten. How did Grandma Yolanda know when the cota was ready to pick? Should Shane snip pieces of the young plant before its yellow flowers bloomed? Should she wait for the flowers to die, the stems tough and mature? Did it even matter?

In an attempt to solve the mystery, Shane envisioned her grandmother returning home with a basket full of cota. She could recall the fine wrinkles pleating Grandma Yolanda's hands, the sunlight spilling through the open front door, the shape of the boxy cedar basket. However, the rest of the memory was fuzzy, like an overexposed photograph. In fact, all her memories of the tea possessed the hazy quality of old dreams, as if that period of Shane's life were less real than the vivid torments after the flood. Why could Shane mentally return to an ICU waiting room in St. Mary Hospital, catalogue every detail of that miserable place, a place she'd only suffered once, the night her father died? But couldn't remember the details of her grandmother's tea, which was a regular part of spring and summer for most of Shane's childhood. The contrast struck her as cruel.

It didn't matter. Lorenza could teach her.

Right?

Would Shane's mother remember how to gather cota, or, like Shane, had the specifics been pushed aside to make room for more urgent skills, the means of survival in a harsh world? After Grandma Yolanda died, Lorenza had poured all her free time into search and rescue, teaching Shane how to deliver other people home.

Hardship had stripped their lives to the bone, resilient but bare. Shane was out of practice at the skills that flourished during peace, and she worried that her mother was, too. Once things settled down, could they re-teach themselves how to thrive? Or was it too late?

Grandma Yolanda knew the answer. In fact, she knew many glorious things, like how to relax in the shade of an oak tree, sew a traditional dress in just two days, and weave a basket for her burdens. And now, Shane was certain that the tea came from her, since it was perfectly sweet, as if measured by Yolanda's strong hand.

Was she watching? Would she answer a single question, if Shane asked?

Was her grandma alone?

No. Grandma Yolanda never trained dogs to pull sleds. But the trio could've been sent by a different ancestor with her. After all, Shane's maternal line was known as skilled animal trainers. And her heroic four-great-grandmother always traveled with a pack of living and ghostly dogs.

Her family was looking out for her.

Her pa, too? He must know that she was Below.

Numbly, Shane stared at the boots in the sled. They'd fit large, like a women's twelve or men's ten, going by the measurements in standard American department stores. How big were her father's feet? As a child, she'd occasionally stomp around the house in his shoes, laughing and stumbling, pretending to be a giant. However, at that age, her parents had adult-sized feet in her mind, with no nuance. She couldn't use the memories as guidance. The boots might be his, might not. Her eyes skimmed the sled's other contents. The firewood could have been collected by anyone; the checkered hat wasn't her father's style; the pelt was from the days of bison, far before his time; he'd been a talented man, but never a weaver, so the blanket had probably been created by another pair of hands. Still walking, Shane spun around, looking for any sign that he was close. She saw nothing. Nobody.

"Don't be sad," she whispered. "I know why you're hiding. I understand."

"What's that?" Bobby cried out, pointing to the sky. He'd finished gulping from the canteen, and now sat with the shell in his lap and the wool blanket around his shoulders. It occurred to Shane that the temperature had dropped in the past five minutes, from warm to coolish. Did that mean they were getting closer to the land of wooly mammoths? Perhaps. However, during the first leg of her journey, the switch from the desert's heat to the freezing tundra had been abrupt, like jumping into an ice bath.

Following the child's finger with her gaze, Shane was confused by the sight ahead. Above the endless horizon floated a mountain range wrapped in flashing, roiling storm clouds.

"Heel," Shane said, considering. The lightning ahead was silent with distance, the sky above them clear. Continuing forward, they might reach the portal before the storm. On the other hand, they might not. Although Lorenza advised against hiking in the rain, she'd taught Shane how to survive a downpour. But it would be a risky and exhausting journey.

Shane looked over her shoulder at the bright and unchanging world they were escaping.

"What are we going to do?" Bobby asked.

Marcos's voice indistinctly whispered from the shell, like the static on TV when the signal evaded its rabbit-ear antennae. What had he said? A question, a suggestion, an update on the time?

"I'm not sure," Shane answered.

In her head, a round, white clock was ticking. To her, time was never going forward. It was always running out.

~ THIRTY ~

Grandpa Hugo, who'd pray to the sun in the morning,

Grandma Yolanda, who knew the good stories,

Grandma Bee, who had a ghost cat.

Our father, my hero.

They're all here. They speak our language and make our food, even though they never hunger like we do when the fields aren't hiring and the pantry runs low.

Am I really lost? Or am I finally where I belong? Maybe this is the only home left for the piteous remnants of an extinct tribe. Isn't that what people call us? People with more power than we'll ever have.

I'm sorry. That was a terrible train of thought. I won't include it in my story, if I get home. Ever since Ma went missing, I've been prone to bad convictions. It's odd, since Ma says I have a knack for hope, Amelia calls me strong, Donnie believes I'm a badass, and you trust me to make everything better. Lately, I wonder: What do I think about myself? If I'm being honest . . . I don't know.

But as I stood there, Marcos, failing to muster an ounce of motivation to carry on with the rescue, I experienced a vivid memory.

An ant, crawling across the rich brown earth, dragging a wing-shaped potato chip that was fifty times her weight.

"OK Nellie," I said. "Let's do this."

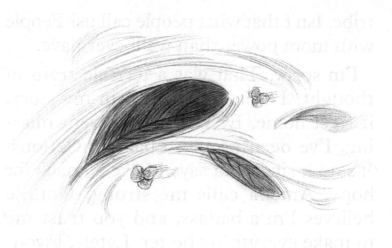

↝ THIRTY-ONE ↜

It would have been difficult to ford the prehistoric river with a child, several ghost dogs, and a sled full of supplies, but fortunately, they didn't have to worry about that, since there was no river anymore. No tundra, either. Instead, the land before them dried up, a slow transition, as gradual as nightfall. Shane couldn't pinpoint the exact moment when the desert engulfed the world, but within an hour, she noticed an arrow made of pebbles on the ground.

"Whoa!" she said, pointing down. "Bobby, check it out!" They were moving at a sluggish crawl, the sled's runners catching and dragging against the clumpy terrain.

"How'd that get there?" Bobby asked, sitting up straight.

"I left it earlier. We're nearly home." They'd gone full circle! Well, the circle was closer to a Möbius strip, but same concept.

Suddenly, one of the runners became wedged against the base of a stout barrel cactus. With a determined push, the three shorthairs strained against their harnesses and forced the sled forward, over the cactus. Bobby cried out in shock as the sled tilted; it was going to overturn!

With a lunge, Shane grabbed Bobby under the arms and pulled him to safety before he could topple onto a clump of pincushion cacti. Her backpack and the sled's other contents scattered across the ground as the dogs dragged the sled, which was now upside down. It resembled a boat gone belly-up.

"Nellie!" Shane called. "Heel!"

The bloodhound trotted to her side, his tail wagging, and Shane lowered Bobby on a clear patch of dirt. In the crook of his arm, he clutched the speaking shell. "Wipeout," Shane commented.

"Yeah, it was gnarly." He raised his voice, "But I'm OK!"

With that, Bobby put the shell on the ground and started gathering the fallen supplies. After watching him a moment, Shane moved to the shorthair dogs and knelt beside the lead on the line. She unfastened his harness, setting him free. He shook the tension out of his body and stretched, bending his front down and his tail up.

"Terrain's too rugged for the sled," Shane called, as she freed the second dog. "We'll have to walk from here."

"Awwwww."

"Your feet are comfy, right?" Thankfully, Bobby wore a pair of high-top black and white Converse, not sandals or uncomfortable dress shoes.

"Uh huh. But! I'm scared of stepping on a scorpion or rattlesnake. Donnie says they hide in plain sight."

"We'll be careful." Now that all the dogs were free, Shane turned the sled right way-up. She neatly placed the wool blanket and bison pelt within its shallow belly for the watchers to retrieve. Everything else, she'd carry to the portal. Bobby could help by holding the shell and one canteen of water. He took them without complaint.

"Walk behind me," Shane continued, tying a bandana around his neck to protect his nape from burning. Unlike Marcos, Bobby had short hair, cut tight against the scalp. "Step where I step. It's like a game. Follow the leader."

Bobby nodded. "What happens if you step on a snake?"

"I'd holler and curse. You better cover your ears, in that case."

"Don't worry," he reassured her. "Donnie taught me the baddest words already."

From the shell, a soft protest: "Did not!"

"Hey, don't tattle on your sister." Shane snickered and shook her head. "C'mon. Let's get moving."

As they followed Nellie by foot, Shane glanced over her shoulder once, to bid the sled and its pups farewell. They'd carried her a long way: across a tundra, over gentle rolling hills, and into the desert, farther than she could've dreamed.

The shorthair dogs sat together, their tails wagging, their ears perked toward Shane. She wondered if they'd meet again someday.

"Goodbye," she said softly. "For now."

Within ten minutes, the dogs and the sled were obscured by distance, folded into the unseen Below. Now a trio, Shane, Bobby, and Nellie trudged onward. It felt like they walked for hours, but Marcos only checked in once. "Nine a.m.," he said, and then he yawned. Had he slept that night? Or had he tossed and turned in the camp along the river, worried that he'd lose everyone?

"What's for breakfast?" Shane asked the shell.

"Pizza," he said.

Amelia called out, "And conchas!"

"The clouds aren't getting bigger or smaller," Bobby remarked, interrupting her chat. "Why's that?"

"They could be moving slowly." With a skip, Shane maneuvered around a young yucca. "Or floating in place like balloons on a string."

"But we've gone miles! Are they running away from us, or what?"

"Uh huh. That's a possibility." She laughed as she looked at him. "Why the frown? You don't want to get caught in a storm, right?"

"No, but a little shade would be nice," he exclaimed, throwing up his hands in a dramatic show of exasperation.

The kid had a point; without the rise and fall of a sun, the desert cast no shadows, except for small patches under horizontal saguaro arms.

"I think we're close," she promised.

"Oww," Bobby rubbed his eye vigorously.

"What's wrong?"

"Got a piece of sand in my eyeball." He lowered his hand and blinked rapidly; a tear slipped down his cheek, carrying the irritant away. The wind had been gaining speed since they entered the desert; a bit stronger, and it might whip into a sand-storm. Puzzled, Shane eyed the distant clouds. They still weren't moving, but the wind might be low-lying.

Suddenly, Nellie halted. He tilted his head, sniffed the air, and then paced in a circle with his nose against the ground, as if searching for a lost trail.

The wind quickened, sharp with sand, like a swarm of biting flies; Shane tied a bandana around her nose and mouth before she helped Bobby do the same. In front of them, Nellie took a couple steps to the right, stopped, turned, and whined.

"I can't hear you, Donnie," Bobby shouted at the shell. He was pressing it against his ear to block out the roar of the Below. Was he successful? Shane couldn't tell. She was too intent on watching Nellie, who still hadn't picked up the trail, as if the wind had scattered their scent, scrubbed it from the land. A gust pummeled her back a step. When she raised a hand to protect her eyes, the wind whipped around and blew from the left, thwarting her defenses.

"What's happening?" Bobby squeaked; he grabbed Shane by the hand, as if afraid he'd blow away without an anchor.

"Let's find shelter. C'mon. Heel, Nellie." Roughly, she remembered the direction Nellie had been travelling before he got confused. Shane didn't want to wander too far, in case they became hopelessly lost, but if a genuine sandstorm occurred, they'd need a shield. Step by step, she and Bobby pushed forward, their heads bent and their stances wide.

The wind swept from right to left. Then left to right. Against her face. Shane felt like a fly batted between the paws of a cat.

She lifted a hand, pressing it against her brow like the cupped brim of a baseball cap.

And for the briefest of seconds, as the wind flagged, she felt a subtle heat against her fingertips . . . faint, so faint. When Shane turned to the right — the east, she thought, even though she had no way of actually knowing — she felt the steady heat against her entire palm. Shane knew the warmth — had felt it a thousand or more times before, when she tilted her face toward the intense summer sun.

There was no sun Below.

The wind whipped low, scattering the sensation of heat, but she thought she had its origin.

"You're smiling!" Bobby exclaimed, and then he made a sour face and spat onto the ground. "Uck! Sorry, I got sand in my mouth."

"That way!" Shane said, pointing with her lips. "I'm sure of it!"

Now that she knew to seek it out, Shane locked on to the heat. Its consistency contrasted with the chaotic and unpredictable nature of the wind. Gentle one moment, furious the next. Nellie's ears blew back like a pair of flags, and he squinted as they walked, his nostrils flaring to process the cacophony of scents Shane could only imagine. Scents carried from the farthest reaches of the world Below: the nameless seas of whales and megalodons; the forests and plains and cities of ghosts. The wind brought them all to him, as if saying: *This is your infinite home, all you're leaving behind.*

And against Shane's face, the sun's warmth intensified, breaking through other distractions. She was jogging, Bobby laughing and still spitting sand, exhilarated, his hair tousled. Maybe he sensed it, too: Earth, within their reach. As she ran, Shane swore she heard a voice in the wind, a prayer to the sun, and then it was her voice, the words her words.

"What are you saying? I can't hear!" Bobby asked.

"I'm thanking him!"

"Who?"

"Sha! The sun!"

"Thank you, sun!" he shouted.

"Xastéyó!"

"Ah stay yo!" he repeated.

Abruptly, two things happened at once: the wind abated, going still; and Shane saw, against the horizon, a familiar twelve-armed saguaro. It was the marker in front of the passageway home.

"We're here!" Shane shouted, so loudly the people at camp must have heard her through the speaking shell, because they responded with a murmur of excitement. "Get ready!"

Nellie yapped excitedly and bolted toward the saguaro; after the wind went still, he must have regained the trail. Shane and Bobby sprinted the final stretch; the heat of the sun was radiating from a two-dimensional juniper shape growing alongside the cactus. The passageway home was a rippling vision of earth's sky, as seen from the river, looking up. In front of the juniper shape, Shane and Bobby stopped to catch their breath, and Nellie trotted to and fro, sniffing the ground and wagging his tail happily.

"Good boy," Shane praised. Then, she took the speaking shell from Bobby to announce, "It's time, everyone! Looks like we'll emerge in the river. Can somebody lean over the tree's shadow, so I know you're there?"

Almost immediately, Donnie's face appeared near the trunk of the juniper shape. The river's ripples distorted her countenance like a subtle funhouse mirror.

Bobby leaned close to the shell and giggled, "I see you!"

From Earth, Donnie beamed and extended her arms, as if reaching for him.

"Here's what we'll do," Shane decided. "Bobby, put one hand through the doorway. Donnie, grab him and pull. That way, nobody gets swept downstream, OK?"

"Ten-four!" Bobby said, nodding. Then, he plunged his right hand through the passage home.

"I got you!" Donnie shouted. Shane watched as Donnie took Bobby by the hand; the girl leaned back, and her brother fell forward, upward, pulled to safety in seconds. Cheers of relief and joy radiated from two places: the shell and home.

For a moment, Shane was overwhelmed by the relief and exhaustion that always overcame her at the end of a rescue: when it was finally time to rest, and all the adrenaline, every ounce of strength that had been fueling her forward momentum, crashed because there was time at last to . . .

No. No, her work wasn't over. No time to rest. Lorenza was missing, and Shane didn't know where to begin searching if her mother wasn't on Earth, but she wasn't Below . . .

She wasn't.

Right?

Shane turned her back to Earth and shouted at the desert, "If you can hear me, I need to know: is my mother here too?"

As she waited for an answer, Shane scanned the horizon for any sign of movement.

Nothing.

"I get why you're being secretive," she added, her voice cracking with the strain of its volume. "You're protecting me. But I promise: even if I know you. Even if I love you . . ."

Again, Shane's voice faltered. She quickly brushed a tear off her cheek.

". . . I don't belong here. Shemáá! I miss her! Somebody help me, please! Pa! Pa, tell them it's okay! The dead can talk to me! I'm strong!"

And from behind the towering, twelve-armed saguaro, a deep, feminine voice responded.

But Shane didn't understand. The woman was speaking in a different language. Lipan? Shane recognized two words: *Lorenza* and *Sheiné łénde*. Their names. But aside from that? Nothing.

"Do you know English?" she asked, circling the cactus slowly.

Nobody was there.

Then, suddenly, from the speaking shell in her grasp, Grandpa Louis spoke: "She said, 'Go home, Sunflower. You know where the sun always shines. That is where Lorenza will be.'"

"Grandpa?" Shane gasped. "How long have you been at the camp?"

"Arrived early morning," he said, his voice lacking its usual humor. "Come home, mija. I don't know what that lady meant, but Lorenza ain't —"

"Oh," Shane gasped, lowering the shell in shock. "Where the sun always shines."

She had her answer.

She'd had it all along.

With a bittersweet smile, Shane looked at Nellie's gentle brown eyes and pet the soft fur on his brow, and down his neck. He pressed his wet nose against the palm of her hand, asking for more pets, so she ruffled his ears one last time. When they returned to Earth, he'd be a sweet shimmer. Perhaps, someday, she could teach him to become visible.

"Pa," Shane whispered to the wind, "it's been hard without you." She took a slow breath, smelled sunflowers. "But I promise that we'll be alright." For him, Shane smiled gently. "I love you. I love you, Pa. I love you, Grandpa. I love you, Grandmas. I love you so much."

With that, she closed her eyes, held her breath, and stepped through the juniper-shaped passageway.

In an instant, gravity flipped, forward became down, and Shane felt a terrible pull, as if the world Below was fighting to keep her. But no. It was the weight of her backpack. Instinctually, she thrashed, trying to slip free. Water blanketed her face, ears, hair.

A strong hand clasped her by the elbow and pulled Shane onto the bank. She gasped in lungfuls of fresh air, which smelled of juniper and lavender. Grandpa Louis, whose checkered sleeve was soaked, didn't release Shane's arm until she was standing. For a second, all was silent; she blinked the water from her eyes, saw Marcos in front of her, and Amelia behind him, with Donnie and Bobby and the Parks and a doctor with a stethoscope who'd been listening to Bobby's heartbeat, but now paused to gawk. And beyond them stood Jose and Gabrielle, as well as the delivery guy whose name she'd forgotten. To the right, a well-dressed man with a silver news microphone posed in front of a bulky video recorder and two of his colleagues. To the left, a group of six college-aged men and women surrounded Assistant Professor Bronson, all carrying clipboards and pens. One student held up a Polaroid camera and snapped a photo with a flash and whir. Furthermore, on the bank and between the trees stood dozens of other people, faces Shane might've seen in passing but couldn't quite place. Men and women of all ages, wearing all manner of clothes, all eyes on her.

At once, a cheer erupted from the crowd of spectators; Marcos threw his arms around Shane and squeezed; the news reporter shoved his microphone toward Shane's face.

"Miss, miss!" He pushed the microphone closer. "What was it like? How did you know young Bobby was trapped in another world? Was it a realm of magic? Who are you?"

Firmly, Shane wrested the microphone out of his grasp and held it against her lips, so her voice would be crystal clear, despite the excited clamor along the riverbank.

"My mother taught me how to save a life," she explained. "Her name is Lorenza Solé. She's five feet four inches tall and was last seen wearing a long pink skirt, hiking boots, and a long-sleeved white blouse. After my father died, Ma learned how to rescue other people." Shane glanced down at Marcos. "Bobby's alive because of Lorenza Solé, and you can quote me on that. It's the last thing I'll say about the matter till she's found."

And she would be found. Yes, Shane knew where the sun always shone. That's what her father called it, the patch of sunflowers behind the old oak tree in la rancheria de los Lipanes. Home. She'd had the evidence all along. Had suspected the truth, deep down, but had simultaneously denied the possibility. After all, when Shane saw the old swing behind the abandoned house in Less Crossing, she'd thought too of her swing on her oak tree. And hadn't she told Donnie, days ago, "You know your family best?" That was true. Everything Shane knew about her mother — and her mother's heart — pointed to home.

But home didn't exist anymore.

Shane felt a tickle on her hand, and, looking down, she saw the transparent shimmer of a butterfly's ghost. Slowly, she smiled.

Home might not exist anymore.

Yet that didn't mean it had to be gone forever.

shimmer of a building's ghost. Slowly, she smiled.

Home might not be there anymore.

Yet that didn't mean it had to be gone forever.

⟣ THIRTY-TWO ⟣

The Singers' house was still perched on the hill overlooking the horseshoe-shaped valley. They'd renovated since Shane last visited, adding a side wing and expanding the garage to fit three cars. There was a new marble fountain in the courtyard, too; fresh water trickled from a fish's mouth. At least, Shane thought it was a fish, though it could have been styled after the scaled dolphins of old Roman sculptures, like the elegant, water-spitting creatures of the Fontana del Tritone. Or perhaps it was an infant sea serpent, which, fully grown, could crush boats within their coils.

To reach the Singers' front door, Shane walked up a freshly paved road that corkscrewed around the hill. She zipped her jacket against the breeze, which carried a distinct chill and the scent of honeysuckle. Near the top, Shane gazed at the valley and tried to locate her old address, which was a difficult task, since very few landmarks and houses remained. The big oak tree had been cut down. Gone, too, were the fields of maize, yucca, sunflowers, and mesquite. In their place were a couple ranch houses with fence-enclosed yards of bright green grass, and monotonous fields of young corn. After a couple minutes, Shane gave up the search.

At the highest point on the hill, the road abruptly turned left and led to the Singers' colonial-style house. Two stories high and built from whitewashed cedar, it was surrounded by a cast-iron fence. Shane bowed her head against the quickening wind and pushed through the creaking gate. From within the house, behind shuttered windows, a dog barked lowly. In response, Nellie made a soft *whuff*.

"Quiet, you," she chided, cautiously walking up the redbrick driveway. As she neared the lamp-lit porch, the barking intensified, causing Shane to hesitate with one foot on the stoop. She adored animals, especially dogs, but wasn't naïve enough to let down her guard around them. Some breeds hunted bears, and even toy dogs had painful bites; in fact, she had a scar on her big toe, thanks to an old coworker's snippy terrier/chihuahua mix. Unfortunately, judging by the deep pitch of the landlord's dog, it was much bigger than a chihuahua.

From within, a man shouted, "Sam, take him upstairs. I can't hear myself think."

A young man responded, "Right, papa."

At the sound of her old friend's voice, which had deepened beyond recognition, Shane hesitated, suddenly unsure. Did he know what his parents had done? Would it shock him to learn that they'd stolen land from grieving families? Perhaps he'd refuse to believe Shane's story. Perhaps he'd forgotten her already.

She lifted her hand to the copper lion-head knocker. However, before she could knock, the front door swung wide open.

There, backlit by the golden lamps in the entryway, stood Mr. Singer. "How can I help you?" he asked.

"I . . ."

The landlord hadn't changed much, aside from the incursion of gray hair at his temples and the slight deepening of his laugh lines. He wore a white shirt, brown trousers, and black suspenders; his feet were bare, and a pair of reading glasses hung from a silver chain around his neck. "What?" he asked.

"Mr. Singer, do you recognize me?"

In response, Mr. Singer looked Shane up-and-down, frowning. "Should I?"

"No," she said, softly. "I've changed a lot in eight years."

"Miss," he said in his heavy drawl, "it's almost dinnertime, and you've agitated our dog. What do you want?"

"Can you answer one question?"

It took a couple seconds for him to decide on a response. "I'm not interested in cookies or a magazine subscription."

"That's fine. I'm not a saleswoman."

"Then ask."

583

"Do you remember my family? We lived in the valley, by the old oak tree. I used to play on the swing with Sam. We're the same age."

He removed his glasses and looked at her hard. "Lorenza's girl. That was a long time ago."

"After you stole my family's land," she said, "my grandmother died 200 miles away from the only home she'd ever known."

"Are you mad?" He shook his head, as if baffled. "I've never stolen anything."

"You scammed a desperate widow."

"Oh, give me a break." Mr. Singer made to shut the door, but Shane stuck out her foot, preventing it from closing.

"How would you describe it?" she asked. "If not theft? If not a scam?"

"I don't know what your mother told you about our deal —"

"She didn't have to tell me anything," Shane interrupted. "I was in the background, listening, every time you came calling. I know all the promises you made. The lies. I'm a witness. We trusted you. We thought you were a friend. Mr. Singer, you may not remember me, but I remember you."

He froze, his shoulders stiffening.

"Honey, who is it?" a woman called from farther in the house. The elegant Mrs. Singer. Shane remembered her, too.

"Nobody," he responded. Then, Mr. Singer pointed into the night. "Get off my porch," he said, taking a firm step forward. "Now. And don't ever harass my family again. I'm not playing games."

"You misunderstood." Shane put up her hands, palms outward, as if surrendering. The landlord was so close, she could smell the home-cooked casserole on his breath. "I'm not here to cause trouble. I just wanted to warn you about the land. It's something you may not know yet. A curse. That's all. But I can leave, if you want. No problem."

She took a slow step backward.

"What curse?" asked Mrs. Singer, stepping into the entryway and standing behind her husband. Framed by a hairspray-teased blonde beehive, her dismay-widened eyes locked on Shane's face and wouldn't look away. In one hand, Mrs. Singer clutched a sudsy dishrag; water dripped on the thick brown carpet.

"Ah. It's a long story —" Shane explained.

"Give us the short version," Mr. Singer ordered.

"We're all connected to the land. People change it, and it changes us. As a farmer, you know that well. In a way, the land carries memories."

He threw up the peace sign. "Groovy." It was difficult to miss the sarcasm in his voice; even the landlady smiled, her fear slowly vanishing.

"You want examples?"

"I asked for the short version, not a lecture. You have one minute before I close this door, so make it count."

"The land remembers my family," she said. "It remembers my ancestors and their ancestors. It remembers you, what you did to us —"

Mr. Singer opened his mouth, uttering another offended protest, so Shane raised her voice to be heard.

"The land cradles my father's body," she said. "I can't visit him, Mr. Singer. I can't say his name. Because he died too

586

soon, and the land knows why. I'm giving you a chance to make things better. Return the homes you stole eight years ago, or —"

"Or what?" the landlady demanded, throwing down her dishrag. "My husband's a gentleman, so he won't hit a girl, but if you threaten my family, I'll beat your bro —"

"Honey, enough," the landlord barked. "I'll handle this. Finish washing up."

Obediently, she grabbed the dishrag and stormed out of sight, her slippers clicking on the polished wooden floor.

"Or what?" the landlord restated, his voice calm.

"Or the memories of this land will curse your crops," she continued, "and your houses, your barns, your stables. All of them. Everywhere. Even beyond the valley." Mr. Singer owned or leased all the farmland in the zip code.

"That's your story?"
She nodded.

"Here's the problem." He leaned forward now, his voice dropping to a conspiratorial whisper. "I don't believe you."

"You should."

"Oh, really?" Mr. Singer put a hand on her shoulder; Shane tensed, but didn't shove him away. Not yet. "Then why didn't the land defend you when it mattered?"

Softly, she replied, "It still matters." Then Shane pulled out of the landlord's grasp and calmly descended the stoop. "I did my part," she called back. "The rest is on you."

When Shane reached the cast-iron gate, she looked back; Mr. Singer stood in the doorway, his silhouette still framed by warm electric light. She put a note in his mailbox — a slip of paper with her phone number — and then left.

Donnie was waiting at the bottom of the hill. She'd brought her grandmother's convertible, freshly painted lawn-flamingo pink. "How'd it go?" she asked, turning down the radio. Shane slipped onto the passenger seat.

"They got angry at me." She rolled down the window and inhaled, noting the air's humidity. Rain was coming. After a summer of droughts, the storm would be good for the crops, not that Mr. and Mrs. Singer would reap its benefits.

"So it went as expected?"

"Yeah."

"Where now?" Donnie asked.

"Anywhere," Shane said. "It doesn't matter which way you go. They own all the farmland in town."

With a nod, Donnie turned off the radio and shifted into drive. The pair crisscrossed down country roads, the sun setting, the air chilling; aside from the purring engine, they traveled in silence.

After all, Shane had to concentrate. Over the next two hours, riding with the window open, she roused the ghosts of aphids; they leech the juice of plants, drain them till they become weak and wither. She called forth larval borers, which grow plump on corn, chewing holes and burrows through leaves and stems. Then Shane invited army worms, grasshoppers, and burrowing grubs to the feast. She knew them — and their hunger — all too well. For when the fertile land was still their home, Shane's parents had taught her how to manage pests. Showed her the devastation of their hunger.

Before long, the air hummed with buzzing wings, clicking legs, and crunching mandibles. Millions of invisible bodies crawled, flew, or hopped through tidy rows of corn, flooding miles of the Singers' fields.

For although they might not need to eat, the dead had a terrible appetite.

~ THIRTY-THREE ~

Shane received the phone call on a Sunday afternoon. She was halfway out the door when the shrill bell trilled: *Brrrrrring!* *Brrring!* A moment later, Amelia called, "Wait! It's for you!"

Although Shane had an appointment in the city today, there was time to spare; she'd take a later bus, if needed. In the living room, Amelia held out the pea-green receiver. She wore a white skirt with a flower-embroidered blouse. Shane's own skirt, a handmade gift from her friend, was bright yellow.

After taking the receiver, Shane pressed it against her ear and asked, "Hello?"

Hope expected her mother's voice on the other end of the line; despair expected a policeman or medical examiner, calling with terrible news. But Shane didn't put stock in either of those internal voices.

"Let's discuss the valley." It was Mr. Singer.

"Certainly." Shane knew full well that he'd been trying to sell the property for a month. Unfortunately for the Singers, there wasn't a hot market for cursed farmland.

"You want it?" he asked.

"You don't live on the hill anymore, do you?"

"We found a better house." He paused. The line crackled. "Just take back your land, before I'm ruined."

"Tell you what," she told him. "I'll buy la rancheria de los Lipanes. How much did you pay my Ma for our old place?"

Mr. Singer chuckled bitterly. "You were there, weren't you? In the background."

"I was."

"So you know the answer."

"Guess so."

"And you're good for it?"

592

It was Shane's turn to laugh. "Sure. It won't be difficult to round up almost nothin' and twenty cans of soup."

An hour later, the zero-four bus hissed to a stop outside the university. After gathering her belongings, a metal tackle box and a manila envelope, Shane squeezed down the narrow aisle to the front exit. If anyone on the crowded bus noticed the shimmer that followed her, they didn't comment.

Campus was busier in the fall than in the summer; students sunbathed on the green and hustled between buildings with arms full of textbooks. This time, Shane didn't need to ask for directions to the Department of Agricultural Sciences, and within ten minutes, she stood outside the office of Dr. Oliver Bronson. He'd left his door open, expecting her.

"How's your mother?" Dr. Bronson asked, waving Shane to sit in the chair across his paper-laden desk.

"She'll be back soon." Shane took a seat, the tackle box on her lap, smiling. "Got a promising call today."

"Good," he said. "I'm glad to hear it."

Slowly, Shane opened the envelope and removed three Polaroids, each containing the image of a small mimic ring. The first was in the shade of a pine tree, half-hidden by needles. The next two were in a patch of well-watered grass at the edge of a golf course. After passing the photos to the professor, Shane explained, "I found those yesterday in Travisville and Laredo. The GPS coordinates are on the back. Me and my friend burned them, but new rings could grow back." She held up the tackle box. "Their ashes are here."

"Which friend? That hairspray girl?"

"Nope. Dr. Richards . . . preeminent scholar of *M. transpose* biology."

The morning after Shane and Bobby returned to Earth, there'd been a loud knock on the door. Expecting another wave of busybody reporters, Grandpa Louis had shouted through the cracked window, "No press, no solicitors!" At the time, Shane had been mixing cornbread batter in the kitchen. However, the moment she heard the crisp response, "Fortunately, I am neither," she'd recognized the voice. "Let him in, Grandpa!"

she'd shouted. "It's Dr. Richards, from the comic place!" By the time Shane stowed her half-finished dish and hustled into the living room, Dr. Richards — in a blue suit and yellow tie — had already made himself comfortable on the sofa. "I took an early flight," he explained, noticing Shane's surprise. "Good to see you again, Bug Girl. And congratulations. According to the news, you saved a life yesterday."

"I was on the news in Colorado?"

"At this point, you're national. They say you pulled Bobby from the Herotonic River, saved him from a magical shadow realm. Curious place for the mimic to send a child, hm?" Based on his knowing smile, Dr. Richards knew that the truth was much more complicated.

"For your ears only, Bobby was transported Below."

"Below what?"

"Afterlife," Grandpa Louis interjected, scratching his beard and yawning widely. "Anyone want a cup of coffee?"

"No thanks, Grandpa."

"I take mine with sugar, thank you." Then, Dr. Richards shook his head with disbelief. "Incredible. Mimics can send people to different . . . what is the afterlife, anyway? An extension of our universe?"

"I'm no expert," Shane had answered, sitting beside him with her hands in her lap, "but in the stories, it's where we came from and where we go."

"Not my area of expertise, either. The child is all right, though?"

"Yeah. Bobby's happy to be home."

"And your mother?" he'd softly asked. "Any progress on her case?"

She'd struggled with the answer for a moment, tilting between "yes" and "no," and finally settling on, "I know where she'll be."

"She'll be? Future tense? You think the ring sent her to a time?"

"To a place," she'd explained. "A place in time."

Although Dr. Richards didn't speak for several seconds, he must've been thinking deeply, based on the distracted *tap*, *tap*, *tap* of his right foot against the carpet. Eventually, he said: "You know why I'm here, Shane?"

Of course she did. "To destroy the mimic sample."

His entire posture had deflated, bent under an invisible weight. "If growing a mimic is the only way to reach your mother, then maybe, under extreme supervision, just this once . . ."

"No," Shane whispered. Then, more firmly, "No."

"No?"

"It'd be useless, if I'm right. The ring sent her home, but there won't be a home until I make it."

"How confident are you in that hypothesis?"

"Knowing my mother," she replied, "and all the evidence we've gathered, it's the only possibility that makes sense. So —"

She'd been interrupted by the squeal of a trumpet from the radio on the shelf. After a flurry of static and music, the FM station number had stopped in the high nineties, where a singer had belted out the lyrics: "*One more dance before we go . . .*"

Click.

Silence.

"An electrical surge?" Dr. Richards had wondered, staring at the radio in disbelief. At least he hadn't blamed the ghost dog.

"Representatives, more like." She'd hopped to her feet and gone to the window to look outside. "Yep." Reggie and Orlanda, still dressed in yellow suits and colorful sunglasses, had come calling too. Orlanda had a clipboard in one hand, and a pen in the other, while Reggie carried a bright bouquet of pink and lavender flowers in a porcelain vase; starlings and gold swirls danced across the glazed surface. A card emblazoned with the words "GOOD JOB!" dangled from one of the daffodils.

"Representatives of what?" Dr. Richards had asked, joining Shane at the window.

"Queen Titania's kingdom, I think." She'd looked up at the scientist, grinning. "Actually, this is perfect timing. You guys need to meet. They'll be interested in your research. Might set up a collab with Merlin the Third."

Outside, in unison, Reggie and Orlanda were waving hello.

Presently, Dr. Richards was back in Colorado, but — based on his latest phone call with Shane — he had already arranged plans to visit the Greatest Kingdoms. Indeed, the fae scientists were interested in his work, especially his belief that an assortment of earth-sourced fungus species could be used as a safer conduit for transportation magic. If he was correct, they wouldn't need to import fungi from the Greatest Kingdoms, thus eliminating the risk of mimic transfer.

"So you found these rogue rings in Travisville and Laredo, you say? Two different towns?" Dr. Bronson asked, going a sickly, bloodless shade, no doubt imagining a future with uncontrolled mimic ring growth.

"Don't worry! These were the only ones left in Texas."

"How could you possibly know that?"

"My ghost dog has a super nose, sir."

Before Shane and Dr. Richards had incinerated the original mimic sample Grandpa Louis collected, they'd trained Nellie to recognize its unique scent. Hadn't taken long. And over the past month, she'd worked steadily on extending his senses on Earth. Now, Nellie could smell a person — or an extradimensional mushroom — that was hundreds of miles away.

"Excuse me, what?" Dr. Bronson's wide eyes locked onto Nellie, who was a faint shimmer near the back cabinet.

"Don't worry. He's a good boy."

"That's not why I'm staring. However — and this may be the oddest sentence I've ever uttered — the ghost dog isn't the most urgent matter. The rings are, still."

"Dr. Bronson, it's been great catching up." With that, Shane stood. "I have lots to do," she apologized, "so can't stay long. But if my dog smells more of those wild rings in Texas, are you the right guy to call?"

"Yes," he reassured her, while also standing. "Yes, I'll make sure they don't spread. Call me any time. Here's my number."

With a grateful nod, Shane accepted Dr. Bronson's business card. She trusted him, truly. Because he'd been kind, and because he understood ecology, and because the thought of wild rings frightened him too.

Even still, Amelia's brothers had set up camp near the pine tree; they'd observe

600

everything that happened at the first set of coordinates. Just in case.

With a whistle, Shane called Nellie to heel and hurried to catch the 2:10 p.m. bus. There was much to do before Lorenza came home.

⤳ EPILOGUE ⤳

With a bemused smile, Shane paused to catch her breath, leaning on her aluminum walking stick for support. Normally, the trek between the comic shop and the dead zone was easy, even with a sore knee; in the eighties, as Tanner boomed from a nowhere town to a city with two McDonald's, the local government installed a proper hiking trail with signage and along-the-way stone benches. Go figure. The dead zone was great for tourism. Everyone who visited the landmark wondered, as they gazed over the circle of gray dust: would this be the day Mr. Brooklyn reappeared?

603

However, Shane had been talking the whole trip, finishing the story of her first solo rescue. Heck, she'd been chatting for days. There wasn't much else to do when you camped in the Colorado wilderness. Fortunately, she had good company.

"What did Great-grandma Lorenza say after she reappeared?" Shane's granddaughter, Ellie, wondered. "I mean, it must've been confusing."

At that, Shane laughed. "At first, Ma said nothing at all. She didn't pop into existence, like you'd expect from typical ring travel. Rather, she seemed to thicken from the air itself, mist and sunlight becoming body and clothes." On that old oak stump, Lorenza had towered over Shane and Marcos, statuesque, like some idol to motherhood; then, she'd held her children tight, all of them standing on the oak stump together.

Shane shook her head, beaming, remembering.

"Ma's first words were, 'Why are you crying?' Thinking of us, as always. I told her, 'Because we're happy.'"

"What a moment," Ellie said, her arms crossed loosely. Beneath a nearby aspen tree, Kirby, Ellie's ghost dog, curled up in a shimmery ball and rested, too. In some ways, he reminded Shane of Nellie. Inquisitive, bright, loyal.

After Lorenza passed away at the age of ninety-one, surrounded by family at home, Nellie, Neal, and Nealey had followed her Below; Shane hadn't seen them since. Lorenza had never adopted a fourth dog; said she had all the pack she needed. Shane's developing allergies might've swayed the decision, too. And Shane, much like Grandma Bee and her ghost cat, had befriended nontraditional animals.

Affectionately, Shane leaned over to pet Kirby's invisible back. The ghost tilted his nose upward to nuzzle against her finely creased hand. When Shane noticed the lattice of wrinkles across her skin, she thought, *Ma's hand*. But it wasn't. It was hers. Curiously, although she mentally felt like an Elder now, Shane's physical self-image hadn't caught up with reality. In her dreams, she was sometimes twenty, thirty, or forty. Rarely fifty. Never sixty. It was a curious sensation, since she liked being older. Age was confidence. Shane didn't know everything. Never would. But experience made life easier.

"Did you first meet your mammoth in the Below," Ellie wondered, "when you rescued Bobby?"

"Yup." Shane nodded. "A few months after Ma returned, I tried to call a butterfly, and the big girl appeared instead. It was like she'd been waiting for an opening. I must've piqued her curiosity."

Feeling ready, Shane stepped onto the dirt trail, which was dappled by afternoon sunlight and the round shadows of heart-shaped aspen leaves. Side by side, she and Ellie continued up the slope at a leisurely pace. The walking stick clicked over the hard-packed ground.

Click, click, click.

As steady as a ticking clock, though slower than a second hand. It was Shane's pace, after all.

"Mom never told me that you went Below," said Ellie. "The way I heard it, you pulled Bobby out of a river 'cause he was trapped in a shadow or something."

"Until last week," Shane explained, "nobody knew the whole truth, except for us who witnessed everything firsthand. Marcos. Bobby. Amelia and Donnie."

Was there anyone else still alive? No, she realized. Not anymore.

"Grandpa Louis tried to convince me to sell the story," Shane continued. "'Sheiné łénde's Adventure in the Afterlife.' He said the news would pay a fortune for the scoop, or that I could hire a ghostwriter and publish an autobiography."

"I take it you shot down his big ideas?" Ellie asked.

"Yup."

"And how'd he respond to that?"

She shook her head, grinning wryly. "Grandpa Louis sulked for a couple days. After I wouldn't budge, he made a couple attempts to sell his side of the fiasco, which was fine with me. He was only there for a small part, anyway. However, he embellished so much, the news didn't take him seriously."

"Oh . . ." Ellie kicked a pebble from the path into the brush.

"You sound disappointed."

"I thought he changed, is all. Became less self-involved."

Had he? It was difficult to say. Aside from the minor sulking, her grandpa had been supportive in the years that followed; he'd traded the station wagon for a camper and lived behind their new house in the valley. When Lorenza and Shane went on search and rescue missions, he babysat Marcos, and during community barbeques, he brought hot dogs and enough stories to entertain the whole neighborhood. Some days, he sat at the dining table and drew penguins, zebras, and elephants. Often bragged that he was the reason Marcos became a painter.

That said, they'd flourished in la rancheria de los Lipanes. It was easy to show up when everything was peaceful, so Shane couldn't say that her trust in her grandfather had ever fully returned. However, when she thought back on those years and his unbroken presence, she felt like smiling.

"He might've changed for the better," Shane concluded. "Based on his actions . . . yes. Yes . . . I think Grandpa Louis did good, in the end. I really do."

She leaned over and unclipped the leather knife sheath on her boot. "And I was reluctant to tell anyone about my experience Below because . . . well. It's like sharing the directions to an active volcano. But I heard that you discovered the route without me."

Ellie had also gone Below for the sake of justice. Wasn't that curious? Their family's ghostraisers all came into their true strength at the age of sixteen, seventeen, eighteen. Perhaps it was just part of becoming a woman.

"Here," Shane said, handing Ellie the hunting knife with the worn wooden hilt. "Grandpa Louis would've wanted you to have this. I'm sure of it."

"Whoa." Ellie slid her fingers in the grip-enhancing furrows. "You think so? What for?" She held the knife up and turned its mirror-bright blade toward the sun; the metal flashed like a beacon.

"Might need to cut a rope someday." Shane smiled fondly. "Or chop vegetables for the camp stew."

Suddenly, there was a loud crunch of a foot crushing dry leaves; Shane looked up to see Donnie jogging down the trail. Visually, out of all Shane's friends, Donnie had changed the least over the decades. She still primarily wore T-shirts and jeans, and her hair, more white than black these days, was still usually teased into a hairspray-enhanced storm cloud. Because of her reliance on hairdryers, she and Amelia were renting a hotel room in Tanner, but they'd spent the day chatting on beach chairs outside Shane and Ellie's tent. "Ladies!" Donnie shouted. "There are major spikes in the chronometric field! Pretty sure this is it!"

"Grandma, you good to go?" Ellie asked.

In response, Shane stepped forward with the help of her walking stick. "Sure am." As they strode the final stretch of trail, she felt a thrill of excitement, grateful that Mr. Brooklyn was returning during her lifetime. That she'd witness the safe return of an innocent man, something Dr. Richards — whose life's work had ensured that Longfire would never happen again — had dreamed of experiencing.

"Amelia's downtown, stuck in traffic," Donnie chattered, "so somebody needs to record this. Can you do that, Ellie? Your phone's better than mine, anyway."

"Easy," Ellie promised. "I'll get everything in 4K." At her side, Kirby wagged his tail and trotted ahead.

"I warned Amelia it was a risky time to go on a coffee run, but to be completely honest, she enjoys the camping experience more than the spectacle of Brooklyn's return, so I don't think she'll be disappointed." Considering that the women had gotten hitched in 2009, Donnie definitely knew Amelia best. But as Amelia's oldest friend, Shane agreed with the assessment.

At the end of the trail, where the tree line ended and the gray dirt began, there was a buzz of activity; authorities had cordoned off the dead zone, so all the tents and spectators were concentrated in a colorful ring around its perimeter. There were about fifty people present inside the site, mostly support staff, researchers, and extended members of the Brooklyn family who'd ensure that Mr. Brooklyn was welcomed to the future and given any help he needed. Earlier that week, when the first irregular chronometric readings began, the public had been removed from the area.

Shane and her family were exceptions: Dr. Richards had asked them to deliver a message to Mr. Brooklyn, a letter in a sealed envelope.

She wondered what it said.

"A whole century," Ellie breathed, her voice tinged with awe and sadness. The three humans and one ghost dog walked up to the yellow warning rope and looked over the gray expanse. "Nothing's grown, in all that time?"

"The dead zone's smaller than it used to be," Shane reassured her. "By a little bit. See?" She pointed with her lips at their feet, where grasses and other plants stretched into the dead zone, determined to spread. "Someday, the forest will reclaim it all. I'll never forget the day Dr. Richards noticed the change. He threw a party in C & C, and half of Tanner was there."

"Look!" Donnie whispered, gently touching Shane's hand. "I see something. Is it . . . ?"

"It's him," Ellie gasped, turning her phone to capture the faint glimmer of a man in a button-up shirt and high-waisted pants; his face was tilted upward, as if toward the stars, and he held a telescope in one hand.

In that moment, as Mr. Brooklyn slowly but certainly appeared within the ring of people, time seemed to constrict like a singing accordion, and Shane relived every homecoming she'd experienced, beginning with the first.

In that moment, in her memories, Shane stood in a field of sunflowers as her mother returned to Earth.

This is not the end.

ACKNOWLEDGMENTS

When I decided to write a book about a Lipan teen in 1970s Texas, I leaned on the wisdom of my mother, who was once a Lipan teen in 1970s Texas and therefore had invaluable insight into the world of *Sheine Lende*. Mom was my first reader, and — in countless ways — an inspiration.

For his patience, editorial guidance, and faith in my book, I want to thank my hardworking editor, Nick Thomas. I put a ghost cat in this for you, Nick. The cat was only mentioned in passing, but if there's a third book in the *Elatsoe/Sheine Lende* universe, I promise to give her a pivotal role.

I am also grateful to the entire Levine Querido team, champions of stories, including Antonio Gonzalez Cerna, Irene Vázquez, Danielle Maldonado, Kerry Taylor, Freesia Blizard, and the extraordinary Arthur Levine.

Thank you to Michael Curry, my agent, for finding a home for *Sheine Lende* (and my other projects, including secret future plans).

To Taran, my love: every day with you is a blessing. Thank you for being my partner in life (and for supporting all the weird author stuff I do). I can't wait to create more stories together.

And finally, to the readers who picked up this book and followed the adventure of Shane, I have one thing to say: xastéyó. <3

A NOTE ON THE TITLE

The Lipan language has no official dictionary, so spellings are generally the result of best attempts to capture a word's pronunciation (which may vary with region and time). Shané łánde and Sheiné łénde are both potential spellings of our word for "Sunflower." Ultimately, I chose the latter because it made the most sense for the protagonist.

Unfortunately, that's when things got tricky.

As you can tell, the title of this book is not *Sheiné łénde*. It's *Sheine Lende*. Sadly, I learned that many aspects of publishing and book distribution do not support the use of diacritical marks in titles. To navigate these challenges, and ensure that readers could find my indie book when they searched for it, I agreed to remove the diacritical marks. At least officially.

619

Levine Querido's design team thought of a creative way to sneak them on the cover. Her name is Sheiné łénde, after all.

ABOUT THE AUTHOR

Darcie Little Badger is a Lipan Apache writer with a PhD in oceanography. Her critically acclaimed debut novel, *Elatsoe,* was featured in *Time* as one of the Best 100 Fantasy Books of All Time. *Elatsoe* also won the Locus Award for Best First Novel and was a Nebula, Ignyte, and Lodestar finalist. Her second fantasy novel, *A Snake Falls to Earth,* received the Newbery Honor, was a *LA Times* Book Prize Finalist, and was longlisted for the National Book Award. Darcie is married to a veterinarian named Taran and splits time between California and Texas.

The employees of Thorndike Press hope you have enjoyed this Large Print book. All our Thorndike Large Print titles are designed for easy reading, and all our books are made to last. Other Thorndike Press Large Print books are available at your library, through selected bookstores, or directly from us.

For information about titles, please call:
   (800) 223-1244

or visit our website at:
   http://gale.cengage.com/thorndike